PRAISE FOR

THE TEARS OF ELIOS
"The first thing that came to mind upon finishing this book is, 'Holy Crap! Is that it?!' I did not want this book to end."

— Starcrossed Reviews

"This was a riveting tale of two couples and an amazing tale of Elgean and it's inhabitants. I hadn't heard much about this book… but I was certainly impressed. This is a quick read as the story just flew by."

— Grave Tells/Undergound Love Addiction

A WALTZ AT MIDNIGHT
"What a lovely read… a historical romance began through letters, involving deceit, high emotions, the baring of souls, and secrets"

— The Book Babe

A Waltz at Midnight a beautifully sweet (and perfectly clean) post-Civil War romance"

— The Historical Romance Critic

HEART OF A HUNTRESS
"Warning: you will not want to put this book down once you start."

— Happily Ever After Reviews

ANGELIC SURRENDER
"The author did such a great job creating my ideal hero that I found myself thinking about him for days."

— Whipped Cream Reviews

KISS OF TEMPTATION
"As Ms. McHugh moves on with her writing of *The Kavanaugh Foundation*, I found this story even more spell binding than first two books."

— Literary Nymph Reviews

A Soul For Trouble

by
Crista McHugh

Book 1 of the Soulberer Trilogy

ISBN-13: 978-1468158748
ISBN-10: 1468158740

Aknowledgements

Thank you to Sherry and Cate, the first crit partners who took a peak at my crazy chaos god and the lives he tormented.

Thank you to Nonny for helping me push the edges on my antagonist to make him more creepy.

Thank you to all the readers who offered suggestions on how to improve Arden, Dev, and Kell.

Thank you to Rhonda for helping me polish this novel and smooth out the rough edges.

Thank you to Nicole, a generous reader with an eagle eye for fiding all the typos I miss.

Thank you to Kim for coming with a gorgeous cover.

Thank to Lee at Iron Horse Formatting for doing a fabulous job on the ebook version of this novel.

And thank you to my family for not thinking I was insane when I walked around the house, muttering to myself about chaos gods and necromancers.

Chapter 1

"Trouble, you have a special customer," Hal said as soon as he entered the kitchen.

Arden Lesstymine, known to everyone in the village as Trouble, slid a sheet of freshly baked meat pies onto a cooling rack. "Please don't let it be Conn again. My ass is still sore from his pinching." She peered out of the cracked door, praying the lecherous blacksmith wasn't sitting in the main room.

"No, this one's a stranger, and a real kook at that." The beefy innkeeper leaned against the door frame, pointing him out. "You must be some kind of magnet for the crazies."

"Why do you think I ended up here?" She smoothed her apron and shoved the swinging door open.

Arden approached the table and studied the new customer. His frail body trembled like the last leaves on the branches outside, and his snow-white hair stuck out in every direction. What troubled her the most, though, was his constant muttering. She waited for a lull in his private conversation with himself, but when it never came, she cleared her throat. "Can I get you something?"

His body jerked at the sound of her voice, and he lifted his head. Feverish bright blue eyes ringed by a yellow-green halo stared back at her so intensely, she took a step back. Yep, definitely crazy. And definitely a foreigner based on his coloring. Most of the natives of Ranello had dark hair, dark skin, and dark eyes. "Yes," he whispered before resuming his low, incomprehensible ramblings.

She flicked her thick braid over her shoulder and went

back to the kitchen. Hal and Jenna, the other barmaid, stifled their laughter as soon as she entered. "Let me guess—you led him right to my table, didn't you, Hal?"

He shook his head. "He walked straight past me as if I wasn't there."

"Besides, you know how to handle his type better than me," Jenna added. "He probably wanted to stare at you or something."

Arden's jaw tightened. Every time she walked in a room, she felt dozens of eyes on her. Her golden hair stood out in the sea of brunettes that surrounded her, along with her blue eyes and delicate features. All gifts from her father, according to her mother. Unfortunately, she'd never had a chance to meet the man who sired her and thank him for making her the only freak in the kingdom.

"I think he's too busy talking to himself." Arden filled a tankard with ale and placed one of the meat pies on a plate. Maybe the aroma of rosemary and mushrooms that rose from the meal would pull him back to reality. "Here's to hoping he pays."

With her chin held high, she marched back into the main room and set the meal in front of the old man.

"Thank you," he said and reached a shaky hand for the pie.

She paused for a moment to take a good look at him. His threadbare cloak hung limply off his bony shoulders, and the skin on his hands wrinkled like onion paper when he moved his fingers. How old was he? *Poor man. He probably has no idea where he is.* "I'll come by and check on you later."

She spun on her heels and collided with a hard mass behind her. A hand grabbed her arm to steady her. "Excuse me," a voice said from under a heavy brown hood.

The warmth from his touch spread through her body like a wildfire. A soft, musical accent marked him as a foreigner as well, along with the bright green eyes that burned from under the hood. When did this little village on the remote edge of Ranello begin to attract so much attention? Not that she minded meeting new people, especially ones who spoke like the new stranger. She'd much rather listen to his ramblings than those of the old man's.

She tried to peer past the shadows and catch a better glimpse of his face. "Can I get you anything?"

The stranger sat at a nearby table and focused his attention on the old man. "I'll have what he's having."

Coarse fur grazed her fingertips, and she looked down at the large red wolf that brushed past her and settled down at the stranger's feet. She resisted the urge to bolt for the door, as did just about every other patron nearby. Everyone, that is, except the old man, who continued muttering to himself while he ate.

"And for your wolf?" she asked in a slightly higher pitch than normal.

The stranger chuckled. "He's already had his fill."

Arden backed away slowly and waited until she was about ten feet away from the wolf before she turned and ran back to the kitchen. "What is going on tonight? Did the moons line up in some unusual formation?"

Hal glanced up from Jenna's overflowing cleavage. "What do you mean?"

"Now we have another foreigner with a wolf in the main room."

"A wolf?" Hal's heavy feet thumped across the wooden floor. "Not in my inn." The kitchen door swung open with a bang, and he stomped toward the hooded stranger. "Sir, I don't know how things are done where you're from, but we do not allow creatures like that in public houses."

The wolf lifted its lips and growled.

"I suggest you remove the finger you're pointing at him before he removes it for you," the stranger replied in a low, even tone.

The color drained from Hal's face. "But I have to worry about the safety of my customers. A wolf is a wild beast."

3

The stranger ruffled his pet's fur with his hand, and the wolf lowered his head. "I have him under perfect control. So long as no one provokes Cinder, you won't have to worry about the safety of your customers."

"I can refuse to serve you."

"It seems like you're a bit late for that." He nodded toward Arden, who'd been watching the entire exchange with a tankard and plate in her hands.

"Trouble, I forbid you to serve him."

The clank of coins on the wooden table sounded behind them, and Hal's eyes grew large enough to reflect the gold in front of him.

"This should cover the inconvenience."

Hal scooped up the coins and retreated to the kitchen without another word.

"You could've bought the entire inn for a few coins more," Arden said to the stranger as she set the meal on the table.

He shrugged. "What would I want with it?"

"No idea. Burn it to the ground so I could leave this town and wouldn't have to deal with Hal anymore?" Even though she was trying to make a joke, the words hit a little too close to what she desired. She knew there had to be a place where she wouldn't draw stares and pointed fingers, but she feared what could happen to her if she dared to strike out on her own. She saw what happened to her mother when she tried it.

His fingers wrapped around her wrist when she tried to leave. Again, the warmth from his touch both soothed and excited her. "You're not from here, are you?"

"I was born here in Wallus."

"You don't look like a Ranellian."

She jerked her hand free. *Just what I needed. Someone else reminding me that I didn't belong here.* "Sometimes variety is a good thing."

The stranger chuckled again. "Perhaps, Trouble."

Damn, she wished she could see his face to know what he found so amusing about her. His rumbling laughter sent shivers down her spine. *Stop it*, her mind ordered. *You're all wound up because he's new in town and doesn't immediately cross the room to avoid you*. Of course, imagining the lean-muscled body under the cloak didn't help matters. Blood rushed into her cheeks, and she returned to the kitchen before he could ask any more questions.

Ale foam coated Hal's upper lip. He wiped it away when he saw her. "As soon as he's done eating, get him out of here, Trouble. You got that?"

"He paid you enough money for a month in your best room. Let him and his wolf eat in peace."

"It's more than the wolf that bothers me. He ain't from around here, and strangers who don't show their faces are usually bad news."

Arden peeked out the door at her customers. The stranger picked at the meat pie and tossed bits of it to his wolf. His attention never wavered from the other foreigner, who remained completely oblivious of anything around him. "I think he's looking out after the old man."

"Which means they're both kooks."

"Why should you care? You've got gold in your pocket, and they aren't hurting your business."

Hal grabbed her face in one hand and squeezed her cheeks until she cried out. "That's enough sass from you. Just remember, I'm the only one in this town who'll tolerate your antics."

Anger flared deep within her, fire flowing through her veins. It burned brighter inside her as his grip tightened. She wanted him to hurt as much as she did, maybe even worse. Flames sparked from her skin.

He released her face with a yelp, blisters already forming on his fingertips. "Why, you little witch!"

"What did she do this time?" Jenna asked.

"She burned me."

Arden took a deep breath and exhaled through her teeth. Damn it, she didn't mean to allow her temper to get the better of her again. She'd managed to go almost a whole year without doing anything that would make people suspect she was a witch. At least nothing caught on fire this time. She grabbed the full pitcher of ale from Jenna. "Take care of Hal. I'll tend to the guests."

She slipped into the dim room, far away from their accusing glares. One of these days, they were going to burn her at the stake if she wasn't careful. She wasn't sure why Hal spared her this long. He either feared her or felt guilty about the way he treated her mother. As much as she hated it here, it was better than being executed or cast aside. She grazed her fingers over her pendant and silently reaffirmed her promise never to make the same mistakes her mother did.

She made the rounds without looking anyone in the eye. The less people knew about what just happened in the kitchen, the better. She finally came to the old man and refilled his empty tankard.

"How much?" he asked.

"Four loras."

He stopped muttering long enough to fumble through his robes and pull out a money pouch. A five-lora coin rolled toward her.

"I'll be back in a moment with your change."

He shook his head. "Still hungry." His gaze appeared as hollow as his gut must have been before he came here.

"I'll see what I can find in the kitchen." She cast a quick glance at her other customer. His tankard remained filled to the brim, but she could have sworn she saw him grinning at her. Fixing her courage in place, she pushed the swinging door open.

"Give me one reason why I shouldn't toss you out on your ungrateful ass right now," Hal said as soon as she set the pitcher down.

Arden brushed past him and cut a slice of apple pie. "Because you need someone like me to keep the weirdoes happy. Besides, Jenna can't see past her bust to do any of the cooking."

Before he could get another word in, she went back

into the main room and placed the pie on the old man's table.

"What kind of pie is it?"

"Apple. Eat up. You need to put some meat on your bones before winter comes."

"My favorite. Would you care to sit with me?"

She looked over her shoulder. It sure beat going back to the kitchen and facing Hal's wrath. Besides, the old man actually seemed coherent now that he had some food in his stomach. "For a few minutes."

The mass of wrinkles in his face parted to reveal a smile. "Thank you."

She sank into a chair next to him and watched his shaking hand stab the flaky crust and dig into the sweet golden filling.

A moan of a pleasure escaped from his lips with the first bite.

"Where are you from, old man?"

He stopped chewing. "A bad place." Then the muttering returned.

So much for trying to find out more about him.

The fork rattled against the empty plate, but the old man pressed his fingers against the crumbs, scooping up every last morsel.

She reached for the plate. "Enjoy it?"

His hand clamped over hers, but it didn't tremble like before. "Very tasty," a deep voice murmured.

Her breath caught in her throat. He didn't sound like the same person anymore. She tried to pull her hand away, but he held on. Her skin crawled from the contact. This was what she got for being nice to a poor old man.

"Almost as tasty as its maker." The yellow-green halo in the old man's eyes glowed brighter. His finger stroked the inside of her palm. "Such a pretty little girl, you are."

"Let go."

He threw back his head and laughed. Behind him, the hiss of a sword being pulled from its scabbard filled her ears between the throbs of her pulse. "I want to stay with you a bit longer," the dark voice said from the old man's mouth.

Arden focused the fire in her mind, but fear held her back. She didn't need to use her magic in full view of everyone in Wallus, but she doubted she'd be able to overpower him any other way. "I mean it, you don't want to piss me off," she whispered.

The grin fell from his face, and his eyes bulged. He slumped forward onto the table, revealing the dagger protruding from his back. Grey stone replaced his flesh, spreading out from the hilt like ink on paper.

She screamed, and pandemonium erupted. Customers bolted from their chairs, running through the front door into the night.

A strangled cry gurgled from his throat, but his hand still clamped around hers in a rock-hard vise. As the stone encased his face, a green mist rolled out of his nostrils and filled the space between them. Cold terror prickled along her spine, and dark shadows flittered on the rim of her peripheral vision. What in the name of the three moons was going on here?

The mist drew closer, filling her mouth and nose. She gagged and tried to pull away from it, but it surrounded her like a shroud, choking her. Her lungs screamed for air. The mist poured into her when she drew a shaky breath. Every muscle in her body tightened, and the room went black.

Chapter 2

Devarius Tel'brien caught the barmaid before she hit the ground, cursing under his breath. No wonder the owner called her Trouble.

She seized in his arms, her eyes rolling back until only the whites showed. His gut clenched. Loku had chosen her instead of him. Once again, he'd failed to protect the Soulbearer. There was nothing else left for him to do but guide her through the transition and take her to Gravaria for more formal training.

His gaze swept over the statue that remained of Robb's body. The poor human was never meant to bear the weight of Loku, and neither was the naïve girl he held.

Cinder growled next to him. Dark figures with glowing red eyes poured into the main room of the inn. Undead. "Great, this night just keeps getting better."

The hiss of an arrow sang in the air, and he ducked under the nearest table. He'd gone from tracking down an escaped Soulbearer to hiding from assassins and zombies. Who had Robb pissed off? He reached for the vials on his belt and launched three of them at the shadows. Grunts filled the air when they exploded. He charged, using the confusion to his advantage. A flash of golden light erupted from his palm, and the walls of the inn rattled from the impact of the undead bodies slamming against them.

"Light up, Cinder."

The wolf's growls grew louder, flames dancing off his fur. He leapt toward the nearest enemy with a snarl.

Dev picked up his sword and swung at the neck of another undead. Up close, the face appeared grey and waxy. Fresh undead. Lucky for him, that usually meant untrained and stupid, even if they were stronger than seasoned soldiers. His blade sliced through the neck of his attacker. The head rolled across the floor, and the body collapsed.

The room brightened as Cinder's flames engulfed another undead, and Dev scanned the room for the necromancer controlling the animated corpses. No sign of him. Just more undead pouring through the front door, surrounding them.

"Cinder, protect the girl."

The wolf retreated behind him and flanked the other side of Trouble.

The undead slowed their steps and formed a semi-circle around them. He counted at least a dozen in the main room of the inn. Who knew how many waited for him outside? Their emotionless faces revealed nothing of their intentions, but the glow of their red eyes intensified.

There were only three ways to kill undead: burn them, behead them, or kill the necromancer responsible for them. Words formed on his lips, and the magic within him hummed to life. It flowed from his center and down his arm like a tidal wave. As the last syllable of the spell hung in the air, a stream of fire rushed forward from his hand, igniting his attackers. They flailed backwards with a high-pitched wail. The flames from their limbs licked the curtains and wooden furniture of the room, and smoke choked the air.

Trouble's body stopped jerking. He flung her over his shoulder and ran for the kitchen. Relief washed over him when he saw the gaping back door. Lady Luck hadn't totally screwed him over tonight.

The blazing inn captured the attention of most of the bystanders on the one dirt road that ran through this town, but Dev stuck to the shadows. No need to entice them to form a lynch mob. Based on the warm reception he'd experienced earlier this evening, a foreigner like him wouldn't have a chance at justice if these simple folk got a hold of him, especially once they realized he wasn't human. He lost count how many times he'd cursed Robb for coming to this backward kingdom.

"My inn!" the burly human who tried to threaten him earlier shouted, his face red. "That witch set it on fire to spite me."

Dev turned his head to the rump that lay beside his cheek. "A witch, eh? When this is all said and done, you're going to have some explaining to do, Loku."

Cinder crept ahead, peaking around corners before he ventured forward. Dev followed him with silent footsteps. The sharp points of the girl's hips dug into his collarbone, but at least she was light enough not to hinder his movements. He slipped through an alley at the edge of the town and found the grove of trees where he had tethered his horse. Once again, Lady Luck smiled on him. The horse was still there.

He tossed Trouble over the saddle and mounted the horse behind her. For a moment, he closed his eyes and tried to sense the presence of dark magic. Years of his knightly training didn't fade when he was sentenced to become the Soulbearer's guardian. Part of him wanted to hunt down the necromancer responsible for tonight's attack. Creators of such atrocities didn't deserve to live.

Cinder's whimper interrupted his concentration. When he opened his eyes, the wolf licked the girl's dangling arm.

"All right, I'll take care of her first." He'd pledged centuries ago to protect the Soulbearer, and Trouble needed all the help she could get.

***

Sulaino hid in the shadows, searching the night for the yellow-haired girl. She either burned to death in the flames or found another way to escape.

A crowd gathered around the inn and tried to douse the fire. A futile effort. It would take a deluge from the heavens to put that inferno out. He could call on one, but why bother? He liked the townsfolk standing in one place, where he could easily pick them off to replace the members of his army who burned inside.

He turned to his minions. "Kill all the men, but bring all the women to me. I must find the girl who trapped the god's soul."

A dozen figures emerged from the nearby shadows, weapons raised. Completely occupied by the fire, the humans didn't notice his undead soldiers until their blades impaled the first victims.

Sulaino grinned while he listened to their screams. *Nothing like the sound of terror on an early autumn night.* He stroked the scar on his left cheek. If his estimations were correct, he'd easily replace the soldiers he lost in the inn. Soon, he'd have enough to challenge King Heodis and have his revenge. And if he could capture the soul of the chaos god, nothing could stop him.

His soldiers brought him the first two women they captured. Tears streaked through the soot on their cheeks, and sobs racked their fragile human bodies. He examined the first one. The wrinkles that lined her face spoke of the many years of life she had lived. She was far too old to be the girl he sought. "Finish her," he said with a wave of his hand.

His soldier remained expressionless as he slit her throat in a quick strike. Blood gurgled out from the wound, and the old woman collapsed into a heap at his feet.

The other woman screamed and strained against her captor. "Please don't hurt me. I'll do whatever you want. Just please don't hurt me."

The necromancer stepped closer to her and tilted her head back so the firelight enhanced the curve of her face. *Such a pretty young thing.* He brushed back the stray curls that fell around her cheeks and glanced down at her generous cleavage. The smell of her fear aroused him. He studied her closer and recognized her from the inn. "What is your name?"

"Jenna," she replied in a trembling voice.

He pressed his lips against the flesh of her neck. She shuddered beneath him, and his cock stiffened. She tasted like smoke and salt. How long had it been since he'd had a woman come willingly into his bed, especially one terrified as she was? "And you'll do whatever I want, Jenna?" he whispered in her ear.

She bit her full bottom lip, nodding. Another tear streaked down her cheek, and he caught it with his lips. So delicious.

"And do you know what I want from you?"

She nodded again and turned away from him.

He reached into her mind, feeding off her fear. She thought he only wanted her body, and she was willing to give it to him. What interested him far more was her dread. To have one person so terrified of what he might do to her thrilled him. Soon, the whole kingdom would share her fear.

"First, tell me the name of the yellow-haired girl."

She wailed. "This is all Arden's fault, isn't it?"

He chuckled. "That's for me to know." He trailed his fingers along her neck, over the tops of her full breasts. "Shall we find a more private place, or do you prefer the streets?"

She glanced over her shoulder where his undead soldiers finished off the last of the townsfolk behind her. Her breath quickened, and her body shook. "Please, let's find someplace more private."

Jenna led him into one of the open houses and up the stairs to the bedroom. The sheets still retained the heat of their former occupant, who was now probably lying dead in the street. Without waiting for his command, she began to remove her clothes and lay still as he climbed on top of her.

A few minutes later, a shudder tore through him as he came inside her. He tightened his grip around her throat and pressed harder, strangling her cries. Her eyes dulled in the moonlight, and her body grew limp underneath him. A wave of euphoria washed over him as he watched the life drain from her pretty face, heightening the pleasure of his orgasm while he consumed the last traces of her soul.

He buttoned his trousers in silence. She had served her purpose well, but now he was finished with her. His mentor, Oztom, always raved about the taste of innocent souls. Sulaino disagreed with him. Innocent souls tasted sweet, but they carried no substance. Thieves and whores were much more filling. Their transgressions supplied more than enough power to fuel his magic.

Now, back to work. First order of business: animating the fresh dead waiting for him in the street below. Then to track down Arden and claim the divine soul residing in her.

***

The last of the three moons sank below the tree line before Dev finally climbed down from his horse and spread out his bedroll. His body ached and demanded sleep, but duty kept him from giving into it. She would have his bedroll tonight. He would stand guard.

Trouble slid from the saddle and landed in a small heap at the horse's feet. If what he'd seen before held true, she would be out until midday. He scooped her up off the ground, arranging her gangly limbs on the soft blankets. His jaw tightened as he examined her and the way her bodice hung loosely on her lack of cleavage. Why had Loku chosen her?

And yet, as he studied her closer, his curiosity increased. He told her earlier that she didn't look like a Ranellian. In the four months he'd travelled this kingdom, the monotony of its citizens blurred together. The same dark hair, dark eyes, dark complexions over and over again. Then this little barmaid collided with him. Her golden hair reminded him of a summer wheat field glowing under the sun. A breath of fresh air in the dreariness.

But more than her appearance caught his attention. In every town Robb visited, the people pointed and stared. A few even threatened to kill him. Yet she'd shown the old man compassion, treating him like a person rather than a raving lunatic.

"Is that why you chose her, Loku? Because she was kind to you?"

Trouble's brows furrowed together, but her eyes didn't open. She rolled over onto her side and curled up into a ball.

More than just her coloring bothered him. His fingers brushed her hair back to reveal her ears. Scars covered the skin on top of them, but they didn't form the distinct points he would've imagined finding. If she had elvan blood, then someone had deliberately tried to hide it.

He traced the length of her ear from the rough scars to the delicate lobes. She moaned in her sleep. He jerked his hand away. What secrets did she keep?

His blood chilled, and he backed away from her. Like the other human Soulbearers before her, Loku's presence would slowly drive her insane. Humans were never meant to contain him. They were too weak, too easily swayed into doing his bidding. No wonder Loku preferred them.

It was just a matter of time before she aged prematurely and started muttering responses to the voice in her head. For the first time in a century, a Soulbearer's fate frightened him.

Chapter 3

The sound of humming interrupted Arden's dreams. It was too early for the drunks to be singing, but the off-key notes continued to invade her thoughts. "*Shut up*," she muttered in her mind.

"*But it's time for you to get up*," a deep voice replied. "*He grows impatient.*"

Her heart rose into her throat. She bolted from her bed. That same strange voice came from the old man seconds before he died.

A warm hand grasped her shoulder, and she screamed.

"Quiet, or you'll have the entire Ranellian Army after us."

The bright sunlight blinded her eyes, but she knew that voice, too. His musical accent was unmistakable. The stranger with the wolf. She swung her arms and knocked him away from her. Then the back of her hand connected with something hard, sending tremors of pain up her arm.

"*Oh, you should see the look on his face*," the deep voice said with giddy amusement.

Arden stumbled to her feet and backed away until she felt the rough bark of a tree behind her. Where the hell was she? Colors swirled in front of her eyes, forming incoherent blobs.

"Trouble, relax. I'm not going to hurt you."

"What did you do to me?"

"Besides save your life? Nothing much."

Her fingers clawed at the tree trunk, and she wondered if she could climb high into the branches until her mind cleared. "Why can't I see anything?"

"It takes a while for the transition to be complete."

"Transition?" A cold tongue licked her hand. She yanked it away.

He sighed a few feet away from her. "Even Cinder's trying to calm you down. Will you please just sit and be patient while I explain what happened?"

The coarse fur prickled her skin through her thin skirt as the wolf leaned against her, effectively pinning her to the tree. The blobs of color began to solidify. She slid down the trunk and pulled her knees up to her chest. How did she get into this mess?

"Finally, you're showing some common sense."

"Where are we?" She looked up at the vibrant reds and yellows above her.

"In the woods, about four hours east of Wallus."

"Why did you kidnap me?" Browns, blacks, and greens began to take the shape of a crouching man in front of her. She pulled her knees tighter to her chest. Until she could see clearly, she couldn't even fathom an escape from her captor.

"Did you want me to leave you in a burning building full of undead?"

Her breath hitched. Memories of the night flooded her consciousness. She'd joined the crazy old man at his table when he grabbed her hand and started speaking in a strange voice. Then he fell over dead, a knife sticking out of his back. "You killed him," she gasped.

"Nonsense. I was his protector."

She tried to rise to her feet, but a low growl stopped her. *Perfect. I'm out in the middle of the woods with a murderer and his wolf. What's he going to do? Feed me to it when he's done?*

Laughter echoed in her mind. *"Cinder doesn't like human flesh."*

Her muscles tensed, and she looked around for the source of the voice. "Who else is here?"

His face slowly came into focus. It could have been a handsome face if the frown hadn't etched creases into his cheeks and forehead. Dark auburn hair framed it, providing stark contrast to eyes the color of evergreens. "It's just me, you, and Cinder."

"Liar. I hear another man's voice."

Her vision cleared just in time to see him quirk one brow. "You hear him already?"

"He won't shut up. Where is he?"

The foreigner lowered his head and traced a symbol into the dirt. The pointed tips of his ears appeared through his hair.

Arden bit into her hand to keep from screaming. The Lady Moon preserve her, he wasn't human.

He jerked his head back up, and a slow smile spread across his lips. "Your vision's back to normal now?"

Words refused to serve her, so she merely nodded.

He chuckled. "You should see how wide your eyes are, Trouble."

His use of her nickname pulled her from her shock long enough to allow her fury to course through her veins. "My name is Arden, not Trouble."

"Arden Soulbearer," he replied. His words caressed her like they did last night. "It has a nice ring to it."

"Soulbearer?"

He stood and offered his hand to her. "It seems I have a lot of explaining to do. If you'll come with me, we can continue our conversation as we ride."

"Why should I follow a man who hasn't even given me his name?"

"I'm Devarius Tel'brien, Knight of Gravaria and sworn protector of the Soulbearer."

"And that's me?"

He nodded. "Of course, I still think you're more aptly named 'Trouble.'"

She ignored his hand and brushed the dirt off her clothes once she stood. "I hate when people call me that."

"But it fits you."

She fiddled with the pendant around her neck, hoping to find some comfort in the familiar object and finding none. "Where are we going?"

"To Gravaria."

Fear coiled in her stomach. He wanted to take her to another kingdom. "No, I want to go back to Wallus."

"Why?"

"Because I have a job there." Not to mention, it was familiar and comforting. Yes, they stared at her and called her a freak, but it was all she'd ever known. Hal had promised her mother he'd look out for her and, despite all his threats, he was bound by blood to his word.

"The inn is a pile of ash."

Her knees wobbled, and she braced herself against another tree. "Sweet Lady Moon, they're going to blame me." Her voice trembled as she spoke. She blinked back the stars forming on the edge of her vision.

"Yes, I heard them calling you a witch as it burned down."

That sealed her fate. If she returned to Wallus, she was as good as dead. "Why didn't you turn me over to them, then? Our laws forbid the use of magic."

He closed the distance between them in three long strides. He cupped her chin in his hand and forced her to look up at him. "I'm the one who set fire to the inn. It was the only way to deal with the undead that were trying to kill us."

The horizon wavered. If he hadn't wrapped his other arm around her waist, she would have passed out. This all sounded like something from a bedtime story mothers told their children to frighten them. She clung to Devarius, welcoming his solid warmth against her. The smell of campfires and spices wafted from his clothes.

"Come along, Arden. The sooner we start moving, the sooner we can get you to Gravaria."

She hesitated. She couldn't go back home, but why should she blindly go along with an elf who'd probably drugged her?

"You can trust Dev," the strange voice answered. *"He's too honor-bound to lie to you."*

19

She weighed the voice's words carefully, wondering if it was some manipulative magic he was casting over her. For now, it was the best option she had until they came to another town. "It seems I might have to trust you."

"You should." He mounted his horse and helped her to the space behind him.

"Why Gravaria?"

"Do you always ask this many questions?" A smile played in his voice. "Gravaria hasn't outlawed magic. You'll be trained by the most skilled mages in the land."

She wrapped her arms around his waist as the horse started walking. "Why would they want to train me?"

"Because you are the new Soulbearer."

"You keep saying that." Annoyance crept into her words. Did he only speak in riddles? "What exactly is a Soulbearer?"

"Do you want the whole story or a quick explanation?"

"How long are we going to ride?"

He remained silent for almost a minute, and she wished she could see his face. "Your body is now the home to the former god of chaos, Loku."

Perhaps it was hunger, exhaustion, or sheer insanity, but Arden began laughing so hard, tears gathered at the corners of her eyes. "I have a god living inside me? You expect me to believe that?"

"Loku, will you please confirm your presence inside your Soulbearer?"

"Hello, my dear sweet Soulbearer," the voice answered in her mind, sounding exactly like the old man did seconds before he died. *"I'm looking forward to getting to know all your secrets."*

She screamed and almost fell off the horse. If Dev hadn't caught her hand, she would have landed in an undignified heap on the forest floor. Her breath flowed in and out in raspy shudders, her body shaking.

"You're not going to have another seizure, are you?" Dev asked.

She wrapped her arms even tighter around his chest. "No," she murmured into his back.

"Do you remember the green mist?"

She nodded and fought the urge to cry. At least she had an explanation for the voice inside her head now.

"That was Loku entering your body. I've seen it five times now, and every time, it's the same."

A few more minutes passed in silence before she finally gathered the courage to ask, "Why does he need a Soulbearer?"

"Are you ready for the whole truth?"

She nodded again, wiping her nose on the back of his cloak. If he was trying to scare her, he deserved a little snot on his clothes.

"Loku is the god of chaos. About six hundred years ago, he decided to challenge the other gods and opened a portal from the plane of chaos to this realm. His careless actions almost wiped all life from the kingdoms of Gravaria, Ranello, and Thallus."

"He's exaggerating. I never came close to destroying the world like he implies. I just wanted to spice things up a bit."

"The other gods fought to destroy the creatures he unleashed, while the Master Mages of Gravaria devised a plan to contain Loku."

"Those arrogant pricks tried to kill a god. Ha!"

"They managed to separate his soul from his body and imprison it inside a mage named Piramus. He became the first Soulbearer, and the other gods destroyed Loku's body after they closed the portal."

"How's that for an eviction notice? Murder and imprisonment. No chance to redeem myself. Just, 'Here's you punishment—enjoy spending the rest of eternity trapped in mortal bodies.'"

"Since then, there have been nine other Soulbearers. Robb, the old man you met last night, was the previous one."

"And I freely admit it was a mistake choosing the poor

guy, but it was either him or Dev."

"Whoa, hold on a minute. Give me a chance to digest all of this, both of you." The two versions of the story seemed to flow together. She needed to figure out who was telling the truth.

"Ah, is Loku giving you his side of the story?"

"Yeah, and it's slightly different from yours."

"As I would expect it to be."

"He said he had a choice between you or Robb. What did he mean?"

Dev stiffened, and the warmth fled from her body. "It was the tradition that the protector would become the next Soulbearer, but Loku had other ideas. I was originally appointed to protect the fifth Soulbearer, an elvan mage named Quertus. Upon his death, I was supposed to absorb Loku's soul and become the sixth Soulbearer. Unfortunately, Loku convinced Quertus to take his own life at the feet of a human guttersnipe named Syd."

Laughter echoed in her mind. *"You should have seen the look on his face when I denied him his chance to be the Soulbearer the first time. It gets more comical each time I do it to him. I convinced the eighth Soulbearer to run away from him and leap off a castle turret, which was how I ended up with Robb."*

Arden gasped and squeezed Dev's ribs. Sweet Lady Moon, what kind of gruesome death did he have in store for her?

"What did he say?"

"He told me how Robb became his Soulbearer," she replied in a trembling voice.

A low rumble spread through his chest like a growl. "That was an unusually cruel end for a Soulbearer."

"Do they all eventually kill themselves?"

Neither one answered her immediately. "Human minds are more fragile than elvan ones. The burden of being a Soulbearer makes them more susceptible to insanity and suicide."

The blood drained from her face. "Stop the horse,

please." The second it halted, she slid off the horse and started running.

Dev called her name. Footsteps pounded behind her, but she only quickened her pace. It didn't matter where she ended up, as long as she got away from Dev and Loku and the promise of her grisly end.

The wolf raced ahead of her, stopping suddenly. She tripped over him and went sprawling across the ground. A pair of hands yanked her up by her bodice and spun her around.

"What were you trying to accomplish by running away like that?" Dev's eyes flashed, and he gripped her arms in an iron vise.

Anger from his rough treatment overpowered her fear. Her hands balled into fists, and she swung at his jaw. His head jerked back, but he didn't release her.

"That's the second time you've belted him. I wonder how much longer he's going to take it from you?"

Fear gripped her heart. As hard as Dev tried to reassure her that he was her protector, she'd felt the muscles that rippled along his body, not to mention the sword and two daggers hanging from his belt under his cloak. He could kill her with a flick of his wrist.

She waited for the blow, but it never came. Silver light radiated from his hands. Her pulse slowed, and a strange feeling of calm wrapped around her. Her fingers uncurled. "Please, I don't want to be a Soulbearer," she whispered. "Can't you take Loku from me?"

His expression fell flat, and he released her. "I'm sorry, Trouble. I wish I could."

"So I'm stuck with him?"

"Until you draw your last breath."

Now she understood why some of the previous Soulbearers decided to kill themselves. The idea of slowly turning into Robb terrified her.

"It's not all that bad. You and me, we'll have fun together."

"I wish I could believe you, Loku."

Dev's hand wrapped around hers. She savored the brief contact. After her mother died, the villagers treated her like a leper, scared to touch her because she appeared so different from them. When they did approach her, it was with fists and threats. Yet here was a man who knew what evil lived inside her and wasn't afraid to hold her hand.

"Are you feeling a bit more rational now?" He waited until she nodded before he added, "Good, let's go. There's a necromancer in the area, and I want to get as far away from him as I can."

Her feet moved in response to the gentle tug of his hand. "Why?"

One auburn eyebrow arched. "Besides the pain of dealing with undead?"

"So you weren't lying about that, were you?"

He lifted her up on his horse and stared at her. "This isn't some wild tale I'm fashioning to scare you. I believe the necromancer was behind Robb's death."

"And if that's true, you're the next target."

Arden froze. What kind of trouble had she gotten herself into now?

Chapter 4

Trouble stopped asking questions for almost an hour after Dev told her about the necromancer. The silence soothed him after all of her hysterics earlier. Thankfully, the calming spell seemed to work on her.

"Are you hungry?" he asked when the shadows began to lengthen from the late afternoon sun.

Her nose moved from side to side against his back.

He cringed at the thought of what she might have wiped on his cloak. "I'm planning on stopping at an inn tonight. You could use a bath and some suitable travelling clothes."

"I smell bad?"

Far from it. Underneath the smoke, she still smelled of warm bread and baked apples. "You're covered in soot and dirt."

She sighed. "I suppose a bath would be nice, and a hot meal."

A hot meal would do her some good. Several meals, in fact. She was far too thin for his liking. The hollowed recesses under her cheeks and along her collarbones made him fear she would snap in his hands.

"Why did you want to return to that place when they treated you so horribly?"

She removed one hand from his waist. Although he couldn't see what she was doing, he suspected she was playing with the thin gold chain around her neck. "It's the only home I've ever known. My mother was from there."

"And where is she now?"

Her body went rigid. "She died ten winters ago."

"And your father?"

"Why are you interested in my past?"

The acid in her voice almost singed him. He had unwittingly stumbled on a touchy subject with her. But at least now he knew why she worked for that bully of an innkeeper. "I was just curious about you. Perhaps if I knew more, I might understand why Loku chose you."

She flinched, followed by a hiss.

"What?"

"Loku said something very crude."

Despite her reaction, he couldn't suppress his amusement. "That sounds like him."

"Have you ever heard him?"

Her body began to relax against his again, and the sensation felt so good, it almost unnerved him. She was the first female Soulbearer, a fact he couldn't ignore. Dev cleared his mind and focused on her question instead of the pressure of her cheek between his shoulders. "I've had a few conversations with him over the years. Occasionally, he'll take over the Soulbearer's body and speak."

"Like last night?"

The image of her face when Robb grabbed her hand and Loku spoke to her flashed in his mind. He'd called her tasty. Odd choice of words for the thin girl riding behind him. Dev had drawn his sword and was about to rouse Robb from Loku's control with a whack on the shins when the assassin's blade lodged itself in the old man's back.

Guilt over his failure weighed down his limbs like heavy chains. This was the first time a Soulbearer had been murdered. He feared what the Mages' Council would say when they learned about it. They would probably strip him of his responsibility. Not that he minded. He'd been risking his life to protect Soulbearers for over a century now, and Loku had thwarted him at every opportunity.

"Why did you choose her over me, Loku?" he asked.

Trouble flinched again.

"What did he say?"

She hesitated. "He said you were too stiff."

"Were those his exact words?"

"Um, no, but I don't want to repeat what he said exactly."

Dev chuckled. He could only imagine what Loku said. "For a barmaid, you seem unusually prudish."

His comment earned him a smack on the back of his head. "Just because I worked in an inn doesn't mean I saw to my customer's every comfort. And if you think you're going to get under my skirt, think again."

His cheeks burned for a second. It had been so long since he'd been with a woman, he'd almost forgotten what it felt like. She didn't need to remind him. His throat tightened, and he cleared it before replying, "You don't have to worry about that. As your protector, I'm never allowed to let my guard down. What I meant to say is that you should be used to such language from your customers."

"Most of them preferred not to speak to me. I think they feared I would set them on fire or something."

The loneliness in her voice almost made him glad he was taking her away from this backwards kingdom. He just wished it wasn't under these circumstances. "So you are a witch."

Her arm tightened around his waist, forcing the air from his lungs. "I never said that."

"There's no reason to hide it from me. I'm a mage, too."

"Then we'll burn together if we're caught."

"The key word there is 'if.' I plan on getting you out of Ranello as quickly as possible."

They emerged from the forest with the sun setting on their backs. An arid plain stretched out in front of them, baked golden in the early autumn sun. Farther up the road, smoke curled from the chimneys of a small settlement. Dev pulled the hood of his cloak lower to conceal his face and ears. The fewer questions asked about him, the better. "When we come to the inn, we're getting one room."

"I want my own room."

He clenched his jaw and counted to five. "No, we're going to share one room. I'm not letting you out of my sight after sunset."

"So much for your gallant promises to leave my virtue intact."

The leather reins nearly cut into his palms from squeezing them so tight. Trouble had a bit more of a sassy tongue than he'd expected. "I'll sleep on the floor in front of the door. Now, stop arguing with me before we draw too much attention to ourselves."

***

One room? What the hell was he thinking? That she would be so grateful to him for kidnapping her—sorry, saving her life—she would willingly throw herself at him? It didn't matter that he was probably the best-looking member of the male gender she'd ever seen. She still wasn't a two-lora whore.

"I bet you'd warm his bed for less than two loras."

Her cheeks burned. *"Loku, will you please get your mind out of the gutter?"*

"I wouldn't have said it if you hadn't been thinking it."

Arden buried her face in Dev's cloak and prayed to the Lady Moon no one would see her embarrassment as they rode into the town.

They stopped in front of a mud-brick building with a thatched roof that towered over its neighbors. The carved wooden sign above the door proclaimed it to be the Happy Hog Inn.

She slid off the horse, wincing. Her muscles ached from the long ride, and the skin between her thighs felt like it had been rubbed raw by pumice stones. Her skirt wasn't designed for riding.

The cool breeze penetrated her weary bones. She welcomed the blast of warmth flowing from the cheery interior. Various travelers crowded around the tables in the main room. A wisp of silence hung in the air as they entered.

A thin man with deep creases folded into his leathery face approached them. He wiped his hands on his apron a little too thoroughly, probably a way to excuse himself from shaking their hands. "Welcome to the Happy Hog. How can I help you, strangers?"

Her spine stiffened. Of course, they would draw attention without saying a word. A hooded man, a yellow-haired girl, and a wolf. Who would find anything normal about that? "We were hoping you had two rooms available for the evening," she replied, hoping her voice sounded calm.

"One room will be fine," Dev growled behind her.

She plastered a sweet smile on her face, ignoring him. "I prefer two."

"One." His green eyes glowed from shadows that concealed his face, and her blood ran cold.

"You've pissed him off now, my little Soulbearer."

"Tell me something I didn't know."

The man cleared his throat. "I only have one room available this evening. The trade routes are full with the harvest going on, and so is my inn."

"We'll take it." Dev discreetly dropped several gold coins in the man's hand. "My apprentice could use a bath and some more suitable clothing for travelling. Perhaps you could assist us with that, as well."

The innkeeper's eyes widened past his droopy eyelids at the sight of gold in his palm. "My boy has a few things he's outgrown that may fit the young lady. I'll tell my girls to start heating up some bathwater as well."

"No need to do that. My apprentice will be fine with a cold bath."

Arden gritted her teeth. So this was her punishment for disagreeing with him. She would have preferred a slap to the face rather than the cool intensity of his glare. At least she'd know he'd gotten his anger out of his system.

"Come this way, and I'll show you to your room."

Dev's hand pressed against the small of her back. She followed the innkeeper to a small corner room with a fireplace and a bed large enough to share. Her gaze fixated on it, and her pulse raced. Would he keep his word and sleep on the floor?

"I hope you'll find this to your liking. Let me light the fire—"

"I can do that." Dev moved in front of the fireplace, blocking the innkeeper. "Just please see to the bath."

He backed away, colliding with the young woman carrying the metal tub. "Of course. I'll be back in a few minutes with some water."

Dev closed the door behind them and crossed his arms. "Why did you disobey me?"

Arden mimicked his posture. She wasn't going to let him know how much she wanted to hide under the bed. "I'm the Soulbearer. You're my protector. If anyone should be giving orders around here, it's me."

"Wrong. Until you complete your training, you're just a little scrap of a girl with a half-crazed god of chaos trying to control your mind and a necromancer on your tail. You need me to keep you sane and alive, so until we get to Gravaria, I suggest you do as I say and not challenge me again."

She lifted her chin, refusing to look away from him. "Or you'll do what?"

His upper lip lifted in a snarl.

"Uh-oh, wrong answer. You're awfully good at pissing him off, my Soulbearer. I'm going to enjoy watching you two in the coming years."

Dev opened his mouth to say something, but the entrance of three people interrupted him. The innkeeper must have recruited every staff member and empty bucket he could find to bring up her bath water. They wasted no time filling the bath two-thirds full, leaving a bar of soap and a towel beside it and retreating back downstairs. It was almost as if they sensed Dev's anger and didn't want to witness the unavoidable explosion. At least they had the courtesy to close the door behind them so they could feign ignorance when it happened.

He snatched her wrist and pulled her close enough to him so his lips brushed against her ear when he spoke. "Now, listen to me, Trouble, and listen well. There are far worse things out there than what you're imagining me to be. The last thing I want to see is a knife sticking out of your back or your eyes glowing red after that necromancer animates your corpse. I will lay down my life before I let that happen, but I would appreciate your cooperation. Do you understand me?"

The intimacy of his touch warmed her, but his words tore at her defenses like an icy blade. She didn't know which of the two left her shaking.

He pulled away, pointing his free hand at the fireplace. Flames ignited the logs, rising high into the chimney.

She tried to smother her gasp by covering her mouth. Yes, he made his point very clear. If he wanted to harm her, he could. But he could also be a powerful ally. It all depended on her. His grip loosened, and she backed away with a nod.

"I suggest you take a bath while I inspect the clothes the innkeeper said he could find for you."

She dipped her fingers into the tub and yanked them out. "It's freezing!"

He chuckled. "Consider it a lesson in learning to harness your magic. You can either take a cold bath, or you can figure out a way to warm the water."

"He's testing you," Loku whispered in her mind, *"but don't worry. I'll show you what to do."*

"And why should I trust you?"

Loku's chuckle vibrated through her body. *"Always so suspicious."*

"I'll leave Cinder here to protect you while I'm downstairs," Dev said. "I doubt you want me in the room while you're bathing."

The heat from the fire crept along her back, but it didn't match the burn in her cheeks or the warmth coiling in her stomach. What was it about this man that made her react this way? She closed her eyes and took a deep breath.

It's only because he's the first man who gave me a second look and treats me halfway decently.

"Keep telling yourself that if you want, but you and I both know the truth."

Dev left the room, and Cinder stretched out in front of the door, forming a barricade.

She waited a moment to see if he would return. When he didn't, she stared at the bathwater. How was she going to get it to a temperature that didn't make every nerve in her body scream from the pain?

"Dip your hand in the water and picture the fire flowing from your fingers into it."

She followed Loku's instructions, biting her bottom lip from the stinging-cold water as it slipped over her skin. Deep inside her mind, she found a small flame. She fed it with her thoughts until it spread along her arm and into her fingertips. The water hissed and bubbled around them, ripples racing to the edges of the metal tub. By the time she removed her hand, tendrils of steam rose from the surface.

She unlaced her bodice and yanked the simple dress over her head. It'd been ages since she'd enjoyed a hot bath. She slid into the tub. Even though the warm water stung the raw skin between her thighs, it eased her aching muscles. She sighed in contentment and leaned back against the metal rim. "Thank you, Loku."

"You're welcome. At last, I get to see the body I'll be inhabiting for the next few years. Yes, I think I'll enjoy having tits."

Arden bolted up in the tub and crossed her arms over her chest, causing Loku to laugh again. She hadn't anticipated the unseen voyeur. "Can you please look away?"

"Nope, and more importantly, I don't want to. I've always been curious what it feels like to be a woman. But I'll try and keep my comments to myself."

Her muscles unlocked, and she sank deeper into the water. If he kept his word, she'd hopefully forget his presence in a few minutes. No reason not to enjoy the bath while she could.

Chapter 5

Dev inspected the tunics and leggings the innkeeper provided for him.

"He outgrew them so fast, they didn't have much time to get holes in them. The boots, too."

The fabric showed some signs of gentle wear, but the innkeeper was right. No holes. He held one of the tunics up in front of him, trying to imagine Trouble wearing it. She was thin, but also tall for a Ranellian woman. The young man's outfit should fit her well enough until they got to Gravaria.

"I'll take them." Dev pressed another coin into the man's hand. "And I appreciate your assistance on this matter."

He turned to walk away when the innkeeper said, "She ain't really your apprentice, is she?"

Dev stiffened at the suggestive tone in the man's voice. "I'm not sure what you're implying."

The innkeeper held up his hands and took a step back. "No offense intended, but it's not often I get a man claiming to have a female apprentice, especially one looking like her. I don't doubt a few noblemen out there wouldn't mind bedding a young girl with hair the color of gold. Lord Yessling, for example, has been known to have exotic tastes in women, if you're looking for a place to sell her."

"Things are handled differently in Gravaria." The growl in his voice made his annoyance very clear to the innkeeper, judging by how the sly smile slipped from the man's face. "Women are not bought and sold like cattle and, more importantly, they are educated to the fullest of their abilities, unlike here."

The man's Adam's apple bobbed up and down several times before he found his voice again. "Very good, sir. Will you and your apprentice be eating tonight?"

"Yes. After she's done bathing and dressing, you can send some food up." Thank the gods this conversation was almost over.

"Of course, sir. Oh, and my daughter reminded me that the young lady might want a comb and a mirror." The innkeeper placed the items on top of the pile of clothes then returned to the main room.

Dev climbed the back staircase, grateful he didn't have to cross the main room again. He tended to draw stares wherever he went in this kingdom for always wearing his cloak and hood in public, but it was safer than letting the people see his ears, especially in this remote corner of Ranello. They'd probably kill first and ask questions later. Or burn him at the stake like Trouble mentioned earlier.

He paused in front of the door, listening. Claws scratched against the floor on the other side, letting him know Cinder was moving away from the door. But no muttering or one-way conversations yet. Unfortunately, it was just a matter of time before she slipped into that.

A shriek filled the room when he opened the door. Trouble reached for the towel and draped it over her chest and the top of the tub. "Haven't you ever heard of knocking?"

"I wanted to prove how easily a killer could sneak up on you." He dumped the clothes on the bed, along with the comb and the mirror.

"Point made. Now let me finish my bath."

"You look like you're almost done to me." Her skin glowed pink, and her wet hair hung down her back in golden waves. The faint scent of roses lingered in the air.

She pulled her hair over her shoulder and twisted it, wringing out the remaining water. The sharp edges of her shoulder blades winged from the movement, and he counted each of the prominent vertebrae along her spine. She needed to be eating, not lingering in a tub. His eyes travelled farther down until he saw the black lines etched onto the small of her back. Loku's symbol. If the greenish-gold ring in her eyes hadn't already marked her as the Soulbearer, this confirmed it. He'd lost count of how many times he wished it wasn't her burden to bear.

"Are you going to stand there and stare, or will you be kind enough to step out into the hallway so I can get dressed?"

He blinked a few times to clear his mind. He didn't like where it was going with her sitting naked a few feet from him. He needed to think of her as the Soulbearer and not as a woman, but his trousers were already growing tight. "Fine, I'll give you three minutes to dry off and put those clothes on."

"Only three minutes?"

The playfulness in her voice almost threw him off guard. Was she planning on challenging him again? Or had she noticed the growing bulge in his pants? He turned his back to her and adjusted himself. He couldn't afford to react this way to her. *Stay focused.* "Yes, three minutes."

He welcomed the cool drafts in the hallway after the heat in the room. He offered a quick prayer to Jussip, the god of soldiers, to keep him from further distractions.

***

Arden jumped to her feet as soon as the latch clicked. The gall of that man, telling her to get dressed in three minutes. It was obvious he hadn't spent much time around women.

"I don't think I've ever seen him with a woman outside of the Mage's Council," Loku said. *"I noticed he got an eye-full of you while he could."*

A flush spread over her entire body. She rubbed the towel over her bare skin with renewed fervor. She refused to be caught naked again.

"You should be flattered he sees you as woman first instead of my Soulbearer."

"Shut up, Loku."

She pulled the leggings on and tied the drawstring as

tight as it would go. Thankfully, their previous owner seemed to be as skinny as her. She had barely smoothed the tunic over her hips when Dev opened the door.

He assessed her appearance and nodded. "So you can follow orders."

She snatched the comb and mirror off the bed and glared at him. "It was either that or let you leer at me like a lecherous old man."

His expression hardened, and he strode past her. He dipped his fingers into the tub. "You figured out how to the heat the water?"

"No thanks to you."

He swirled the water with his hand. The soap and grime vanished, leaving the water crystal clear. Steam rose from the tub once again.

Arden gasped. He made it look so simple. When she looked up, he'd already removed his cloak and was loosening his leather jerkin. "What are you doing?"

"I figured I'd take a bath, too."

Her skin burned, and not even the water dripping from her hair soothed it. "Perhaps I should go downstairs to give you some privacy."

"No, you're not leaving this room. It's dark out. That's when the necromancer will be at full power."

She dug her fingernails into her palms and ran toward the door. Cinder blocked her exit. When she whirled back around to give Dev a piece of her mind, he removed his shirt. Her mouth refused to make spit. Sweet Lady Moon, he was as gorgeous as she had imagined. Corded muscles rippled down his back, from his broad shoulders to his lean hips. He turned at his waist, allowing her a peek at his carved chest and stomach. Her gaze followed the line of reddish-brown hair that disappeared into his trousers, and an odd ache formed in the pit of her stomach.

"And you accused me of staring."

Her eyes snapped back to his face. His lips twitched, but the tips of his ears appeared pinker than normal.

"I didn't expect you to shed your clothes so quickly."

"Not that you minded the glimpse."

The god's taunt added to her embarrassment. With a huff, she sat in a corner of the room so her back faced the tub. The last thing she needed tonight was to have her insides turn into mush over the sight of a naked man, even if it was Dev. She held the mirror up in one hand and started combing her hair with the other.

"If you angle the mirror a bit to the left, you might enjoy the view."

Before she could stop herself, the mirror tilted, and the image of Dev's well-defined behind lowering into the tub came into view. Her breath hitched. It was a crime for such an annoying man to be that tempting.

"I told you you'd enjoy it."

"Shut up, Loku!"

Arden dropped the mirror and continued combing her hair. "The clothes are a little too big," she said, trying to act like he wasn't sitting naked in the tub a few feet away from her.

"They're going to be more comfortable than that dress you were wearing. Besides, it's only temporary. We'll find you more suitable clothes when we get to Boznac."

The splashes of water filled the silence while she braided her hair. Thoughts of the coastal town filled her mind. "I've never seen the ocean before."

"It's vast and as blue as your eyes."

A smile played on her lips. "Was that a compliment?"

"No, just stating a fact," he said matter-of-factly. "Hopefully, we can catch a ship bound for Gravaria before the winter storms hit. I'd rather take my chances on water than going over the mountains. It's faster and, more importantly, free of undead."

"You keep talking about the undead. How do I know you're telling the truth?"

"Do you want to meet one?"

A chill snaked down her spine. "Not particularly."

"Smart girl."

"You said undead attacked Hal's inn last night. What

exactly happened after I passed out?" she asked with a flick of her braid.

"You inhaled Loku's soul and starting seizing, just like every other Soulbearer before you. Then the undead poured into the room. Cinder and I tried to fight them, but there were just too many. So I set the inn on fire and dragged you out."

"Why did you set the inn on fire?"

"Because burning an undead to ashes is one of the few ways to kill them."

She hugged her knees to her chest. This conversation left her feeling like she'd just plunged into an icy lake. "What are the other ways to kill undead?"

"You can cut their heads off, or you can kill the person controlling them."

"There are more ways than that, but most mortals can't summon the power to kill them."

Loku's statement did little to comfort her. "Do you think the necromancer is really coming for me?"

The splashing ceased for a moment. "I think he's after Loku."

The god sighed. *"Everybody wants a piece of me. It's no fun being this popular."*

"Why would he want to have some perverted deity living inside him, slowing driving him insane?"

"Ouch, that was harsh. You don't like our little arrangement?"

She could almost picture the pout that came with Loku's reply.

"Trouble, you have a god living inside you. Do you understand the potential power you could extract from him? Of course, it comes at a cost. The more control you surrender over to him, the less control you have over yourself."

"And the sooner I turn into Robb."

"Exactly."

The water in the tub rustled, and she reached for the mirror. Once again, she was granted full view of the backside of his body while he dried off.

"Hoping for a frontal view? You are a naughty girl, just like I thought."

Arden jerked the mirror back to her face. Redness seeped into her cheeks for being no better than what she'd accused Dev of being minutes before. The new golden rings around her irises startled her, and she dropped the mirror.

Dev rushed to her side. "What's wrong?"

"My eyes look different."

He tightened the towel around his waist. "It's one of the marks of a Soulbearer."

She closed her eyes, remembering how the strange yellow-green rings glowed when Loku spoke through Robb. Great. If she wasn't already a freak, this made it worse. "Will they always be there?"

"Yes, as will the other mark."

Her skin crawled. "What other mark?"

"Loku's symbol on your back."

"Think of it as a tattoo claiming you as mine."

She flew to her feet. Everything was happening too fast. In less than a day, she'd witnessed a murder, been accused of burning down an inn, been kidnapped, told she had a god living inside her who would slowly make her crazy, and now she'd been branded like a cow. Sweet Lady Moon, please make this stop. There was a time in her life when she would've given anything to be normal. Now, all she wished was to have her old life back.

Warm hands rubbed along her shoulders and upper arms. "I know this is a bit much for a young girl like you to bear—"

She wrestled away from him. "Quit talking to me like I'm a child. I'm twenty-one, not twelve."

"I'm sorry. You seem so young to me."

Her hand itched to slap him, but when she focused on his face, she stopped herself. The downward tug of his mouth and the way his brows bunched together spoke more of sadness than mockery. "Why?"

He backed away and reached for his shirt.

"He's more than ten times your age, my Soulbearer. That's why. Talk about a dirty old man."

"And how old are you?"

Dev flinched. "I'm three hundred twenty-three years old, if you really want to know."

Her breath came in sharp gulps from his reply. She'd heard elves lived a long time, but over three hundred years? "Are you immortal?"

"Only gods are immortal, you silly girl."

"No, I'll eventually grow old and die, but at a much slower rate than a human."

"If you were a human, how old would you be?"

"Are you going to watch me dress while you ask me all these questions?"

She dutifully faced the corner again. For a three-hundred-year-old man, he looked damn good. Almost too good. And he would continue to look good while she turned into an old crone, so it was best she push any stupid thoughts out of her head.

"To answer your question," he continued, "I guess I would be about thirty or thirty-one."

"Oh. That doesn't seem that old to me."

"Why? Do I look older?"

"Only when you frown."

He laughed. The sound of leather sliding through a metal buckle let her know he had finished dressing. "I asked the innkeeper to send dinner up here. I hope you don't mind eating in private."

Someone knocked at the door as soon as the words left his mouth. The innkeeper silently set two plates of steaming food on the small table. A barmaid appeared a second later with mugs of ale and followed her boss out of the room.

Arden reached for hers and gulped half the contents. The cool liquid soothed her dry throat, warmed her belly.

"Slow down with the ale. I don't need a drunk Soulbearer."

She peered at Dev from over the mug. "Sorry, but I haven't had anything to eat or drink all day."

"That's my fault. I should have forced you to eat something earlier today. It won't happen again. Now, eat before your food gets cold."

She cut a small slice of meat and popped it in her mouth. The juices coated her tongue with flavor, and she sighed. "This is so good."

Dev tossed a sliver of meat to the wolf. "I've had better."

"It's the best meal I've had in months." She reached for a chunk of bread to sop up the gravy.

"Who's Lord Yessling?"

The bread stopped inches away from her mouth. He wasn't threatening to sell her to him already, was he? "He's a local nobleman."

He cocked a brow and waited for her to continue.

She dropped the bread. "He likes women and tends to go through them quickly. Most of the farmers around here know they can fetch quite a few loras by selling their daughters to him, especially if they're pretty."

"And what happens to these girls?"

"They're put to 'work,' is the politest way to say it. Sometimes they come back. Sometimes they don't."

"How do you know so much about him?"

"Why are you asking?" When he didn't answer her question, she added, "Hal always threatened to sell me to him because I looked so different from most of the girls around here."

He frowned but didn't say anything else for the rest of the meal. When their plates were empty, he stood and ran his hand along the door. Blue light peeked out from the gaps.

"What are you doing?"

He repeated the same action with the lone window. "Sealing the room."

Arden rolled her eyes and flopped down on the bed. "I promise I won't try to run away."

"It's not to keep you in—it's to keep others out." He stared through the window at the town below for a few seconds, probably searching for the supposed necromancer who was chasing them.

"And I thought I was paranoid."

"It's my duty to be paranoid," he replied with a grimace. "I am your protector, after all."

"Well, I'm going to get some sleep. I'm exhausted after the long day." She looked over at Cinder and patted the mattress next to her. The wolf jumped on the bed.

"What are you doing to my wolf?"

She laughed and stretched out next to the warm mass of fur. "Spoiling him. You know, there's a bit more room on the other side of him, if you want to sleep in the bed."

The mattress sank as he sat down on the edge. "I thought you were worried about me taking advantage of you?"

"There's a wolf between us. I think I'm safe."

As she drifted off to sleep, she heard him whisper, "Don't get used to this."

Chapter 6

The darkness in Dev's dreams parted, letting a beam of light fall on Arden. She stretched in the bed as if waking up. The silk sheets slid through her fingers, caressed her bare skin. His mouth went dry as he watched in the darkness, memorizing the curves of her body.

The light brightened, casting his shadow on her. She sat up and backed away, the sheet clutched to her chest as though she was embarrassed to be caught naked. "Who's there?"

His skin flamed, but his tongue refused to form his name. *I shouldn't be staring at her.* He turned away.

"Don't speak, then, Dev. Just come closer. "

His heart pounded. He wasn't quite sure what he heard in her voice—fear, anger, lust—but his stomach tied in knots. He crept toward her with apprehension tempering his steps. The innocent girl from earlier had vanished, leaving a vixen in her place.

"I know what you want, what you desire, and I'm willing to give it you."

He stuck to the shadows, hiding his face from her so she couldn't read his emotions. The light shimmered off her hair, and her pale skin shown like moonlight. Desire coursed through his body as he lowered onto the edge of the bed. His fingers itched to touch her, to see if her skin felt as silky as the sheets around her, but he balled them into his fists. *Even if this is a dream, I will not cross the line.*

She chuckled and crawled next to him, leaving the sheet behind. "Is that what you want?"

Her hair draped over his shoulder, burning deep gold. He reached up to brush it out of his face. *So soft*, he realized with a shock. Softer than he could possibly imagine.

She traced the lines of his back, working her way to his chest, and he realized with a start that he was a naked as her. Her touch started out light, more like a whisper at first, before massaging his weary muscles. The firm globes of her breasts pressed against him, teasing him, coaxing him to turned around and cup them in his hands. His mouth watered as he imagined how sweet those tiny pink nipples would taste, how she would moan in pleasure as he took her into his mouth.

He caught her hand and threaded his fingers through it, forcing it to the bed. "Trouble, there's no need to do this."

"You're lying. I can see that you want me."

By Jussip, a woman had never tempted him like this before. If she continued, he might just throw her to the mattress and ease the throbbing in his dick.

"Relax, and let me show you pleasure like you've never known."

Her lips brushed against his ear, and he moaned. The fire in his veins intensified. He tried to pull away, scared he would burn from his desire. Soulbearers had tried his patience in the past, but this made them all look like innocents.

"You can't hurt me unless you deny me what we both want. Please, Dev, give yourself to me."

The temptation became too much to bear as she nibbled at the corner of his mouth. He seized control of the seduction, completely covering her lips with his own. Her arms snaked along his neck, pulling his head closer to her. He didn't want this kiss to end. His tongue traced the outline of her lips, and she opened them. Slow and sensual, he explored her mouth, coaxed her to do the same with his. The sweet scent of her skin nearly overwhelmed her, but he noticed she no longer smelled like roses and fresh bread.

She was the one who ended the kiss, breath coming quick as she gasped for air. "You taste like honey and apples."

It's just a dream, he told himself. *I would never kiss her if I were awake. I would never let my guard down.* But in his dreams, he allowed himself the indulgence he could never enjoy when he was awake.

Her hand wriggled free from his and travelled lower, coming dangerously close to the part of his flesh that longed for her touch.

"You don't have to tell me what you want," she said. "I already know."

"Do you?"

His mouth silenced her before she had a chance to speak. He pressed his body against hers as the kiss deepened, lowering her onto the mattress. His hands roamed over her skin, along the flat planes of her stomach and over the soft curves of her buttocks.

She lifted her hips, allowing him access to the part of her that was now slick with desire. "Please," she whispered.

"Do you have any idea how beautiful you are?"

She met his gaze, the wicked smile on her face telling him she knew exactly how much power she had over him at that moment. Her greenish-gold eyes burned with such intensity, he threatened to melt under the heat of their stare.

His brows drew together. *Aren't Trouble's eyes blue?*

He released her and backed away, desperately trying to ignore the cold sweat that beaded on his skin. *Something is wrong about this. Very wrong.*

His body jerked, and his lover vanished.

Chapter 7

Dev's eyes jerked open and he stared into the darkened room.

"So close, and yet you resisted," a familiar voice said next to him.

His hands balled into fists. He didn't need to turn his head to know its source. Loku already had tormented him enough times in the past.

"Dev, you disappoint me."

Anger flooded his veins, almost making him forget about the aching hard-on that remained from his dream. "Why? Because I didn't fall for your little trick?"

"No, because you deny yourself pleasure when you can so easily grasp it."

Dev took a deep breath before he rolled his head to the side and looked at Trouble. Just as he had figured, she lay perfectly still, staring at him with bright yellow-gold eyes that never blinked. "Let go of her."

The chaos god laughed. "And miss out on a new way of tormenting you? Never!" The eyes flickered to Dev's groin. "I see my little dream got you more worked up than I'd first thought."

Dev bunched the covers over the evidence of his desire, hoping it would conceal it, but Trouble's features morphed into a smirk.

"It's going to be so easy for me to gain her trust, especially with you treating her like she's a flea on your back. You should feel the power she possesses. As soon as I tasted it in that run-down little inn, I knew she had to become my next Soulbearer."

His fingers dug into his palm. So help him, he refused to see Trouble follow in the same path as Robb. His words came out in a low, even growl. "Let her go right now."

"Or you'll what? Slip your hands under her tunic? Or better yet, into her pants? I know exactly what you were dreaming, Dev, because I put it there."

"Why you sick son of a—" Dev stopped short, his fist raised in the air, and looked into the horrified blue eyes of Trouble.

***

Arden had no idea why she was pulled from a sound sleep, but she awoke to see her so-called protector on the verge of striking her.

She did the only thing she could think of doing at that moment—she screamed.

Cinder shot up and wedged himself between them, knocking Dev out of the bed. He landed with a loud thump on the floor.

She wrapped her arms around her furry hero and held on to him for dear life. Her racing pulse began to slow, but her lungs still sucked in air as quickly as they could. Sweet Lady Moon, what had she just witnessed?

"Trouble, are you all right?"

"Yes, I'm fine, no thanks to you." What else could she say?

She cast a side glance at him. He stayed on the floor. Pain tightened his features, but he refused to look at her.

"Why were you trying to punch me?"

He pulled himself into a seated position and ran his hand through his hair. His pupils stretched the green in his eyes into thin emerald rings, and his chest heaved up and down. "It's complicated."

Loku's laughter filled her mind as she shrank farther away from Dev.

"I was curious at first when I discovered that Dev was dreaming of doing naughty things to you, but now that I see how worked up he got from our conversation, I'd say it was worth it."

She grabbed her pillow and wanted to rip the feathers out of it. *"Loku, you bastard! How dare you use me like that?"*

"Oh, come now, I'm sure you would have enjoyed it if he acted out his fantasies."

His words produced a hum throughout her body. Images of Dev's dream flashed through her mind, of them lying naked in a bed, his lips trailing along her throat. Her mouth went dry and her breasts grew heavy as she imagined what they would feel like in his hands.

"You are a lusty wench after all. And more importantly, it looks like you almost had Dev persuaded to neglect his duty for one night. He has quite the tent pole in his pants." More laughter reverberated through her mind.

She hurled the pillow at the opposite side of the room.

"Trouble, what's wrong?"

Her cheeks flamed. Had Dev really been as aroused as Loku said? And if so, how did he manage to keep his hands to himself when she was sleeping mere inches away from him? "I'm sorry I screamed like that," she whispered.

"Let's face it. You're just like your mother."

Rage burned inside her stomach, making her forget every second of pleasure she had experienced moments before. "Shut up, Loku!"

"Ah, so he's tormenting you now."

"Loku was the cause of all this? Was that why you looked so angry?" She hugged Cinder even tighter and buried her face into his warm fur.

"He took control of my dreams and…" His voice broke.

He didn't need to finish. She already had a good idea what kind of dreams Loku had given him.

"I should have expected something like this from him. I think he gets some kind of thrill from tormenting me."

"How right he is." Loku chuckled like a devious child. *"At least I woke you up before he struck you."*

"Loku, I have half a mind to slit my throat in front of Dev just so you'll have no other option but to take him as

your Soulbearer."

"But think of all the fun we'll miss out on. He'll never thrill you like I can."

"You're determined to drive me insane, aren't you? Just like all the others."

"No, my sweet Soulbearer. I have other plans for you."

She ran her hands through Cinder's fur. The solid warmth under them reminded her that this was real, and that thought comforted her. "I'm sorry, Dev. I don't know how I let him gain control of me like that."

A bitter sound that resembled one note of laughter burst from him. "Loku is tricky. He'll weasel his way into your mind and seek out your deepest desires. Then he'll use them to seduce you into surrendering your free will to him."

"I guess I should be happy Cinder woke up when he did."

"Yeah, me too," he muttered.

The hair on the back of her neck stood up. Something in the atmosphere changed, and an icy prickle of dread crawled down her spine. The scent of rotting meat assaulted her nose. "Dev, do you smell that?"

He sniffed the air. "No, I don't smell any—" His words broke off, and his body stiffened. "Trouble, get your boots on now."

"What?"

"I said, *now.*"

His fierce tone made her jump. She obeyed without asking any more questions. Whatever she sensed unnerved him, too.

Chapter 8

For once, she's listening and not giving me any sass about it. Dev paused from strapping a dagger to his thigh to watch Trouble. Her pinched face spoke volumes. She sensed the danger, too, but he doubted she knew what it was.

He pulled a slim blade out of his boot. "Here, take this."

Her eyes widened. "I don't know how to use a weapon."

"I figured as much, but I want you to at least have something in case we can't avoid the undead."

"Undead?" she squeaked.

Great. She's certainly living up to her name. Getting her out of this alive might be more than I bargained for.

Satisfied he had an adequate arsenal attached to his body, he armed himself with a short sword and lowered the ward on the door. "Stay close to me, and don't speak until I tell you to."

He opened the door and peeked out into the dark hallway. Every muscle in his body tensed, ready to spring into attack if necessary. Silence greeted him. After checking both ways for any shadows, he stepped out of the room and motioned for Trouble to follow him. The wolf padded silently ahead, scouting out the back staircase.

Much to her credit, she knew how to sneak out of a building without being heard. That was one thing he didn't have to teach her. But based on the awkward way she gripped the knife, she'd be more likely to stab herself than anything else. He paused in the kitchen long enough to adjust the handle and give her a brief, wordless demonstration on how to use it.

The aura of dark magic almost threatened to smother him by the time they made it to the stable. He saddled his horse and pulled her up behind him.

At first glance, the streets looked deserted, but he knew better than to trust his eyes. The necromancer had to be close by to cause the twisting in his gut that made him want to double over. He nudged the horse forward, aiming for stealth rather than speed.

A shadow slithered out of the corner of his eye, and he barely had to time tell Trouble to duck before an arrow sailed over their heads. So much for avoiding a confrontation. He dug his heels into the horse's side.

Another arrow shrieked past him, bathing his cheek in an icy breeze. He veered the horse down a side street toward an open field. Normally, he would have preferred having a wide area to fight, but the three arrows that sank into the side wall of the last building in town reminded him that he'd be a prime target. He pulled on the reins, turning the horse sharply to the left and back toward the main road to Boznac.

Five pairs of glowing red eyes stared back at him from the shadows of the building, the stench of undead filling his nostrils. Trouble's arm squeezed his waist, easing his own terror and reminding him of his duty. She was his only priority. He urged the horse to run faster as a volley of arrows danced around them.

Strangely enough, no more arrows followed. He listened for the sounds of more hooves but only heard the ones beneath him. Unease knotted his shoulders. It was almost too easy to escape.

The horse's sides heaved from carrying the weight of both of them during the wild gallop, and he was forced to slow down before he killed the beast. An empty plain dotted with boulders stretched out in front of them under the light of the three moons.

Trouble loosened her grip around his waist. "Do you

think we lost them?"

His skin still crawled, but he wanted to test her ability to sense dark magic. "What do you think?"

"I can still smell them."

"What do they smell like?"

She shifted behind him. "Like something even vultures refuse to eat."

He bit back a laugh. "Do you sense anything else?"

"I can't really describe it, but yes." Her fingers twisted in the fabric of his cloak. "It's like I'll never feel warm or happy again."

That's one way to describe it. "Remember these sensations. If you have them again, you'll know that undead are nearby. It may be the only warning you get."

A few minutes of silence passed before her muffled voice said, "Thank you for getting me away from whatever was shooting those arrows."

"Are you finally starting to believe me?"

"Possibly."

He almost groaned. This girl was more stubborn than any previous Soulbearer he'd protected before. The gods must have sent her to try his patience.

One of the boulders shifted in front of him. The hair stood up on the back of his neck, and he rubbed his eyes. *Lady Luck, please let me be seeing things.* The boulder moved again and raced toward them.

***

A tingle shot down Arden's spine a split second before the horse reared and tossed her to the ground. Pebbles dug into her flesh, and the stars danced in the sky above.

"Get up before you get killed," urged the voice in her head that was becoming all too familiar.

She rolled to her side in time to see a pair of hooves kick up the dust in front of her. Fear rushed through her body, and she scrambled to her feet to escape the frenzied horse. The smell of rotting flesh intensified. Shadows coated the darkened surroundings, deepening the chaos around her. The clang of swords echoed nearby.

"Trouble, behind you!"

A shriek escaped from her mouth when she turned to see the man wielding a scythe. The blade sliced through the air. She jumped back. A whoosh of air rippled her tunic from the near miss. *Sweet Lady Moon, he's trying to kill me.*

"This brainless minion won't kill you yet. I think he wants that honor."

"Who wants that honor?"

The grey-skinned man swung the scythe again, forcing her back to avoid the blade.

"The necromancer is standing about twenty feet behind you."

Her chest tightened. It was all true—everything Dev had tried to warn her about. Undead. Necromancers. And now they wanted her.

"They only want you to get to me," Loku continued.

She twisted to avoid the blade and changed her direction. Like hell she was going to be herded like a mindless sheep. "That's rather conceited of you to think that," she said to him through clenched teeth while she focused on her attacker.

"Didn't I ever tell you that the world revolves around me? Life is dull without chaos."

If she weren't inches from being slashed into ribbons by a man with glowing red eyes and scythe, she would have laughed. Her hand wrapped around the handle of the knife Dev had given her. The slim blade would probably shatter if she tried to block a blow with it, but at least she could flash it around and let her waxy-faced attacker know she wasn't going to give up without a fight. Maybe she'd even be lucky enough to draw blood.

Other than her own, that is.

A burst of flames ignited nearby, chasing away the darkness. Her heart pounded in her throat. Cinder was on fire. She ran toward the glowing wolf with the intention of extinguishing the inferno but stopped when she realized he was wasn't in pain. Quite the contrary, actually. He seemed to attack the undead around them with renewed vigor.

"Trouble!" Dev pointed behind her.

Scythe-man caught the end of her braid as she whipped around, and her hair tumbled into her face.

Several small pyres burned around her, and the number of attackers grew smaller. Dev struggled to avoid three of them while Cinder attacked two more.

"Remember what Dev told you. Fire can kill undead."

"But how—"

"Gather it up inside you like you did in the inn and launch it at him."

If only she had a few seconds to cast the spell. The curved blade hissed through the air. Its wielder took a step toward her, directing her toward the dark-cloaked figure waiting on a boulder behind her.

Fury at becoming a pawn in his game gnawed at her stomach until it burned. The heat travelled through her body from her core to her fingertips, building in intensity until her fingernails glowed like white-hot coals. With a strangled cry, she released the magic. Six fireballs erupted from her hands. Scythe-man moaned as the flames consumed his face, and he dropped to his knees.

Arden grabbed his harvesting tool, swinging it with all the strength she could muster. The blade cut cleanly through the undead's neck, and his head rolled across the ground.

Waves of nausea enveloped her. What had she just done?

"Very impressive, young Soulbearer," a gravelly voice murmured behind her. "Loku chose well this time."

Although her lungs burned for air, her breath froze at the end of a shaky exhalation. She lifted her head. The necromancer glided toward her like a shadow of a large bird. An icy chill gripped her. Her hands shook when she raised the scythe. "Back away, or you're next."

His laughter felt like thousands of ants crawling on her skin. Sparks of black lightning zapped between his fingers.

"You think you can destroy me?"

"Uh-oh. Time to put up a shield."

Before she understood what Loku meant, a bolt of the black lightning struck her. The scythe fell from her hands as she doubled over in pain. Searing blades tore at her insides, clawing their way to the surface. A black veil descended over her vision and, off in the distance, she heard her own screams.

She had never prayed for death until that moment.

An orange glow bloomed in front of her, and the torture ended. She slowly opened her eyes. A circle of flames surrounded the necromancer. Hooves thundered toward her.

"Get your shield up now before he has a chance to mount another attack."

"A shield?" A haze of exhaustion clouded her mind.

"Imagine a barrier covering you that will block any magic that comes toward you."

She focused on the idea of a blanket wrapped tightly around her, one that could drive away the cold dread nibbling at her soul. She stretched it further, covering her head and limbs in its warmth. Her muscles unlocked. When a rough hand grabbed hers and pulled her onto the horse that galloped past her, she willingly molded her body to the task. The blanket doubled in size, enveloping Dev and his horse.

Something collided with the shield. Her body jerked forward as if she had been punched, but her back and chest remained pain-free. She tightened her grip around Dev's waist, burying her face in the folds of his cloak.

The wind carried a whisper that penetrated her shield, coiled around her ear like a tendril of smoke. "Very impressive, little Soulbearer, but don't worry. You'll soon come crawling to me, and Loku will be mine."

Chapter 9

Dev's jaw began to unclench when the next farming town came into view. He had underestimated this necromancer, and Trouble had almost gotten killed because of it. The threat that followed them on the breeze served as a challenge.

A yawn behind him also reminded him that he'd also underestimated the new Soulbearer. It was one thing to shoot a single fireball at an enemy, but six? Either she'd received some training in the magical arts, or she was more powerful than he first thought. Judging by Ranello's hostile attitude toward mages, he placed his bet on the latter. He remembered what Loku had said about being drawn to her power. What did the god have in mind for her?

He shook his head. Too many questions without answers. Fatigue sagged his shoulders, reminding him of how little sleep he'd gotten tonight. Maybe in the morning, the answers would appear more readily than they did now.

Trouble yawned again, and the warm glow of her shield retreated from him. Its absence left a chill in its wake. He savored the remnants that pressed against his back. Yet another thing puzzling him. "Where did you learn to cast a shield?" And more importantly, why hadn't she cast it before the necromancer attacked her?

"Loku taught me." Sleep laced her words.

"Stay awake until the sun comes up. We'll be safe then."

Her arms tightened, but she didn't say anything else. She must be weary not to ask her usual barrage of questions. He slid his hand over hers and let it linger there, enjoying the faint pulsations of her arteries that vibrated through his fingertips. The fact that this naïve little barmaid had managed to stay unharmed so far amazed him.

"Your hands are warm," she murmured.

"Cold?"

"I'm the one without a cloak here."

He chuckled at the return of her sarcasm. "And does Loku have a suggestion about how to get your own cloak?"

A few seconds later, she tugged on the bottom of his cloak. She reached her arms under it and pressed her body close to his back. "Mmmm, better."

"Is this what Loku suggested?"

She paused before drawing out the word, "No."

His curiosity rose, washing the fatigue away from his body for a brief while. "What did he suggest, then?"

"You don't want to know."

The memory of the way her body writhed in bed caused him to inhale sharply. He had a pretty good idea of what Loku suggested. Blood rushed to his groin, and he shifted in the saddle to find a more comfortable position. Why did he torture himself this way? He should know better than to have such thoughts about the Soulbearer. Just because she was a woman didn't change the fact that he was sworn to protect her, not take advantage of her.

In an effort to distract himself from the temptation, he started forming a mental list of things he needed to get when they came to the next market town. Arden needed her own cloak, and they'd reach the coast quicker if his horse didn't have to carry two people. Provisions for the road. Maybe even look into getting her a small sword.

They rode until the first rays of dawn appeared on the horizon. The weak sunlight illuminated the tall red grass that waved in the breeze around them, turning it into a flaming sea. A necromancer's powers weakened during the day, so Dev finally surrendered to his weariness. It would be safe to snatch a few hours of sleep while they could.

He turned his horse off the road and cut through the grass toward a lone fig tree in the middle of the field.

"Why are we stopping?"

His lips twitched in response. "Would you rather sleep on horseback or on the ground?"

"At this point, I don't care."

He stopped the horse, dismounting. Once he secured the reins to the tree, he placed his bedroll on the ground and helped Trouble down. "You can sleep here."

She cocked her head to the side and blinked a few times. "Where will you sleep?"

"Probably next to the tree."

Her brows furrowed together, but she stretched out on the bedroll and curled her thin body into a ball. "There's still frost on the ground." Her breath formed a white mist in the air when she spoke.

"Do you want my cloak?" he asked as he removed the horse's saddle.

"But how will you stay warm?"

Good question. As if he knew what they were talking about, Cinder lay down and leaned against her back. Not perfect, but his fur would at least keep her back warm.

He closed his eyes so he wouldn't have to watch her shiver. An idea formed in his mind, but he wondered if he had the willpower to carry it out without letting his guard down. He took a deep breath. Duty came before everything else, and right now, the Soulbearer was suffering.

He sat next to her. "Would you mind sharing my cloak while you sleep? I promise I won't do anything that will make you uncomfortable."

"You mean you want to sleep with me?"

Her large blue eyes focused on him, and he winced at her accusation. "No, I meant more like sleep next to you. But if that makes you cringe, I can go back over to the tree."

"No, wait." She grabbed his wrist and pulled him

toward her. For a few seconds, she studied him before she added, "I trust you."

If only she knew some of the thoughts that had crossed his mind last night.

He wrapped his cloak around the both of them. When he lowered his head, she cuddled closer to him.

He shifted so his arm cradled her shoulders and the side of her face pressed against his chest. His muscles relaxed. Instead of being awkward, she fit so well next to him, it almost frightened him.

She stopped shivering after a few minutes, and her warm breath tickled the side of his neck. Sleep claimed her, but before he joined her, he tried to ignore the nagging feeling that he could get entirely too comfortable with her presence.

***

When Arden awoke, she was surprised to find herself sandwiched between Cinder and Dev. Not that she minded, initially. She appreciated the warm coziness of the situation. Then she realized she had draped her thigh over Dev's and wrapped her arm around his chest. Perhaps there was such a thing as too cozy.

"Admit it, my little Soulbearer. You like sleeping next to him or you wouldn't have agreed to it."

She bolted up, but Dev's hand snatched her wrist and pulled her back down against his rock-hard chest. "You're not planning on running away, are you, Trouble?"

"I will if you don't stop calling me that." She yanked her wrist free, sitting up. The sun shone high overhead through the branches of the fig tree, and the breeze rustled the red grass around them. "How long do you think we were asleep?"

He raised his head and squinted at the sun. "I'd say about six or seven hours."

Thoughts of what happened the night before haunted her, and she pulled her knees up to her chest. The necromancer wanted her. She had called upon magic she didn't know was possible for her to wield, and she had slept next to a man who hadn't taken advantage of her. What was the world coming to?

Laughter rang in her mind. *"You wouldn't have stopped him if he tried to take advantage of you."*

"You're wrong." She cast a sideways glance at Dev, and her cheeks burned. Would she have minded if Dev kissed like her like he had in his dream?

"You are *a wench in prude's clothing,"* Loku replied, followed by more laughter.

Her hands bunched up into fists. *"Will you stop implying that I'm nothing more than a common whore? I'm beginning to think the reason why the others went insane is because they had to listen to your constant stream of lewd insinuations."*

"Is Loku misbehaving again?" Dev held out a piece of dried meat to her.

She took it and tore off a bite. When it was soft enough to swallow, she replied, "How can you tell?"

"The ring in your eyes flashes, followed by this expression on your face that can only be described as one of pure annoyance."

"Yes, you can say he's pissing me off."

Cinder rested his head on her lap and fixed his ocher gaze on what was left of the piece of meat in her hand. She tossed it to him. It was too tough for her liking, anyway.

"You're going to spoil him if you keep doing that."

"And what's so bad about that? I'd rather stay on his good side." The wolf licked her fingertips. When he finished she ran her hands through his thick, rust-colored fur. No burns, no blisters, no evidence of what she'd witnessed last night. "Dev, did you heal Cinder?"

"What do you mean?" He dropped the saddle and knelt next to them. Concern etched his face as he examined his pet. "Was he hurt?"

"One of those undead set him on fire last night. How could you have missed that?"

He threw his head back and laughed. "Cinder's a fire wolf. He can ignite himself and use it to attack others, but the flames never hurt him."

The wolf panted with his tongue hanging out of his mouth like he was laughing at her, too.

"I've never heard of such of thing."

"I'm not surprised," he replied. "Fire wolves can only be found in the extreme northern reaches of Gravaria. About ten years ago, Robb killed one, leaving three young cubs without a mother. I took Cinder and found homes for the other two."

"He's getting up in age now, isn't he?"

That muffled chuckle answered her. "Cinder's still a pup. Fire wolves easily live into their fifties."

She stood and combed through what was left of her tangled hair. Until last night, it had reached her waist. Now it fell just past her shoulders, reminding her of how close that scythe had come to her neck. "You wouldn't happen to have something I could use to tie my hair back, do you?"

"No, but I'm sure we'll find something if we can make it to Pasella before nightfall."

"But Pasella is three days away from Wallus."

Dev tightened the saddle to his horse. "Yes, and in case you've forgotten, this is our third day together."

Her shoulder blades jerked back like someone had poked her in between them. Had they really been running for three days now? "Are we going to stay the night at Pasella?"

"Absolutely not. From now on, we ride all night and sleep during the day somewhere off the main road. It's safer that way."

A frown tugged at the corners of her mouth. All her life, she'd heard stories of the large market town, and she wanted to have some time to explore it.

"Yes, let's linger there and wait for the necromancer to catch up with us. Brilliant idea. I can't wait to spend eternity trapped in his body."

A shiver raced down her spine. No, she wasn't in any hurry to meet up with the necromancer again. "Fine, we'll keep moving.*"*

"If it's any consolation, there's plenty to see in Gravaria for the first-time tourist. Me, I'm rather bored with it all, but that doesn't mean you won't enjoy it."

She grinned and began wrapping up the bedroll. *"Uh-oh, if we're going to travel like this all the way to the coast, I'm not sure I want to have to huddle next to Dev every night for warmth."*

"Liar."

"Dev, do you think we'll be able to find me a cloak and bedroll in Pasella?"

He mounted his horse and extended his hand to her. "I've already thought of that. They're both on my list of things to buy while we're there."

She hopped up behind him. "What else is on your list?"

"Food. A horse for you."

"What? You don't like me being this close to you as we ride?" She wrapped her arms around his waist.

He flinched. "I, um, think we'll be able to travel faster if we didn't wear out my horse."

"Now he's the liar."

Arden giggled at Loku's observation. "I agree. It will be nice to have my own horse, especially if we need to outrun anyone looking for us."

"Are you comfortable handling a horse?"

"Of course. Before I worked in the kitchen, I used to work in the stable."

His shoulders relaxed, and they cut through the field to get back on the main road toward Pasella.

Chapter 10

The sun hung low and red on the horizon when they entered Pasella. Despite the late hour, the markets still bustled with activity. Merchants shouted out the daily specials from their booths. The pungent scents of exotic spices mingled with the odors of meat and fish. Children wove in and out of the traffic in the streets, laughing as they kicked a ball between the wheels of a passing cart.

It boggled Arden's mind to think the people could stand to be so close to their neighbors and not become permanently irritated. The constant jostling by the crowds in the street already had her wanting to smack someone.

"Your knuckles are turning white," Dev said as they rode through the crowded street.

She unlocked her hands from around his waist and allowed the circulation to return to her fingers. "I've decided I don't like the city."

"And you wanted to stay the night here." That mocking chuckle rumbled through his chest.

"Point made. Can we please buy what we came here for and leave? I feel like everyone is staring at me."

"They are."

"Thanks for trying to soothe my nerves."

"You'll be more comfortable once we get to Gravaria."

She rolled her eyes. "Promises, promises."

A small child pointed at Cinder and screamed, "Wolf!"

The crowd parted around them and pressed against the sides of the buildings.

With a quiet groan, Dev stopped the horse and dismounted. He ruffled the fur on Cinder's neck and told the child, "He's just a large dog. Completely tame." Then he grabbed the reins and pushed his way through the masses.

Arden took advantage of having the horse all to herself and slid forward into the saddle. "Ahh, it's good not having to endure a horse's ass the entire ride."

"And what is that supposed to mean?" he asked tightly.

She smiled sweetly in return. There was more than one way to define horse's ass.

As Dev led the horse through the crowds, most people gave them the same amount of leeway as they would a plague-bringer. At least the stench of unwashed bodies and urine wasn't as overwhelming now. The scents of spices and leather trickled up from the stalls in the market. The merchant trains that came through Wallus twice a year seemed pitiful compared to the variety here.

They stopped in front of a clothing booth, and he began inspecting the cloaks hanging there. Her gaze fixed on a deep blue one that would match her eyes and compliment her hair. Absolutely perfect. She stroked the buttery-soft wool, admiring the silver embroidery along the edge.

"This will do." Dev shoved a plain brown cloak into her hand, ignoring the merchant who counted out the coins behind him.

"But I like this one." She reached for the blue cloak again.

"I don't care what you like. I'm paying for this, and you'll take what I think is practical."

How dare he order her around like she was his blood? A few choice words sat poised on the tip of her tongue, but his glare silenced her. For now, anyway.

At the edge of the market, they found a blacksmith with several horses in a pen next to the shop. "Any of them look good to you, Trouble?"

"Why are you asking me? You're paying for it, so just pick the one you think is most practical."

A muscle rippled along his jaw, but he didn't say anything else.

"That was rather sassy."

"He deserved it. After all, I was just repeating what he told me earlier. He can't complain that I'm not listening to him."

She slid out of the saddle and began to inspect the horses. Two of them looked like they'd keel over dead before they reached the coast. A solid black stallion pranced around the pen with so much nervous energy, she feared she wouldn't be able to control him. That left the small roan near the water trough.

Dev stood next to her. "I think the roan will work best for you," he said almost apologetically. "Do you agree?"

She glanced at him out of the corner of her eye. "For once."

His lips twitched, and he went to search for the blacksmith. The two men haggled over the price of the mare, leaving her alone with her thoughts. Perhaps she shouldn't have given Dev such a hard time. After all, he was spending more money on her in one day than Hal had in the last ten years.

With Cinder at her side, she approached the roan with her hand extended. The horse snorted and shied away from the wolf initially, but with a few coaxing words, she came close enough to nuzzle Arden's hand.

"My apprentice seems to have taken a liking to that one," she heard Dev say behind her. "I'm not interested in the others."

"Apprentice, eh? Is that what they're calling them these days?"

Every muscle in her body locked. Now people thought she was Dev's whore. She should have expected it, though. Anyone with eyes could tell she wasn't his blood, and she doubted they'd believe she was his wife.

"Wife. Whore. The only difference between the two are

a few words. Oh, and the binding commitment that
shackles you to another person."

"Thank you so much for sharing your unique outlook
on life."

"When you've lived as long as I have, you'll
understand my perspective."

"You mean to say you're not going to drive me to
suicidal insanity any time soon?"

"No, my little Soulbearer, I have big plans for you."

The sensation of fingers grazing the curve of her neck
sent a shiver through her body. She was about to ask Loku
exactly what those plans were when Dev motioned for her
to join him. The blacksmith hurried toward the ramshackle
barn on the other side of the pen, the gold coin in his hand
glinting in the fading sun.

"You know," she said, "you shouldn't flash your
money around like that. You're asking to get robbed."

The corner of Dev's mouth quirked up in a half smile.
"I'd like to see the human foolish enough to try and rob
me. He'd probably run screaming once he saw Cinder light
up."

She snuck her arm around his waist and carefully
lifted his money pouch. Her fingers brushed against the
cool metal inside and hooked three coins into her fist.
"Only if you knew you were getting robbed."

His hand clamped down on her wrist. "What are you
trying to prove?"

"That if a more skillful thief picked your pocket, you'd
lose a lot more than just a few coins." She opened her hand
to show him the gold in her palm.

His eyes darkened, and a sliver of fear pierced her
chest. "You're a thief in addition to a bar wench?"

She tried to yank her hand free. The gall of that man!
"I don't know what you're implying."

He pulled her closer. "I saw the other wench flirting
with her customers. I just assumed you also saw to all your
customer's needs."

Blood pounded in her veins. "And that's where you're

mistaken. My duties were confined to the kitchen, not upstairs." She finally wrestled free of his grasp and hurled the coins at his face. "I'm neither a whore nor a thief."

"Arden, don't storm out of here like a sulking two-year-old."

She froze at the sound of her name. And all this time, she thought he didn't know it. "Apologize first."

"I'm sorry," he said through clenched teeth.

That's his idea of an apology?

"Enjoy it while you can. He's not a man that apologizes often."

"I guess I'll have to." "Apology accepted. Now, what did you want to show me?"

"This way." He led her deeper into the shop, where several weapons hung on the wall. He grabbed a short sword with a thin blade and tested it for balance. "This feels like something you should be able to handle."

Laughter nearly choked her. "You want to buy me a sword?"

"You need to learn to protect yourself in case something happens to me. I would be neglecting my duty if I didn't at least prepare you for the worst." He held the sword out to her. "Here, try it out."

Her hand trembled as she grasped the hilt of the sword, a thing she'd always been forbidden to touch. Her muscles tensed, preparing to wield the weight of the weapon, but it was lighter than she imagined. Only a few pounds. Gaining confidence, she swung the blade through the air a few times.

Dev dodged the tip of the blade as it passed mere inches from his stomach. "Hey, watch where you're pointing that thing."

Arden giggled and continued to mimic the fighting maneuvers she'd seen the men of her village practice with over the years. The rush of having a weapon excited her, and she threw more power into her swings. It felt so comfortable in her hand, like it had been made especially for her. "I want this sword."

A loud crash sounded behind them, and the hilt slipped through her fingers. The sword landed with a dull clang. She whirled around.

"What is the meaning of this?" the blacksmith asked, his face red with anger.

"I was wondering how much the sword was." Dev's cool and collected voice soothed her but had little effect on the blacksmith.

"I don't sell weapons to women. They need to know their place. You should have better control of your whore."

Dev crossed his arms, and the silent intimidation that he'd used on Hal before seeped into the room like an invisible fog. "What I teach my apprentice is none of your concern. Again, how much is the sword?"

The color fled from the man's face, and his mouth flapped open and closed like a fish. "It ain't right, I tell you. Women should respect their blood, and even when they've been cast aside like her, they still need to be taught their place."

Dev's brows furrowed together. "What a strange kingdom this is. I ask to purchase a sword, and I have a merchant who's unwilling to sell it to me and keep his family well fed for the next month."

The blacksmith picked up the sword, his eyes darting back and forth between them. The struggle over money versus his ideals played out in his face. Finally, he said, "Two hundred loras and your word that she won't use it."

A tight smile stretched on his lips as Dev reached into his pouch and counted out enough coins to equal double the asking price.

The smith's eyes widened at the sight of the money, and he gave Dev the sword in exchange for it. "I found a saddle for her. Let me put it on the mare--"

"I can saddle my own horse," Arden interrupted. Leave it to a man who thought she was nothing more than a whore to not tighten the straps properly, in hopes she'd fall and break her neck. One less cast-off for society to deal with.

"I don't think you're a cast-off at all. In truth, you are far more special than any of those fat and content women who are slaves to their blood. Out of all the people in the inn that night, you're the one I chose as my Soulbearer."

She closed her eyes and allowed the compliment to wrap around her like a warm hug. *"Thank you, Loku. I needed to hear that."*

Dev fetched the horse from the pen, leading it to her. Within a few minutes, they saddled the horse and prepared to leave Pasella. He sheathed the new sword into a leather scabbard, tucking it into her bedroll.

"I thought you gave your word I wouldn't use it."

"Did you hear me agree to that?" He winked at her. "Would you like to stop at an inn for a hot meal before we leave?"

Her stomach growled, but she shook her head. "No, I just want to leave this place."

"That was very inappropriate for him to say those things about you. I fought hard not to disembowel him when he called you a…" His voice froze.

"When he called me the same thing you accused me of being only a few minutes before?" she finished for him.

He lowered his head and turned away. "I suppose I'm no better than him."

Guilt gnawed away at her mind. Somewhere underneath all the gruff orders and biting sarcasm was a good man, and she'd just punched him in the stomach with shame. "Dev, don't worry about it. Maybe one day, I'll explain our traditions and why he said those things. In the meantime, let's go before the necromancer catches up with us."

Chapter 11

Dev blocked another swing and added one of his own. Trouble's sword barely met his before he tapped her shoulder. Sweat dripped down her face, and her breaths came in loud pants now. In the distance, lightning flashed and thunder rumbled. She spun around, trying to attack him once again. He stood back, calmly parrying her assault.

This was their third night of combat training. So far, she'd proven to be a quick study. He only had to show her a maneuver once or twice before she mastered it. Aided by her cat-like reflexes, she was becoming a formidable opponent in short stretches of combat. The only thing she needed to work on was her stamina.

She swung and missed, leaving her body open for attack. He whacked her on the flank with the flat of his blade.

"Ow!" Her sword fell from her hands.

"You get sloppy when you get tired. Take a break."

She walked to a tree stump, still clutching her side, and sat with a grunt. "That's going to leave another bruise."

"Consider it a lesson learned. It's far better to be alive with a few bruises than to be dead."

"I'll try and keep that in mind when I can't find a comfortable sleeping position in the morning." She wiped the sweat off her face. "I'm just glad that spell of yours keeps the blades dull, or I'd be full of holes by now."

"Only by your own blade. In case you haven't noticed, most of my hits on you haven't been with the sharp edges."

She grimaced. "I've noticed. They leave bigger welts."

He studied her once again for any subtle signs of madness while she rested. Thankfully, he hadn't seen any yet.

His mind drifted back to the blacksmith's comments in Pasella. He waited for her to explain it to him, but so far, she hadn't. "Trouble, what did the blacksmith mean the other night about women obeying their blood and being cast aside?"

She flinched like he'd slapped her, and he realized too late that he shouldn't have asked. The insults were still too fresh. By Jussip, why had he insinuated that she would sleep with men for money? Deep inside, he knew the answer. She'd wounded his pride by proving she could pick his pocket without him noticing it, and he wanted to knock her down a few notches. And it had backfired.

To his surprise, she answered him. "In Ranello, women are under the control of their nearest male relative, or their 'blood.' Everything we have is owned by our blood. They arrange our marriages for us, and if they determine we can't be married off or if we bring shame to the family, they cast us aside." Her eyes never left the ground as she spoke.

"What a strange custom that is. In Gravaria, women have the same rights as men. In fact, our ruler is a woman, Empress Marist. But why did he call you a whore?"

Her head snapped up, and her mouth tightened into a thin line. "Women who've been cast aside have only one option available to them to keep a roof over their heads and food in their bellies. And since it's quite obvious we're not related, he assumed the worst."

Dev shook his head. The sooner he got her out of this kingdom, the better.

She reached inside her tunic, playing with the gold pendant around her neck. Another bolt of lightning lit up the sky, followed by a roll of thunder a few seconds later.

"Who is your blood? Your father?"

She froze. The halo in her eyes flashed golden, and her fist clamped around the pendant. "The man who sired me cast my mother aside and left her. Hal, my mother's cousin, took her in when she returned to Wallus pregnant with me, even though he wasn't obligated to do that. She'd left the village to foolishly find a better life for herself in Trivinus. Instead, all she got was a broken heart and bastard child."

"So, you have no idea who your father is?"

"Why should I care?" She jumped up to her feet and grabbed her sword. "That asshole took advantage of her."

He barely had time to grab his own sword and block her swing. The force of the blow sent vibrations up his arm into his shoulder, and he braced for the next thrust as he jumped to his feet.

Her upper lip curled in a snarl. Tears gathered in the corners of her eyes. "He gave her fancy gifts and told her he'd love her forever in order to seduce her into his bed, and then he left her when she needed him the most. It was all a lie." She continued to swing her weapon in a blind rage, forcing him on the retreat.

Whoever her father was, he feared for the man's life if she ever found him. Her anger toward the man poured into her strikes.

"Even though Hal took her in, he never let her forget she'd been cast aside, and he resented having to be responsible for me. He forced her into other men's beds for the money to keep me fed and clothed. She would have never become a whore if my father had been man enough to take responsibility for his actions."

After a few more hits, fatigue set in. Her swings became less precise. At last, she made a mistake that allowed him to grab her sword arm and pin it behind her back.

"Let go of me! I'm not ready to surrender."

He pulled her closer to him so her body pressed against his. Tears streamed down her face, and a dull ache formed in his chest. So much pain in someone so young.

She wrestled against him, but he held her even tighter. Her anger would continue to fester inside her and drive her closer to the abyss of insanity if she let it. She needed to be shown that if she let go of the past, she'd have so much to look forward to. And he vowed he would help her see that.

Her body stilled. The softness of her curves pressed against his chest. He stared down at her trembling lips. Why would anyone ever cast her aside? Lightning lit up the sky, driving away the shadows on her face for a brief second. The beauty of her spirit called to him. The sudden urge to kiss away her fears overwhelmed him.

The first raindrops pelted them from the heavens, but neither one of them moved. His head inched closer to hers. She lifted her chin, yielded to him. Just before she closed her eyes, the golden-green halo in them flashed, and she gasped.

Dev released her and backed away as if she'd burned him. Dear Jussip, what had he been thinking? She was the Soulbearer, and he'd almost given into his baser desires and kissed her. And judging by the flash he'd seen, Loku had witnessed his moment of weakness. Some protector he was turning out to be. Sometimes he couldn't even keep his head on straight when he was around her.

"I refuse to end up like her," Trouble whispered. Her shoulders sagged under the weight of her confession. The rain ran down her hair, forming tiny rivulets along her clothes.

For the last century, he'd questioned the gods' wisdom when they'd punished him and made him the Soulbearer's protector. His duty had exposed him to the worst in humanity—the weakness, the greed, the cruelty. All things he had seen in himself at one point, but magnified threefold. And yet, as he stared at this fragile girl in front of him, he finally understood why fate had chosen him—to save her. "And you'll never have to, Arden. I promise you that."

A scream pierced the night, followed by the distant clang of swords. The familiar coldness of undead crawled up his spine.

Dev tightened his grip on his sword.

Chapter 12

Arden spun around. Her wet hair lashed against her cheeks, and the smell of rotting corpses filled her nose. All the blood drained from her face. It had taken the necromancer three days to catch up with them, and now he was nearly on top of them.

Distant voices shouted between the sounds of fighting. Some unsuspecting party had stumbled across the undead. Would they have any idea how to kill them?

Loku snorted. *"Ranellians refuse to believe undead exist. What makes you think they'll know what to do when they meet them? It will be lambs to the slaughter."*

Dev grabbed her arm and steered her to the horses. "Let's go before they find us."

"But what about the others?"

"They'll slow the necromancer down and give us a chance to escape."

She wrestled free from him. "But they'll die unless we help them."

"Better them than us."

"How could someone who calls himself a knight think that way?"

His face hardened, and he reached out to grab her again.

She ducked out of his grasp, refusing to be affected by his cowardice.

"I'm a knight of Gravaria, not Ranello. I owe no loyalty to this kingdom. My only duty is to keep you alive and unharmed. Now get on your horse, and let's go."

"He has a point, my Soulbearer. Best to run away now

and live to see another day."

They both told her to run, but her heart kept her feet planted in the ground. Why would the Lady Moon give her these powers and allow her to become a Soulbearer if she couldn't use her gifts to help others when they needed her? She'd faced the necromancer once. She knew how to destroy the undead.

"Don't even think about it. You're already exhausted from your training. There's no way you can fight him on your own and win."

"Then you'll just have to help me," she told Loku. To Dev, she said, "You may not owe any loyalty to this land, but you're sworn to protect me, and I'm a Ranellian." She grabbed her sword and ran in the direction of the fighting, ignoring Dev's shouts for her to come back.

The wind whipped through the trees, causing their branches to claw at her face like dozens of spindly hands. The clouds blocked any light from the moon. The rain came at her sideways now, so she lifted her arm to shield her face.

She paused at a clearing. A bolt of lightning illuminated the scene in front of her, and her heart jumped into her throat. A score of undead with their glowing red eyes shining in the darkness battled an equal number of humans in the storm. *"Sweet Lady Moon, what was I thinking?"*

"I was wondering the same thing. You wanted to help them, so do it."

The smell of death drew closer, and she turned just in time to see an undead plow toward her. The fat in his face had obviously vanished days ago, leaving the loose skin clinging to his prominent facial bones. What had once been a man was now reduced to a skull, with a sinister light radiating from his hollowed eyes.

She tightened her grip on the hilt of her rain-slicked sword, bracing for his attack. The clang of steel echoed in her ears, and she took a step back to keep her balance. *"Either Dev must have been holding back on me, or this undead is stronger than him."*

"The first, I'm certain. Aim for the head."

"What?" she managed to ask before she dodged another swing of the undead's sword. His miss opened him up enough to allow her blade to slash through the bloated stomach. He stumbled back as his guts spilled onto the ground but continued to attack.

A death cry pierced the night, accentuated by a peal of thunder. The humans began to fall while she struggled just to keep one from slicing her to shreds.

"You can hack at them all you want, but until he loses his head, he'll keep swinging."

"What about fire? That worked before."

Loku's laughter grated on her already frazzled nerves. *"I'd like to see you cast and fight at the same time. Even Dev needs to pause before he casts."*

A growl drew her attention to her left. Cinder lunged at the back of an undead's neck, hauling him to the ground so Dev could decapitate it. They made it look so easy.

"Arden, look out!"

She snapped her head back to her attacker and spun out of his way. A line of fire blazed down her back where the blade traced along her skin, forcing the air out of her lungs.

"Keep spinning with your sword up."

She followed Loku's command, and her blade embedded into a solid mass. The resistance she met there slowed her down, but it didn't stop her from sawing through the bones and sinews of the undead's neck. His head rolled off into the darkness.

Her lungs burned as she leaned over and sucked in the cool, damp air. She stared at the black blood that coated the sword. *"I liked the scythe better. It made a cleaner cut."*

"Perhaps we should steal one from the next farm we come across."

Despite the violence raging around her, the corners of her mouth twitched. *"I'd look pretty funny riding through the kingdom with one."*

"But you'd make a memorable impression, my Soulbearer."

Another cry caught her attention. She straightened to her full height. Even though she'd destroyed one undead, the others kept fighting. She drew upon the fire that ached along her back, feeding it down her arms. A flash of lightning provided her with a glimpse of her targets, and the fireballs flew from her fingers.

Instead of consuming the animated corpses like before, the flames fizzled out in the downpour. The sound of gravelly laughter echoed around her—laughter that wasn't Loku's. A chill raced down her spine.

"Did your mentor not inform you that fire spells are useless in the rain?" he asked.

Arden turned in the direction of the voice. A familiar cloaked figure stood a few yards away from her. She threw up her shields before the Necromancer could hit her with another one of his agonizing spells.

"At least he taught you how to block a spell."

The words, although softly spoken, echoed in her mind and surrounded her like a plunge into an icy river. "What do you want with me?" she asked, hoping her voice didn't waver from her shivering.

"Arden Soulbearer, didn't you know you're a unique individual with powers that surpass most mages in this world? Only you can control a god."

"How do you know my name?"

"You left something behind at our last meeting." He held up a thick, golden braid. "Now that I have something of yours, I know where you are. I can find you, learn your secrets, help you fulfill your deepest desires."

She reached to grab her hair back from him, disgusted to know he had a piece of her, but Loku stopped her. *"It's a trick, my Soulbearer. He wants you to lower your defenses so he can attack. Don't fall for his threats."*

Something invisible poked at her shield, looking for weak spots. She reinforced them and glared at the

Necromancer. "You speak nothing but lies."

From under the hood, two red orbs flashed. "I can speak to you of the true horrors of this kingdom. Have you seen what the king does to witches like you?"

The image of five people tied to trees while flames licked at their writhing bodies filled her mind. The odor of burning flesh made her stomach heave, and the victims' screams drowned out the battle around her.

"Get him out of your mind, Arden."

With a whimper, she shut her eyes and forced the image away, knowing it would haunt her later. What if she was caught before she made it to Gravaria? Was this the fate that waited for her?

"Yes, horrific, wasn't it? King Heodis forced me to watch as he reduced my family to ashes for practicing magic. But we could change that. Wouldn't you like to see justice dispensed?"

Her thoughts turned to Hal. She'd love to see him on his knees, begging her for forgiveness after everything he had done to her and her mother. She laughed as Jenna and all the other people in Wallus who called her a freak cried out for mercy when she had her revenge.

"It's all an illusion. Don't believe anything he says."

The Necromancer took a step toward her, and a new wave of magic assaulted her shields. "I can help you. I can free you of Loku."

"The only way you can free me of Loku is by killing me."

"That's what your mentor wants you to believe. I have the power to free souls. I could teach you how to do it if you come with me." He held out his hand, beckoning her.

To be free of Loku? To no longer be a Soulbearer, but to have the chance to live a normal life? Was it even possible?

"Your soul is bound to mine. He'll not only remove my soul, but yours as well, leaving you a hollow husk of what you once were. You'd be like the other undead you see around you. An animated corpse forced to do his bidding.

His slave."

She gritted her teeth. "I refuse to be anyone's slave."

"You choose to believe the god of chaos over me? Who's to say he doesn't want you for his slave? A body forced to do his bidding." The Necromancer tilted his head back and laughed. The dim light caught on a scar that stretched from the left corner of his mouth and disappeared under the shadow of his hood. "Pick your fate, Arden, but know I won't lose this battle. I always get what I want in the end."

The words had barely left his lips when Dev called her name. Keeping her shields up, she searched for him in the stormy darkness. Her heart raced when she couldn't find him. "Dev," she shouted back.

The Necromancer's mouth curled up into a snarl. "Perhaps I can help you make up your mind." He pointed past her and said something in a rasping language she didn't understand. Four undead stalked a lone figure with a wolf at his side.

"Stop playing games," Loku said. "We need to end this now."

"We?"

"You have to trust me. Let me help you defeat him."

"But if I give in to you—"

"If you don't, Dev will be killed and turned into an undead. Do you want that?"

Her mouth went dry. What would she do if Dev became her enemy? He seemed to be her only ally in the craziness that filled her life over the last week. The seconds ticked by as she watched the four undead surround him and begin attacking. He and Cinder tried to hold them off, but fatigue labored his swings. He wouldn't last long against them.

"What do you have in mind?"

"There's more than one way to kill an undead. Coat your hand with the blood on your sword and trust me."

As she smeared the black goo across her palm, Dev's voice cried out. One of his attackers' blades sliced through his thigh, and her protector fell to the ground.

"Give yourself to me now, Arden."

She closed her eyes and surrendered to Loku. He seized control of her body. Magic like she never imagined coursed through her veins. Ice crystals coated her hand, and the wind whipped around her with renewed fury. All she could focus on was saving Dev. Her lips began to move, and words she'd never used before tumbled from them.

The power welled up inside her, threatening to explode. Fear gripped her. Her pulse raced in her ears. What had she agreed to do? The storm intensified. Sleet stung her cheeks. Her knees wobbled. How much longer could she bear this before it destroyed her?

"Don't worry, my Soulbearer. I could never harm you." A pair of invisible, strong arms encircled her, keeping her hand up while Loku continued to cast through her. She leaned back against the warmth and security he offered and let the oblivion consume her.

She lost track of time. Seconds could have passed, or hours. When her consciousness returned, her body felt like all the life had been drained from it, leaving her a limp rag doll. She fell to her knees and slowly opened her eyes.

An eerie silence hung in the clearing. Even the rain had stopped. Tendrils of white fog swirled around her, parting to reveal the Necromancer encrusted in a block of ice in front of her.

She gasped, stumbling back into the mud. What had they just done?

The crack of glass shattering broke the silence. "The undead are frozen," a voice shouted through the fog.

"Destroy them while you can," Dev answered, and the tinkle of more ice breaking reverberated through the clearing.

"We turned them into ice, Loku?"

"I told you there was more than one way to destroy undead."

Her eyes grew heavy, and her sword slipped from her

fingers. They had beaten them. Dev was still alive. And the Necromancer had been stopped. She would have laughed in delight if she could've found the strength to do so. But all she wanted to do now was curl up into a ball and sleep. Her enemies were all ice sculptures now. There was nothing to fear.

A loud crack rumbled the ground under her, and something hard smashed against her temple. A red flash of pain filled her vision before the blackness descended upon her.

Chapter 13

When Dev saw the first cracks in the ice surrounding the Necromancer, he ran toward Trouble as fast as he could with his injured leg. Magic illuminated the fissures forming in the ice, and the resulting explosion catapulted fist-sized chunks through the air. He dropped his sword and dove for her, but he couldn't get to her before one of the blocks connected with her temple. Her eyes widened for a second before they rolled back, and she collapsed into the mud.

He shielded her from the rest of the debris with his body and his magic, exhaling with relief when he felt her warm breath on his hand. He still couldn't believe what he'd just seen. Trouble, the little slip of a barmaid he'd rescued less than a week ago, had turned the Necromancer's army into statues of ice. Of course, she didn't do it alone. Her eyes glowed bright yellow-green while she cast, and her voice deepened when she recited the incantation. Loku had seized control of her.

His shields buckled, and he looked up. Even though the rain had stopped for the moment, lightning still illuminated the sky and the face of their enemy. The scar that ran along the Necromancer's left cheek added a new level of sinister to his snarl.

"Give her to me," he whispered.

"You'll have to kill me first."

Shadows emerged from the darkness around them. "I won't have to, mage. The Ranellians will do that for me. You know how low their tolerance for magic is."

"So you can expect the same treatment from them."

The Necromancer laughed, sending a chill into the very core of Dev's body. "Sooner or later, I always get what I want." He produced a dagger from under the folds of his cloak and held it out for Dev to examine. The same dagger that killed Robb.

The memory of his failure tore at him like a barbed whip. He lifted his body, muscles poised to spring, but stopped himself. The Necromancer wanted him to lower his shields and attack. That was the only way he could get to Trouble. He cradled her in his arms, pulling her closer to his chest. Whatever happened to him, he refused to let her suffer the same fate as the prior Soulbearer. "As long as my shield holds, no one will hurt her."

"And how long will it hold with your leg bleeding like that?" The Necromancer's hand tightened around the dagger's hilt. "I can feel your magic weakening with each beat of your heart."

The Ranellians circled them, coming close enough to where he could see the stark lines of their features in the night.

The Necromancer ignored them. "As long as my shield holds, we can continue this stalemate for days, Protector."

Dev sized up the humans. He needed to make sure they were on his side. "And who do you think they'd attack first? You, who ordered the undead to attack them? Or me, who came to their aid?"

"The law of the kingdom still stands." He inched closer so that his shield butted against Dev's. "King Heodis is not known for his mercy."

From the crowd, a voice replied, "And I intend to carry out the King's justice."

Steel flashed through the air and sliced through the Necromancer's wrist. His screams echoed off the trees as his hand fell to the ground, the fingers still clutching the hilt of the dagger. Before the Ranellian could come in for another attack, red magic exploded from the Necromancer's other hand, knocking all the humans to the ground.

"Tell Arden I look forward to seeing her again soon," he growled as his body faded into mist.

The Ranellian responsible for cutting off the Necromancer's hand jumped to his feet and swung his sword through the shadowy remnants left behind, dispersing them into the wind. "What the hell just happened?"

"He dissipated," Dev replied. He wrapped his arms tighter around Trouble and reinforced his shields around them. The Ranellian's blade had pierced the Necromancer's shields, and he worried that if he didn't cooperate, they might become the next victims to experience the King's justice. "It's a spell most master mages know."

"Where did he go?"

"I have no idea. It's not like we're best friends."

The hand in the mud burst into flames and turned into a pile of ashes within seconds. Only the dagger remained. The Ranellian picked it up.

"Be careful with that," Dev warned. "It's cursed. The last person who felt its point ended up encased in stone."

The Ranellian dropped it and raised his sword. The tip pressed against Dev's shoulder through the shields, the blade obviously holding some enchantment stronger than any magic he could wield. "Why should I believe anything you say?"

"Because my apprentice and I seem to be the only ones who can help you defeat the Necromancer."

The Ranellian's blade grazed Dev's neck. "Who are you, and what is your business in Ranello?"

"I'm Sir Devarius Tel'brien, Knight of Gravaria." No need to add the "Sworn Protector of the Soulbearer" and rouse their suspicions further. The fact that he was a foreign elf who could use magic would be enough to cause him to lose his head. "I was sent by the Empress to follow a Gravarian who'd escaped to Ranello and bring him back."

The clouds parted, and a beam from one of the three moons shined down on them through the trees. Damp curls clung to the Ranellian's broad face, and the royal crest of Ranello stretched across the armored plate covering his chest. One of the King's soldiers. "And where is he?"

"The Necromancer killed him before I could capture him."

Something warm and wet dripped onto Dev's hand. He turned his attention to Trouble. The gash on her temple continued to bleed, trickling down her face onto her shoulder. He contemplated the danger of healing her in front of a hostile audience or waiting until later and praying he wouldn't be too late. His leg throbbed in response, reminding him of his own wounds. He lowered his shields, since the Ranellian had already proven he could slice through them. "May I ask your name?"

The Ranellian's eyes widened in surprise. He withdrew his sword a few inches. "I'm Kell." He waited a moment, the expression on his face full of self-importance.

Dev gave a curt nod in acknowledgement but nothing more. The name meant nothing to him. As far as he was concerned, the man was just another backwards Ranellian. "Well, if you don't mind, my apprentice and I need to find our horses and be on our way to Boznac."

"You're not going anywhere. Like Sulaino said, magic is forbidden in Ranello. Your apprentice gave us quite a display of her power."

"She did it to save your lives, you ungrateful humans."

His retort resulted in three news blades poking his back.

Kell narrowed his eyes. "The law is still the law, and only the King can overturn it."

A familiar growl sounded behind him. The Ranellians jumped back as Cinder forced his way through them, sitting between Kell and Trouble. Dev used the momentary distraction to heal the gash at her temple. The blood stopped, but she didn't stir.

Cinder licked her cheek and whimpered.

"I'm beginning to think you like her more than me," he murmured to the animal.

"Is this your wolf?" Kell asked. His sword wavered slightly in front of them.

"Yes. He's tame," he replied before adding under his breath, "for the most part."

"Sir Devarius, I have no desire to remain here in the mud with my sword pointed at you all night. You and your apprentice both look like you could use the attention of a healer."

Dev choked back a laugh. He would rather rot in a shallow grave than face the primitive healing the Ranellians offered. Although it took more magic to heal himself than it did to heal another, at least he wouldn't have to worry about rusty needles and dirty bandages. "I'll take care of her." He brushed her wet hair back from her temple to inspect the injury. Not even a scar remained. "She is my responsibility."

"Perhaps I didn't make myself clear. You are both under arrest for using magic in Ranello. According to the law, I have every right to burn you both at the stake right now." Kell knelt in front of them and lowered his voice. "I'm grateful you came to our aid, which is why I'm showing you what mercy I can. I can't overturn the laws, but I can plead your case to the king and ask him to set you free."

A smirk pulled at Dev's lips. "Or you and your men could say we escaped and forget about this whole incident."

"My gratitude doesn't extend to making me look like an incompetent fool in front of my men."

He scanned the small band of soldiers, calculating his odds of escaping without getting either one of them killed. He could always use magic to confuse and detain the Ranellians, but he had to factor in that he was injured and Trouble was unconscious. He doubted he could make it back to their horses before they overtook him.

He closed his eyes, took a deep breath. He hated when

Lady Luck stacked the odds against him. "It seems I have no other choice in the matter," he said at last.

"I'm glad we could reach a consensus without more violence." Kell stood, sheathed his sword, and turned to the man standing next to him. "Lord Bynn, will you relieve Sir Devarius of his apprentice and take her to my tent? She'll have some privacy there while the healer tends to her injuries."

"Yes, Your Highness," Bynn replied with a bow.

Dev winced at Kell's title. Just perfect. He'd been exchanging barbs with the youngest of the Ranellian princes. So much for improving relations between their two kingdoms. At least that explained why the man thought he might be able to sway King Heodis into pardoning them. Saving a young princeling had to count for something.

Bynn reached for Trouble, causing Cinder to growl. Dev didn't stop him.

Kell sighed and rolled his eyes. "We can't help you if you don't let us."

"I'm trying to decide whether or not to trust you and your men." *Especially when your reputation with women is legend even in Gravaria.*

"Are Gravarians always this suspicious?"

"It wouldn't be the first time a Ranellian has double-crossed us."

Kell's mouth became a tight line. Some stories history never seemed to forget, no matter how many times they were rewritten. More than three centuries had passed since Ranello refused to come to Gravaria's aid when blight raged across the land. Instead, the king blamed the use of magic for the failed crops and closed the borders between the two kingdoms. Thousands died from starvation before a ritual to end it was found. By then, the blight had crossed the mountains into Ranello. Gravarian mages came to help the Ranellians when they begged for mercy, only to be executed by the king for breaking his new law banning magic within the realm.

"I give you my word as the Third Prince of Ranello that no harm will come to you or your apprentice from me and my men."

His gaze travelled between the two men in front of him before coming to rest on Cinder. "Do you mind if he follows her?"

What little color the pale moonlight gave Kell's face fled. He cleared his throat. "And what if your wolf attacks us?"

"As long as you don't hurt her, he'll behave. He's quite attached to her, after all."

The Ranellians exchanged glances. Bynn cleared his throat. "I have no problem with the wolf, Your Highness. He seems tame enough."

When Bynn reached for Trouble again, Dev gave her to him. The nobleman carried her with ease toward the other side of the clearing, with Cinder on his heels.

Dev watched them until they disappeared from view. His heart pounded, and he hoped he'd made a wise decision trusting the prince. With his lap bare, he got a closer look at his thigh. Blood oozed from the wound, and a wave of dizziness blurred his vision.

Kell leaned over and offered his hand. "I think the healer needs to tend to you before your apprentice."

"I'll be fine." A grunt escaped Dev's throat as he came to his feet and tested his leg. He could put a little weight on it, but he stumbled forward when he tried to walk. Pain snaked up his thigh like a dozen hot daggers.

A strong arm caught him and kept him from sprawling in the mud. "Are Gravarian knights as stubborn as they are suspicious?" Laughter laced Kell's voice.

Dev ground his teeth to keep from telling him exactly what he thought, but he worried the cries of pain would overshadow his words if he opened his mouth. Instead, he accepted the prince's aid and limped across the clearing.

"Sir Devarius—"

"It's Dev, if you don't mind." He already felt nauseated enough without having to deal with excessive formality.

"Dev, I truly do appreciate your help tonight fighting Sulaino."

"You have your work cut out for you if you think you can defeat a necromancer without magic."

"Which is why I want to see you and your apprentice live. We could use your assistance."

He stopped and refused to budge. "What makes you think we'll stay and help?"

Disbelief crossed Kell's face, revealing his youthful idealism. By Jussip, he and Trouble were two of a kind. A few decades' worth of experience would temper it.

"The only reason I'm here is because I went chasing after Trouble," Dev continued. "She's the one who came up with the crazy idea she could stop the Necromancer you call Sulaino. If I had my way, I would've thrown her over her horse and been several miles down the road by now."

The frown on the prince's face deepened. "You call yourself a knight, and yet you would not come to the aid of others when it was needed? What about honor and chivalry?"

"I don't know where you Ranellians get your definitions of honor and chivalry, but in Gravaria, honor means upholding my oaths. I pledged my service to the Empress of Gravaria, and I swore an oath to protect Trouble. That's it. I'm not obligated to help you at all."

Kell shoved him away and reached for his sword. "You're a man without honor."

Dev held his arms out to his sides. "And you're willing to attack an injured and unarmed man because he speaks the truth. How honorable is that, Prince Kell?" He almost spat out the last words.

The prince's fingers unwrapped from the sword's hilt one by one. "Point made. Let's get you to the healer before I have to drag you through the mud."

A still figure emerged from the shadows, and the smell of death wafted in the breeze. Dev tensed. Could Sulaino have already sent more undead to attack them? He stopped, nodding toward it.

Kell stared at it for a minute then turned away. "It's one of my own men. He was killed in the fight, and Sulaino changed him. I couldn't bring myself to destroy him."

Water steadily dripped off the figure. If he didn't act soon, the undead would thaw out of his icy shell and continue to follow the Necromancer's orders. Dev limped toward it, raising his elbow. The head of the ice statue cracked under the force of his first blow.

Kell grabbed his arm. "What do you think you're doing?"

"I'm setting his soul free. As long as his body remains intact, it'll be tortured by that fiend." He wrenched his arm free and managed to shatter the head into dozens of shards before Kell flung him to the ground.

"But he was one of my men."

Dev struggled to his feet. "No. The moment Sulaino animated him, he became his slave. He has no memories of his friends and family. He exists only to carry out his creator's bidding."

A muscle rippled along Kell's jaw. He glanced at the jagged torso and legs that remained. "Perhaps I was foolishly wishing your apprentice could reverse the spell."

A bitter note of laughter answered him. "Trouble's powerful, but there's only one way to bring the dead back to life, and you've already seen it."

Kell traced the sharp edges of the ice. "It seems like the apprentice is more powerful than the master."

Resentment surged through Dev. He didn't like the idea that the prince thought his powers inadequate. In truth, Trouble had demonstrated strong potential in the elemental magics even without Loku's influence, but the only reason she succeeded tonight was because of the god's power. "All the more reason to get her to the Mage Primus in Gravaria so she can complete her training under someone whose skill matches hers."

"Are you sure she's your apprentice and nothing

more? After all, not many women would travel alone with a man unless they were on, um, intimate terms."

Dev resisted the urge to punch the insolent grin off the prince's face, especially after his question reminded him of how close he came to kissing her earlier this evening. "My duty takes precedence above everything else," he replied woodenly, "and she lives up to her name."

Kell's smile widened. "It'll be interesting to see how things play out then." He turned to the soldier who approached him and said, "Lassandro, please help Sir Dev to Cero's tent so he can have that leg sewn up."

The soldier bowed and led Dev in the opposite direction of the prince.

He frowned. Why did he feel like he'd just inherited a whole new set of problems?

Chapter 14

Kell rubbed his chin as he reviewed his conversation with the Gravarian knight. Dev was holding something back, but what? His gut told him it had something to do with the girl, and he was determined to get to the bottom of it, especially after seeing Sulaino's interest in her.

Inside Kell's tent, Bynn stood back, drawing something on a piece of paper.

Cero had just finished tying a knot in the bandages around the girl's torso. "Now, let's take a look at her head," the healer said after nodding in acknowledgement to the prince.

"I can take care of that," Kell said. "Please tend to the other men. Some of them have more serious wounds than hers."

Cero assessed him with keen eyes. "You look like you got nicked a few times yourself, Your Highness."

The scratch along his cheekbone stung as he ran his finger across it. "It's stopped bleeding."

"Any other injuries?"

"Nothing more than a few bruises."

The grey-haired healer nodded, satisfied that his work was done. "I'll leave a bit of my salve so that wound won't leave a noticeable scar."

"But the ladies like men with scars," Bynn said with a grin. "Especially pretty little wounds like that. They'll give the prince a roguish air."

"Would you like a matching one?" he teased back.

"Only if you think it will help me get into Lady Ralena's bed when we return."

"I think I've heard enough from you two young men." Cero gathered his supplies with the aid of his assistant. "I'll be in my tent if you need me later tonight, Your Highness."

As soon as they were alone, Bynn's face grew serious. "Come take a look at this, Kell."

He leaned over his friend's shoulder at the odd symbol sketched on the paper. "What is it?"

"I don't know, but when Cero lifted her tunic to tend the cut on her back, I saw this." He dropped the paper on a small table and lifted the girl. "See for yourself."

Underneath her tunic, Kell saw the same black symbol drawn on the small of her back. "I've never seen anything like this."

"Nor have I." Bynn laid her back down on the cushions and pulled the blanket up to her chin. She continued to sleep, unaware of their examination.

"I have a feeling Sir Devarius knows what it means."

Bynn didn't miss the note of sarcasm in his voice. "Were you able to learn anything from him?"

"Only that her name is Trouble."

He snorted. "Fitting, I suppose. Let's hope she's a nice witch when she wakes up. I'd hate to end up frozen, too."

"According to Dev, it was her idea to come help us." He turned the paper around, wondering if the symbol made sense upside down. "If she wanted to hurt us, she could have done so. The only things affected by her spell were the undead."

"I admit I feared for my life when she started casting, though. Did you notice how her eyes glowed?"

Kell looked from the drawing to the girl. "No, I was more focused on keeping debris from blowing in my eyes and worrying about my bits freezing off." He shivered at the memory of the storm she conjured. He'd never felt wind that cold before.

Bynn laughed. "With you, it's always about your bits."

"I have a reputation to uphold."

"Yes, I can imagine the ladies of the court wailing in

grief if you were missing what they've come to love."

Despite their banter, Kell saw signs of his friend's weariness. "I'll take care of her from here. Go get some rest."

"Are you sure you'll be safe alone with her?"

Kell flashed a grin. "I think you should be asking if she's safe alone with me once she wakes up."

Bynn chuckled. "So full of yourself. If I didn't know you better…" His words drifted off as he shook his head.

"You know me better than most, my friend. I'll call for help if I need it."

"You never struck me as the type to share."

"There's a first time for everything, I suppose."

Bynn was still laughing as he left the tent.

Kell dipped a cloth in the water basin and began removing the dried blood along the side of her face. Under the layers of dirt, she was actually kind of pretty, in an odd way. Her golden hair, creamy skin, and heart-shaped face captured his attention after years of staring at the dark features and oval-shaped faces of the ladies at court. Perhaps introducing Gravarian ladies to the court would finally entice his father and the other lords to re-open negotiations with the neighboring kingdom.

He laughed in spite of himself. Here he was, inches away from a powerful Gravarian witch, and all he could think about was what she would look like cleaned up and in a fine dress sitting next to him during an official dinner. How many men would stare at him in envy?

"This is all nonsense," he murmured. *I should be thinking about how to convince her to help us defeat Sulaino and how to keep my father from burning her at the stake, not thinking about how her hair is the color of fresh honey.*

A rustling sound caught his attention. Kell looked up to see the wolf creeping closer to them. He jumped back and tensed, waiting for the animal to attack. Cinder's glittering yellow eyes locked with his for almost a full minute before the animal yawned and rested his head on her stomach.

Kell inched closer to her, restraining the tremble that wanted to work its way down his arm into his hand. He had seen what timber wolves did to a man, and this monster made them look like pups. "I'm just going to finish cleaning her up, if that's agreeable to you. I'm not going to hurt her."

Cinder tilted his head to the side, and his tongue flopped out, giving Kell an unobstructed view of his fangs. He didn't think it was meant to be an intimidating gesture, but it sure didn't put his fears to rest.

With delicate swipes, he resumed cleaning the blood matted in the hair at her temple. He expected to see a stellate wound that would take him the better part of an hour to sew back together, but when he got to the surface of her skull, the skin showed no signs of injury. Not even a goose egg.

What in the name of the Lady Moon was this? Judging from the amount of blood on her face and clothes, there should be something. He ran his hand through her hair, searching for any wounds, lumps, or indentions. Nothing. No signs that a huge chunk of ice hit her hard enough to knock her out.

His search became more desperate, trying to make sense of what he was seeing. But when a soft moan vibrated through her cheek, he froze. Cinder lifted his head and watched her, stretching his neck so his nose almost pressed against her chin.

She turned toward Kell and opened her eyes.

His body refused to move. Few things in life had shocked him to the point where he had to remind himself to breathe, but this moment was one of them. He'd never seen eyes the color of sapphires before, especially with the odd halo of pale green around the edges. *What kind of witch is she to hold me prisoner with just her gaze?*

Then to his surprise, she smiled. "Who are you?"

Those three simple words unlocked his muscles. He pulled back from her. "I'm Kell."

"Kell." The soft way she repeated his name felt like a massage working down his back. "Where's Dev?"

"He's in the healer's tent, having his leg sewn up."

Her pale brows knitted together. "Was he hurt badly?"

Her concern for her mentor mirrored the worry he'd seen on the knight's face earlier, convincing him they were closer than a typical mentor and apprentice. "It looked like a deep cut, but he was awake and trying to leave as soon as he could."

She chuckled. "That sounds like him." When she tried to sit up, her body wobbled. He caught her and caused her to hiss through her teeth when his hand pressed against her back. "Sorry, it still stings. And I wish the room would stop spinning."

"You took quite a blow to the head. Perhaps you need to rest." He lowered her to the cushions.

A heavy sigh escaped her lips. "I suppose you're right."

"Of course I am."

"Why do men always think they know what's best for everyone else?" The corners of her mouth twitched.

He listened to her speak, noting she didn't have the same accent as the Gravarian knight. In fact, she sounded like a typical Ranellian. "Because sometimes, we do."

"Or so you think." She ran her hand through the wolf's thick fur. "Did we stop him?"

"You stopped his soldiers, but he got away."

"I'm sorry. We'll try harder next time." She curled up next to the wolf and drifted off to sleep, leaving Kell with more questions than answers.

He replayed their conversation and found nothing threatening in her words or demeanor. They needed magic if they were going to have any chance against him, and although her innocent ways put him at ease, he still wanted answers.

Grabbing the drawing, he stood and strode out his tent. "No one goes in or out," he ordered the guard outside. "Is that understood?"

"Yes, Your Highness."

He crossed the camp to Cero's tent. When he entered, two men were holding Dev's arms behind him while the healer sat on his legs with a needle in his hand. "Please sit still, Sir Devarius, so I can sew the wound closed."

"I told you I don't want any of your primitive healing." He tried to buck Cero off his legs.

"But your leg is still bleeding. You're just making it worse."

"Do you want us to knock him out?" one of the men asked Cero.

"No," Kell answered in place of the healer. "I want to ask him a few more questions. Go tend to the other men for now."

The healer's mouth hung open in disbelief, but he didn't protest the prince's command. The men released Dev and walked away, their faces showing a mixture of disgust and frustration. The Gravarian wasn't making many friends so far.

"What do you want?" Dev asked while he tied a fresh bandage over the oozing wound. With his head tilted down, the pointed tips of his ears protruded from his hair.

Kell tried to muffle his gasp. He hadn't seen an elf in Ranello in over twenty years, not since Gravaria sent a diplomatic party to the palace when he was a small boy. Back then, he only managed to catch a quick glimpse at them when he escaped from his nanny's grasp.

Dev looked up, and his green eyes narrowed. "What's the matter, Your Highness? Never seen an elf before?"

"On the contrary, I have. But it's still not something I see every day."

He hid his ears under his hair and crossed his arms. "I'm waiting for your question."

A jolt of anger stiffened Kell's spine. How dare a prisoner talk to him this way? His insolence alone would have cost him his head if they had been in Trivinus. But the gleam in Dev's eyes told him the knight felt quite comfortable challenging him. In fact, he seemed to welcome confrontation. The complete opposite of the quiet acceptance the man's apprentice had given him a few minutes earlier.

"I wanted to speak to you about your companion." He couldn't figure out if she was truly his apprentice or his whore.

Dev raised a brow. "The girl, or the wolf?"

"The girl, mostly." He held up the drawing. "What does this mean?"

"You work fast," he replied, anger lacing his voice. "I've heard of your reputation, but I didn't expect you to have her out of her clothes this quickly, Prince Kell."

Heat burned his cheeks. He freely admitted to having his fair share of women in his bed, but Dev's accusations almost embarrassed him. "She's sleeping, fully clothed, in my tent with the wolf next to her."

"Then how did you discover that?" He pointed to the drawing.

"Cero had to lift her tunic to treat the wounds on her back."

"She had other injuries?" The cocky arrogance vanished from his face, and panic replaced it.

"Yes." He waved the paper in the air. "Back to this."

"But she's fine now?"

A slow smile spread across his lips. So, he'd found Dev's weak spot. "Yes, for now."

His shoulders drooped. He leaned back against the saddle someone had left behind. "Good."

"Are you going to answer my question?"

"I'm thinking about it, Your Highness."

"Why the hesitation?"

"Because there are some things that aren't meant to be shared with Ranellians."

Kell gnashed his teeth together. He'd probably have better luck waiting for the girl to wake up and answer his questions. That was, if he could keep her away from Dev long enough to extract them from her.

"Prince Kell, there you are," Bynn's voice said from

the entrance of the tent. "Come take a look at this."

Dev feigned sleep, but the small slits left open between his lids told Kell he was watching his every movement. If the knight was still in the camp come dawn, it would be a pleasant surprise.

Kell stepped outside to where Bynn stood. A beam of light fell on the sword in his hands.

"I found this." He tilted it so the light fell on the blade. "Notice anything unusual about it?"

Etched on the flat of the blade was the same symbol that was branded on Trouble's back. Kell wanted to shake away the icy fingers of dread that grabbed him. "Very interesting."

"Yeah, they're a perfectly matched pair. Must be part of some kind of cult in Gravaria."

"She's Ranellian."

Bynn's jaw fell slack for a second before he forced a laugh. "You're joking, right?"

"I wish I could say I was, but she sounds like one of us. No accent like him." He took the sword from his friend's hands and examined it. Perfectly balanced. A thin blade made of some metal other than steel. The artistry of the hilt could rival even his father's swords. Overall, too fine a weapon for a simple knight.

"She woke up?"

"For a few minutes. Long enough to ask about the knight and then apologize for not stopping Sulaino."

"This is an interesting twist." Bynn ran his hands through his hair. "It sounds like we have more to worry about from him than the witch. Strange, huh?"

"Not as strange as the fact that I couldn't find any evidence of a head injury on her when I was cleaning up the blood."

"Magic?" Bynn's face paled. "Are you sure you want to take them back to Trivinus? Something tells me they may become as big a problem as Sulaino."

"I don't think we have any other option." Kell rested the tip of the sword in the mud and leaned the hilt against

Crista McHugh

his hip. "The girl wants to help us—I can feel it. It's just convincing him to go along with the plan."

"And you think he will eventually?"

"It's not going to be simple." It should be easy enough to seduce her to his cause. Once she came to his side, Dev would follow, just like he did tonight when she ran to help them. He curled his lips up into a smile. "But I'm already forming a plan."

"May the Lady Moon shine in your favor, because you're going to need all the help you can get."

"If I don't defend the kingdom from Sulaino, who will?" He tried to sound nonchalant, but he knew time was running out. It had taken him over a year to convince his father there really was a necromancer operating in the realm, and now Sulaino had grown too strong to stop without some kind of magical aid. Tonight had proven that.

"Do you want me to take the sword back to your tent?"

Kell lifted it and let the light flash on it. "No, I think maybe I can use it to get some answers from Dev."

"You never struck me as the type to resort to torture, unless you include your lousy jokes."

"Ha-ha. But something tells me he'll want his sword back."

As soon as Kell ducked through the flap back into the tent, Dev's eyes opened a bit wider.

Kell stood over him and positioned the blade so the engraved symbol faced the knight. "Now, back to this symbol."

Dev sat up and held out his hand. "Thank you for finding my sword."

"Not so fast," Kell replied as he moved it out of reach. "I want answers."

"You wouldn't believe me if I told you the truth." He examined the bandage on his leg and grabbed a fresh strip of linen to layer over the soaked bandage. "You Ranellians are slow to accept things you don't understand."

102

Kell knelt so they were at eye level. "Was it difficult convincing Trouble to believe you?"

"Why do you keep going back to her?"

"Because she's obviously powerful enough to challenge Sulaino. Maybe if I understand this symbol, it will help your case when I present it to my father."

Dev squeezed the cloth tight enough around his thigh to cause blood to drip down on the dirt floor from the underlying bandage. He winced in pain and then repeated the procedure. After taking a deep breath, he said, "It's the symbol of the god Loku."

"Who?"

"Just because you Ranellians cling to your moon goddess doesn't mean there aren't more deities out there. Loku is the god of chaos."

A strangled laugh formed in his throat. "This is ridiculous. You don't actually expect me to believe that, do you?"

Dev cocked a brow. "I said you wouldn't believe the truth. What were you expecting? For me to tell you we were members of some cult or part of the mythical Gravarian Special Forces?"

"Do you have the same symbol on you?"

"Are you planning on strip-searching me?"

"It depends—are you planning on escaping tonight?"

The knight gave a half chuckle filled with bitterness. "Do I look like I'm in any condition to run away? Besides, you still have Trouble."

"And she's got the wolf."

"Why do you think I sent Cinder with her?" He rubbed his face. "I don't bear Loku's mark. She's the only living person with it. I have the same symbol on my sword because I'm her protector."

"Why does she bear his mark, and why does she need a protector?"

Dev eyes glittered, and his hand gripped the top of his boot. "I'm not allowed to tell you that."

Kell couldn't help feel like the tables had suddenly

turned. Something predatory lingered in the knight's expression, and if pressed further, he'd attack.

"But you can only guess why she needs a protector. She isn't called Trouble for nothing." Dev released his boot and reclined against the saddle. "Now, if you don't mind, Your Highness, I need to rest so I can heal."

"You'd be better off letting Cero tend to your wounds."

"Over my dead body."

Kell stood, taking the sword with him. The voice of his tutor echoed in his mind. Small victories would end up winning the war, and he had to be satisfied with the outcome of tonight's battle of wills. "This conversation isn't finished."

"That's what you think."

Chapter 15

The pale light of dawn filtered through her eyelids, but Arden wasn't ready to open them yet. Her head still throbbed. She ran her hands over the silk cushions under her and immediately cursed, wondering if Loku was playing the same trick on her that he'd played on Dev.

"No, my Soulbearer, you're not dreaming. I'd have you naked if you were."

The damp wool of her tunic rubbed against her shoulders, answering her next question. Her thoughts turned to the face of the man she saw last night. Kell. His dark brown hair curled at the ends and framed his square jaw when he looked down on her, and his brown eyes danced with amusement. He even had a dimple in his left cheek when he smiled. All and all, it was a handsome face. One she wouldn't mind seeing again. *"Loku, did I dream him up?"*

The chaos god's laughter filled her mind. *"Is that where your tastes roam?"*

"No, not usually, but I liked the look of him."

"I'll have to remember that if I decide to tempt you."

Kell intrigued her. Maybe it was because he actually seemed warm and friendly to her, a sharp contrast to Dev's cool and distant demeanor.

A mixture of metal clanging and conversation began to fill her ears. She tensed. Wherever she was, she wasn't alone. Then something furry stretched next to her, and she relaxed. Cinder had stayed by her side. But where was Dev?

She called out his name and opened her eyes.

"He's still in the healer's tent," an unfamiliar voice answered.

Arden shot up and immediately wished she hadn't. The room spun in circles, matching the swirling in the pit of her stomach. She crumpled back down on the cushions.

A face swam above her. "Still dizzy?" Cool fingertips brushed her hair from her face, and the man from last night came into focus. "Should I send for the healer?"

Her tongue refused to cooperate with her and form an answer. She didn't know if her speechlessness was from the fact that he didn't appear to regard her as some kind of freak or that he was probably the most gorgeous Ranellian she'd ever seen. She licked her dry lips and found her voice. "I think if I try to sit up slowly, the dizziness won't hit me as hard."

"Then let me help you." A pair of arms encircled her and lifted her back off the cushions. "Tell me if I'm moving too fast."

If he had been a customer at the inn, she would have some sarcastic reply to that, but he was one man whose touch she welcomed.

"Enough to let him under your skirt?" Loku asked.

Her cheeks burned. Leave it to Loku to take her attraction and add some perverted twist to it. *"Why does everything have to come down to sex with you?"*

"Because it's the one thing all you humans seem to have in common. It's what drives your species forward. I have a feeling you'd enjoy it if you ever gave it a chance."

"Absolutely not. I don't want to be labeled a whore and end up with a bastard child."

"Always picturing the dreariest outcome, huh?"

Her gaze flickered to the man at her side. His brows knitted together as he studied her.

"Will you just shut up so he doesn't think I'm completely crazy?" She forced a smile on her face. "Thank you," she told Kell. "The dizziness is slowly going away."

"I'm glad to hear that, Trouble."

Her body flinched at the sound of that name. "My

name is Arden, not Trouble," she replied with a bit of steeliness in her voice.

"That sounds like a more respectable name. May I ask why Dev calls you Trouble?"

"Because he can't get it through his thick head that my name is Arden."

He laughed wholeheartedly. "Yes, he seems like a stubborn man."

"You don't know the half of it." His arms still steadied her, even though her initial vertigo had passed. "You said your name was Kell, right?"

"You remember that from last night?"

"Bits and pieces." She refused to tell him that the only things she remembered after Loku released her from his control were Kell's name and his face. "What exactly happened?"

"A group of undead ambushed me and my men as we were making camp. You and your protector showed up. Sulaino and you had a little conversation, and then you turned all the undead into frozen statues. Sulaino broke free of the ice that surrounded him, and you got hit in the head."

"I wonder why the spell didn't work on him," she whispered aloud and immediately froze. Her eyes felt like they were stretched to their limits, and her throat tightened. Sweet Lady Moon, she didn't just admit to using magic in front of him, did she?

She listened to the pounding of her heart, waiting for him to shove her aside and call her a witch. When nothing happened, she met his gaze with caution. The accusation she feared shown from his eyes. *May the goddess protect me*, she prayed.

"Who needs that silly moon goddess when you have me? Say the word, and I'll reduce him to a pile of ashes."

Magic welled up inside her, and her heart beat faster. *"No, not yet, Loku. If he wanted to burn me at the stake, he would have done so by now."*

The tingling in her arms and chest retreated. *"Very*

well. But I will not tolerate anyone hurting you while you still carry my soul."

The silence between them stretched too long for her comfort. "Um, so, everyone's all right?" she asked.

"For now," he replied, still staring at her. His mouth formed a thin line, and he pulled his hands away from her back.

Wonderful, she inwardly groaned. *He's one of those guys who wants you to be in perfect health before he begins his torture, isn't he?*

She jumped to her feet. The sudden movement made her sway, and she grabbed the small table nearby until she regained her balance. Sweat prickled along the nape her of neck, but it was a small price to pay in order to get away from him.

He reached for her. "Take it easy. I don't want you hitting your head again."

"I'm fine." She swatted his hands away. "Where's Dev?"

"I already told you—he's in the healer's tent."

"Take me to him now. I need to speak to him" Her voice trembled. Dev would know what to do. He'd know how to get them out of this mess before they both burned for it.

"There's no need to be frightened. I'm not going to hurt you."

"How do I know that?" She stumbled toward the opening of the tent, with Cinder leaning heavily against the side of her leg. "Go find Dev," she ordered the wolf.

Cinder sniffed the air and bolted for the flaps. Arden followed him, startling the guards posted outside the tent. The wolf paused to sniff the ground before loping toward a tent across the clearing, allowing her time to catch up to him. Two soldiers stood in front of it. They both cocked their crossbows and aimed them at the snarling wolf.

"Let them enter," Kell said behind her.

"Yes, Your Highness," they replied simultaneously, lowering their weapons.

"Ooh, a prince. You did well this time, my little Soulbearer."

The sarcasm in Loku's voice singed her already wounded pride. She closed her eyes and inhaled through her teeth. *Perfect. Now he can add 'disrespecting royalty' to my list of crimes.*

Inside, the smell of blood and unwashed bodies burned her nostrils. She resisted the urge to pinch her nose while she scanned the faces of the men inside. In the far back corner, she spotted Dev and rushed to his side. "Thank the goddess you're alive."

"Feeling better this morning, Trouble?" he asked dryly.

A quick glance over her shoulder told her the prince was standing right behind and listening to every word she said. "I've been better."

Dev's one-note laugh broke some of the tension. "Has His Royal Highness finished his interrogation of you yet?"

The bones in her spine locked. He hadn't asked her many questions. Had he already made up his mind?

"I was trying to find out more about your apprentice when the sudden desire to check on you seized her."

Dev rubbed the back of his head. "Nice to know she appreciates me."

"Of course I appreciate you." She examined the mound of blood-soaked bandages on his leg. "That looks horrible."

"I tried to convince him to let my healer sew the wound up, but he stubbornly refused."

"I have my reasons," Dev muttered.

"Dev doesn't trust traditional healers," Loku replied before she could vocalize her question. *"He prefers to be healed by magic. Faster healing, no infections, and no scars."*

"How do you heal someone with magic?"

"If you can cast magic, you can heal yourself, although the wounds knit together at a snail's pace. It's much faster if someone else heals you."

She glanced down at his thigh and cringed. How many days would that take? *"Show me how."*

"Just touch the area around the wound and picture it healing. The magic will flow from you and do what needs to be done."

"What are you thinking, Trouble?"

Dev's words jerked her from her conversation with Loku. She couldn't just announce that she was going to cast a healing spell, not in a room full of Ranellians. They'd probably have her tied to a tree within minutes with enough kindling around her ankles to build a nice bonfire. But she couldn't leave his leg like this either.

She took a deep breath, then pressed her fingertips against his thigh just below the bandages. Magic stirred inside her chest. She directed it toward her hand. "Do you trust me to examine your wound?"

He hissed when she released the first trickle of magic and stared at her in disbelief. His gaze flickered to Kell before he nodded. "Just be careful."

"I will." As she untied the layers of dirty linen, she increased the steady stream of her healing spell. In her mind, she saw the angry red depths of the wound and the beginnings of infection in the surrounding tissues. "Why do you have to be so stubborn?"

"Because I know what I need to do."

She tugged at a knot that refused to come undone and sent of jolt of magic toward him, causing him to wince. *Good, let him suffer a bit.*

"Do you have to be so rough?"

"I need a knife to cut through the last few layers."

"No, don't," a new voice said. A grey-haired man knelt next to her and pulled her hands away from the bandages. "You'll risk disrupting the scab and restarting the bleeding."

"Let her do what Sir Devarius wants, Cero." Kell pulled a knife from the sheath on his belt. "At least he's allowing her to address his injuries."

She took the knife and shimmied it under the bottom

layer. After another surge of the healing magic, she angled the blade up and began sawing through the stiff linen.

"Careful where you point that thing," Dev said through clenched teeth. "I have no desire to be castrated."

Her cheeks burned long enough to disrupt her concentration, and she waited until she regained her composure before she continued. "The tip isn't that close to your, um, groin."

"That's what you think."

Part of her wanted to aim the knife at his throat. "Why do men always seem overly concerned about that one area of the body?"

"Because if it were injured, the ladies wouldn't want us as much," Kell replied with a smirk.

Great—now she had both of them obsessed with their dicks. She tried to imagine why ladies would want that flaccid collection of appendages between men's legs. "It's not that impressive."

"That's what you think. Perhaps I should come to you tonight and finish what I started with Dev."

Arden paused, took a deep breath, and bit her tongue. Once her anger subsided, she resumed cutting the bandages with renewed fervor. She didn't miss the amused light in Kell's eyes as she worked. Fine. Let him assume she was Dev's whore. As long as she could finish healing her protector and get the hell out of here, she didn't care what the prince thought of her.

The blade sliced through the final layer of the bandage. She pulled back the material with caution. Her heart pounded in her chest like she'd just run a mile, and fatigue crept into her joints. *"Please let my spell have worked."*

Kell's breath warmed the back of her neck as he peered over her shoulder, raising her guard. Was he trying to collect more evidence for her trial? If she got one, that is.

A smile formed on her lips. No evidence of the wound remained, not even a scar. "Seems you made a big fuss over nothing."

"Impossible." Cero shoved her aside and examined the wound. "I saw the wound last night. How did it heal so quickly?"

"Has it ever occurred to you that maybe I can heal on my own?" Dev hugged his knee up to his chest and then straightened his leg several times. "As Prince Kell so kindly pointed out last night, I'm not human."

Arden's pulse slowed, and she wished she could lie down on the silk cushions in the other tent. Every spell she cast seemed to leave her exhausted when she finished.

"It will get easier with practice, my Soulbearer."

"I don't care right now. I just want a nap."

"Did you use magic?"

She held her breath when she heard Kell's question but slowly released it after she saw him focused on her patient, not her.

Dev stood and tested his leg, hopping up and down on it and appearing satisfied with the results. "Did you see me cast any magic?"

"No."

"Then you'll just have to be satisfied with the theory that elves can heal themselves."

"Dev, please stop arguing with the prince." Her head grew heavier by the second, and she feared that if she didn't get moving soon, she'd curl up into a little ball and fall asleep. "Let's just find our horses and get on the road to Boznac."

Both men stared at her with frowns on their faces. "I take it His Royal Highness hasn't informed you that we're under arrest."

"I was going to get to it," Kell said, glaring at Dev.

"When? After you wrung all the information you could out of her? Or after you added her to the notches in your headboard?"

Her cheeks burned. Did they really think she'd hop in his bed because he was a prince?

The familiar sound of swords being unsheathed

echoed around her. "How dare you speak to the prince that way?" one of the soldiers demanded.

Kell motioned for his men to lower their weapons. "He's just full of piss and vinegar. Not appropriate behavior for a man who calls himself a knight. I guess Gravaria holds their knights to a lower code of behavior."

The scowl deepened on Dev's face, but he didn't say anything else.

"Why are we under arrest?" Arden already knew the answer, although it didn't hurt to play innocent.

Kell raised one brow. "As if you didn't know. No matter how good your intentions were, the law clearly forbids the use of magic in Ranello, and I doubt any man present will deny what you did last night was magic."

"Just keep your mouth shut for now," Loku interjected. "Arguing will only make it worse."

"Why?"

"Because you don't want to piss off anyone else. I know Dev, and he's already forming a plan. He's more than your grouchy protector, after all."

"But we need to get to Boznac before the winter storms," she pleaded.

"And we will." Dev grabbed her hand and pulled her to her feet. "Come along, Trouble."

Kell crossed his arms and blocked their way. "You sound awfully confident for a man whose fate is out of his hands."

"That's because I know a few things you don't, Your Highness."

"Dev, please stop." She closed her eyes for a moment and waited for the room to stop spinning. Was it due to her head injury or her recent exertion from the spell? "I'm still not quite myself, and I'd prefer to not hear you two arguing if you don't mind."

When she took a step away, he tightened his grip on her hand and pulled her closer so her head pressed against his chest. The possessive nature of his action both angered and comforted her. She didn't belong to him, after all, but she also appreciated having him near. She tucked her head under his chin and enjoyed his warmth for the moment.

"Agreed," Kell said at last. "I'd prefer to get back to Trivinus as soon as possible and report last night's activities to my father. If we leave soon, we might be able to reach Lord Pryan's keep before nightfall. I'm sure we'd all appreciate sleeping with a roof over our heads for one night." He stepped closer to them. "Arden, I regret that I have to uphold the law, but I have no other choice in the matter. Please know that I'll do all in my power to convince my father to pardon you when we get to Trivinus."

A turmoil of emotions swirled inside her. Part of her told her the only person she could trust was Dev, but something in the prince's voice soothed her. "Well, since I'm not a roasted carcass yet, I suppose I should believe you," she replied with a bit of cynicism in her voice.

The corners of his mouth twitched. "It seems you've been teaching your apprentice how to be sarcastic, too."

"No, she comes by that naturally." Dev placed one hand over her head, brushing the stray strands of hair back from her face.

"If you two will excuse me, I have some things to attend to as we break camp." His gaze flickered between them. "Please don't try anything foolish."

Dev's half chuckle vibrated through his chest. "I'm not a fool, Your Highness."

At this point, any energy she might have had for foolishness had abandoned her. She closed her eyes again and surrendered to Dev's embrace.

Chapter 16

As soon as the prince left the tent, Dev turned his attention to Trouble. She wilted in his arms, and his gut clenched with worry. "What's wrong?"

"So tired," she replied with a yawn. "And my head aches."

He found the spot where the block of ice hit her temple and released a small stream of magic. Now he had the time to heal her as completely as she had him.

She sighed in contentment. "Thank you."

"You're welcome. I can't do much about your sleepiness, though."

"I know. Loku explained that part to me."

Bile rose into his throat. He hated that she'd formed such a strong relationship with the disembodied god that he was the one giving her lessons in magic now. But what bothered him more was his visceral reaction whenever another man, flesh or not, tried to win her trust. Jealousy could be just as blinding as desire.

He took a deep breath and loosened his hold on her. "That was a risky decision you made."

Puzzlement filled her large blue eyes when she looked up at him, so he guided her hand to his thigh. Her mouth formed a perfect circle. "I had to do it."

He couldn't argue with her there. The idea of riding all the way to Trivinus with his injured leg kept him up as much as his pain did last night. "I'm the one who should be thanking you."

"We have to take care of each other, especially after last night." She swayed slightly.

He caught her, guiding her to the ground. "Let's rest while we can."

Cinder approached them and licked her face before settling his head in her lap. Dev almost laughed. At least there was one male with whom he didn't mind sharing her.

"Kell said the necromancer got away."

The way Sulaino's eyes glowed red when he demanded Dev give Trouble to him haunted his memory for a moment. For someone who was nothing more than a simple barmaid less than a week ago, she'd suddenly become one of the most popular women in the kingdom. Not only did the necromancer want her, but the prince, too. Although Dev suspected the latter desired more than just her magic.

Three men entered from outside. "Everyone out so we can pack away this tent."

"We can discuss this later. Come on." He helped Trouble to her feet and noticed she seemed to sway less than before.

Ten minutes later, they rode toward Trivinus surrounded by a group of soldiers.

***

In the afternoon, one of the soldiers broke away from the procession and galloped up the road. Dev's hand automatically reached for his sword, only to grasp air.

"What is it?" Trouble's shoulders slumped forward as she rode next to him, displaying her fatigue. Her lids hung half closed over her eyes.

"A rider broke off from our group in a hurry."

"The prince probably sent him ahead to warn Lord Pryan that we were stopping at his keep tonight," a soldier answered. "That will give the cooks enough time to prepare a decent meal for all of us."

The tension in his thighs and shoulders loosened. After spending the last week dodging Sulaino, he always suspected the worst when he noticed a change around him. He glanced over to Trouble, who practically draped herself over the horse's neck as she rode. If undead came near them, would she notice their presence?

"Dev, do you think it will be safe to stop somewhere overnight?" she asked.

No, his mind immediately replied. As soon as night fell, they'd be sitting ducks for the necromancer and his army. "We don't have much say in the matter. We're prisoners, remember?"

He looked over his shoulder in the direction of Boznac. They had been so close—only a few days' journey to the sea by his estimation. Now, with their diversion to Trivinus, they'd be lucky to catch the last ship for Gravaria.

He studied Trouble for any cracks in her sanity. So far, she seemed calm and sensible, perhaps even more confident than when he'd first met her. But he also sensed Loku's growing influence over her. Not only did she surrender to him last night and allow him to cast through her, but she also turned to him for instruction on how to use healing magic. If this continued, she'd end up like Robb in a matter of weeks. Time was running out for them in more ways than one, and the sooner he secured her within the walls of the Mage's Conclave, the better.

His thoughts turned to formulating an escape plan. He considered the soldiers around him, noting the location of their weapons and the gaps in their armor. He examined their faces and categorized them into two groups: those who would be easily overtaken and those who had a few more years of seasoned combat behind them. He noticed the location and the severity of their injuries, if they had any. After calculating his odds, he decided he needed the element of surprise if they were to successfully escape from the prince and his men.

About an hour later, the stone walls of a small keep appeared on the horizon. The men around him relaxed, and smiles appeared on their weary faces. Dev wished he could share their relief at its sight. To him, it was nothing more than a stone cage that would hold them until Sulaino launched another attack.

As soon as the prince crossed the bailey, a man appeared at the doorway and bowed with a flourish. *Obviously a nobleman familiar with the life at court.* It almost surprised Dev to find the lord at home to greet them.

Kell dismounted, immediately launching into a light-hearted conversation with his host. The two men disappeared inside the main building, followed by Lord Bynn.

Trouble stared at the ramparts and visually traced the walls. "Do you think they'll keep him out?"

"I can only hope."

She flinched, and he didn't miss the brief glow of the ring in her eyes. Loku.

"Don't listen to him. I'll keep you safe."

Her laughter irked him. "Funny, he was telling me the same thing."

Dev's jaw tightened as he hopped down from his horse. Trouble already had one protector—him—and that upstart of a chaos god was trying to usurp his position. Usually, Loku tried to entice the Soulbearer with power, not security. "His protection comes at a cost."

She cocked her head to the side and slid out of her saddle. "I suppose you're right, but it is comforting to know I won't be completely alone if something happens to you."

Before he could reply, the soldiers surrounded them and shoved them forward. They might not be bound, but they were still prisoners.

His eyes adjusted to the dark interior faster than hers, and he caught her when she tripped over a bump in the dirt floor. A brief jolt raced through him from her touch, but he released her as soon as she regained her footing. To hold on to her any longer might lead his thoughts astray.

Inside, thick tapestries hung on the walls, insulating the large room from the chilly evening air. The prince and the two lords sat near the fire, too engrossed in their own conversation to notice their entrance.

The soldiers broke the tight ring around Dev and Trouble once they reached the middle of the room, but the shuffling of feet behind them told him they still blocked his way to the door. Not the best time to make a run for it. Maybe later, when everyone slept.

He guided Trouble to a nearby corner. "Rest while you can. I'll wake you if they decide to feed us more than strips of dried meat."

She sniffed the air. "I certainly hope so. Whatever they're roasting in the kitchen is making my mouth water." Her stomach growled to confirm her hunger.

"If I have to steal it from the prince's plate for you, I will."

Creases appeared in her forehead. "Please don't make any more trouble with him."

"Why are you defending him?"

She plopped down on the floor with a huff. "Why don't you just come out and say it?"

"Say what?" *That I want to keep you as far away from him as possible?* He knelt next to her.

"That it's all my fault we're in this mess. If I hadn't run off to save the prince and his men, we'd be free and on the road to Boznac now." She bit her bottom lip and pulled her knees up to her chest.

Her theory blindsided him. "Do you really think I blame you for this?"

"Just say it and get it out of your system."

"The prince orders you to eat, sir," a soldier interrupted before Dev could explain things to her. He shoved a wooden trencher with steaming meat and bread at him. "He invites the girl to join him at his table."

He bit back the warning poised on his tongue, that the prince would just use her and toss her away like he was rumored to do with every woman that crossed his path.

Trouble peered over his shoulder at the table closest to the fire. The halo in her eyes flared to life, and her private conversation with Loku lasted long enough for the soldier to clear his throat. "I'd like to stay here tonight," she said.

"Please give my apologies to Prince Kell."

The soldier walked away.

Dev released the last of the breath he'd been unconsciously holding. "I'm surprised you turned down an invitation to sit near him, seeing as how I'm being such a grouch tonight."

"Shut up, Dev." Her hands balled up into little fists, and he moved far enough away to avoid her right hook. Twice was enough for him to learn that she knew how to punch a man. "I have my own reasons for my decisions."

The soldier returned with another trencher for Trouble, containing a better cut of meat than the gristle-laced hunk in his. "Prince Kell expresses his disappointment that you declined his invitation. He hopes you'll join him tomorrow night." The wooden way the man spoke revealed his disapproval over his prince getting cozy with a witch, even though she probably saved his life and the lives of his comrades.

Despite his attitude, she took the trencher and gave him a small thanks. With her back leaning against the wall, she began eating, never looking up from her meal.

The food tasted like dust to him, even though it smelled enticing, and he knew the reason why. How had she managed to get under his skin like this? He'd never cared what the other Soulbearers thought of him. But then, none of them had been like her. The fact that she had put others before herself shamed him a bit. He tossed a chunk of the meat to Cinder and wiped the grease off his hand.

"You need to eat, too, if you're going to protect me," she reminded him.

"I don't blame you for our predicament. If I feel anything about your actions last night, it's a combination of fear, awe, and admiration." There. He said it. Now maybe his conscience would let him enjoy the rest of his meal.

The slice of bread in her hand paused halfway between the trencher and her mouth. "What was that?"

"You heard me, so don't pretend you didn't. It's my

duty to protect you, and it doesn't make my job easier when you put yourself between a group of strangers and a necromancer who wants to kill you."

"Ah, so you were just worried about your reputation? Yes, having the same man kill two Soulbearers in less than a week would look bad on your record."

By Jussip, she knew how to make his temper flare faster than any person he knew, including Loku. Anger coursed through his body, heating his face. "I didn't mean it that way."

"Then what did you mean?"

Damn, she wouldn't be happy until she got a full confession out of him. "Did it ever occur to you that maybe I want to keep you alive for reasons other than my reputation as your protector?"

"Oh," she whispered, and her cheeks flushed.

"It took courage to run to the aid of those men last night, especially when you knew what you were facing. And it bothers me now that I resisted going. As you and Prince Kell have reminded me, I make a sorry excuse for a knight."

Her face softened. The halo flashed again, and her eyes widened as she inhaled sharply.

"What did he tell you now?"

She flinched at the growl in Dev's voice, and the halo grew brighter. Just perfect. Now he was pushing her even closer to Loku.

Dev took a deep breath to calm himself. "Never mind. I'm sure you'd rather listen to him than me anyway. He'll tell you what you want to hear."

"Actually, he told me you were sentenced to be a protector as a punishment."

For a moment, he couldn't look her in the face. Even after a hundred years, his actions still haunted him, still reminded him of a time when he let greed and pride turn him into a knight who'd lost his honor. He'd only retained his title because of his willingness to protect the Soulbearer, and he'd spent the last century trying to regain what he'd lost.

"What did you do to deserve this punishment?"

The image of Minius' face as the life ebbed from his body flashed in front of his closed eyes. He wanted to tell her before Loku gave his version of the events, but he hesitated. Her trust in him was fragile at best. What would she think if she knew he'd murdered someone?

A warm touch of her fingertips on his jaw pulled him from his cold memories. "We shouldn't let past mistakes dictate our actions now."

Odd of her to say that, since she'd spent most of her life trying to avoid the same mistakes her mother made. Or maybe she had some truth in her words. Maybe he could rise above the past. He slid his hand over hers and pressed it closer to his cheek. Her acceptance soothed him for now.

Two pairs of hands seized her and jerked her to her feet, ending the precious moment between them. "Come with us, witch."

Chapter 17

Arden attempted to wriggle free from the two soldiers who grabbed her, but they held tight. Her lungs refused to move. Calling her a witch wasn't a good sign. Sweet Lady Moon, what were they planning to do to her? Burn her as part of tonight's entertainment?

"Let her go." Dev plowed into one of the men, and all four of them tumbled backwards onto the dirt floor.

The men closest to the disturbance jumped to the defense of their comrades. She covered her face to shield it from the flying fists and feet. Any moment now, she expected to hear to clang of steel and feel the warm, sticky ooze of blood.

"Stop this immediately," a man's voice boomed over the ruckus.

The soldiers froze at the command.

She dared a peek at the situation. Three soldiers pinned Dev to the ground, and a fourth pressed the tip of a sword into his cheek just inches above the spot her fingers touched him seconds ago. Cinder stood between her and another soldier, his teeth bared.

"So that's Dev's imitation of a pincushion."

"Shut up, Loku."

Prince Kell stood over them all with a royal frown on his face. "This is disgraceful behavior for members of the royal guard, especially when we've experienced such gracious hospitality from our host. Is this how we return it? By engaging in a bar fight under his roof?"

"He started it, Your Highness," one of the soldiers started to explain.

"He threatened my apprentice," Dev countered.

"I did no such thing. I merely—"

"Enough." One word ended the conversation, and his men stared at the floor. "Can't you see you've frightened the young lady?"

A nearby cough told her not all of his men agreed that she was a young lady. Nor would she give him the satisfaction of letting him know the fight frightened her. She grew up in an inn, after all. Instead, she wiped the dirt off her palms and stood.

Kell held her gaze and waited for her to say something. When she didn't, he asked, "Are you unharmed?"

"Aw, he's such a gentleman. Next thing you know, he'll be offering to cover mud puddles in your path with his cloak."

"I seriously doubt that." To give Kell some credit, he played the part of a gentleman well. Of course, she scarcely believed his concern was genuine. "I was fine until two of your men grabbed me and insulted me."

He turned to the two soldiers who'd accosted her and glared at them. "I'll make sure that won't happen again."

A grunt from Dev reminded her he still had a blade on his face. "Could you be so kind as to order your men to release my protector, Your Highness? He was just performing his duty."

The corners of his mouth twitched. Kell must've gotten some kind of sick pleasure from seeing Dev eating dust. If she wasn't fearful for her life, she might have joined him in his amusement. "Only if he agrees not to cause any more trouble tonight."

"If your men behave, I trust he will."

With a nod, Kell consented to her demands. The soldiers backed away from Dev, throwing a slight shove as they did so.

Her protector stood and moved between her and the prince. The rigid set of his shoulders matched the way his fingers curled into fists. "Where were they planning on taking her?"

"Since she's the only lady in our company, I thought it only appropriate that she have a private room. I'd asked my men to escort her there."

"Oh, a private room. You lucky girl." Loku's sarcasm made the muscles in her neck twitch. *"Now, the next question should be if you'll be alone there."*

"Escort?" Dev's half laugh pierced the space between the three of them. "Is that what you Ranellians call it?"

"Perhaps my men were a little rougher than I intended, but in their defense, they are soldiers and unfortunately only know one way to handle prisoners."

Dev's knuckles crackled, and his lips pressed into a thin line.

Before he could launch another string of insults at the prince, she intervened. "I appreciate your concern for my comfort and reputation, Your Highness, but I'll be quite fine spending the night here."

"I'm afraid I can't allow that."

"Then I'm coming with her." Dev closed the gap between them so she smelled his scent of leather and spice.

She took a deep breath and savored his familiarity. *Mmm, I wouldn't mind that."*

"Of course you wouldn't. You'd love to share your bed with Dev, you naughty girl. Maybe I don't need to visit you in your dreams tonight, eh?"

Blood gathered in her cheeks. *"I didn't mean it that way. I just meant it would be nice having him nearby so he'd, um, stay out of trouble."*

"Liar."

"I'm afraid the space reserved for her isn't very large. You should be quite comfortable down here, provided you don't start any more fights with my men."

"And what guarantee do I have that they won't start anything with me?"

Arden rolled her eyes. Would these two ever learn to let things rest? "I'll agree to go peacefully under three conditions."

"Which are?" The evident amusement on the prince's face irked her. It felt like he was indulging some headstrong child.

"One: Dev will be alive and well in the morning when I come back."

One dark brow rose. "Fine. If he causes trouble, though, my men have every right to defend themselves short of killing him."

Damn, she didn't expect him to be good at negotiating. *"And you're some kind of expert in this field?"*

"Two: I get to take Cinder with me."

"He's a wild beast, more fit to spend the night outside the keep than inside a room."

"If you deprive me of one protector, I demand another."

Kell approached her. "You don't trust me?"

Her heart skipped a beat. The way his dark eyes studied her face as they were searching for her secrets made her tongue feel thick and clumsy. "Not completely, Your Highness. The whole kingdom knows of your reputation, which brings me to my third condition. I refuse to stay the night in this private room if you're in it."

A snicker broke loose from the crowd behind Kell. The sly grin fell from his face. A little thrill rushed through her. *Take that, Your Highness.*

"I wonder if any woman has ever refused him before?"

"I don't care. I'm not as easy as the women at court appear to be."

"But aren't you curious to see if he's as talented as the rumors say he is?"

A flush spread through her whole body. *"Don't be ridiculous. What interest would he have in a common-born witch like me?"*

"Your body betrays you. Admit it, my Soulbearer, you have a wanton woman buried deep inside you wanting to break free, and you don't seem to care if it's Dev or Kell who satisfies that need."

Anger throbbed deep inside her. She lowered her eyes, afraid Kell would see the flashing of the halo while she told Loku exactly what he could do with his crude accusations.

A forced laugh broke the silence. "You don't have to worry about that, Arden, and as long as your wolf doesn't tear holes in the cushions, he's welcome to stay there, too." He crossed his arms. "Satisfied?"

"I suppose so."

"I'm not." Dev blocked her from following the prince. "I need to know where she is in case we're attacked or the keep burns down. Her safety is my only priority."

"As was getting her to Gravaria, if I remember correctly. I promise that I'll personally see to her safety if those things occur."

Dev's eyes narrowed.

"The prince is smarter than we gave him credit for. It seems he knows exactly what Dev was planning to do."

"I don't care at this moment. I just want to go to sleep. I'm still exhausted from healing Dev this morning." "Dev, I'm not completely helpless." She placed her hand on his shoulder and let the heat from her fire magic penetrate his skin.

His winced from the sting of it but nodded his head in agreement. "True, and you'll have Cinder with you."

"Exactly. Rest tonight. Tomorrow starts fresh."

"Good." The smile that reappeared on Kell's face seemed less forced this time. "Now that we've resolved this situation, I agree that we could all benefit from a good night's sleep. Arden, please allow Lord Pryan's steward to show you to your room."

She followed the dour-faced man out of the great hall, casting one more glance at Dev before she passed through the doorway. *Please don't let this be some kind of mistake.*

"There's only one way to find out," Loku answered.

They climbed the wooden stairs to a narrow hallway. The sprigs of dried lavender hanging from the rafters did little to conceal the dank odor that clung to the stone walls.

She doubted the noblemen would be sleeping in this part of the keep tonight.

"In here," the steward ordered.

The room was hardly more than a closet, but the same silk cushions from the night before waited for her on the floor. A lit candle flickered on the small stand with a pitcher of water and basin. A sigh of delight escaped her when she spotted the cake of soap sitting near it. Now she could scrub away the mud that matted her hair and darkened her fingernails.

"I'll fetch you in the morning." The door slammed shut, followed by the click of the lock.

Panic rose into her throat from the thought of being trapped in this room, but she swallowed it down. *I'm still a prisoner, after all. And being treated very well for one, I suppose.*

"If you had agreed to warm the prince's bed, I bet you'd be on your way to Boznac in the morning."

"I'm not going to stoop to that level." She poured the icy water into the basin and reached for the soap.

Chapter 18

Kell sat at the head table and surveyed the great hall.
The soldiers' plates rattled above the din of their voices,
but his attention focused on one person in particular. The
Gravarian knight sat alone in his corner, his gaze fixed on
the main doors while he ate his breakfast of bread and
cheese.

He'd taken a gamble last night by accusing Dev of
plotting to escape, but the way the elf scouted the keep
when they arrived roused his suspicions. Luckily, he'd
been right.

Arden entered the great hall behind Pryan's steward.
The morning sunlight fell her hair as she passed under a
window, making it flash like polished gold. Porcelain skin
that had been hidden under layers of dirt now glowed from
a fresh washing. She stood out like a rare bloom. One he
would've wanted to possess if he didn't know how
dangerous she could be.

"See something you like?" Bynn teased.

"Possibly."

"You're playing with fire, Kell. She made it quite
clear last night she's on to your games."

The sting of her refusal resurfaced. Years had passed
since a woman had denied him, and no one had ever done
it like that in front of a crowd. Despite that, she still
intrigued him. "What if I want to play a new game?"

"What are you suggesting?"

"First, I need to earn her trust."

"Then what?"

"Then we'll see what happens." He nibbled on a piece
of bacon and grinned. The order of his plans varied with

his moods, but they all involved convincing her to stay in Ranello long enough to help him defeat Sulaino.

The steward led her to the head table. She stood in front of him with a mixture of curiosity and resentment in her face. "Good morning, Your Highness."

"Good morning, Arden. Please join us."

Her deep blue eyes flickered to her protector. "If you please—"

"That was an order, not a request."

For a second, he wondered if his imagination played a trick on him. The pale green halo in her eyes flashed, and her upper lip curled slightly. By the time he blinked, however, a smooth mask of composure had settled over her features. She sank into a chair, her gaze never leaving him.

Sweat prickled his skin. He'd never had a woman's unwavering attention fixed on him like that; or at least, not with his knowledge. What was worse, he wasn't sure if his attraction toward her or his fear of her power added to his unease. The weight of Dev's glare only added to it. He was a prince, damn it. He should be used to being the center of attention.

He pushed the discomfort to the back of his mind and flashed his most charming grin. "What would you like to eat?"

She surveyed the offerings on the table, then looked behind her. "I'll have what Dev's having."

"You wouldn't like a bit of bacon or perhaps a bit of preserved fruit to put on your toast?" He imagined licking the remnants of the sweet berry preserves off her lips, and his hunger grew. But not necessarily for breakfast.

The pink color in her cheeks deepened. "I'm not on the menu, Your Highness, so you can quit looking at me like that."

Bynn almost choked on his food from laughter, and embarrassment killed any desire Kell felt for her at that moment. "I could have your head for speaking to me like that."

She shrugged, reaching for a piece of bread. "Beheading is more merciful than being burnt at the stake."

"And you think by antagonizing me, I'll be more merciful?"

"I'm not purposely trying to antagonize you, Your Highness. I'm just treating you like I would anyone else. We aren't exactly schooled in how to address members of the royal family where I come from."

He leaned forward. "And where is that?"

"Wallus." She folded her bread around a slice of cheese. He had to wait until she finished chewing her bite before she continued. "It's a small village in the southwest corner of the kingdom. You've probably never heard of it."

"And who's your blood there?"

The bread and cheese slipped from her fingers.

Bynn exchanged a knowing look with him. No wonder she clung to Dev like she did. He was the only one who would claim her. "Why were you cast aside?"

The rosy flush deepened into red anger. "Who says I was cast aside? Did it ever occur to you that I left home because my blood mistreated me?"

"Your father mistreated you?"

She threw the remains of her meal on the table and rose from her chair. "I don't like the way this conversation is heading."

Although she kept her voice low, her actions attracted attention from those around him. He gestured for her to sit. "If I promise not to ask any more about your father, will that convince you to finish your meal without making a spectacle of yourself?"

She slumped down into her seat and reached for a piece of bacon.

He waited a few seconds for her to calm down before asking, "How did you meet Dev?"

"He came into the inn where I worked and saved my life when the necromancer attacked it."

Two pearls of information from her response. First, that Sulaino had spread the reach of his attacks further south that he'd realized. Second, that Dev found her in Ranello. It almost made his story of being her protector a bit unbelievable now. "How did he go from saving your life to becoming your protector?"

She cast another glance in Dev's direction. "I think he'd be the best one to explain that."

"You'll blindly follow him without completely understanding your situation?"

"I never said that, Your Highness. I understand my situation all too well, both now and before we ran into you the other night."

"Then why won't you answer my question?"

"Because it's none of your business."

Bynn had the courtesy to cover his mouth this time when he snickered. The sassy witch had provided enough fodder for his friend to tease him with all the way to Trivinus.

"Fine. You're dismissed." He'd reached his limit of humiliation for the day.

"Thank you, Your Highness." The deepness of her curtsey matched the sarcasm dripping from her voice.

When she joined Dev, Bynn released the laughter he'd kept bottled up inside.

***

The soldiers set up camp as the last rays of the autumn sun filtered through the red and gold canopy of leaves above them. Despite their injuries, Kell didn't notice much of a disruption in the way they worked. They were all seasoned professionals, the elite of the royal guard. And he thanked the Lady Moon he'd only lost one of them during their skirmishes with Sulaino.

His attention turned to Arden. If she hadn't unleashed her magic against the undead… A shudder disrupted his thoughts.

She reclined back on her elbows, soaking up the last of the sun's warmth. With her eyes closed and a blissful smile on her face, she almost resembled the paintings of the goddess he'd seen in the temple.

"Now I'm being ridiculous," he muttered, retreating into his tent. It was one thing to concede she was pretty in her own way and to be in awe of her power. It was another to give her a divine association.

"Any changes in your plans for the witch?" Bynn asked the moment Kell sat down. "Admit it—she proved to be a bit more difficult than you suspected."

The muscles in his neck began to twitch. "Patience is all it takes."

"Like you have any."

"Considering the circumstances, I'm willing to gain some. She's like a siege. It won't be easy to break through her defenses." He massaged the knots forming in his shoulders.

Bynn poured a glass of wine and handed it to him before pouring his own. "And I suppose your usual strategy of sneaking past those walls and undermining her defenses isn't going to work like it usually does."

He snapped his head up. "What is that supposed to mean?"

"It means you've finally met a woman who won't fall victim to your charms, which has you more riled up than you care to admit. Look at you. You can't get comfortable, and you can't get her off your mind."

"She's a woman," he replied with a laugh.

"She's a challenge."

"Sooner or later, she'll cave. I just need to find her weakness like I found the knight's."

"What if *he's* her weakness? Have you ever thought of that?"

The image of Arden and Dev lying in bed together caused his stomach to tighten. He remembered the way she rushed to find Dev when she woke up in his tent and her demands that he be left unharmed last night. He stood and paced the room, trying to ease his discomfort. "She's been cast aside, and he's the closest thing she has to blood now.

Of course she attached to him."

"Attached? Or something more?"

"I don't know, but I'm going to find out. If I know their connection, I know how I can use it to my advantage. In the meantime, I plan on keeping them separated as much as possible. Dev's waiting for the right moment to grab her and run for the borders."

Bynn swirled the contents of his glass and stared at the resulting vortex. "And why should we stop them, other than the brief humiliation that you let them escape?"

Kell stopped and turned on his heel. "Do you seriously think we can defeat Sulaino without her?"

He looked up from the wine. "I think you're pinning all your hopes on a witch instead of coming up with an alternative. How do you know we can trust her?"

"Why would she come to our aid if she meant to harm us?"

"Dozens of reasons. She could've had it out for Sulaino and wanted to defeat him so she could eliminate a rival. Hell, she could be in league with him, and the other night was all just a show so she could infiltrate our group and gain access to the palace." He placed his glass on the ground. "Have you even considered that?"

Kell took a deep breath and tilted his head back. Could the two prisoners be underhanded enough to plan such a thing? "No, I haven't," he admitted.

"Your Highness, may I enter?" a man's voice called from outside, interrupting their conversation.

"Enter."

The flustered captain of the guard strode in with a snatch of weeds in his fist. "Your Highness, I caught her trying to poison us with this."

"I was doing no such thing." Arden came in right on his heels, not pausing to ask permission. "I simply wanted to add some herbs to the meat to make it taste better."

Kell studied her face, looking for the slightest tell of a lie, but found none. "Let me see them."

Larenis released the greenery. Bynn came over to sniff

a sprig with green, needle-like leaves. "Rosemary."

Picking up a different one, Kell held it to his nose and inhaled its slight lemony scent. "Is this wild thyme?"

"Yes," she replied with a hint of irritation on her voice. "It's not my fault your men can't recognize basic herbs."

He examined the rest of the bundle to make sure she didn't slip something else into it but found nothing. "Larenis, you have nothing to worry about. These are herbs, just as she said."

The captain stared at the ground. His voice trembled slightly when he said, "Yes, Your Highness. I apologize for the interruption." He didn't wait to be dismissed before hastening out of the tent.

Arden took the bunch from his hand. "Thank you, Your Highness."

"Wait a moment." She stopped, and he closed the space between them. "Where did you learn to recognize wild herbs?"

"I'm a woman. Normally, we amuse ourselves with things like cooking, in case you failed to notice. But I guess the ladies of the court aren't as well-versed in this subject because they have servants who tend to these mundane matters for them."

"For someone who claims to be baseborn, you seem to know quite a bit about life in court."

Her face scrunched up like she'd just eaten a lemon. "My mother used to work at the palace." She lifted the flap and disappeared before he could ask more questions.

Another gem of information. Kell turned to Bynn to discuss it but paused when he saw the frown on his face. "What's wrong?"

"That's only a taste of what's going on out there. The men are on edge. They don't trust her or Dev. If you're not careful, you may have a mutiny on your hands."

"They wouldn't dare disobey my orders."

"So I hope." His shoulders slumped as he crossed the room. "I'll speak to Larenis and some of the other men and reassure them. Maybe that will keep them from using your witch for kindling."

"You think I'm wrong to keep her alive, don't you?" Kell held his breath, hoping to keep his doubts to himself.

Bynn shook his head. "I have my concerns, but no, I don't think you were wrong to spare her life. It was a tough decision to make, and I'm not sure I would've had the courage to do the same."

His friend's words echoed in his mind for the next few hours. Anxious to be free from his doubts, Kell stepped out of his tent to get some fresh air. Outside, the men gathered around the large bonfire, watching two figures in the center. The light from the fire silhouetted them, obscuring their faces, but their graceful movements hypnotized him as they had the others.

"Who's giving the swordplay demonstration, Larenis?" he asked once he neared the captain.

"The two prisoners, Your Highness. Seems the knight demanded he continue the witch's lessons." He spat on the ground. "It's bad enough that she's a witch, but now he's trying to teach her how to use a sword. You wait and see— tomorrow morning, we'll all be slit from nose to navel by the two of them."

"I seriously doubt that. If they wanted to kill us, they would have done it already. Or better yet, left us alone in the first place so Sulaino and his undead could do it."

Larenis' jaw dropped. "Are you saying that we couldn't have handled them on our own, Your Highness?"

"You were there. How well did you think we were doing?" When the captain closed his mouth and crossed his arms, Kell knew he'd discussed this long enough with him. "By the way, what did you think of dinner tonight?"

"It was better than usual," he begrudgingly admitted.

"Yes, I agree. The herbs added a nice touch to the meat." One battle down for the night. If he could convince Larenis that Arden wasn't a threat, maybe the rest of the men would follow.

He moved around the crowd until he could see her

face. She remained focused on her mentor and the stick in his hand, expertly blocking his blows with her own. A smile stretched her lips to their limits, plumped the apples of her cheeks.

Something strange curled in the pit of his stomach as he watched her glee from the swordplay, but he couldn't place it. Fear? Admiration? Envy?

Dev lunged for her, but Arden danced away and whacked her stick against his neck. "Gotcha."

Although they both gulped for air, Dev gave his one note laugh. "Finally."

"That had to be one of the most impressive displays of swordsmanship I've seen in years," Kell said as he waded through the crowd and approached them. "I hope maybe we can engage in a little match once we get to Trivinus."

"Why wait until then?" Dev tossed his stick to him. "You verses Trouble."

Snickers rippled through the men until he glared over his shoulder at them. "You're asking me to fight your apprentice?"

"Yes, I am." The knight moved to the edge of the circle and sat next to his wolf. "She needs all the practice she can get."

"What's the matter, Your Highness?" Arden teased. "Scared to take on a girl?"

His answer became choked in his throat. Dev had purposely insulted him by declining his challenge in favor of Arden. If he backed down, he'd lose his men's respect. "I'm worried that I may harm you."

"These are sticks, Your Highness, not real swords."

"And don't worry about her," Dev added. "She's tougher than she looks."

Although he had his doubts, he raised his stick and stood *en garde.* "I'll try to be easy on you."

She laughed, mimicking his stance.

When she didn't move, he swung his stick. She blocked his attack with the speed of a master swordsman and continued with the momentum of the maneuver, twisting away from him. The shadows on his peripheral vision hid her. He turned to follow her, only to feel the sting of her stick as it slapped against his chest.

"Gotcha." Triumph glowed from her face, and her lips twitched as if she was trying to stifle her laughter.

Kell's face burned. The last time an opponent had taken him down in under a minute, he'd still had his nanny present in the room. This time, he didn't have the excuse of his youth. And he'd lost to a woman.

He thought he saw an odd green light flash in her eyes before she spoke again. "In all fairness, Your Highness, you were going easy on me. Shall we say best two out of three?"

Her offer gave him a chance at redemption. "Sounds fair enough."

They both took the ready positions again. Someone behind Kell whispered his prediction of this match to a comrade—less than one minute again, but with the same result. Anger and pride swirled together in his gut and shot out to his muscles, giving them the fire he needed. He'd be damned if he let her out of his sight again.

She attacked first. When he swung his stick up to block her, the weakness behind the swing surprised him. He parried her next two blows and frowned. Something was different this time. Perhaps fatigue had taken hold of her. When he finally attacked, he easily knocked her stick out of her hands and pressed his against the center of her chest.

"Well done, Your Highness." She bowed when he withdrew his weapon.

He picked up her stick and leaned close when he returned it. "You weren't as quick this time," he said low enough for only her to hear.

Although her face remained blank, her eyes mocked him. "I figured I should at least let you win once so you could save face in front of your men."

She let him win? Of all the arrogant things to say. Who did she think she was? He cast a glance at Dev, noting how his amusement at the situation mirrored Arden's. They were two of a kind, and they needed to be shown he wouldn't stand for this.

"Play fair this time, Trouble," Kell warned.

Her mirth faded when he used that name.

Good, let her get angry. Maybe she'll get sloppy.

The second she assumed the *en garde* position, he attacked. This time, he held nothing back. He treated her like an enemy, and he wanted blood. To his amazement, she either blocked or dodged most of his blows. Her quick reflexes startled him, but when her stick came within inches of his face, he snapped out of his daze.

She retreated as he continued to swing at her, breaking the circle of men surrounding them. Free of their confines, her movements took on the grace of a dancer. She twisted and pirouetted, using her slender body to its best advantage while her weapon whizzed through the air. What she lacked in strength, she made up for in speed. And as he chased her around the campsite, his admiration for her multiplied. He had to admit he'd never fought an opponent like her before.

They reached the tree line. Her movements stiffened. He continued to attack, pushing her farther back. She was running out of room, and unless she found some way to escape soon, he'd have her.

Her feet tripped over an exposed root. Now was his chance. He surged forward, pinning her free hand between her back and large tree. With his other hand, he grabbed her wrist and twisted it until she dropped her stick. A grin formed on his lips as he prepared gloat over his victory.

Then the light from the three moons illuminated her face. His breath caught. His anger melted, leaving behind an odd emotion he'd never experienced before.

His brother, Therrin, once told him that falling in love was like falling off a horse. He never saw it coming, and when it happened, it knocked the wind out of his lungs and left him stunned.

Kell felt that way now as he stared into her eyes.

Whether she'd used magic or not, he fell completely under her spell. His lungs burned for air. His heart beat in perfect rhythm with hers. Her curves pressed against him as her body yielded. He focused on her lips, drawn to them as if they alone could provide the life-giving air he needed. He leaned closer until her warm breath caressed his mouth.

In that moment, he no longer feared losing his heart.

Chapter 19

Arden braced herself, her pulse quickening. She'd never been kissed before. *Please don't let me swoon like some of those idiot girls I've seen.*

"*It all depends on how well he kisses,*" Loku replied.

Before Kell's lips could brush hers, a very annoyed voice interrupted them. "I think you've made your point. You can release my apprentice now."

Her cheeks burned from the acid in Dev's order. *This is ridiculous. I shouldn't feel this way from losing a swordfight.*

Loku laughed. "*My dear Soulbearer, this is more than just swordplay, and you know it. It's foreplay.*"

"*Foreplay? We were fighting, not flirting.*"

"*Fighting, flirting—there's not much different between the two. It's all about dominance, and I have a feeling Prince Kell has a sword he wouldn't mind letting you play with.*"

"*Shut up, Loku.*" Yes, she found Kell attractive, but she knew better than to allow him any liberties with her body. Her mother fell into that trap, and she refused to follow in her footsteps. That did little to soothe the fluttering in her chest, however.

Kell held her gaze as he backed away. Something had changed. His expression lost the cocky arrogance he'd extruded earlier. He seemed as shocked and uncertain as she did. He spun around on his heel, pushing his way through the crowd. His men followed him with their eyes and fell back into place, concealing his escape route.

Her lungs sucked in the cool air, and she slid down

along the tree. Her hands trembled as she brought them up to her flaming cheeks.

Dev knelt beside her. "Did he hurt you?"

"Who?" Then she understood his question. "No, he didn't hurt me."

He examined her wrists before tilting her chin up to search her face. "Are you sure? Because if he did—"

"No, Dev, I'll be fine in a few moments. Just let me catch my breath."

He continued to watch her with an intensity that made her fear he'd read her mind. "You're acting strange."

"I'm not going insane, if that's what you're worried about." At least, she hoped not. No, everything she had experienced was physical, not mental.

"It's called lust, and it's about time. I was beginning to fear you'd remain a frigid virgin for the rest of your life. My only question is, who are you going to turn to, to satisfy the need inside you? Dev or Kell?"

"Neither."

"Keep fooling yourself, but we both know better. Just be careful. If you don't make a decision soon, they'll decide it for you."

"Don't be ridiculous. Dev doesn't feel that way about me."

"No? Then why does he look like he wants to castrate Kell?"

She focused her attention on Dev. Lines carved into his face around his mouth and between his brows. "No, I don't think you're showing signs of insanity." He released her. "Yet."

"Meaning?"

"The sooner I get you to Gravaria and away from the prince, the better." He stood and offered her his hand.

"I told you he was jealous."

"And I still find that hard to believe." She took his hand and stiffened her legs, ignoring the fatigue that threatened to turn them into dough.

"Do you realize what you did wrong?" he asked.

Besides almost letting Kell kiss me? "Um, no."

"You lost awareness of your surroundings. You let him back you into a corner, and then you failed to notice the exposed roots on the ground. If he'd been an enemy with a real sword, you'd be dead now." He led her back to where Cinder stood guard over their belongings.

"And then Loku could torment someone else."

Dev halted and spun around. "For someone who's collecting death threats, you seem very nonchalant about all this. I'm trying to teach you what I can so you'll stay alive long enough to get to safety."

"And I appreciate it—really, I do." She placed her hand on his arm. "I'm sorry I disappointed you."

His lips curled up into a smile. "I wouldn't say your performance was a complete disappointment, Trouble. I had to keep from laughing when you got the prince in less than a minute."

"So, I'm learning something, right?"

"Yes, you're learning quicker than I thought, which is a good thing, considering you have a necromancer hunting you." A serious expression replaced any mirth that he'd allowed to show on his face. Back to business once again.

He didn't say anything else, much to her relief. Whatever happened between her and the prince was just a one-time thing, and life showed signs of returning back to normal. She sank to the ground by her saddle, reaching for her bedroll. The rush from the battle and almost getting kissed seeped out of her body, taking all her energy with it. She'd sleep well once she quieted her mind.

She had just unrolled her blankets when Dev cursed under his breath.

The prince's right-hand man, Lord Bynn, approached them. "Come with me."

"Both of us?" Dev's sarcasm held an edge as sharp as any blade.

"Just the girl."

Her heart skipped a beat. *"He's going to punish me for publically humiliating the prince, isn't he?"*

"If he tries anything, I'll make him regret it. Dev probably would, too."

"Why?" her protector asked. His hand slid down his leg to the edge of his boot.

She remembered the slim knife he concealed there from the one night he removed his entire arsenal in front of her. How many other weapons did he still have on his body?

"Prince Kell's orders. He wants to make sure she has a safe place to sleep."

"She's perfectly safe next to me."

A smirk appeared on the noble's face. "I'm afraid the prince disagrees with you."

Arden found a break in the conversation and jumped in with her opinion. "Why? Because he thinks I'll be safer next to him?"

"You won't be sleeping in his tent, if that's what concerns you," came the clipped reply. "You can either come with me peacefully, or I can have the men take you like they tried to last night."

Dev's fingers disappeared into his boot, but she stopped him before he could retrieve the weapon by covering his hand with her own. "It's fine, Dev. I'll take Cinder with me again."

Bynn didn't look very pleased at having to accommodate both her and the wolf, but his annoyance eased when she rolled her blankets back up and stood. Dev's expression, however, remained unchanged; he still looked like he wanted to gut the young lord standing in front of him.

"This way." No thanks for defusing a potentially explosive situation. No mention of her name. Nothing.

"Where are we going?"

"You'll stay in my tent tonight."

Arden dug her heels in. "Listen, I've already told the prince I'm not going to warm his bed, and I sure as hell won't be passed around his friends. You got that?"

He grabbed her wrist and pulled her so his face was

inches away from his. "For someone in your position, you have a lot of nerve speaking to anyone that way. I should order you whipped for that arrogant display earlier this evening, witch."

"You mean the one where I wounded the prince's pride?" *And almost made him kiss me?* "Come now. He's a big enough boy to fight his own battles and lick his wounds afterwards."

"Right now, he's the only thing standing between you and a pyre, so I suggest you mind your tongue and show him some respect."

His words chilled her blood enough to where she kept her mouth shut after that. He led her to a small tent and pointed to a corner, telling her to sleep there. He lay down on the opposite side, blocking her exit. Sensing there was nothing else she could do that night, she let her mind drift into sleep.

***

"Arden, I see you."

The eerie voice roused her from her dreams. She knew Loku's voice as well as her own by now, but this wasn't him.

"Do you think the prince and his men will keep you safe? Or do you tragically place your trust in your protector?"

She lifted her head from the ground and looked around, trying to determine where the voice was coming from. *"Loku, if this is some kind of twisted joke…"*

"It's not me—I promise." The alarm in his voice only added to her panic.

"You'll be mine before the end of the fortnight." The sinister voice danced around her like a hummingbird, whispering in one ear and then the other. *"You and the soul of the god who lives inside you."*

"Don't listen to him," Loku urged. *"He'll just eat away at your mind until he finds enough holes to worm his way into it."*

Lord Bynn rolled over onto his side, snoring louder

than ever. The noise blocked out the eerie voice long enough for her to build a shield around her mind.

"It's the necromancer, isn't it?" She pulled her knees up to her chest and began rocking. As perverted as Loku was, he didn't seem to mean her any harm. She could almost touch the cold malice in the new voice. How had the bastard gotten into her mind?

"Go to sleep, my Soulbearer. I'll keep him from haunting your dreams."

"Too late." The experience rattled her nerves to the point that sleep became impossible. Instead, she sank her hands into Cinder's fur and clung to it as if it offered some kind of magical protection. The wolf licked her hand and went back to sleep, leaving her to stare out into the darkness.

An unknown amount of time passed, but by the time the sun rose, Arden's eyes stung like she'd just gotten caught in a dust storm. As soon as Bynn sat up, she dashed out of the tent. She needed to tell Dev what happened.

She cleared the flap and collided into a rock-hard body. "Excuse me," she began and froze.

"Anxious to leave?" Kell asked.

Her tongue acted like it was twice its normal size as she tried to reply. She took a step back and moved to the side so she no longer stood between the two men. "I wanted to speak to Dev about something."

"Your face is pale. What happened?" The prince gave his friend an accusing glare.

Bynn raised his hands in the air, palms out. "I promise you, I didn't harm her in any way."

"Lord Bynn was every bit the gentleman as expected by his title." *And acted like a total ass.*

"Then what troubles you?"

Besides the fact he still had the strange glow in his eyes from the night before? Despite Kell's insistence that she trust him, there was only one person she did. "I'd prefer to tell Dev."

He tried to stop her, but Cinder growled in warning.

She ran to the spot where she left her protector, relieved to find him still there.

Dev jumped to his feet when he saw her approaching. "What did they try to do to you?"

"Not them," she replied between pants. "He's in my head now."

His mouth hardened into a thin line. "What does he have of yours?"

His question surprised her. It took a full three seconds before she could reply, "My hair."

"Do you know how to raise shields around your mind?" His fingers curled into fists, blanching the skin of his knuckles.

"I've had them up most of the morning." And thankfully, they seemed to be working.

"Keep them up. And if we run into Sulaino again, remind me to retrieve your personal effects from him."

"Personal effects?" Kell asked behind them. Suspicion now filled his eyes.

Arden welcomed his changed demeanor. "We had our own skirmish with him before we ran into you, and one of his undead cut off the end of my hair while I was fighting him."

"He used it last night to contact her," Dev added.

Kell's dark brows furrowed together. "I'm not following this."

"Of course not." Dev packed his belongings as if the prince wasn't standing there. "You have no concept of how magic works. Sulaino is concentrating his magic through something that belonged to Trouble—in this case, her hair—and using it to invade her thoughts."

"Should I worry that he'll try to influence her?"

A chill rippled down her spine. "The only way he'll influence me is if I'm dead and reanimated."

Dev nodded in agreement. "She's aware of the threat and has taken measures to ensure he'll hit a few walls if he tries it again."

The prince seemed confused with their answers but

walked away without asking any more questions.

As soon as he was out of earshot, Dev squeezed her upper arm in an iron vise. "You're telling me the truth, right?"

"Why would I lie about something like this?"

"Tell me everything. Every word he said. Every threat he made. Leave nothing out."

She tried to wrestle free from him. "Let go of me, and maybe I will."

His hand relaxed, and she recounted the entire night's events.

***

Arden kept her mouth shut the rest of the day. Keeping her shields up required too much concentration, even though both Dev and Loku reassured her Sulaino was less likely to make contact with her during the day since his powers were weakest while the sun shone.

They stopped that night at the edge of an apple orchard. The first frost of winter hadn't coated the trees with its sparkling crust yet, and the thin branches remained heavy with ripe fruit.

Dev sank into a dark mood, one she knew better than to disturb. His attention travelled back and forth between the men setting up the camp and the orchard while he drew lines in the ground beside him.

She ventured into the trees. A few minutes away from the stares and accusing glances would ease her worried mind. Besides, she needed to find a couple of sturdy sticks for tonight's lesson.

"What are you doing?" Kell asked a few feet away from her.

She almost jumped out of her skin. Dev's voice filled her mind, lecturing her about being aware of her surroundings. She'd been so engrossed with finding the perfect stick that she didn't hear the prince sneak up on her. "*A little warning would have been appreciated, Loku.*"

"*Why should I warn you about him? He doesn't mean*

any harm."

"Depends on your definition of harm." "What does it look like I'm doing?"

"You're either gathering firewood or tearing down trees." The playfulness had returned to his voice. He picked a rosy apple off the branch and bit into it.

She stiffened her spine and placed three long strides between them. If she wanted to keep from giving away any more of her secrets, she needed to keep her distance. "I have enough respect for whoever's orchard this is not to steal from him or destroy his livelihood."

His mouth froze, poised to take another bite from the apple. "And what does that mean?"

"I'm not surprised these things never cross your mind, Your Highness." She fought hard to keep the steely edge in her voice. "You're a prince. You've never had to do an honest day's work in your life. You just help yourself to whatever you desire because you know it'll be given to you."

He tilted his head to the side. "Are you mocking me?"

"Mocking the Third Prince of Rancllo would certainly cost me my head."

"Then why the lecture?" He took another bite of his apple and leaned against a tree.

"Did it ever occur to you that you're stealing? That you're taking food out of a child's mouth or money out of a man's purse by eating that apple without permission?"

He shrugged. "I'm the prince. If I asked for it, the owner would have given it to me."

"And you just made my point. You're so used to getting what you want that you don't even consider the cost to your subjects." She dove deeper into the orchard, eager to place a few more feet between them.

Loku's snickering stopped her in her tracks. *"That's right—hurt his feelings and run away. Tell yourself he's an ass if you think it will help. But when his breath brushes against the back of your neck..."*

The words came true as soon as he said them. The

warm air tickled her skin, made her breath catch. What kind of game was Kell playing?

"Do you really think I'm that spoiled?"

She licked her lips while her mind fought with the rest of her body. "Yes, I do."

"I don't always get what I want." He slowly turned her around until she faced him.

"Give me one example."

"Politically or personally?"

In the past, she would've slapped a man's face if he looked at her the same way Kell did, undressing her with his eyes and making no pretense about it. She knew she should have answered, "Politically," but the other option tumbled out before she caught herself.

His finger meandered along her cheek and down her jaw, stopping at the tip of her chin. "What if I told you I want you?"

Her heart fluttered in her chest. "I find it hard to believe a prince like you would be interested in a common-born witch like me." There. She said it. Her spine straightened, and she hoped she might resist his charms.

"I think you underestimate what eyes the color of sapphires can do to a man." He leaned forward, brushing his lips against hers.

The bundle of sticks in her arms fell to the ground. Arden became as frozen as the undead from the other night. It wasn't even a real kiss—a tease, to be precise— but it threw her entire world upside down.

"They make him question everything he's ever known." This time, he really kissed her, his lips pressing against hers for a second.

Fire flowed through her veins, and her breath caught. *What is wrong with me?*

"Stop fighting him and enjoy it."

"They make him want to be a better man," he continued.

A twig snapped behind them, and Kell pulled away before he could kiss her again.

The tip of her tongue darted out to assess the already swollen bit of flesh. The taste of apples lingered there. A sinking sensation formed in her chest as though she'd done something to betray Dev.

"There you are, Kell." Bynn stood in the lengthening shadows, his hand resting on the hilt of his sword. "I was wondering where you had gotten off to."

"Just keeping an eye on Arden." He winked at her before sauntering over to his friend.

Bynn's eyes narrowed. "You shouldn't place yourself in danger."

The lord's open hostility pulled her from her thoughts. No matter how nice she played, the suspicion aroused by her appearance and power would always stay the same. "Surely you don't think I'm a threat to the prince's life, do you?" She snatched the last stick from the grass and shoved past the two men. When Bynn didn't answer, she strode back to the camp in a huff.

Chapter 20

Kell watched Arden disappear through the trees. The gentle sway of her hips mesmerized him until the world around him faded from view. He doubted she knew what a tempting creature she could be sometimes. But the questions she roused inside him almost made him forget the sweetness of her lips. She was different from any other woman he'd tangled with before. He actually meant it when he said she made him want to be a better man. If only he knew what she wanted from him.

Bynn snapped his fingers in front of his face. "Should I even ask what happened?"

An easy smile curled the corners of his mouth up as they wandered back to the camp. "I might have had a bit more fun if you hadn't interrupted us."

"And is your curiosity sated for now?"

"I've just whetted it." Arden captured his mind more than any other woman he'd met. Her uncertainty when he turned her to face him. The way she dropped the branches in her arms when their lips touched. Her hesitancy when he'd kissed her. All the signs of a woman who'd never been with a man before. He inwardly winced at how he'd thought she was little more than Dev's whore before this afternoon. "She's more innocent than I gave her credit for." *And I'm the one trying to corrupt her.*

"Or she's just a really good actress. Sometimes I wonder which one of you is trying to fool the other."

Kell halted. "What do you mean?"

"I know you're trying to seduce her so she'll stay and help you defeat Sulaino, but I'm beginning to think she's playing the same game with you. If she joins you in your bed, would you set her free?"

Anger flashed through him, locking his muscles as the current passed over them. "What do you have against her, Bynn?"

"I'm just trying to be a good friend. I've never seen you act this way around a woman before. You're obsessed."

Obsessed? He chuckled at the idea, his temper cooling with each note. "Maybe I've found someone who amuses me more than those simpering ladies of the court."

"Are you sure she hasn't cast some kind of spell on you?"

"Would she be so resistant if she did?"

"I suppose you're right. But I still wonder about the recent change in you. Last night, for example—"

"I'm perfectly aware my behavior has you and the other men concerned, but you have nothing to worry about. *I'm* in control of this situation, not her."

He refrained from telling his best friend about the odd ache in his chest every time he stared into her eyes, or the way he almost forgot about everything but her when they kissed. Hell, he even held back on the kiss for fear he would startle her. He'd never done that before.

"As long as you know what's going through my head. I'll be watching both of you."

Kell couldn't suppress his grin, finding some levity in this conversation at last. "You never struck me as the voyeuristic type before."

Bynn's expression mirrored his, and the tension between them eased as they continued toward the camp. "Are you suggesting I could learn a thing or two from you?"

"I'm having to handle her differently. The last time I met this much resistance from a woman was when I stole a kiss from your sister about ten years ago."

"Which neither one of us has forgiven you for doing, by the way."

He laughed. "Yes, I still remember the black eye she gave me."

Larenis approached them with worry tightening the planes of his face when they returned to the camp. After a quick bow, he said, "Your Highness, I hate to bother you, but I thought you should see this."

Kell gritted his teeth, expecting the captain of the guard to accuse Arden of poisoning them again, but he silently led him to Cero's tent instead.

The smell of rotting flesh hit him as soon as they walked into the enclosed space, curdling the contents of his stomach. The healer bent over a man and wiped a cloth over his patient's upper arm.

Larenis waited until Cero reached for a pot of salve. "I brought the prince."

"Your Highness." Cero started to rise, but Kell ushered him back down.

"Continue your work." He knelt next to the soldier and examined him. Glassy eyes stared back at him. Foul-smelling yellow pus oozed from a jagged gash on his upper arm, and the underlying flesh varied from an angry red to a sickening shade of black. "What happened to Ortono?"

"He was wounded in that last battle, and I haven't been able to stop the infection." Guilt laced the healer's words, mingling with the shame in his face. "I'm at the point where I may need to amputate his arm to save his life, and even then, there are no guarantees."

"No." Ortono shoved Cero away from him. "No cutting."

"But if it can save your life—"

"No!"

Larenis restrained the soldier's fist before it connected with the healer's jaw. "This is why I brought it to your attention, Your Highness. He won't listen to me or Cero, but if you said something, maybe he would concede."

"I don't care if the king himself ordered it—no one's cutting off my sword arm. I'd rather die than be a cripple."

Ortono's panting from the short exertion quickened until he retched and lost the watery contents of his stomach.

Kell leaned back, worried for a second he might mimic Ortono's actions. The acidic bile burned the inside of his nose. He jumped to his feet. Once outside, he gulped in the fresh air.

Bynn and Larenis joined him. "What should we do, Your Highness?"

He took a moment and cleared his mind. "He has a wife and children, doesn't he, Larenis?"

"Yes, Your Highness. Three small boys, all younger than five years."

"And if he can't work as a member of the Royal Guard, what will he do? How will he support them?"

Bynn frowned. "How will he support them if he's dead?"

"We have the widow's fund," the captain of the guard admitted with some reluctance. "It helps take care of the family of any member of the Royal Guard who dies in service to the crown."

"So, in his eyes, it's better for his family if he dies rather than lose his arm." Kell tightened his jaw until his teeth hurt. "I'm not sure what we should do, to be honest."

"Are you saying you'd consider letting him die because he refuses to have his arm amputated?" Bynn said, his jaw slack. "Look at him—he's so fevered, he's not thinking rationally."

"No, I think his mind is working quite well. And until we can think of another option, I have to respect the man's wishes."

"These are his only two options." Larenis' spine jerked into a ramrod straight position. "Cero has tried everything."

His gaze drifted to the corner where Arden and Dev examined the sticks she gathered. "There may be another alternative."

The other two followed his direction, and a snarl appeared on the captain's face. "Absolutely not. I will not let that witch touch him."

"What are you thinking, Kell?" Bynn's face couldn't hide his disbelief. "Magic?"

"I think she healed Dev."

"You have no proof."

"Other than knowing what his wound looked like the night before and how well it healed the next morning. I don't believe for a moment elves heal quicker than humans."

Larenis blocked the entrance of the tent with his body and crossed his arms. "I'm sorry, Your Highness, but in the best interest of my men, I won't allow her to come near him."

Kell raised one brow. "You would defy my orders?"

The knob in the captain's throat bobbed up and down. "I hope I won't have to, Your Highness."

Kell weighed the pros and cons of consulting Arden and Dev on this matter. Even if she managed to save Ortono's life and arm, would it cause a mutiny among his men? Or would they finally see she meant no harm? He cast another glance at her. "Let's see what happens overnight. If I were you, Larenis, I'd pray long and hard to the Lady Moon for a miracle, because Ortono's going to need one."

***

As soon as he awoke the next morning, Kell headed straight for Cero's tent. "Any news on Ortono?"

The dark circles under the healer's eyes showed his lack of sleep. "He's worse. Shouting in his sleep all night, none of it making any sense. The area around the wound has gangrene. Even if I amputated his arm right now, I fear we're too late."

"Are you at least making him comfortable?"

Cero nodded. "I've been trying to force a few sips of poppy juice down him whenever I get a chance."

He closed the space between them and lowered his voice so only the healer could hear his words. "What is your stance on asking Arden to take a look at him?"

"The witch, Your Highness?"

He nodded, watching Cero's expression fluctuate between hope and fear.

"You of all people know that magic is forbidden."

"Yes, but I might be able to turn a blind eye to it if the ends justify the means."

"Be careful, Your Highness. You walk along a slippery path."

"As long as I know ahead of time, I can prepare for it."

He crossed the camp to Bynn's tent. Inside, he found Arden sitting in the corner, massaging the wolf's back. Her eyes met his, and he froze. He would be asking a lot from her, and he prayed she'd show as much mercy for his men as she had before.

I can't afford to hesitate right now. He shook his head and nudged his friend with his boot. "Bynn, wake up. I can't think with all the noise you're making."

The corners of her mouth rose. "Imagine trying to sleep here."

Kell made a mental note to find another tent for to her sleep in tonight. "Arden, may I have a word with you in private?"

She cocked her head to the side, seeming more curious than anything else. He welcomed it over Bynn's dark frown.

"Kell, don't even think about it."

"It's too late. I have thought about it, and now I'm going to ask her."

Bynn jumped to his feet. "And you think we can trust her?"

"We've run out of options."

"I'm glad to know I'm your last resort," she said dryly. "What did you want to talk to me about?"

She didn't stand when he entered the tent like most women did at court. She didn't move when he told her he wanted to speak to her privately. And she didn't speak to him with the respect any other commoner would have. If she'd been anyone else, he would have made an example of her rude behavior. But she only intrigued him further.

He crouched in front of her. "Arden, answer me truthfully: did you heal Dev with magic?"

Her fingers curled so tightly in the wolf's fur that Cinder nipped at her hand. She yelped and jerked it away. "Why are you asking?"

"Answer me first."

"If this is some kind of trick to gather evidence and bring up more charges against me—"

"No tricks. One of my men is on the verge of death from an infected wound. I was wondering—hoping, actually—you'd be able to help him."

"And you think magic will do that? Even if I could use magic to heal someone—which I'm not saying I can— what makes you think I'd risk breaking the law to help you out again?"

"Because I trust that somewhere deep inside you, you're a good enough person not to let someone die when you can help him. I promise no charges will be brought against you."

The rings in her eyes flashed before she closed them and inhaled a long, slow breath through her teeth. She held her breath until her face turned red then exhaled just as slowly. "I'll take a look at him."

The wariness in her expression said it all. She saw this as a trap. He wished he could convince her otherwise. Instead, he smiled and said, "Thank you."

Cinder stayed so close to her side, she stumbled a few times on the way to Cero's tent. Apparently, the wolf shared her wariness. The protective loyalty the animal bore her spoke of her character and eased some of the doubts swirling in his mind. Everyone else thought he was a fool to ask her to help Ortono, but he would prove them wrong.

Arden wrinkled her nose when they entered the tent. The stench of rotting flesh seemed to have doubled in the few minutes he'd been away.

"Sweet Lady Moon," she said under her breath. "Is this the man?"

Kell nodded. "His name is Ortono."

She inched closer, her face turning slightly green. He prayed she wasn't the puking type. "What have you been treating it with?"

Cero didn't look up from his work. "Everything in my arsenal. Marigold and honey salve. Imported tea tree oil from Thallus. Willow bark tea for the fever. I even tried cauterizing the wound yesterday morning in hopes I would burn the infection out. Nothing's worked."

Holding her hand up to her nose, she knelt between the healer and the patient. "What is your prognosis, healer?"

He finally turned and acknowledged her. "I fear he'll be dead before this evening, witch."

She frowned at the name, but that didn't stop her from pressing her hand against Ortono's flushed face. "Ortono, can you hear me?"

"Don't waste your time. He's so deep in his fever, he hasn't made a lick of sense all night." Cero began tearing strips of linen to form new bandages. "I should have amputated his arm last night."

"No cutting," came the feeble reply. Ortono fixed his fevered gaze on her and clasped her arm. "Please don't let him remove my sword arm."

She chewed her bottom lip. Wetness gathered in the corners of her eyes. "What would you have me do?" she asked him.

"Please help me, goddess."

A bitter laugh burst from her lips. "Now I know he's seeing things." She brushed his sweat damp hair back from his face with the tenderness of a mother tending to a sick child. "Your Highness, you ask a lot of me."

"Only because I know you can do it." Her gentle compassion for Ortono stirred something deep inside him. Someone with an evil heart wouldn't be moved to tears at the sight of a dying man. "He has a family back in Trivinus who need him."

She played with the gold pendant around her neck. The struggle on her face intensified. Her voice quivered. "I have your word?"

"If you can help him, I don't think any man here will bear you ill will."

Bynn silently turned on his heel and stormed out of the tent.

She watched him leave and withdrew her hands from the patient. "Why are you testing me this way? You're only going to make things worse for the two of us." She tried to rise, but Kell caught her and held her next to Ortono.

"Arden, for some reason beyond any of our understanding, you've been blessed with an incredible gift. Not me—you. I'd give anything to be able to heal one of my men. Don't tell me you would selfishly choose to keep this gift all to yourself."

She pressed her lips together in a thin line. "Dev's not going to like this." She touched the skin along the wound. "Ortono, will you let me heal you?"

Kell sensed a change in the atmosphere. The air became charged like a storm was brewing. He could almost taste the thick veil of magic that surrounded them, ready and waiting for her to gather and use.

The glazed sheen in Ortono's eyes vanished. "Yes, I trust you."

She nodded. "He's given his permission. Will anyone stop me?" The tone of her voice issued a challenge to those in the tent.

Kell looked at Cero. The healer's mouth hung open, but he backed away with his head lowered. "I've done all I can. I turn my patient over to you."

He scanned the rest of room. Cero's two assistants stood on edge, not sure if they should drag her away from the patient or follow their master's lead. One nodded, then the other.

She now waited on him. "You have my word," Kell said as he released her.

"Please don't interrupt me. I need to concentrate." Her eyes glowed with an intensity that made the hairs on the back of Kell's neck stand up. All the powers she'd held in check flamed to life within her. The air practically crackled with magic now. She closed her eyes and pressed her fingers into the flesh around the wound.

He expected Ortono to cry out in pain, but a sigh of relief came from him instead. The ominous atmosphere vanished, replaced by warmth that rivaled the sunniest of days. Unlike the time she healed Dev, she made no effort to conceal the spell she cast.

Cero's strangled cry jerked his attention from Arden. The healer pointed a shaking finger at the wound. If Kell wanted proof that she could heal with magic, he had it.

The discolored skin grew pink, erasing all signs of the gangrenous flesh that rotted away at Ortono's arm. A river of pus erupted from the gash. Once it flowed away, the wound cleaned itself from the blood and debris, leaving only healthy tissue behind. It knitted together as easily as darned socks. A shiny white ridge of skin covered the opening, sealing it up in a neat scar that the soldier would carry the rest of his life.

"What are you doing to my soldier, witch?" a voice bellowed behind them. Larenis tore through the tent and knocked her to the ground with the back of his hand.

Kell reached for his sword at the same time Larenis grabbed his own. The sound of steel against steel rang in the air when he blocked the captain's blade. A low growl filled the silence that followed as Cinder flashed his fangs at the men gathering outside.

Arden stared at the ceiling with a blank expression on her face. He couldn't tell if she was stunned, scared, or still under the influence of the spell. An angry red welt formed on her cheek.

Kell's rage threatened to choke him. "How dare you strike her?"

"She was bewitching one of my men," Larenis replied through gritted teeth. A vein on his forehead throbbed, and he leaned his weight forward.

"And how did you know she was here?" Out of the

corner of his eye, he saw Bynn hover at the entrance and look away from the scene. An admission of guilt, if he ever saw one.

"Stop this immediately," a new voice ordered. Ortono reached between them and shoved them aside with a strength that surprised everyone in the tent.

Larenis dropped his weapon. His eyes widened like he had seen a ghost. "What kind of spell is this?"

"One I accepted." The young soldier stood between Arden and the other men. "She healed me, and I owe her my life. If any man harms her, he'll feel the edge of my blade."

The captain of the guard backed away, his face sheet-white.

Dev burst into the tent. "What happened?" He didn't have to raise his voice to send shivers down Kell's spine. The low, even tone spoke volumes.

"She was an angel of the goddess and healed me," Ortono replied.

Dev narrowed his eyes, focusing his glare on Kell. "Why?"

"Because I knew she could save his life."

The knight's fingers twitched, and his gaze flickered to the swords in the men's hands. "I'll deal with you later." With a swift grace that humans could only dream of having, he picked up Arden and carried her out of the tent.

Ortono jumped to his feet and followed them. Any signs of his illness lingered only in the memory of those who had seen him on the verge of death. The newly healed soldier looked like he could take on any member of the Royal Guard and win.

Kell's pulse pounded in his ears from the mixture of fear and anger that flowed through his veins. He tightened his grip on his sword's hilt. "Larenis, I have half a mind to place you under arrest for drawing a weapon against me."

Two bright spots of color appeared on his weathered cheeks. "You would be within your bounds to do so, Your Highness."

He crossed the tent in three long strides to address the men standing outside. "For those of you wondering what happened, I asked Arden to help one of your comrades. Ortono's wound became infected to the point that he probably wouldn't live to see Trivinus again. Any of you who are battle-hardened know what it's like to watch one of your fellow soldiers die from a gangrenous wound."

A few heads nodded in the crowd.

"Although she had no obligation to help him, she offered to heal him. Ortono gave her permission to use magic on him, and he's alive and well now because of it. If any of you feel she deserves death for her actions, speak now."

Silence answered him.

"Then let it be known that I second Ortono's threat. If any one of you so much as lays a finger on her, I'll make the undead seem merciful." He turned and went straight for Bynn. "I thought I could trust you."

His friend stubbornly looked him in the eyes. "I acted as I saw fit."

"So you questioned my judgment and told Larenis what she was doing?"

Bynn opened his mouth to speak, but no words came out.

"We are treading upon a fragile ledge here," Kell said. "One false move, and we could all die for it. And you and Larenis just started the equivalent of an avalanche. When she comes to her senses, let's hope she's in a more forgiving mood than her protector, or we'll all know a witch's wrath."

He sheathed his sword and proceeded directly to his tent. His rage waned with each step, leaving just his fear in its wake. He'd sensed her power in the tent, and the intensity of it terrified him. Now more than ever, he needed Arden as an ally, not an enemy.

But something else bothered him—his growing admiration for her. It took someone with real courage to risk her life to save another. She'd done it twice now, not because she wanted to gain his princely favor, but because it was the right thing to do.

And that left an odd ache in his chest.

Chapter 21

Dev couldn't decide if the new, self-proclaimed guardian of the Soulbearer was more of a nuisance or an overly eager helper. Either way, he didn't like the way the young human fawned over Trouble. He glared at the ring on the soldier's finger. "Don't you have a wife?"

The human had the decency to blush. "Yes."

"And what would she think if she saw you looking at Trouble that way?"

The color deepened until his ears practically glowed. "She'd probably smack me."

He grunted in agreement and bent over Trouble. Her blue eyes stared blankly ahead. A curse broke free under his breath. Either Loku had finally pushed her over the edge of sanity, or she was still wrapped up in her casting. And he didn't want an audience watching when he tried to determine which one it was. "Go get me a cloth and some water."

The soldier jumped to his feet, running to fetch the items.

One problem taken care of. Now for the next one. He pressed his palms on either side of her face. "Trouble, can you hear me?"

The rings in her eyes intensified until the green overwhelmed every hint of blue. "Worried, Dev?" Loku's voice said from her mouth.

Although the rest of his body jerked in response to hearing the chaos god speak, his hands remained fastened to her face. "Let her go, Loku."

Her lips curled up in a sly grin. "That's where you

have it all wrong. I'm trying to bring her back, just like you."

"Where is she?"

"Here, but a bit stunned from having her spell interrupted. You know how disorienting that can be."

"Enough with the games." He focused his magic toward her mind, searching for a way to snap her out of her trance. He sensed another magic within her, dark and green and filled with random disorder. They both searched for cracks in her shield, poking at them when they spotted one.

He closed his eyes, applied more force on a particularly large crack. *Arden, wake up*, he silently ordered. His heart skipped a beat. He hated to admit how much he worried about her. It made him think irrationally. He almost slaughtered the prince for doing this to her. But once he brought her back to reality, he would settle the score with Kell.

The shield shattered, and she bolted from the ground. He didn't move fast enough to avoid the collision of their heads. The impact sent a jolt of pain from his forehead all the way down his neck.

She moaned and covered her temple. "I knew you had a hard head, but I never realized how hard."

He mirrored her posture. "I could say the same for you."

The soldier returned with a water skin and a damp cloth. When he saw Trouble sitting up, a huge grin split his face. "You're awake," the man said, offering her the cloth.

Much to her credit, she smiled back at him and pressed the material to her forehead. "Ortono, right?"

"Yes, m'lady."

Dev raised a brow at her new title. *If he only knew how little of a lady she really was.*

"Is your arm better?"

He opened the slit in his shirt and proudly displayed the neat scar snaking along his bicep. "Better than it's ever been, thanks to you."

"Will one of you please explain what happened?" Dev sat back on his heels so the smell of gangrenous flesh that clung to the soldier's clothes wouldn't overwhelm him.

"Prince Kell asked me to heal Ortono."

"And why did you agree to do a foolish thing like that?"

Ortono looked pissed off enough to punch him, but one touch from Trouble calmed him. She moved the cloth to the handprint on her cheek. "Because it was the right thing to do."

"You and your overpowering sense of morality," he muttered under his breath. "One day, it's going to cost us our heads."

"And you call yourself a knight." Ortono almost spat the words.

Dev could barely resist the laughter welling up inside him from the young soldier's disgust. "Once again, I think you Ranellians have a different code of behavior when it comes to knighthood." He reached out and ruffled Cinder's fur. "Then what happened?"

"Captain Larenis struck her, but Prince Kell stopped him from killing her."

Now that was an odd twist in events he didn't expect. Maybe he should thank the prince for protecting her. After he roughed him up a bit for placing her in that situation to start with, though. "So the prince was the good guy here?"

Ortono nodded. "Everyone else wanted to cut my arm off, but he wouldn't let them. Then he brought this angel of the goddess to my aid."

The cow-eyed admiration with which he looked at Trouble broke all restraints. Dev laughed long and loud enough to earn an ill-tempered swat from her. "Trouble? An angel of the goddess? That's the funniest thing I've heard in over a century."

"Just because you consider me the bane of your existence doesn't mean everyone else shares your opinion." She tried to stand but swayed as soon as she got to her feet.

Both he and Ortono reached out to steady her. "I think I have her under control," Dev told the solider. "Don't you have to report back to duty?"

"From now on, I'm not letting her out of my sight."

Trouble's cheeks turned a tempting shade of pink, and he wanted to wrap his arms around her and claim her as his. "Um, that's really not necessary. Dev's my sworn protector and—"

"He can't be everywhere at once."

"True, but—"

Ortono shook his head. "I feel obligated to repay you."

She bit her bottom lip and turned to Dev for assistance.

He pulled her closer to him, her skin still too clammy for his liking. "I have her for now. You can help by keeping your eyes and ears open. If you so much as hear a whisper of someone wanting to hurt her, let me know."

She nodded. "If you can help us get safely to Trivinus, that will be thanks enough."

"Are you sure? What about tonight?"

"We'll deal with tonight when it comes."

Ortono nodded. "Of course, Sir Devarius."

As soon as he turned to leave, Trouble rested her head against Dev's chest and sighed. "Don't say it. I already know what kind of a mess I've gotten us into with this one."

He loosened the tie at the end of her braid, combing his fingers through it. The faint scent of roses filled his nose. If he could just hold her and ignore the rest of the world, life would be near perfect. "You've earned his respect and admiration. That's nothing to apologize for."

"So I was just imagining the annoyance in your expression?"

"You never cease to amaze and frustrate me."

She lifted her face. "Is that meant to be a compliment?"

His lungs stopped moving as he stared at her. The back of his mind screamed at him to stay in control, but his body savored the way her curves hugged his body. The contact between them stirred something inside of him. She was like a siren calling to the very depths of his soul. If he gave into temptation, would he regret it?

He closed his eyes and took a steadying breath. There would be time to think about such matters once they were safe in Gravaria. Until then, he couldn't let his guard down for any reason, even if it meant pushing her away. "If you consider the fact that you've caused me more headaches than your previous two predecessors combined, then yes, you can consider it a compliment."

Her eyes narrowed, and she shoved him away. The magic of the moment passed, much to his relief.

***

Dev leaned against the wall of the inn and watched Ortono run back and forth across the great room. Despite her reassurances she didn't need anything, the young soldier insisted on fetching Trouble's meal and a blanket to drive off the night's chill. Dev bit back a grin. As soon as she sat down, she curled up in a ball and fell asleep.

"Lady Arden, I brought you…" Ortono's voice trailed off when her eyes didn't open. "Is she lost in another trance again?"

"No, this is just the usual exhaustion that comes from using magic."

"But she needs to eat."

"You're welcome to try and wake her, but I doubt she'll be in a pleasant mood."

His head sagged, showing the subtle signs of the soldier's own weariness. "What am I going to do with her meal?"

Dev took the bowl. "I'll eat it."

"Where do you want me to stand guard?"

He gritted his teeth. Ortono took his vow to protect her a bit too seriously. And as well-meaning as the human was, Dev couldn't afford to have him nearby if he wanted his plan to work tonight. "Perhaps you should mingle with your comrades and make sure they aren't plotting anything against her. We're indoors tonight, so I won't have to worry about something sneaking out from the trees."

"Good idea." He joined several other soldiers at a table. They regarded him with a bit of suspicion at first but then welcomed him into their conversation, playfully ribbing him a few times.

Dev reached into his pocket, pulling out a small piece of chalk. Time to show Kell he can't keep Trouble hidden from him every night. After he drew a circle on the floor, he recited a spell in a murmured rush of words. The circle flashed in response. *Let's see Kell's sword try to get through this.*

Full and sleepy after eating the stew, he was preparing his own bed when Kell dragged a chair over to his corner. A curse flew from Dev's lips, and the prince balked for a second.

"I take it you don't want to deal with me at the moment?" Kell's dark eyes danced in amusement, much to Dev's annoyance. He would have to do a better job of intimidating him in the future.

He wrapped his cloak around him, covering the front of his body. "I'm not sure I even want to look at you. It might upset me."

"I'll take my chances." Kell flipped the chair around and straddled it. "How's Arden?"

"Sleeping, and you're not going to wake her."

"But I have a nice room set aside for her."

"Not a chance, prince-boy. She's staying with me tonight. The last thing I want is for you to test her magic again so someone else can smack her around."

Kell looked away, but not before Dev caught a glimpse of some of the shame that hung on his features. "If I'd known that was going to happen, I would've taken more precautions."

"Well, it did happen, and she's sporting a nice bruise on her cheek to show for it."

Kell's whole body winced. "I'll have Larenis standing guard duty for a month for that."

"That still doesn't change the fact that you used her. From now on, she isn't leaving my side. I have an idea what your plans are for her, and I don't like them." He glanced down at the circle, wondering if it would crumple like his shields if the prince drew his sword. "If you want her, you're going to have to take her from me."

"You're challenging me?" His fingers curled into fists, and his jaw hardened.

"Call it what you want, but I have my duty, and no one—not even a self-absorbed Third Princeling—is going to get in my way."

Kell jumped out of his chair and lunged at him, only to have a spark of lightning send him sprawling across the floor when he reached the circle's barrier. The nearby soldiers rose and drew their weapons. He lifted his head, wiping the blood away from his mouth. "You think you're pretty clever hiding behind magic, don't you?"

"You're the one who attacked. If you could control your temper, you wouldn't have a busted lip right now."

"Your Highness, are you all right?" a soldier asked

"Fine, just fine." Anger burned in the prince's face. "I fell out of my chair."

"Are you finished, Your Highness?" Dev grinned and reached up his sleeves under the cover of his cloak. His fingers caressed the daggers hidden there.

Kell righted his chair and sat in it. "No, I was just getting started. I want to know more about Arden."

"I've already told you more than enough." He withdrew his hands from his sleeves and relaxed.

"What happened to her after she healed Ortono? I was worried."

"You have an odd way of showing your concern, considering you waited until now to inquire about her health."

"I saw you had things under control."

Dev snorted. In truth, he was glad Kell didn't witness his brief conversation with Loku. If he had, they'd be roasting now. "If someone interrupts a caster in the middle of a spell, it continues to draw energy from that person, even if the spell is complete."

"Is that why she didn't move after Larenis interfered?"

"Yes. It's also why she's sleeping like the dead, so I hope this settles your curiosity for now. Good night." He tried to lie down, but Kell didn't get the hint.

"Will she be like this every time she casts a spell?"

The damn prince almost treaded upon his last nerve. He took a deep breath and counted to ten before he answered, "Why the sudden interest in her magic?"

"I'm worried I asked too much of her this morning."

The concern in Kell's voice seemed too genuine to keep Dev's rage burning. "I'll try to make this as simple as I can so your Ranellian mind can understand it. Think of magic as a well you can draw on. Some mages have deeper wells than others, meaning they can cast more powerful spells."

"And Arden's well is shallow?"

Dev chuckled. "On the contrary, she has one of the deepest wells I've come across in years. If she'd been born in Gravaria, she would've started training at a young age and would probably be a member of the Mage's Council by now."

"Then why does she have trouble keeping her eyes open after she casts?"

"Because she's still learning to efficiently draw magic from her well. Remember when you first learned how to wield a sword. A few minutes of combat probably left you sore and winded. But as you practiced and increased your stamina, you were able to fight longer and harder. Using magic is similar to that."

"Do you think she'll be able to repeat the ice storm again if Sulaino attacked?"

Dev's shoulders tensed. *So that's what he wants to know, huh?* "The ice storm was a dangerous spell for her to cast."

"Why? Because it would dry up her well?"

"None of your business. I've already told you more

than you need to know."

Kell rubbed his chin. "Do you really think she won't be able to take on Sulaino, despite how powerful she is?"

"She's not the weapon you want her to be, and I won't let her take the risk."

He jerked his head up. "Just because you're her Protector doesn't mean you can control her decisions. She seemed perfectly capable of making up her own mind this morning."

"I'm charged with keeping her safe and bringing her back to Gravaria. I'm sorry if this interferes with your plan to bed her and then use her to fight your battles for you."

"You overstep your bounds, knight." His face twisted into a snarl, and he almost lunged for Dev again. "And you assume too much."

"No, I know exactly what you want from her. Don't think I missed the little exchange you two had the other night. She's naïve enough to be led astray, but I'll be watching you. And now that I have Ortono as backup, I don't think you'll be getting her alone any time soon."

"And I think you underestimate your ward." A cocky smile smoothed over any traces of the prince's anger.

Dev's fingers reached for his dagger. As much as he wanted to lodge it in the middle of Kell's throat, a soft sigh stopped him. They both watched as Trouble rolled over on her back and smiled in her sleep. He swallowed his rage, removing his hand from his sleeve once again.

"This is the last time I'll warn you, Your Highness. Stay away from her. You have no idea what you're messing with."

"Worried I might steal her from you, Dev?" The swagger returned to his step as he crossed the room and climbed the stairs.

Dev rolled over and watched her dream. Worried was putting it lightly. Terrified would be more accurate. And if he didn't lose her to Kell, Loku could always claim her if he wasn't careful.

"What am I going to do with you, Trouble?"

Chapter 22

Arden awoke to an arm tightening around her waist. This was the second morning in a row that she'd found herself wedged in between Dev and Cinder, but she didn't complain. Their warmth drove off the damp chill of the river fog that swirled around them. She snuggled closer to Dev.

"Cold?" His sleepy voice startled her, but his arm kept her from rising.

"A little."

"Here." When he wrapped his cloak around her shoulders, his hands left a trail of heat along her arms. "Better?"

She nodded and continued to enjoy lying next to him. A slow-burning fire crept along her limbs, relaxing her muscles in its wake.

Other noises filtered through the fog. As much as she wanted to stay nestled in his arms, she knew they'd have to get up and ride until sunset again. Ever since she'd healed Ortono, Kell seemed more anxious than ever to return home. This translated to long hours in a saddle, pushing their horses to exhaustion. The supply wagon that followed them usually arrived two hours after they'd chosen a camp site, and the men pitched tents by torchlight.

She sat up. Even in the murky morning light, she could see the frown that tugged at Dev's mouth. "The sooner we get up and moving, the sooner we work the chill from our bones."

"You're unusually cheerful this morning, Trouble."

"That's because you woke up in the arms of a warm, virile man," Loku replied.

Her cheeks flamed from his accusation, but she didn't deny it. "Perhaps because I'm sleeping better."

"You'd sleep even better if you let him fuck you to exhaustion."

"Shut up, Loku. You know that's never going to happen with Dev."

"True. He's too reserved, too bound to his duty. Kell, on the other hand..." His voice trailed off into a snicker, and she knew why.

Kell had been so focused on getting them to Trivinus that he'd avoided her. At least, she hoped that was the reason why she hadn't seen him in the last two days. It was silly of her to hope he might actually be interested in her as something other than a bedmate. The pessimist in her listed dozens of other reasons without Loku's help. Maybe her magic frightened him into regretting his decision to help them escape the pyre.

"I suspect his avoidance has more to do with your lips than your magic, my Soulbearer."

"I wonder if he knew I'd never been kissed before."

"Most likely, but he didn't seem to mind."

"Then why won't he even look at me?"

"Ask Dev." More of the chaos god's deep laughter echoed through her mind.

She paused from rolling up her blankets and studied him. Could his new attentiveness have discouraged the prince's attentions? And in truth, was it a blessing? She couldn't seem to think clearly when she was around Kell.

"So young, so naïve. I'm enjoying having you as my Soulbearer, Arden."

"What is Loku telling you now?" Dev continued packing his things as if there was nothing unusual about her having a conversation with someone in her head.

"How do you know he's telling me anything at all?"

"The rings in your eyes flash, and you get this distant look on your face."

All the blood drained from her head. "Is it really that obvious?"

"Only to me." He looked up and gave her a weak smile. "Remember, I've been watching Soulbearers for over a century."

"Good morning, Lady Arden," a cheerful voice greeted through the fog.

She resisted the urge to roll her eyes. Although she knew she'd done the right thing in healing him, she could do without his constant fawning. "Ortono, be careful. I don't think Dev's lowered the circle yet."

His nervous laughter reached her before his face appeared. "Right. Definitely don't want a repeat of yesterday morning."

A muffled snort came from beside her.

"Dev, if you'll lower the circle, I'll tend to the horses."

"Not alone."

"I'll take Ortono."

He raised a brow. "That reassures me," he said sarcastically. "Just make sure you don't fall into the river. I have no desire to spend the rest of the day wearing wet clothes if I have to fish you out." He waved his hand, and the hum of magical energy that had surrounded them all night dissipated.

Arden grabbed the horses' reins. "Come on, Ortono."

She moved through the trees, listening carefully for the rush of water over the rocks. Ortono's muffled steps followed her, but he said nothing. Perhaps he'd run out of things to talk to her about. So far, she'd heard about his youth, how he met his wife, and every single detail about his three sons. His love for his family was like a knife that twisted in her heart. Her father didn't want anything to do with her. The cold gold of her pendant stung her skin as she reflected on his abandonment. Ortono would never do that to his family.

Dev's horse whinnied. She slowed down, feeling her way to the river's edge with her feet. The soft earth changed into a bed of pebbles. She traced a small drop-off with the toes of her boot, splashing the water around it. She dropped the reins and knelt on the bank. While the horse drank their fill, she washed her face in the icy water.

When she heard the sound of someone approaching, she assumed it was Ortono. Instead, another voice drawled out, "Good morning, Arden."

She froze. How did Kell sneak up on her like that? "Good morning, Your Highness."

"Dismal weather this morning. I hope it clears up so you'll have a nice view of Trivinus."

A frog hopped around in her stomach when she heard his news. "We should see Trivinus today?"

"More than see. We should be inside the palace well before dinner."

The ground seemed to slip out from under her feet. If Kell hadn't caught her arm, she might have fallen into the river. Her heart raced.

"Are you still exhausted from healing Ortono?"

"No." *More like wondering when I'll be burned alive.*

"You really think he'll let you burn? I mean, besides in lust for him?"

"Your hands are trembling." He pulled her closer to him.

"The cold, Your Highness." She buried her hands in the thick wool of his cloak. The ripple of his chest muscles made her mind wander in a very different direction.

"You may call me Kell when we're alone." His husky voice sent a delicious shiver through her body.

"We're not alone. Ortono—"

"I sent him back to the camp to help pack. He seems to think you're safe with me."

"And am I?"

"What do you think?" He closed the space between them until his breath tickled her forehead.

"I think it depends on your definition of safe." She pulled away.

"Do I frighten you?"

She laughed to cover up her unease. Her growing

attraction toward him frightened her, even if it was only physical. But she couldn't let him know that. "You're the one who's been avoiding me. If I didn't know better, I'd say you were afraid of me."

"I won't deny that your magical abilities humbled me a bit."

"You? Humble?"

"It's the truth. I needed a few days to regain my confidence to approach you again."

Part of her wanted to call him a liar, but a tiny fluttering in her chest hoped that he told the truth. "Am I that intimidating?"

"In a way." His hand stroked her hair. "You're beautiful, you're powerful, and you've been occupying my thoughts far more than I care to admit."

She closed her eyes and savored his compliments. So this was what it felt like to have the most desirable man in the kingdom want you. After being stared at and called a freak her entire life, it was strange knowing Kell of all people saw her as something special, someone worth thinking about. "I'm sure you say that to all the girls."

"What do I have to do to convince you otherwise?"

"There's no shame in giving in to him, you know," Loku whispered. *"You might actually enjoy it."*

She leaned her body against his. The hunger in his eyes roused her curiosity. Dev never looked at her this way. Dev tolerated her because he had to. Kell actually seemed to want to spend time with her. But why? She'd made it very clear she wasn't as easy as the women he normally pursued. Most men would've given up by now if they were only looking for a quick fling.

With some hesitation, he brushed his lips against her. Energy crackled where their skin touched, sending shockwaves down into the pit of her stomach. When she tried to pull back, Kell threaded his fingers through her hair and crushed her lips against his. His mouth pleaded with hers to take the kiss deeper. She parted her lips. His tongue coiled around hers like a dancer, moving in time to the rhythm of their pounding hearts. She wrapped her arms around his neck, scared her legs may falter if this continued.

A soft moan rose in the back of her throat. *Sweet Lady Moon, the man could kiss.*

She would have been happy to spend hours locked in his dizzying kiss, but Dev's voice echoed through the fog.

They pulled away from each other like two children who'd been caught with their fingers in a pie. As much as she had enjoyed the kiss, guilt nagged at the edges of her mind.

"Trouble, where are you?"

She silently cursed. What would Dev say if he knew she'd been kissing the prince?

Kell leaned forward and whispered, "Later," before his lips brushed her cheek. Then he disappeared into the fog, leaving her alone and breathless.

"Trouble." Dev sounded like a bear growling the second time he called her name.

"Over here." She grabbed the reins and led the horses in the direction of his voice.

He grabbed her elbow as soon as he saw her. "Where were you, and why were you alone?"

She sent a silent prayer of thanks to the Lady Moon he didn't stumble across Kell in his foul temper. "I was down by the river, letting the horses drink." *And making a wanton slut of myself with Kell.*

His eyes filled with suspicion, and she wondered once again if he could read her mind. "Why are you out of breath?"

"I stumbled and almost fell."

"Not far from the truth, but you should add that you fell into Kell's arms."

"There are some things I don't think Dev should know about. This is one of them."

Loku squeaked in delight. *"Already deceiving your protector? You're learning quicker than most of your predecessors. Let's start thinking of other ways we can torment him, shall we?"*

Loku's words chased away the heat from her interlude with Kell and left an icy chill in its place. *"If you think this will get you closer to taking control of my mind, think again. I'm not going to let you drive me insane."*

Dev inspected every inch of her, looking for injuries. "At least you're not wet or covered in mud."

"No, I caught myself in time."

He focused on her face, and his mouth formed a tight line. She licked her lips, noting how swollen they felt. *Damn, he knows.*

"You should be more careful, especially in weather like this. Someone could sneak up on you and catch you off guard." He stomped off into the fog.

"I can always raise a shield," she said as she followed him.

"Obviously not quick enough."

"Why are you so ticked off this morning?"

He spun around on his heel so quickly, she collided with him. His hands gripped her shoulders. "The sooner we get to Trivinus, the sooner I can get you out of Ranello and away from those who would use you for their own selfish purposes. Until then, I would appreciate your cooperation."

His words struck her like a slap in the face. Did he really think she was stupid enough to let Kell use her? She wriggled free from him. "Well, you'll have your wish. According to Kell, we should arrive at the palace in time for dinner. I hope you have a solid plan in place, because I'm not sure we'll be leaving."

She shoved past him and barely glanced at Ortono when he fell into step beside her at the edge of camp.

A Soul For Trouble

Chapter 23

Arden stared straight ahead at the road, noticing how it widened over the day. Every time enough room to accommodate another rider appeared on either side, her heart thudded to a stop.

Ortono cast a worried glance in her direction. "Is something troubling you, m'lady?"

She fiddled with the reins instead of reaching for her necklace. She didn't need to be reminded that she was conceived in Trivinus. "I was wondering what the city was like."

"You've never been there?" He asked the question like she was some kind of backward hick.

"Wallus was too far away to make casual trips there."

Her sarcasm erased the dumbfounded look on his face. "Then you're in for a treat. Trivinus is the most beautiful city in Ranello."

"It better be if the king chooses to live there," Dev muttered under his breath.

The young soldier began to list all the wonders of the city, from the palace on top of the hill to the artists who lined the perimeter of the city green. Although she could sense his awe of the city, she didn't share it. It sounded too big and complicated for her liking. Who would've thought she'd miss tiny, insignificant Wallus?

"Look ahead, Lady Arden. You can see the palace on the horizon."

Ortono's word chilled her, but she forced her eyes up. The morning sun had burned away the fog enough to reveal a stone garrison large enough to hold all of Wallus.

181

Her breath caught. Her cold fingers wrapped around the reins and squeezed them.

"Relax, Trouble," Dev said.

The lump in her throat made talking difficult. "But we're almost there, and…"

"When are you going to learn to trust me?"

She pulled her attention away from the city looming ahead and focused on the deep green of his eyes. Her terror lessened enough for her to say, "I'm scared."

"I know you are, but try not to worry so much. I have a few tricks up my sleeve."

She leaned over and reached under his tunic sleeve until it touched the metal hilt of a dagger. By a few tricks, she hoped he meant more than his small arsenal of concealed weapons.

One corner of his mouth quirked up before he guided her hand down. "One day, I'll have to teach you how to play lansquenet. The first rule you need to learn is never let your opponents know what cards you hold in your hand. The next rule is never let them know what you have up your sleeve."

"You talk like a professional gambler."

"At one time, he was."

The little tidbit of information Loku let slip matched the grimace on Dev's face. He widened the gap between them so she couldn't touch him anymore. "If you've lived as long as I have, you would've picked up a few things."

"What happened?"

The grimace morphed into a scowl. "None of your business."

"Fine. I'll just ask Loku."

Dev directed his glare to the rider on her other side. "Ortono, make yourself scarce for a few minutes."

The soldier blanched, but nodded and rode ahead.

"Listen to me." His voice practically seethed with anger. "If you want to get out of this alive, the less people who know about the conversations in your head with a god they don't acknowledge, the better your chances. For all you know, they probably think you're possessed by some demon."

She nodded, unsure what to say. Whenever he spoke to her this way, she always wished he would shout instead. He seemed more dangerous when he tried to control his rage.

"As for my past, you have no right to inquire about it. I'm sure you've done things you don't want me to know about, but you don't hear me asking about them. I would appreciate the same respect from you."

"So you were a gambler."

"I've made a few bets in my day," he tightly replied. His body tensed as if he were bracing for her next question.

She studied him for almost a whole minute before deciding it was better to drop the subject for now. "Thank you for answering my question. Perhaps we can revisit this subject in a few weeks."

"Or not."

She sighed. "You ask me to trust you, but you insist on keeping secrets from me."

"I'm not the only one with secrets."

"Meaning?" Sweat prickled at the base of her neck.

"I know you weren't alone at the river this morning, Trouble. If you think seducing the prince will work in your favor, think again. It's his father who holds our lives in his hands, not Kell."

"I wasn't trying to seduce him." She fought hard to keep her voice quiet when she wanted to yell and scream in frustration.

"Consider this a piece of friendly advice: don't fall for his tricks."

Arden pulled her hood lower to cover her burning cheeks. Embarrassment over being caught stung her pride. Then Dev's accusation that Kell was only toying with her bruised it. *My life would be much less complicated without men in it.*

"Ah, but it would also be very boring. Admit it—don't

you feel a little tingle of joy knowing you have two men fighting over you?"

"Fighting? Over me? Are you sure you're not the one going insane, Loku?"

"You haven't heard them exchange words over you while you were sleeping."

"And you have?"

"My dear little Soulbearer, just because I'm confined to your body doesn't mean I'm confined to your experiences. I'm a god, after all. All-knowing and all-powerful."

"Except I'm your jailer."

"A minor inconvenience. But I see and hear things you don't, and I don't need sleep."

"And you expect me to believe that Dev and Kell fought over me?"

"You underestimate your appeal to them."

"They certainly have odd ways of showing it."

"Kell's rather transparent, or did you miss the way his pants strained to contain his cock this morning?"

No, she didn't miss it. Her skin flushed when she remembered the way he'd pulled closer to her. She sucked in a deep breath. Her gaze wandered to Dev. Would he react the same way if she kissed him?

"There's only one way to find out."

"He'd probably pin me to the ground if I tried it. Besides, I have some idea where I stand with Kell. He desires me, but he'll probably lose interest once he beds me. Dev, on the other hand, has made no effort to show anything other than annoyance for me."

"Dev cares for you more than he lets on, and in your heart, you feel the same way. Perhaps you should practice your kissing with him instead."

She almost snorted at the ridiculousness of his suggestion. Yes, she found Dev attractive—she always had. And the few times he'd shown her kindness, her heart warmed to the point where she could feel like she could trust him completely. But affection? Love? She doubted

Dev knew the meaning of those words.

Of course, she doubted Kell knew the meaning of them either. He reminded her of a wildfire on a gusty day. What started off as a single spark would consume her within seconds if she let him take advantage of her. After spending most of her life intent on avoiding the same mistakes her mother made, she came dangerously close to falling into that trap this morning. She knew what she felt for him: pure lust.

Dev, on the other hand, conjured up images of steel and granite in her mind. Cold, strong, dependable. He took a long time to warm up, but when he did, he soothed and steadied her. Kell's fire could destroy her, but Dev would still be there when the flames were extinguished. And that made her want to cling to him all the more.

"Yes, love and lust are two very complicated emotions, my Soulbearer."

"I just wish I knew how to handle them."

"Time and experience are all you need."

"I'm sorry I lost my temper with you, Trouble."

Dev's quiet apology jerked her from her thoughts. "No, I shouldn't have pried into your past. After all, you probably have a colorful one, considering you're over three hundred years old."

He shrugged. "That has nothing to do with what we're facing now. I do have something planned, but I wish to keep it quiet for now. The less people know about my plan, the less likely they are to interfere."

"But you'll tell me, right?"

His eyes flickered over her, and a grin played on his lips. "If I need to. Part of me wants to retain some of your innocence."

"It's that bad?"

"It's political, and if you haven't learned by now, nothing soils your hands like politics."

She stared ahead at Kell, Bynn, and the captain of the guard, Larenis. Ever since she'd healed Ortono, the tension among them intensified. Lord Bynn regarded her with

185

increased suspicion, but at least he didn't look like he wanted to slit her throat like the captain did.

"Do you think we'll be on the road to Boznac tomorrow?"

"If I can have a private audience with King Heodis tonight, possibly."

"That confident?"

His grin widened. "Yes."

His cockiness roused her curiosity. He could be very handsome when he smiled. Too bad he spent most of his time in a pissy mood.

They rode in silence until they reached the outer walls of Trivinus. Her fingers tightened around the reins, and her stomach tied in knots.

Dev leaned over and rested his hand on her thigh. "Relax, Trouble. Everything will work out in the end."

A wave of calm washed over her. Was it magic, or simply Dev's presence?

The city of Trivinus surged forward from the palace walls and down the gently sloping hillside. Ortono told her that behind the palace, the hill dropped off into a sheer cliff that ended at the river. A series of horseshoe-shaped walls divided the twisting streets, telling the history of the city's expansion.

The entire party filed through each narrow gate and continued riding up the hill. The closer they got to the palace, the grander the buildings became.

Arden followed Dev's example and kept her hood pulled low over her face. If the ring of soldiers around them didn't draw attention, her golden hair certainly would. When they passed the third gate, her skin crawled. The smell of rotting meat nearly knocked her off her horse. "Dev—"

"I feel it, too."

He didn't need to say more. "But you said they only come out at night."

"No, I said they were stronger at night."

They both searched their surroundings for a half-rotted

walking corpse, but the streets provided too many hiding places. "Should we alert Kell?"

"And tell him what? That we sense undead? That won't help our case."

"But…" She paused as the stench vanished. "It's gone."

"I know." He twisted in his saddle to look behind him. "Either we moved past it or it went deeper into hiding."

"Whatever the case, I don't like the idea of having one so nearby."

"All the more reason to get out of here while we can."

"And leave the problem for Kell to handle alone? Dev, what if—"

"Quiet." He pointed at the guards listening around them. "One problem at a time."

Her stomach churned at the idea of leaving the Ranellians at the mercy of Sulaino and his army of undead. It couldn't be a fair fight. Even if they told every soldier how to destroy undead, battling magic without magic would lead to a massacre.

"Don't feel guilt over something you can't control."

"I can make a difference."

"But at what cost?"

In order to defeat Sulaino, she'd need Loku's help. The cost? Her sanity.

"I doubt letting me take out a necromancer will turn you into Robb."

"I'm sure you say that to all the Soulbearers."

"But in this case, I mean it. I have no desire to be captured by that creature. I'd much rather stay cozy with you and enjoy the power of having a set of tits."

She hunched over and resisted the urge to cover her chest.

"There's no reason to be ashamed of them, although I must say, they are a bit on the smaller side."

"Shut up, Loku. Here I am, worried about a half-crazed necromancer, and you want to talk about my lack of cleavage."

"Fine. Be serious and gloomy if you want. Dev's becoming a bad influence on you."

The conversation ended just as the party reached the palace. This time, they waited while the heavy iron gates rose just high enough to allow them to enter. Her heart beat double-time with each clank of the gears. What waited for her on the other side? A dank dungeon filled with rats until they gathered enough wood for a pyre?

They rode into the courtyard and dismounted with everyone else. A man in a deep red tunic ran out of the two-story doorway and pulled Kell into a hug. The strong resemblance between the two men marked them as family. "Who's that?" she asked Ortono.

"Prince Therrin, the Second Prince."

"Nice guy?"

"From what I've been told, yes."

A third man joined the two princes. He, too, had the same straight nose and wide jaw, but his face was leaner and he wore his hair so short, it almost looked shaven. He stood back with his hands clasped behind him and began speaking to Kell.

"Another prince?"

Ortono nodded. "Prince Gandor, the First Prince and heir to the throne."

"He doesn't look too friendly."

"More like he has something stuck up his ass," Loku added.

"I wouldn't want to cross him, if that's what you mean."

Kell waved them forward. Her breath came in hesitant shudders when she met the determined gleam in his eyes. *Please don't let Prince Gandor decide our fate,* she whispered in her mind.

"These are the charged?" Gandor's voice held no warmth.

"Yes, but due to the special circumstances of their crime, I wish to speak to Father immediately," Kell replied. "Until he decides what we should do, I would prefer to treat them as special guests."

His eldest brother raised one thin brow. "Special guests?"

Kell nodded. "House them in their own rooms under heavy guard."

Arden released the breath she'd been holding. Rooms under heavy guard sounded much nicer than a dungeon cell.

"And what's to stop them from using their magic to escape?"

"If they wanted to do that, they would have done it already. Please, Gandor, let's take this discussion inside and see what Father thinks."

She didn't need to ask what Gandor thought. She could see the flames dancing in his eyes. At least Therrin gave her small smile.

"Very well. It shouldn't take long." Gandor snapped his fingers, and a man in well-made robe approached him. "Take them to east wing and see they are made comfortable for now."

The man bowed. "Yes, Your Highness."

"Might I request a private audience with King Heodis?" Dev asked as though he had every right to do so.

His request surprised all three princes, but Kell nodded. "I'll ask him about it."

"It would be poor form for him to refuse to see a representative of Empress Marist. That might cause a strain on the already fragile diplomatic relations between Gravaria and Ranello."

Gandor's eyes narrowed into thin, brown slits. "You'll have an audience with my father, but don't think it will be on your terms. It could just be your sentencing."

"Your father is a wise man. I hope he won't let pride interfere with the wellbeing of his kingdom."

Shut up, Dev. Arden fidgeted between her protector and the royalty who could condemn them in a moment's notice.

Kell caught her eye and nodded. "Sir Devarius, your

apprentice seems weary after the long ride."

"Please, Dev, I'm longing for a hot bath and a nap." She pressed her hand against his chest and hoped he'd end his standoff with Gandor.

"That's right—tempt him with your naked body and a possible romp between the sheets."

Blood rushed into her cheeks. *"Loku, you're not helping matters."*

"But I think he got the idea."

Dev took her hand, staring down at her with confusion. Could he be thinking that? The warmth spread to her ears as she remembered their first night together. She wouldn't mind a second glimpse of his naked body, either. She lowered her eyes in case he could read her thoughts.

"I look forward to meeting King Heodis tonight." He pulled her in the direction of the well-dressed servant, leaving the princes standing in a huddle in the middle of the courtyard. She knew he wouldn't take no for an answer, but she hoped his attitude wouldn't cause more problems down the road.

Chapter 24

Kell watched Arden disappear into the palace, the wolf tight on her heels. He had to suppress a grin when the first squeal of terror echoed down the stairs. The servants might have a difficult time adjusting to Cinder's presence.

Therrin cocked his head to the side. "Is that a fire wolf?"

His brother's question pulled Kell away from his thoughts of Arden. "A what?"

"A fire wolf. I've read about them, but I thought they were just a myth."

Gandor rubbed his nose in disgust. "It's a smelly beast, and I'll have it destroyed with the other two as soon as Father gives the order."

"Not if I have anything to say about it." Kell shoved past his older brother and proceeded straight to his father's chambers in the west wing. It mattered who whispered in the King's ear first, and he wanted to make sure it was him.

He didn't bother knocking when he came to the inner chamber doors. One nice perk about being a prince. And, if his father's treatment of him was any indication, he was also the favorite son.

"Did you bring me Sulaino's head?" Heodis asked without looking up from his papers. His large body matched his desk—massive, regal, and imposing. The grey in his hair and beard did little to diminish his bearing.

"Unfortunately, no. Something else came up, but I think you'll be happy to hear I have a better plan for stopping the necromancer."

By this time, his brothers had entered the room. Therrin discreetly closed the doors behind them while Gandor lounged in a plush leather chair.

Heodis lifted his head. "Speak, before I get more wrinkles."

Kell grinned. As gruff as Father tried to sound, he knew he had his respect. He described his battle with Sulaino's undead and how Arden stopped them, making sure he spared no detail over the depth of her power. "I never realized how much we needed her help until I almost lost my head that night."

A scowl darkened his eldest brother's face. "She still used magic in the realm. The witch should burn in accordance with the law."

"So you think one minor violation of the law negates all the lives she saved that night and her potential to save even more lives?"

"The law is the law." Gandor held his gaze. "If we bend it now, we'll have all sorts of witches coming out of the woodwork and wrecking havoc."

"Might I get a word in?" Therrin stopped pacing in front of the floor-to-ceiling windows and rubbed his chin. "There's more to this than just dealing with a witch who reportedly has powers strong enough to defeat the necromancer by herself. What about the other prisoner? He claims to be a representative from Empress Marist."

Heodis leaned back in his chair. "An interesting twist to your story, Kell. When were you going to tell me about him?"

He didn't miss the triumphant gleam in Gandor's eyes. "I was coming to that. Her companion is an elf who calls himself Sir Devarius and claims to be a knight of Gravaria."

"An elf?" Therrin practically hopped up and down like an eager child. "I haven't seen one of those since—"

"Since the last so-called diplomatic envoy," Gandor finished. "You remember how well that went, don't you, Father?"

The king's face hardened, but he said nothing.

"This isn't a diplomatic envoy this time. Dev told me he came here to retrieve someone who had escaped from Gravaria. Unfortunately, this person was killed before he could capture him."

"And the witch? How did she become his whore?"

Kell ground his teeth at Gandor's question, not wanting to remember how he thought the same thing when he first met Arden. He took a deep, calming breath before answering, "She's his apprentice. He's determined to take her back to Gravaria for more formal magic training."

"So, we have a Gravarian knight coming into our kingdom without permission to sneak out a witch, and you want to treat them like 'special guests?'"

His hands curled into fists. If they were fifteen years younger, he might have punched his brother. The idea still tempted him. "He's very tight-lipped about his real mission, but he mentioned something about being a servant of Loku. They both bear this mark." He reached into his pocket and pulled out Bynn's sketch. "He has it on his sword, and she has it on her lower back."

"Already got her naked, Kell? My, you do work quickly."

"Can you offer something other than sarcasm, Gandor?"

Therrin peered over his father's shoulder and studied the symbol. "Loku, you said? Hmm…"

"You know something about this pagan god?" Heodis turned the symbol upside down, his grizzled brows furrowed together.

"Just an old legend I stumbled across in a Gravarian text."

"There's usually some truth in legends." The king laid the sketch aside. "Tell me, do either one of them seem unbalanced?"

Kell shook his head. If anyone seemed unbalanced, it was *him* every time he came near Arden. "Both are very sane and very intelligent."

"And what do you think they desire?"

"Desire?" The word caught him off-guard. Did she desire him as much as he desired her? Or did her heart and body already belong to Dev?

"Yes. You need to truly get inside your enemy's mind if you want to defeat him. Find out what he desires, and you'll know his weakness."

"I already know his weakness: her. He claims to be her Protector, and as long as we control Arden, he won't give us too much trouble."

Heodis steepled his fingers under his chin. "Until he gets pushed to his limits."

Kell nodded, remembering the few times when Dev's thinly veiled rage caused him to reach for his sword in case the knight attacked. "I've been trying to avoid that by working on Arden."

"The witch?"

"Yes. I know she wants to help us—she's a Ranellian—but Dev has somehow convinced her that she needs to go to Gravaria as soon as possible or something bad will happen."

"Do you think she'd be willing to help you hunt down Sulaino?"

"I'm almost sure she would."

"Almost?"

His father's question tugged at every thread of doubt he had, threatening to unravel his plans. "I just need to get her away from Dev long enough to convince her to do what she knows is right."

"That should be simple enough. Kill the elf, and she's all yours." Gandor wiped his hands as if cleaning them from the problem. "Then, depending on how helpful she is, we can decide if she'll live or not."

"Nothing is ever as simple as you expect it to be," the king replied tightly. "It's something you need to learn before you inherit my crown, boy."

"Exactly," Kell added, somewhat giddy at seeing Gandor knocked down a few notches. "She's very attached to Dev. If you kill him, I'm afraid of what she may do in retaliation."

"You bring me a very tangled knot to unravel, son. What would you do in my place?"

"I would consider what's best for my kingdom and my subjects. Sulaino is the real threat. I've seen the villages he's desecrated, and who knows how many undead he has by now? We can't defeat him without either a huge loss of life or the help of magic."

His father nodded. "Go on."

"I've found two individuals who know how to fight undead using magic. Although Arden knew the risk she took when she used it, she did it to save the lives of her fellow Ranellians. And if her behavior earlier is any indication of her conscience, she'd help us again if needed." Kell crossed his arms, dreading his next few words. "Although I hate to admit it, Gandor did bring up a good point. She did break the law, and in order to maintain order, we need to show good reason to bend it in a particular instance. I suggest we offer Arden her freedom in exchange for her promise to help us with Sulaino."

He anxiously watched for his father's reaction, but the king's face remained unreadable. "Well thought out. You make some interesting points. I'll need time to consider them, as well a few things you've neglected to consider."

"Such as?"

Hcodis chuckled. "There's more to being king than just wearing a crown."

Jealousy over the king's praise of Kell twisted Gandor's mouth into a snarl. "The arrogant elf demanded a private audience with you, Father."

"Another thing to consider. I'm sure I might learn a few things from him that he's refused to share with you."

Envy coiled in the pit of Kell's stomach that his father might be able to glean information from the elf when he'd failed. "Will you grant him an audience?"

Gandor jerked up in his chair. "Consider the consequences, Father. He could be an assassin sent by

Marist to kill you."

Heodis threw his head back in laughter. "The young empress may be called many things, but vengeful wouldn't be one of them. It would take more than one elf to kill me, anyway." He turned to Kell. "If I agree to grant this knight a private audience, what will you do with the witch in the meantime?"

The twinkle in the king's eye almost made Kell laugh out loud. Among the many things he'd inherited from his father, his appetite for women was one of them. Members of the court still whispered about how quickly Heodis wooed and married his second wife, especially after Kell was born less than seven months after the first queen's death. "I'm sure I can think of a few things."

The first thing that came to mind was how pretty Arden would look in a court gown. His breath hitched. Usually, his thoughts of women centered around how quickly he could he could get them out of their dresses, not into them.

The king's brows rose as though he noticed Kell's confusion. "I'll give it some thought."

"Come now, Father, this is ridiculous," Gandor spat.

"The only thing that's ridiculous is your closed mind. Now, all of you, leave me alone for a few hours. I need to figure out exactly how to handle this situation, and I don't need to hear any more of your bickering." Heodis dismissed them with a wave of his hand.

Once they closed the door to the king's private chambers, Gandor whipped around to face Kell. "What exactly are you trying to do? Take over the crown for yourself?"

He grinned, knowing his lack of anger would aggravate his older brother even more. "Why? Worried Father may name me his heir instead of you?" He laughed. "You shouldn't feel intimidated by me. I'm just the Third Prince, remember? Perhaps if you listened to what Father has been trying to teach us over the years, you'd win his respect, too."

Gandor grabbed Kell's tunic and bunched the material up in his fists. "Your cockiness will be your undoing. I'm watching you. One false move, and I'll never let you live it down." He released him with a shove and stormed down the hall.

"Give him a few hours," Therrin said, patting him on the shoulder. "He'll calm down like he always does."

He smoothed out his tunic. "Nah, you know he's always hated me for one reason or another. I dread the day he becomes king. I might have to run across the borders to save my head."

"Trust me, I fear the day he becomes king, too. He has no love for the people." A small smile appeared on Therrin's round face. "Perhaps we'll flee together."

"And what does Winnie think of that plan?"

His brother still blushed at the mention of his wife, even though they'd been married over three years. Their relationship was the one thing that made Kell believe in true love. "You know how easygoing she is. I think we'll be happy wherever we are as long as we're together."

"Yes, I'd believe that."

They turned down the corridor toward their own chambers. Arden's suggestion of a hot bath sounded tempting now. Too bad she couldn't join him in the tub.

Kell ducked into his room. The corners of his mouth rose when he saw the steaming bath and fresh clothes already laid out for him. He'd deal with Arden later. First, he needed to soak all the dirt off his skin and dress like a prince again.

Chapter 25

Dev glanced over his shoulder to make sure no one was spying on him. He folded the piece of paper and sealed it with wax. Satisfied that he was alone, he held the letter in his hands, murmuring a spell. The letter disappeared just before a fist pounded against his door.

"Let's go. You don't want to keep the king waiting." Captain Larenis burst into the room accompanied by two well-armed guards. "Maybe he'll sentence you and your witch to a more merciful form of execution than being burned alive."

He stood and smoothed any imaginary wrinkles from his clothes. "Maybe he'll listen to reason."

The captain's jaw dropped when he saw Dev's attire. "Where did you get that?"

For once, carrying a spare set of clothes in his saddlebags paid off. The dark green tunic he wore tonight had slashed sleeves to reveal the immaculately white linen shirt underneath. A pair of fitted black trousers slid into boots that had been shined to a mirror reflection. He plucked a piece of lint off his sleeve. "A true knight is always prepared." His fingers brushed against the small switchblade hidden between the folds of his tunic. *Prepared and ready to fight, if needed.*

Larenis closed his mouth and narrowed his eyes. "I bet you stole those clothes."

"Weren't you the one who said we shouldn't keep the king waiting?"

They escorted him to the next chamber. A girlish giggle greeted them when they knocked on the door. Dev's gut clenched. Trouble never seemed like the giggling sort.

A pink-cheeked maid opened the door. "She'll be ready in a minute. I need to finish pinning her hair." The maid turned around and went back to her client.

"Dev, are you ready?" Trouble asked. Her back was turned to him, but she held up a hand mirror and angled it in his direction.

"Just waiting on you."

"And we're done." The maid slid the last pin into Trouble's hair, securing the ornate tangle of braids that adorned the rippling mass of gold that fell around her shoulders. It looked so soft, he wanted to run his fingers through it.

She laid the mirror down and twirled around. "Do I look presentable?"

A lump formed in his throat. She looked more than presentable. Delicious would be a better word to describe her. The sapphire blue dress made her eyes sparkle, and its tightly laced bodice transformed her small breasts into two tempting mounds of creamy flesh. "Where did you get that?"

"Prince Kell sent her a few things to wear," the maid answered. "Said I was to take good care of her while she was here."

Dev fought hard to keep his emotions under control. Even though he didn't want to tear his eyes away from Trouble, he didn't like the idea of the prince sending her gifts, especially when the flush in her cheeks told him she enjoyed the attention.

"She seems a bit overdressed for a witch," Larenis muttered.

"She's dressed appropriately for an evening at court." Dev offered her his arm.

A shy smile appeared on her lips as she slipped her hand into the crook of his elbow. "Is that a compliment?"

The scent of flowers rose from her skin, and he fought the urge to bury his nose into the hollow of her neck and inhale deeper. "No, that was a statement of fact. If I had said, 'You look very nice,' that would have been a compliment."

"And do I look nice?" She tilted her head up, waiting for his response.

His voice almost broke when he admitted, "Yes, you do."

The halo in her eyes flashed, and she giggled again.

"His Majesty is waiting."

The captain's coarse reminder pulled him away from drinking in her appearance. Business first. Then, maybe once they were safely in Gravaria, he could indulge in the pleasure of spending time alone with her.

They filed out into the hallway, with Larenis in front and the two guards in the rear. When Trouble ordered Cinder to stay behind, the wolf's ears wilted, and a sad whine rose from his throat. The damn wolf already liked her better than him.

She leaned close to Dev. "So, what's your plan?"

His free hand pressed the heavy gold seal in his pocket against his thigh. The cold weight reassured him he'd at least get the king's attention with that. "Patience, Trouble. Wait and see."

"You can't keep me in the dark forever."

"Continue to think that if you want."

Her bottom lip jutted out in a pout. "Are you always going to be this stubborn?"

"I could ask you the same thing."

She started to withdraw her hand from his arm, but he caught it and held it in place. The warmth of her skin did little to smother the longing that flowed through his veins. It made him crave the silkiness of her naked body against his. *I can't afford any distractions tonight.*

"I understand."

His shoulders jerked to attention at her reply. Could she hear his thoughts? The more time he spent with her, the more that puzzled him. He glanced down and noticed the small gold pendant around her neck. "Still wearing your necklace?"

She covered it. "I never take it off."

"Why?"

"It reminds me not to make the same mistakes my mother did."

Her fingers parted to reveal writing on the flat square surface. He peered closer at it. "What does it say?"

Her brows knitted together, and she balled her hand around it. "It doesn't say anything. Just some odd scratches on one side and an engraving of a rose on the other."

They crossed the grand staircase and entered the west wing of the palace. He'd have plenty of time to examine her pendant closer once they left here. A whole lifetime, in fact. The problem was, how long would she have to live? Hours? Years? His spine stiffened. He'd rather be drawn and quartered alive than to see her burn.

Her fingers dug into his bicep as they walked deeper into the royal living quarters. A set of guards stood at each doorway along the long tunnel of rooms. If push came to shove, he'd have a bit of trouble getting out this way. He counted twelve guards before they finally came to the set of closed, gilded doors.

The few times he'd suffered coming to the Gravarian court, he'd had a much different experience. His entrance into the Ranellian court seemed less welcoming. A servant slipped inside the room and reappeared a minute later, nodding his head. No introductions were made. The doors opened, and Larenis strode inside with a grim face.

The crowd of overly dressed nobles parted like he and Trouble carried the plague. No one wanted to touch them, but that didn't stop them from staring. He bet they made quite a show—the Gravarian elf and the yellow-haired witch. Laughter welled inside his mind, and if she didn't keep trying to bury her face in his arm, he would've vocalized his amusement.

"Appear confident and smile, Trouble. You've done nothing wrong."

His murmured words of reassurance worked. Her

spine straightened, and she threw her shoulders back. The halo in her eyes burned bright. "We have a back-up plan," she whispered.

It was a statement, not a question, and his gut clenched. Her blind trust in Loku grew stronger every day. "Hopefully, it won't come to that."

"But if it does—"

"It won't."

The captain halted and dropped into a low bow. "Your Majesty, I bring you the prisoners."

When he stepped aside, Dev bowed. Trouble dipped into a curtsey. He met the hard, dark eyes of the king.

The king straightened on his throne and stroked his neatly trimmed grey beard. "The charges?"

He expected Kell to answer, not Larenis. "Using magic within the realm."

The only movements in the room were the flicker of the king's eyes between them and the rise and fall of Trouble's chest.

"Names?"

Before the captain of the guard could reply, Dev said, "Sir Devarius Tel'brien, Imperial Knight of Gravaria, Sworn Protector of the Soulbearer, and son of Lord Arano Tel'brien. This is my apprentice, Arden."

Heodis leaned forward at the string of titles. "Tel'brien, eh?"

Gandor sneered from his position next to the king. "Father, surely you don't pretend to recognize that name?"

His face darkened. "Boy, don't presume to know everything I do." He turned back to Dev. "I understand you requested a private audience with me, Sir Devarius. On what grounds?"

Dev pulled the seal out of his pocket. Although it had been passed down from Protector to Protector over the last five hundred years, it still gleamed like a newly minted coin. He displayed it in his palm. "This."

Trouble's eyes widened to match the king's. So far, so good. His plan was working. When Kell climbed down to retrieve it for his father, she whispered, "Where did you get that?"

"That old thing? I've had it for years."

Heodis examined the seal closely. His cheeks grew a shade paler when he flipped it over to the back and saw the intertwined symbols of Ranello, Gravaria, and Thallus. "Sir Devarius, I wish to speak to you alone." When the eldest prince opened his mouth to protest, he added, "I said alone, and I meant it." He gripped the hilt of his sword as he stood and entered a room behind the thrones.

"Wait here," Dev whispered to Trouble.

Her hand shook when she released him, but she nodded.

As soon as they were ensconced inside the private room, the king's rage exploded. "What is the meaning of this?" He held up the seal.

"You know as well as I do. It grants me diplomatic immunity as long as I act in protection of the Soulbearer."

"You, yes. But it doesn't save her."

"It all depends on your definition of protecting her. For example, if you were to order her execution, it would be my duty to do everything possible to save her life."

"Just because I can't charge you with a crime doesn't mean I won't kill you if you try any funny business."

Dev crossed his arms and sat in a chair while the king paced the room. Courtly etiquette be damned. He had the king backed into a political corner, and he knew it. "Of course, you could always do the just thing and pardon her. She did save your son's life, after all."

Heodis spun on his heel, aiming his dark gaze in his direction. "You're not making this any easier for me. I have half a mind to make a lesson out of both of you. This is still my kingdom."

"Until Sulaino animates enough undead to take it from you."

"Don't you dare bring him into this."

"On the contrary, he's as much a part of this as she is. Sulaino attacked your son. Trouble used her magic to fight him and save the lives of over twenty of your men. Or didn't Kell already tell you that?"

"Diplomatic immunity doesn't excuse you from rude behavior."

Dev stood, deciding it was best to humor the king for now. "Excuse me, Your Majesty. *Prince* Kell."

"Yes, Kell told me everything he knows. By the way, do you really expect me to believe she's the Soulbearer?"

"She bears Loku's mark."

"So I've heard." He leaned against a small table. "But I still find it hard to believe in such nonsense. Why would a god want to live in a mortal's body?"

"If you remember your history correctly, he didn't have much choice in the matter."

Heodis combed the grey streak in his beard. "My son seems to think she's the key to defeating Sulaino."

"And I keep telling him she's not a weapon to be used. The consequences could be dire."

"The same could be said if we don't stop that maniac. Lady Moon above, I should have killed Sulaino when I had a chance."

Dev's head jerked to attention. This was an unexpected revelation. "You've had a run-in with him in the past?"

"You could say that. I ordered the execution of his family for witchcraft and made him watch."

"Why did you spare him?"

"Because at the time, he didn't show any magical abilities. I thought I would be merciful, and it came back to bite me in the ass."

"And you're worried the same thing might happen if you spare Trouble?"

"Odd name for the girl, but it fits. And yes, I am worried about that. Whether I like to admit it or not, having her on our side when we hunt down that necromancer will make our job much easier." Heodis eyed him up and down. "If I had known you were a Tel'brien, I would have been better prepared. You're as wily as your old man."

"He warned me about you. He once told me you're the reason why he refuses to take part in any more of the Empire's diplomatic missions."

"Yes, we had some heated arguments back then." His face relaxed for a moment, taking years off his face. He cleared his throat. "But back to the matter at hand. Because of this stupid seal, I can't press any charges against you. You're free to go."

"And you know by the nature of my duty, I can't leave without her." He took the seal back and placed it in his pocket.

"I haven't decided what I should do with her. I might need to mull over it for a few days."

"And in the meantime?"

"In the meantime, you can keep your impertinent mouth shut and leave me to my thoughts. I understand Kell has you staying in the east wing as special guests."

Dev nodded. "Complete with servants, armed guards, and locked doors."

"We spare no expense for our special guests. For your safety, though, I'd suggest staying in your rooms. I've already received quite a few recommendations for your heads."

"May I at least stay in the same room with her?"

A sly grin parted Heodis' beard. "Is that how it is between you two?"

He closed his eyes, remembering how tempting she looked tonight. "Duty comes before all else, Your Majesty."

"But I can tell by the look on your face it's crossed your mind. No need to hide it from me—we're both men. And judging by the way Kell was devouring her with his eyes tonight, you might have competition."

"So I've noticed. If your son lives up to his reputation, his interest will die down in a few days."

"The boy's a bit too much like his father, but once I met his mother, I was hooked. There hasn't been another woman for me since then. If Kell's determined to have something, he usually gets it."

A stone landed in his stomach. He'd left Trouble alone out there, giving Kell the perfect opportunity to seduce her. A curse escaped his lips. He needed to find her and lock her in a room.

"Worried?" Laughter edged the king's voice.

"Only for her safety. She's resisted your son's charms so far. I have faith she'll continue to do so."

"So you hope." He straightened. "I'll announce that I'm still considering both of your fates. No need for the court to know about your special privileges."

"I appreciate your consideration of this matter." He tried to keep his voice calm and steady, even though he couldn't wait to get out of here and snatch Trouble back from Kell. He bowed and waited for the king to exit the room before following him.

Chapter 26

Arden's heart thumped in her chest as Dev followed the king out of the throne room. The chill of abandonment surrounded her, leaving her naked and exposed to the crowd. Once again, she became the freak everyone stared at. The men turned away from her, their expressions something of fear mixed with contempt. The women with their fancy clothes and kohl-lined eyes openly glared her. One in particular looked like she wanted to rip the dress from Arden's body.

She searched the room until she found the one friendly face she could count on—Kell's. He smiled and strolled down the stairs to join her. "May I suggest a turn in the garden?"

"Please." She took his arm and hurried toward the open doors, not caring how many people she shoved aside to get there. Once the night air embraced her, she breathed a sigh of relief. "Thank you."

"You're very welcome, Arden." His gaze swept up and down her body. "You look ravishing tonight."

She lowered her eyes and smoothed her damp palm on the silk skirt. "It has to be the dress."

"My dear Soulbearer, do you know how to take a compliment?"

"I've never had much experience with them until recently."

"Don't discount Dev's compliment, either. He's very spare with his praise, and you should be very proud you weaseled one from him."

Her smile widened and, for a moment, she forgot that

she could be minutes away from a pyre. Right now, she imagined she was just another lady of the court who'd happened to catch the attention of the prince.

A shrill voice came through the open doors. "That little witch must have stolen it."

"Uh-oh." Kell's mouth angled down, and he led her down the stairs onto the garden paths. "Perhaps we should hide in the labyrinth until Elslyn calms down."

"Who?" She'd forgotten how easily her legs got tangled up in full skirts until she tried to match his pace.

"Elslyn, Gandor's wife. You're wearing one of her discarded dresses."

"Oh." Her heart sank a little. She wore a princess's cast-off, not a gown that belonged to her. The truth reminded her that she was nothing more than a skinny barmaid playing dress-up.

He stopped at the opening of a tall hedge. "You sound disappointed. Do you not like the dress?"

"No, I love it, but I don't need any more enemies."

His lips brushed against her forehead. "Don't worry so much about her. Everyone in the palace knows Elslyn's a spoiled bitch. If she dropped dead tomorrow, there would be great rejoicing."

The gentle kiss soothed her more than his words, but she fought back a laugh. "So I've heard from Katie."

"Katie?"

"The maid you sent to help me this evening. She's a delight."

"I'm glad I caught her in the hall, then." His lips trailed along the side of her face, and he tilted her chin up. "I want you to enjoy your time here."

She didn't know if Kell's touch or the tight laces of her dress made it difficult to breathe, but her head swam from lack of air. "Why is that?"

A quick grin flashed on his face. "Come deeper into the labyrinth with me and find out."

A little voice inside her head warned her not to trust him so easily, but she took his hand and followed him through the tall hedge maze.

"Yes, Prince Kell certainly has swept you off your feet."

She stopped dead in her tracks, cursing under her breath. Leave it to Loku to remind her of her foolishness.

"Arden, are you all right?"

She struggled for air. Everything was happening too fast. She'd spent twenty-one years avoiding men, and now in the last few weeks she was intrigued by two of them. *"Loku, is this part of your plan to drive me insane?"*

"Nonsense. On the contrary, perhaps you'd be happier if you learned to play with fire and feel alive for once instead of always playing it safe. The chaos of the unknown is what makes life exciting."

"And terrifying."

"Take deep breaths," Kell instructed. He brushed a few stray hairs from her face. "I suppose I shouldn't have made you run in that dress."

"He's probably enjoying the sight of your breasts straining against your bodice."

She pulled away and covered her chest with her hand. "It's a bit tighter than I'm used to."

"We'll walk from here to the center." His arm circled her waist, and they strolled down the path.

"You know how to get there?"

"Of course. I have this whole labyrinth memorized."

She wondered how many other women had walked along this same path with him, anxiously hoping for a romantic tryst once they reached the center. "What will we do when we get there?"

"Whatever you want to do. There are still a few roses blooming, I've been told. And there's a private arbor with a wide bench for you to rest on."

He didn't need to mention he wanted to continue where they'd left off this morning. His promise of "later" still rung in her ears and made her pulse race.

"How about letting him fuck you into oblivion?"

Her cheeks burned at Loku's suggestion. *"I'm not*

losing my virginity in the middle of a labyrinth, thank you very much."

His laughter vibrated through her mind. *"We'll see about that."*

She took another breath, clearing her mind. She needed to focus on getting out of Ranello alive, not wondering if Kell was going to try and kiss her again.

The twists and turns grew tighter as they ventured deeper into the labyrinth, forcing her to press her body against his several times. She savored the hardness of his body. How would he compare to Dev if she saw him naked?

She shook the stray image from her mind. Why did Dev keep creeping into her thoughts like that?

The hedges opened to a wide circle. She backed away from Kell, taking it all in. The sweet smell of roses wafted in the breeze, mingling with the spicy scent of the fading gardenias. A vine-covered arbor sat next to a gurgling fountain in the center of the clearing, and lit torches bathed everything in golden firelight. "It's beautiful," she whispered.

"I'm glad you like it." He led her to the bench under the arbor.

The sights, smells, and sounds of this little piece of paradise captured her attention and didn't allow her to think of anything else. "What I wouldn't have given to have a place like this growing up."

"Why is that?"

They sat next to each other, their knees barely touching. "Wallus was very small. If I got into trouble or made a mistake, I had no place to hide."

"You don't like being the center of attention?"

She shook her head. "I absolutely hate it. Do you have any idea how many times I've tried to darken my hair or wished my eyes were brown just so I could blend in with everyone else?"

"Ah, but what makes you different makes you beautiful." He stroked her hair, his gentle fingers not disturbing any of the pins Katie had so carefully placed in it. "The rare rose that blooms in winter."

"Except that I'm an accused witch with—" She caught herself before she mentioned the chaos god living inside her. Kell didn't need to know about all her eccentricities. She stared at her hands in her lap.

"With what? A cranky protector?"

She giggled in spite of herself. "That's one thing."

He inched closer to her. "A necromancer hunting you?"

The cold feeling of dread from this afternoon danced across her skin. "Please don't remind me of him."

"Then I won't." His hands caressed her arms. "You know you are safe here with me?"

"Am I?"

"Completely safe." He kissed the hollow of her neck.

Sweet Lady Moon, this didn't fit her definition of safe. Every touch threatened to unleash the wanton woman buried deep inside her. If he continued, she'd give into the reckless need building within her body. "Kell, I don't want to be the next woman you toss aside once you've gotten what you wanted from me."

He pulled away, and a cool breeze chilled her scorching skin. "I see my past bothers you."

"You have a reputation for certain things." Being a damned good lover was one of them. Could she handle the aftereffects of their affair? Memories of her mother weeping into her silk gown still haunted her. She reached for her pendant and tried to push them aside.

"Do you believe people can change?" The cocky air he normally carried disappeared, making him appear just as scared and confused as she felt.

"Sometimes, if given the right motivation." She cleared her throat. "I'm surprised you didn't have an angry father demanding you marry his daughter."

"Most of them throw their daughters at me. Besides, I always take precautions not to sire a child."

Unlike my own father, whoever he was.

He ran his finger along her jaw. "You're different than most of the ladies in there."

"Why? Because I told you no?"

He laughed. "Partly, yes." The levity left his face as he added, "I'm also a little envious of what my parents have and my brother, Therrin, and his wife have."

"And what's that?"

"Love, built on trust and respect. I've never truly seen two people so well-suited for each other. No head games, no politics. Just a man and woman who can't get enough of each other."

Her mouth went dry. She wanted to trust this softer side of him. "Is that the truth, or are you just saying that to win me over?"

"Would I share it with you if it wasn't true?"

"Why did you share it with me, then?"

"Because, I…" His brows knitted together like he was searching for the right thing to say. He cupped her cheeks in his hands, stared at her lips like he wanted to kiss her again.

Her bodice felt too tight again. After this morning, she knew what he was capable of doing if he wanted.

Instead, he released her, a frown tugging at the corners of his mouth. The look she'd come to recognize as desire still smoldered in his eyes, mixed with the strange gleam she'd seen the night of the sword fight. "Do you have any idea what you're doing to me?"

His face struggled to contain his emotions while he waited for her answer.

"What are you afraid of, my Soulbearer?"

"Getting hurt in the end."

"Do you think you could love him? Or is it Dev who holds your heart?"

Kell embodied danger. He'd known his share of women and, despite his words, a tiny shred of her still wondered if he meant what he said.

"But you don't trust your heart with anyone yet, do you, my Soulbearer? Not even me."

"What are you saying?"

"No rewards come without risk. If everything in life was simple, certain things would never be cherished."

"Kell, I…" Words failed her much in the way they failed him earlier. A plethora of emotions tumbled in her heart, making it almost painful to breathe. She wished she could let go of her fears, but there was too much at stake. Even if she was pardoned, how could she tell him about the chaos god living inside her?

"I understand." Defeat creased lines into his cheeks, weighed down his shoulders.

"No, it's not that—" she started to say, but when the hope returned to his dark eyes, she forgot what she was trying to tell him. Could he really care for her?

"What?" When she didn't answer, he held her hand and whispered, "I'm glad you aren't like the other women here."

Her heart stopped. "Why?"

His eyes squeezed together as if he fought to stay in control of his desires. "Because for once, I don't want to rush things. I want to know you want me for me and not because I'm a prince and you think it'll help you escape sentencing. You already know I'll fight for your freedom after you saved my life."

Her mouth went dry when he accused her of trying to seduce him. But on the other hand, he sounded like he wanted more than just her body.

Before Arden could respond, voices filtered through the thick hedges. They wouldn't be alone much longer.

"Let's examine the roses, shall we?" He offered her his hand and led her to the bushes on their right.

She followed, lowering her head to inhale the bouquet of a deep red bloom just as a pair of lovers stumbled into the center of the labyrinth.

Kell cleared his throat, and they both jumped in surprise.

"Your Highness, we didn't know…" The man's voice trailed off when he spotted her.

"No need to apologize. We were just leaving." He offered her his arm. "The arbor is all yours."

She avoided eye contact with the lovers as she and Kell plunged back into the twisting paths of the labyrinth. Tomorrow morning, the whole palace would probably think she'd slept with the prince. But then she caught a glance of his profile and remembered the things he'd shared with her. She tightened her arm in his and smiled. Underneath his rakish swagger, Prince Kell had the makings of a true gentleman.

Chapter 27

The engorgement in Kell's trousers subsided by the time they exited the labyrinth, much to his relief. The last thing he needed was for the entire court to know Arden had left him more frustrated than any woman he'd ever known. He silently cursed at stopping himself when he had her right in the palm of his hand. In the privacy of the labyrinth, it would have been so easy to steal another kiss from her, to press her soft body against his, to caresses those curves he longed to hold.

But when he saw the relaxed smile on her face, he knew he'd done the right thing. Holding back now would only strengthen her trust in him, maybe even give him a chance of finding what Therrin had. The prospect of that warmed his blood like the finest brandy. *Small battles win the war,* he reminded himself.

They'd barely crossed the lawn before Dev ambushed them. "Where the hell have you been?"

"In the labyrinth," she answered nonchalantly. Her ability to ignore her protector's ire never ceased to amaze him.

"Since you left her alone to the vultures in there," Kell interjected, "I decided to rescue her and show her the late-blooming roses at its center."

The bright light from the throne room shimmered off her hair like sunlight. "It was very beautiful, Dev. The crimson ones are especially fragrant."

"Your consideration is appreciated, Prince Kell," Dev said through clenched teeth. He pulled her closer to him, staring at her lips as though making sure she hadn't been kissed. The murderous fire in his eyes dimmed, and his face softened as he looked at her. "Trouble, get inside. King Heodis suggested we stay in our rooms until he makes up his mind."

"For once, I'd have to agree with Dev. My father's suggestions are to be treated like orders." Kell brought her hand up his lips and kissed it. He didn't want to stop there.

She nodded, licking her lips. Damn, did she know what such a simple gesture did to him? "Thank you for showing me the labyrinth, Your Highness."

Dev tucked her hand in his arm and led her away.

Two guards silently filed in behind them when they entered the palace through another set of doors. As soon as she vanished from his sight, his muscles turned to warm wax. He returned to the throne room, dropping into a chair. Normally he only reached this level of exhaustion from a full romp under the covers.

Bynn approached him and gave a small bow. "Interesting turn of events, I hear."

"How so?"

"Your father didn't order them away in chains."

Kell laughed, the last of the tension leaving his body. "I knew he wouldn't make a rash decision."

"What did Dev give him? Judging by the elf's arrogant expression, you'd think it was some sort of blackmail."

"It looked like a seal of some sort. Probably something Empress Marist gave him to legitimize his title."

Bynn pulled up a chair and sat next to him. "Whatever it was, the king seemed pretty annoyed by the discussion when they emerged from the back room."

"My father is always annoyed when someone tries to tell him what to do."

"In the meantime, how did Arden like the labyrinth?"

"Oh, so now you're calling her by her name?"

Bynn looked away and chuckled. "Yes, I admit I'd been a little hard on her."

"Exactly what I've been trying to tell you this whole time. When are you going to get it through your thick skull that I'm right nine times out of ten?"

"When I forget about the one time you're wrong." He lowered his voice. "So, how was she?"

His brows rose simultaneously. "Excuse me?"

"Come on, Kell. You only take women into the labyrinth for one reason."

"This time was different," he replied with some hesitation.

Bynn's jaw dropped "She really has you wrapped around her finger, doesn't she?"

Kell's chest tightened. "Maybe it's the other way around."

"No, I've seen this before in other men. I just never expected it from you."

"What?" His heart raced, waiting for the answer he feared was coming.

"You've fallen for her."

He pushed the lump in his throat down into his stomach, where it sat like a brick. "Don't be ridiculous."

"Then why else would you not take advantage of her like you've done with dozens of other women?"

"Because I have to handle her with care."

Bynn nodded. "Yeah, because you're so smitten with her, if she told you to jump off one of the turrets, you would."

"Now you're really exaggerating."

"Say what you want, but I know you well enough to notice the change. If she left tomorrow, how would you feel?"

Like a vital piece of me was missing. He cursed when he realized Bynn was dead-on. As much as he tried to downplay it, she'd gotten under his skin, and he wouldn't let her go without a fight.

Bynn clasped his shoulder. "What are you going to do about it?"

The reality of the situation sobered him like a funeral. "Find a way to keep her here. Winter will be upon us soon enough, and no ship will leave Boznac during the storm season."

"And do you think it's safe to keep her here?"

"People's opinions change over time. Look at you."

"True, but I don't think Elslyn will ever forgive Arden for looking better in that dress than she did."

Laughter pushed away some of the dark clouds that swarmed around him. Between the necromancer and Arden, his life had suddenly become far more complicated than he cared to admit.

***

The small wooden box beside Sulaino glowed like a candle. He threw the lid open and tore off the wax seal on the letter with his one hand. The contents filled him with enough giddiness that he ignored the throbbing ache in his stump of an arm for a few moments.

He turned to the man hanging spread-eagle from the chains on the wall. "What do you think of this, Lord Yessling? The little Soulbearer is within the palace walls. Talk about making my life easier. I can kill her, absorb the chaos god's powers, and destroy Heodis all in the same place."

Lord Yessling grunted through his gag and rattled his chains. Although the man had quite a reputation for his harem of women, he was annoyingly loyal to the crown.

Sulaino nodded to one of the farm girls who'd been sold to the nobleman. She flicked the cat-o-nine-tails across Lord Yessling's chest. A mixture of fear and retribution lit up her dull eyes when he cried out, and she waited for permission to do it again.

He stood and approached his host. "Lord Yessling, although I do admit I've been a pampered guest these last few days, I'm afraid I must be leaving soon. You see, I'm needed at the palace." He showed him the letter.

His host's eyes widened when he saw the signature at the bottom. He tugged at his chains with renewed vigor. The gag continued to muffle his words, but Sulaino had a good idea what he was saying.

"Don't think we'll get away with this, huh? Do you

have any idea how long I've been planning this? What you see here is only a fraction of my army."

More grunts came from behind the gag, and this time, Sulaino removed it.

"I hope Prince Kell carves you up bit by bit, beginning with your other hand and ending with your head," Yessling growled.

He examined the partially healed stump. "Thank you for reminding me to let Prince Kell know how much I appreciated his attentions."

Yessling answered by spitting in his face, earning him another lash from the whip.

"I shall be taking my leave of you this evening. I appreciate the use of your keep and your girls while I recovered from my injury. So much, in fact, I'd like to take you with me."

He grabbed a knife off the table and slit the nobleman's throat. The sound of gurgling blood played a delightful melody to his ear that beat in time with the last twitches of Yessling's body. Death could be so beautiful at times.

He consumed the decadent lord's soul, relishing the taste of years of lust, gluttony and sloth that fed it. Yes, naughty souls always tasted better. Magic bloomed inside him, and the skin sealed over his stump.

He pressed his finger against Yessling's forehead, casting a familiar spell. The black lightning zapped through the corpse, and a pair of glowing red eyes looked up to meet him. "Welcome to my army, Lord Yessling."

The girl screamed and ran for the door. Another spell knocked her to the floor before she reached it.

"Going somewhere?"

Tears streaked down her cheeks. "You told me if I obeyed you, you'd let me live. Please let me go."

Sulaino knelt beside her and caught a tear on the tip of his finger. Her fear aroused him, but he'd already overindulged his desire for women's flesh in the last few days. He needed tainted souls to destroy Heodis. "Did you enjoy whipping Lord Yessling?"

She trembled, but nodded.

"Good girl. And don't you agree he's met a fitting end?"

She glanced over at the undead stretched by the chains. "That bastard deserved everything that came to him."

He smoothed her tangled brown hair. "Would you like to continue to help me?"

Her face paled, and she recoiled from his touch like he'd burned her. "Please let me go home. My family—"

"Your family sold you to him. Do you really think they'd take you back now?"

"We could kill them."

The vengeful snarl of her mouth intrigued him. Corruption marred her soul long ago. He licked his lips. She'd probably taste just as delicious as Yessling. "I have something else in mind."

He plunged the dagger in to her black heart and sucked in every last morsel of her soul while the light bled from her eyes. A belch escaped his lips when he finished.

The undead Yessling stared straight ahead, his waxy face emotionless.

"Are you ready to leave?" Sulaino asked as he stood.

Obedient silence answered him.

He unlocked the manacles that bound his new servant's wrists and ankles. "I have room for a few more souls before we depart. Let's go find your naughtiest girls."

Chapter 28

Dev jiggled the knob again and pounded on the door when it refused to budge. "The king said I could stay in the same room with her."

"I'm not sure what the king told you, but my orders are from Captain Larenis, and he's said to keep you two separated."

Damn guards. He paced the room, trying to decide if picking the lock later tonight would be worth it. If he heard snoring on the other side, he'd go for it.

A knock came from the wall that divided them. "Dev?" a faint voice asked.

He rushed to source of the sound and pressed his ear against it. "Trouble, are you alone?"

Muffled laughter answered him. "Don't worry. It's just me and Cinder."

He relaxed a bit and leaned against the wall. "Do you know how to cast a ward?"

"I can learn."

"Forget it. I don't want you taking any more lessons from him."

"Are you two going to shut up and sleep, or do I need to move one of you to a different room?" the guard shouted from the hall.

"Don't worry, Dev. I'll be safe tonight."

He listened for anything else from her, but silence filled the void. He'd gotten so used to her body lying beside his, he feared he couldn't sleep without her. He sank onto the bed and listened to the guards. When the clock chimed, the brisk footsteps and increased rumble of conversation told him a new set of guards stood outside. So much for catching them asleep.

If he really wanted to escape, he could knock them out with magic and blow away the door. He had diplomatic immunity, after all. But Trouble didn't, and that's where things got tricky. Whatever he did, he had to make sure she wouldn't pay the price for it. By Jussip, when did things become so complicated? But he already knew the answer. It all started when he ran into a yellow-haired barmaid in a tavern on the other side of the kingdom.

He lay there until the clock chimed again, trying to find a way to get into her room. Too bad he couldn't just walk through a wall.

He bolted up in bed. That's it. As much as he hated ritual-type magic, this was the best solution he could come up with at the moment. He grabbed a piece of chalk from his bag and drew an outline of a door on the wall between their rooms. Then he sat cross-legged on the floor and started casting.

***

The grey light of dawn shone through the windows when the outline of the door finally shimmered to life. Dev stood and stretched, wincing as he discovered new knots in his back and shoulders from sitting still for so long. He extended his hand toward the wall, smiling when it passed through without difficulty.

He crossed the portal and found Trouble sound asleep in her bed. Cinder stretched out next to her and only raised his head when he entered the room. He frowned. "Don't get used to this," he whispered to the wolf. "When we get back to Gravaria, you'll be sleeping on the floor where you belong."

He grabbed a chair and carried it to the side of her bed, muttering under his breath the whole time about how she was spoiling his wolf. How much effort would it take to shove him off the bed and take his place?

Cinder bared his teeth as if he knew exactly what Dev had been thinking.

The damn wolf was too smart for his own good. "Fine, you can stay there tonight. But tomorrow…"

He placed a paw across her stomach in a possessive gesture.

Great, so now he had to compete with Cinder as well as Kell and Loku. Trouble certainly lived up to her name.

He flopped in the chair and stretched his legs out in front of him. It might not be his ideal choice of sleeping positions, but at least he knew he could keep an eye on her.

"Very clever, creating a portal like that."

The deep voice almost caused him to knock his chair over. A pair of glowing yellow-green eyes stared at him from Trouble's face. "What do you want, Loku?"

"What do we all want? Gold? World domination? A warm body to cuddle next to every night?"

"Cut the crap and get to the point. You usually don't have conversations with me without a reason."

"Would it bother you to know that Kell almost declared his feelings for her tonight?"

Dev's jaw tightened, but he kept his mouth shut.

"Of course, I suspect she would have let him kiss her again if he tried. Maybe even more."

His gaze travelled the length of her body. Temptation spread through his veins and gathered in his groin. He wanted to be the one tasting her lips, not Kell. If he wasn't sworn to protect her, he'd crawl into the bed and get some relief for the continual string of hard-ons he'd had since he met her.

"Tough to resist, huh?"

The taunt reinforced his resolve not to touch her. "I'm her protector, not her lover."

"So true. And if you keep pushing her away, she'll end up in Kell's arms."

The thought chilled him to the bone. "What makes you think I would care if she did?"

"Where do I begin? Shall I start with your response that night I came to you in your dreams? Or the way your jaw clenches every time you see her with Kell?"

"I won't cave to my baser instincts."

"You're a man, not a marble statue."

"Why are you so interested in my feelings?"

"Besides the fact that I'd love to see you head-over-heels stupid for her? Maybe because if I have to share with anyone, I'd rather share her with you."

Now the chaos god wanted to play matchmaker. How sweet. "I'm not falling for your head games, Loku."

"Very well. I suppose Kell wins." The eyes closed, leaving Trouble subject to her dreams.

Dev stood and paced the room, too wound up to sleep. Could she really fall in love with Kell? The tightness in his chest told him the chaos god knew more about her thoughts than he did.

***

A cold fog clouded Arden's vision. Shards of ice hung in the air, glistening like diamonds in the faint beams of light that broke through. A chill crept along her spine, threatening to drive away any happy thought she had. Then the scent of rotting flesh rolled in.

Her heart jumped into her throat as she searched for the glowing red eyes of the undead. She rubbed her arms, hoping to warm them.

"Arden." The voice carried on an invisible breeze, but she immediately recognized it.

"Get out of my head!" She struggled to raise her shields.

"I'm coming for you." The voice invaded her mind like a pack of rats searching for any glimmer of fear to feast upon. "Soon, Loku will be mine."

A pair of blood-red eyes as large as her head raced toward her through the fog. She held her hands up to her face and screamed.

***

The scream still echoed off the walls when Arden bolted up in bed. Sweat dripped down her face and neck, soaking the nightgown. Sweet Lady Moon, it was just a dream.

A pair of strong arms pulled her against a firm chest. The familiar scents of smoke and spice comforted her. Dev was here.

"Another dream?" he asked.

Wetness gathered in the corners of her eyes, and she nodded.

"Sulaino?"

She nodded again. "How did he get through my shields?"

Dev's arms tightened in response. "Did you let them down at any point?"

"I don't think so."

His silence left Arden swimming in a sea of doubt, but as long as she could cling to him, she refused to go under. Minutes passed before her breathing slowed and the awkwardness of remaining in his arms stole upon her. She pressed her hand against his chest. His heart beat faster than hers, although she had no idea why. When she lifted her eyes, some sort of internal struggle tightened Dev's face as he stared off in the distance. "What's wrong?"

Her question jerked him from his thoughts. His face relaxed. "Nothing for you to worry about, Trouble."

"He's getting stronger, isn't he?"

"Perhaps." He stroked her hair, and she nestled back into the confines of his embrace, relishing the soothing safety it offered. "Tell me what you saw."

"Fog, mostly. Very dense so that only a few beams of light broke through. And at the end..." The memory of the undead eyes racing toward her sent a shiver down her spine. "He's coming for me."

"Over my dead body."

The fierceness of his voice, coupled with the possessive nature of his hold on her, sent another shiver down her spine, but this time, in anticipation rather than fear. Dev would draw blood if Sulaino came for her. He'd protect her to his last breath. Knowing this chased away her dread of the necromancer and left an odd feeling behind. What would she do without Dev?

"Would you miss him, my little Soulbearer? Are you really that attached to him?"

Her heart thudded three times before she answered, *"Yes, Loku, I'd miss him dearly."*

"You have Kell."

"But I trust Dev. He's the one person I've come to count on during all this craziness."

"You underestimate your abilities. You don't need anyone. Everything you need is inside you."

"You mean you?"

"No, silly girl. Why do you think I chose you as my Soulbearer? Because you're the one person I've met in the last few centuries who can survive being alone."

"Let's hope it doesn't come to that."

"I agree," Dev replied with a grim smile. He loosened his arms. "Feeling safer now?"

Dev sat on the edge of the bed next to her, still dressed in his clothes from the night before. A flush crept along her skin. She pulled the covers up over her nearly transparent nightgown. "Are we still prisoners?"

He chuckled. "For now."

"How did you get into my room?"

"Do I have to reveal all my secrets to you?"

"Maybe." Something hard and cold bumped against her thigh. She reached down and traced the outline of a large coin in his pocket. Her fingers wrapped around it, weighing its heaviness. "What did you give the king last night?"

He pried her hand away from the contents of his pocket. "You can call it my ace of spades."

"Or maybe a lucky pair of dice," she added, picking up on his gaming reference.

"It came in handy last night when I gambled with King Heodis."

"What exactly happened between you two?" When he started to rise, she pounced on him and pushed him back into the pillows. "Please tell me."

He wrapped his fingers around her wrists like he wanted to yank her off him, but instead began massaging tiny circles into her palms. A strange sensation zinged up her arm, causing her nipples to form stiff peaks under the thin linen gown. His eyes flickered briefly to them, but otherwise, his gaze remained locked with hers. An eddy of veiled emotions swirled in the dark green depths in perfect rhythm to the motion of his thumbs.

The current traveled into the lowest part of her stomach. She gasped at the throbbing response. The only other time she felt this way was when Kell kissed her, and Dev recreated the same effect just by looking into her eyes and rubbing her skin. What would happen if she dared kiss him? She lowered her lashes and leaned forward to find out.

Dev tossed her aside and jumped off the bed like it was made of steel blades. He pressed his fingers to his temples. "Do you have to know everything, Trouble?"

She pulled the covers back up to her chin, hugging her knees to her chest. *What the hell just happened?*

"Dev has issues with conveying his emotions."

"But he threw me aside like I repulsed him."

Loku laughed. *"More like his own reaction to you repulsed him. Or, to be entirely truthful, it scared him."*

She studied the two bright spots in his otherwise pale cheeks and the agitated way he paced the room. *"I don't believe you. He won't even look at me."*

"You are so delightfully naïve."

She sat quietly until Dev calmed down. Cinder licked her cheek, and some of the tension eased from her muscles. At least the wolf still liked her.

Dev sank into the chair by her bed. "Sorry." That was it. No explanation, no excuse. Just a grumbled apology.

The morning's early light filtered through the thick fog outside the window, and Arden shivered as she remembered her dream. "Do you think the king will let us go now that you've shown him that large coin?"

He pulled it from his pocket. "It's a seal."

"May I see it?" She waited until he nodded and studied it like an eager treasure hunter. On one side, a large symbol dominated the face of the seal. On the other, three symbols surrounded by interlocking loops rose from the shiny gold surface. She recognized one as the royal crest of Ranello. "What does this stand for?"

"Read the writing."

Shame burned her cheeks. She turned away and gave it back to him. "I can't read."

He took it and pressed his lips together in a thin line. "That's something we'll have to remedy soon." He pointed to the large symbol. "This is Loku's mark. It identifies me as the Soulbearer's Protector." Then he flipped it over. "These are the symbols of Ranello, Gravaria, and Thallus. They're meant to remind others of the treaty forged over five centuries ago."

"What treaty?"

"It was the last time all three countries agreed on one thing."

"Which was?"

The corners of his mouth rose slightly. "Do you really need to ask?"

"Those bastards got together and figured out a way to trap my soul," Loku hissed. His anger rolled over like a lit torch. *"If I could go back in time, I'd fry them all in their cradles."*

His rage continued to grow as he shouted threats into her mind, and Arden slipped further and further under his control. Trying to stop him felt like grasping water. Fear churned in her stomach, and bile rose into her throat. She cast one desperate glance at Dev before a red haze settled over her vision.

A pair of icy hands clamped around her cheeks. "Stop it this instant." Dev shook her like a rabbit caught in a wolf's mouth. "Let her go, Loku."

Fire raced down her arms and gathered in her fingertips, ready to be unleashed at a moment's notice. Her pulse pounded in her ears, but that didn't stop her from hearing the deep voice that came from her moving lips. "Or you'll what?"

"Help me fight him, Arden."

Dev's plea came seconds before a soothing breeze rushed along her skin. It cooled Loku's ire long enough for her to start squeezing him deep into the center of her consciousness. Her sight cleared, and when everything came into focus, Dev's strained face loomed in front of her.

She reached up to touch his hand. "He's gone."

He released the breath he'd been holding. The cool breeze vanished, but he didn't let go of her face. "Is he really?"

She nodded, and he pulled her back into his arms. His heart thudded through his chest. The salty taste of sweat clung to her lips. Her body trembled, and a sob threatened to force its way out of her throat. "Thank you," she whispered as hot tears leaked from her eyes.

Dev rocked her back and forth, and they both struggled to catch their breath. "Shh, relax."

"I don't know if I can. He came up on me so quickly..."

He brushed the wetness from her cheeks. "He's like that. Now you know why we have to get to Gravaria—so he won't do this to you again. Imagine what would have happened if he had stayed in control."

Images of blood-splattered walls and torn bodies littered her mind. A creature crouched in the room, licking claws as long as her arm. She gasped and buried her face in his chest again. *"Loku, how could you?"*

No answer came, and for once, she was glad not to feel the presence of the chaos god. Losing control of her mind terrified her more than anything she'd ever known, even Sulaino and his horde of undead.

He began prying her away. "I hear voices outside."

She choked back a laugh. "I suppose you don't want to be caught in the same room as me."

The corners of his mouth twitched. "I'll be back later.

Ask your maid for some ink and paper, and I'll start teaching you your letters. It's the only practical education I can give you here."

Excitement dried her tears, filled her with the promise of better things. "You're going to teach me to read?"

"You need to learn." He let go of her and took a few steps back. Shadows darkened his face, making him appear every minute of his three hundred years. "Don't lose hope, Trouble."

Katie's voice came through the door, and he bolted for the wall between their rooms. Her breath caught when he disappeared through it like it wasn't there.

Cold crept up her nightgown and rose from her thighs up to her breasts. She crossed her arms over her chest. "You can't see through there, can you?"

Dev's one-note chuckle answered her.

The doorknob turned, and a cheery Katie entered with a steaming breakfast tray. "Good morning, m'lady. Sleep well?"

Until Sulaino invaded her dreams, she'd slept very well. Now, after her strange reaction to Dev and Loku's stunt, she was left feeling more confused than ever. She cast one more glance at the portal before answering, "As well as can be expected."

Chapter 29

Arden finished copying the last letter in the sentence and frowned. Her writing appeared as awkward and clumsy as a newborn foal compared to the sleek, flowing lines of Dev's. "I'm done with this passage."

He peered over her shoulder, nodding. "Getting neater. Can you read it aloud now, too?"

"The cat ran to the girl." For the past two days, she'd soaked up Dev's reading and writing lessons. He'd write a sentence, read it aloud to her, let her copy it, and then make her repeat it back. Now, she was beginning to recognize common words and sound out the ones she didn't know. It made the day go by faster.

"Good." He bent over the desk, sending a wave of his scent in her direction. A spark of attraction raced through her body. "Try this sentence."

"What does it say?"

A grin broke the harsh lines of his face. "You have ink on your cheek."

She glanced down at the letters before the realization of his sentence hit her. Blood rushed to her cheeks. "Where?" she asked, grabbing a mirror.

"Here." He brushed his thumb across her cheekbone. "And here." He rubbed another spot on her forehead. "Don't worry, though. I've cleaned them up."

Her skin tingled where he'd touched her. When she checked her appearance, the smudges were gone. "How did you do that?"

"Magic." He wiggled his fingers in front of her. "Now, back to your lesson."

Her concentration wandered while she copied the sentence. It drove her crazy that Dev seemed so calm and collected when she could barely control her reaction to him. But what really had her off-kilter was Loku's absence. Who would have thought she'd miss his endless stream of lewd comments?

"Dev, what did we do to Loku yesterday?"

He stiffened. "We contained him."

"But he's still inside me, isn't he?"

"Yes. The only way to be rid of him is death."

A ripple of unease flowed through her. "And how long will he be contained?"

Dev frowned. "I can't say. This is the first time I've ever tried to contain him, and I couldn't have done it without your help."

She returned to the piece of paper in front of her, not wanting to dwell on this any longer. "Next sentence, please."

"Insatiable, are you?"

"I want to learn all I can."

The corners of his mouth twitched. "You're learning quicker than I expected."

"I'm not a child. I hope I'd grasp certain concepts faster than one."

"No, you're definitely not a child." The tone of his voice made both her breath and her pulse hitch. He stared at her for a moment. The only sound in the room was the air entering and leaving their lungs. Sweat prickled at the base of her neck from the hungry intensity of his gaze. Then his usual cold mask of composure slipped back into place. "Are you up for a challenge?"

He would tie her stomach in knots at this rate. At least she knew what Kell was thinking. Dev remained a riddle that she never discovered the answer to. "Of course."

He grabbed the piece of paper and laid it on top of a book. The quill in his hand practically flew with each deft stroke. A playful glint appeared in his eyes when he handed her the paper. "Read this."

A mash of lines, curves, and dots formed strange symbols on the page, none of which resembled the letters he'd made her copy over and over again yesterday. "Is this some kind of trick?"

"No, those are words."

She raised one brow and wondered if he'd lost his mind.

"In Elvish," he added.

She studied the new form of writing. "I have to learn another set of letters?"

A faint smile appeared on his lips. "Only if you want to. Most of the documents in Gravaria are in Human. There aren't many elves left to make a difference."

A hint of sadness peeked through his mask, tugging at her heart. "What happened to them? I thought elves lived a long time."

"We do, but many have died off or mingled their blood with others. Some just disappeared over the mountains."

"Why?"

He shrugged, but the tightness in his shoulders told her he knew the reason.

His sober expression sucked the happiness out of her, and she changed the subject. "But back to this—what does it say?"

"Nothing." He snatched the paper from her and tore it in half. "Let's start with a new sentence."

A lump formed in her throat. Every time she felt like she made a new discovery with him, she only scratched the surface. The man was far more complex than she ever imagined.

A knock on the door spared her from his brooding. Kell stuck his head in. "Am I interrupting anything?"

She grinned. At last, some company. "Dev has been teaching me to read and write."

Dev said nothing. He crossed his arms and gazed out the window.

"The guards let him in?"

"Well, um…"

"Yes," Dev answered for her.

Kell's eyes flickered between them, narrowing. He suspected something but didn't press the issue. Instead, he approached her and nodded at the crystal vase on her desk. "I see you got the roses I sent. I remember you showed a particular interest in these."

The sweet scent of the crimson roses reminded her of his careful restraint that night. "Yes, thank you."

"Any news from your father, Your Highness?" Dev's clipped words sliced through her thoughts like an ax.

"I heard him mention something about wanting to speak to you again."

Dev turned away from the foggy landscape outside the window. "He's reached a decision?"

"If he has, I know nothing about it."

"I'd think you of all people would be privy to your father's thoughts."

"The old man still keeps some secrets from me. The contents of your previous meeting with him, for example."

The corner of Dev's mouth quirked up into a smirk. "Irritating to be left in the dark, isn't it?"

A knock sounded from the other room. A few seconds later, a string of curse words erupted from whoever entered the room.

"Guess they found you missing?" Kell heaved a dramatic sigh. "I suppose I'll clear up this mishap, but you owe me." He stepped outside.

Dev grabbed her arm as soon as they were alone. "Be careful with him."

Arden focused her fire under his fingers, causing him to release her with a yelp. "I'm getting rather tired of you ordering me around. I trust Kell. In case you haven't noticed, he's the one person in this place who wants us to get out of here alive."

Dev shook his hand to cool his singed fingertips and scowled.

"Here we are." Kell opened the door wide to reveal a

very pissed-off looking Captain Larenis.

"How did he get in here? My guards had specific orders to keep them apart."

Dev's scowl melted into a mocking grin. "Are you sure they've been paying attention?"

The captain's hand gripped his sword until his knuckles whitened, pushing all the blood up into his florid face.

"Larenis, you've found him. Don't keep my father waiting."

He released his sword and bowed his head. "Yes, Your Highness. Sir Devarius, King Heodis requests another audience with you." The venom in his voice made it clear he would've preferred a good brawl instead of following orders.

"By all means, let's do as Prince Kell suggests and not keep him waiting."

As soon as the door closed behind them, Kell took her hand in his and pressed his lips against her knuckles. A shiver raced up her arm, making her cheeks flames as he turned her hand over to press his lips against the inside of her wrist. The look in his eyes stated he wanted to kiss more of her.

A growl sounded behind them, and Kell jumped away. Cinder raised his upper lip to reveal his fangs and growled again.

"Some watchdog," he muttered and released her hand. "Sorry, but I haven't been able to get you out of my mind since the other night."

"Then why didn't you come by sooner?"

"Politics," he replied with a grimace.

More like head games. He probably found someone else to occupy his bed. She kept a few feet between them in case he tried to take her into his arms again. "Poor Prince Kell."

"Trust me, I'd rather be here with you."

For a second, she almost believed him. "I've been trying to find a way to pass the time."

"With Dev?"

His jealousy shot an arrow straight into her gut. "He's my protector and teacher."

"And what has he been teaching you in your bedroom?"

Her heart fluttered, and her palms grew damp. "Just what you see before you. Nothing more." *Although there'd definitely been a few times when I wanted more.* "It's not like you walked in on us naked and rolling around in bed, did you?"

His pupils dilated. "I wouldn't mind seeing you naked and rolling around in the bed with me."

Cinder growled again.

"You're refreshingly transparent, Kell. Thank you." She turned away and began straightening her papers. Damn him! Just when she thought he was more than just a man-whore, he reminded her he only wanted one thing.

A pair of warm hands covered her shoulders, followed by lips gently pressing against the back of her neck. "There's no need to hide my desire for you. I told you before that I'm willing to wait."

Her knees wobbled. If he only knew what effect his touch had on her. "What's the real reason you came here, Kell?"

"The truth?" He glanced at the bed, grinning.

She broke free of him and stood closer to Cinder. "Don't you ever get your mind out of the gutter? You're almost as bad as—"

"Who? Dev?"

"Hardly."

"Then who?"

She bit her lip. *Damn it, I almost told him about Loku again.* "None of your business. I'm sorry to disappoint you, Your Highness, but I'll have to decline your invitation." She held her breath and prayed he wouldn't try to force the matter.

"Actually, I came here with the intention of offering a much different invitation."

"What?"

"Would you like to join me for dinner?"

Her stomach growled. She covered it with her hands, hoping to smother the noises.

"I take that as a yes?"

"As long as you don't give me indigestion." She smoothed her hands over her soft wool gown. "Am I properly attired for dinner with a prince?"

"I don't have a stringent dress code in my private chambers. Of course, this might help dress you up a bit." He pulled an object wrapped in a cloth from his pocket.

"What is it?"

"Open it and find out."

She peeled back the layers of fine linen to reveal a sapphire-studded gold comb. Her breath froze. "It's beautiful."

"I saw it and thought of you." He placed it the center of the elaborate hairstyle Katie had woven this morning. "The gold matches your hair, but the sapphires pale in comparison to your eyes."

She grabbed her mirror, admiring the way the dainty comb sparkled in her hair. How did she respond to a compliment like that? "I don't know what to say, Kell."

"'Thank you' would be a good start."

Any hostility she held toward him melted. She lowered the mirror. "Thank you for letting me borrow the comb tonight."

"Arden, I think you misunderstood. It's a gift."

"You mean I get to keep it? But Kell, it's too expensive. I can't possibly accept—"

"Please, let me spoil you while you're here. It's a simple gift, but the joy in your face increased its value for me far more than you can imagine."

She leaned closer to him. "Are you trying to bribe me?"

"Possibly." He stopped so their faces remained mere inches apart.

"Perhaps I should tell you I can't be bought." She

waited for Loku to call her a liar, but the only thing she heard in her mind was her inward plea for Kell to kiss her again.

"Pity."

His teasing only fanned the flames of curiosity burning inside her, and she succumbed to the need to kiss him again. She started soft, barely pressing her lips against his. When he tried to seize control, she pulled away.

His hands hovered over her shoulders like she was a fragile bubble that would pop as soon as he touched her. "The Lady Moon help me, I don't know if I can handle this torment much longer, Arden."

"What torment?" She ran her thumb along his bottom lip.

"Being on my best behavior when you—" His voice cracked, and his eyes pleaded with her.

She brushed a stray lock of hair from his face. "You are trying to be good, aren't you?"

"Only for you."

Cinder growled at Kell.

"Stop it, Cinder. Bad boy!" Her scolding probably would have been more forceful if his actions hadn't startled her.

The wolf turned to watch her, but the moment Kell took a step in her direction, his hackles rose with another growl.

Arden retreated a couple of steps. As long as the wolf stayed in the room, she and Kell wouldn't touch each other. *Probably a good thing.* She waited for Loku to add something, but his silence worried her. What had she and Dev done to him?

He offered his hand to her, his expression one of caution as he eyed the wolf. "Come along. Dinner's getting cold."

"Dinner sounds lovely." She offered him a smile as an apology for Cinder's behavior.

"And maybe for dessert—"

The low growl prevented him from finishing his

sentence. Cinder leaned against her leg and glared at the prince.

"I wasn't thinking of that kind of dessert," Kell replied with annoyance.

As if he understood what she said, the wolf trotted ahead to the door and waited for them. Wherever they went, he was coming along, too.

She smiled. "Sorry, but Cinder's rather fond of me."

"At least you know you have an overprotective wolf."

"Unfortunately, he's a bit confused on who's a threat and who isn't."

Kell raised both brows. "So I'm no longer a threat now?"

"On the contrary, I think you can be just as dangerous as Sulaino."

"Scared I'll turn you into some mindless slave?"

"Possibly." The more time she spent alone with Kell, the closer she came to understanding her mother's mistakes. Even the gift of the comb made her think of the pendant around her neck. But she began to recognize why her mother had surrendered to her lover, how a touch or a kiss could cause a lapse in judgment. Her fingers curled around her necklace. Would her mother ever forgive her for judging her so harshly?

The heavy rush of footsteps echoed down the hall. They stopped in front of the windows at the top of the large staircase that separated the east and west wings of the palace to allow the runner to pass. A beam of moonlight fell on the drawn face of a member of the Royal Guard. He jerked to a stop when he saw them and bowed. "Your Highness, I was sent to fetch you and the witch."

She winced in spite of herself. Would she ever get used to that term?

"Why?" Kell tightened his grip on her arm and turned his body so he stood slightly ahead of her. His protectiveness almost drove away the fear gathering in her chest.

The guard pointed a shaky finger to the window. Icy

fingers of dread crawled up her spine. Her body stiffened. She didn't need to look outside to know what waited for them. Instead, she reinforced her mental shields and bit back the fear that rose into her throat.

"Sweet Lady Moon," Kell gasped.

She squeezed her eyes together, not wanting to see it. Her heart pounded. The stench of rotting flesh invaded the palace walls. A tremble struggled to seize control of her body. She took a deep breath and opened her eyes. Time to face what she feared the most.

Thousands of glowing red eyes stared back at her from outside the city walls.

Chapter 30

For once, Arden was glad to have an empty stomach. At least she wouldn't have to worry about vomiting in front of Kell or his father.

The guard led them to a large office and closed the door behind them. Inside, the king, his sons, Larenis, and Dev waited for them. She wanted to hide behind something when they all turned to her.

Dev rushed to her side. "Shields up?" he whispered in her ear.

She nodded and dug her fingers into his arm. Thank the Lady Moon he was here. His presence helped ease some of the sick terror swirling in her gut. She scanned the room and saw a few more unfamiliar faces, but they all wore the same expression when they looked at her: fear mixed with suspicion.

King Heodis leaned forward in his chair. "Good. Now that everyone's here, let's discuss our options."

"May I ask what's happened so far, Father?" Kell squeezed her hand before crossing the room to the king's massive desk.

Larenis stood at attention. "Sulaino has surrounded the city, Your Highness. When the fog lifted about half an hour ago, we spotted them. He's sent what's left of Lord Yessling to the main gate to negotiate terms of surrender."

"Like I would ever surrender to that horse's ass." Heodis pounded his fist against the table. He nodded for the captain to continue.

"His request was simple. He wishes to speak only to the heir to throne and assures us that he will be returned safely."

"Alive or undead?" Dev's steely words caused a few people to grimace.

"Let's hope alive," Gandor replied. "Father, let's at least hear him out, perhaps find some way to buy us some more time."

"You're actually considering negotiations with a necromancer?" Dev's face darkened. "Do you have any idea what you're dealing with?"

"For a foreigner, you've been extremely opinionated about what we should do."

"Enough, you two. I have a throbbing headache, and your snipes aren't helping." The king massaged his temples. "What are your thoughts, Kell?"

She didn't miss the way the eldest prince scowled when the king asked his youngest son for advice. Sibling rivalry took on a whole new meaning here.

"If Gandor's willing to meet with Sulaino, it might buy us enough time to come up with a plan and learn what the necromancer wants."

Dev pushed her behind him. "I can tell you what he wants. He wants Trouble first, and then he'll use her powers to destroy the kingdom."

"Your theory is plausible, Sir Devarius, but I can't rest all my options on it."

Gandor stood and approached the desk. "With your permission, Father, I would like to engage him."

"With troops or peacefully?"

"I'll hear him out, but if I smell trouble, I'd like to have men just inside the walls waiting for my signal."

The king leaned back in his chair and stroked his beard. After a few seconds of silence, Heodis straightened. "Larenis, I want all of our archers on the wall, watching every move Sulaino makes. If they see anything that remotely appears like a threat to my son's life, turn Sulaino and his abominations into pin cushions. Is that understood?"

The captain snapped to attention. "Yes, Your

Majesty."

"Gandor, take three men you trust with you and watch your back."

"Yes, Father." He bowed and left the room with Larenis.

Arden couldn't shake the feeling that the prince seemed a little too confident. She leaned closer to Dev. "Shouldn't he have appeared a bit more worried?"

He nodded. "I agree. Something's wrong about this, and I don't want you going anywhere without me until we figure it out."

"Now, to form a plan. Any ideas?"

"Father, I stand by my original plan," Kell said. "Arden knows Sulaino's weakness. If we can find a way to have her use her magic– "

Dev shoved her behind him. "Prince Kell, how many times do I have to tell you that she's not a weapon for you to use?"

"But she's been the most effective opponent so far. We're simple men. We have our blades and our courage, but you know as well as I do that is no match for the army of undead surrounding us."

"And you have no idea what you're asking of her."

Anger mounted deep inside her, and the involuntary rush of fire flowed down her arms. She took a deep breath to steady her temper before she engulfed the room in flames. "Stop it, both of you. I'd like to make my own decisions without you deciding my fate for me."

"Come here, Arden."

Her heart skipped a beat at the king's command. She turned, walking toward the desk like it was her pyre. Her voice wobbled when she asked, "Yes, Your Majesty?"

"Since you claim to be able to make your own decisions, I'm going to ask you directly. Do you know how to defeat Sulaino?"

"I know how to kill undead, Your Majesty."

"And their creator?"

Doubt seeped into every pore of her skin, oozing into

her blood. "*Loku, can I do this alone?*" She prayed for answer, but none came. "I'm not sure."

Heodis furrowed his brow. "Not sure, or not willing?"

"Not sure, Your Majesty. When I battled Sulaino before, I had help. But now, I don't know if I'll have it again."

He turned to Dev. "What is your estimation of her abilities?"

"She is powerful, but untrained. To ask her to draw upon the help she mentioned could lead to catastrophic effects."

"You mean Loku?" Prince Therrin finally asked.

Dev gave a sobering nod. "The god of chaos has his own agenda, and when he grants you a favor, it usually comes at a cost."

She opened her mouth to add that he'd been unusually silent, but a sharp glance from Dev kept her quiet. She wanted to keep Sulaino from turning her homeland into a blight of undead. But her lack of confidence undermined her. She needed Loku in order to defeat the necromancer.

Heodis studied her with his dark eyes until she felt she had nothing left to hide from him. "What other options do we have?" He turned his attention to the other men in the room, who replied with a chorus of suggestions.

Her knees buckled. If Dev hadn't been at her side, she would've swooned.

"Let's sit in a corner until you've got your wits about you again," he said.

Relief washed through her now that she was no longer the center of the king's attention. How could she summon enough courage to take on a necromancer but have a mere mortal reduce her to a pile of cowardice by a simple glare?

Cinder sat beside her, watching her with worry in his yellow eyes. She scratched behind his ears to reassure him and held onto Dev's hand like her life depended on it.

The men continued their debate without them, talking about ways to summon troops and where the best places would be to fortify the walls. Several of them boasted how the unique design of Trivinus would require Sulaino to break through a series of gates before he'd reach the palace. But as she listened, Kell seemed the only one who raised concerns about the citizens in the outer walls. The rest of the unknown advisors negated them as necessary casualties. Her nausea returned in full force when she heard this.

Nearly an hour passed before Gandor returned. A strange light gleamed from his brown eyes, forming a stark contrast to his paler than normal face. She turned to Dev to see if he saw something worrisome in the prince, but her protector kept his emotions hidden.

Gandor held out a scroll. "Here are his terms."

The king took the paper and read it. A frown tugged at his lips from under his beard. Wordlessly he gave it to Kell. "His demands are simple. He claims he only wants Arden. If we hand her over to him by midnight tomorrow, he'll leave without attacking the city."

"For now," Dev bitterly added. "Once he's done with her, he'll be back."

"Dev's right. I don't trust Sulaino. He's bent on revenge, and he'll stop at nothing until he has it." Kell tossed the note on the desk in disgust. "There's a reason why he wants her. She's the only person who can defeat him, and he's playing on our fears of witchcraft."

"But you're the one always saying it's our duty to protect our people, Kell." Gandor pointed his thin finger at her. "Sacrificing her will save us and the people of Trivinus. What's the life of a witch compared to the safety of thousands?"

The room started to spin as all the blood rushed from her head. The pyre would be a kinder fate than being turned over to Sulaino.

Kell pushed his reddened face into Gandor's. "You're only thinking short-term, my nearsighted brother. You forget that with your enemies, you have to think three steps ahead."

"Boys, you forget the lady is still present." The king's

sentence brought an awkward hush into the room. "Sir Devarius, please accompany Arden back to her room and see that she stays there for her own safety. No one is to enter or leave her room without my permission. Violate this command, and you'll be the first person tossed over the city walls to that horde."

Heodis' threat wrapped around her like a cloak, shielding her from those willing to exchange her life for theirs. She took Dev's hand and left the room as quickly as she could without running. They rushed through the silent halls with Cinder on their heels, not daring to speak in public or delay their course.

Once inside the room, Dev cast wards on the door and windows. "We're safe for now."

Her heart fluttered so fast, she feared it would try and break free of its bony confines. "And how long will 'now' last?"

"I'm not sure." His grim expression told her "not long." "I need my sword."

"They still have it."

"I know, but at least I'm not entirely unarmed." He reached into his shirt sleeve and pulled out a switchblade. "Keep this with you at all times. There are rats in the palace, and I want to make sure you have something to skewer them with if they break in here."

She took it. The cold metal sent a chill up her arm. "Dev, I'm scared."

"Don't be. We're in this together, remember. And you still have Loku."

"No, I don't. I think we've driven him away or offended him or something because I haven't heard a peep from him."

"He's just contained. If you really need him, he'll break free. He seems to be rather fond of you." He brushed her hair back and looked like he wanted to add that he was fond of her, too, but she knew he'd never admit it. "Can you undress without your maid?"

"Yes, but why?"

"Remember how much fun it was to ride in a dress? Now consider making a quick escape in one."

She nodded, remembering the way hours in the saddle chafed her thighs. "I'll change into the boy's clothes."

"Good. I'll be on the other side of the portal if you need me." He disappeared through the wall, leaving her alone with Cinder.

She laid out the tunic and leggings and began to untie the knot in her laces. She'd just unraveled the first layer when a knock sounded at her door.

Dev stuck his head through the portal. "It's warded."

"Arden, are you in there?" The handle jiggled, followed by more persistent knocking. "Answer me," Kell's voice pleaded.

"I'm here," she replied.

"Why won't the door open?"

She cast a glance to Dev. "Um, maybe it's stuck?"

Kell rammed his body against the door. It shook, but the wood remained intact. "Arden, please, no games right now. I need to speak to you privately."

Dev entered her room through the portal. "Do you have your father's permission?"

"Ha-ha. Very funny, Dev. Let me in. It's important."

He waved his hand in the air, and the blue outline of the ward vanished.

Kell fell into the room as the door banged open. He pushed up on his elbows, wincing. "Let me guess— magic?"

Dev simply smiled and reclined in a chair. "Say what you came here to say."

"I believe I said I wanted to speak to her privately. That means alone, without you." He stood by the open door and waited for Dev to leave.

For once, she wouldn't have to worry about lust getting the better of him. Tension drew lines on Kell's normally carefree face. "I'll be safe with him, Dev. If I need you, you know how to get in here."

His jaw tightened. Her dismissal obviously perturbed

him, but he complied by leaving through the open door. "I'll be just on the other side of the wall."

Kell didn't repeat his behavior from earlier this evening. As soon as they were alone, he stood guard by the door instead of wrapping his arms around her. "I won't let Sulaino take you."

"Thank you. Is that all you wanted to say?"

"No." Anger replaced some of his anxiety, and he took two long strides in her direction. "Why aren't you willing to fight?"

"Kell, it's not that simple."

"Tell me why you have all this power at your fingertips, yet refuse to use it. I thought you were better than that."

Tears gathered in the corners of her eyes. "Please, don't judge me. You don't know half the story."

"Apparently not." He spied her travelling clothes laid out on the bed. "Planning on going somewhere?"

His accusations grew more and more bitter with each word. She fought hard to keep her voice from betraying her. "I thought it best to be prepared."

"Why are you doing this to me? I've done everything I can to convince you to stay and fight with me. I've seen to your safety. I've pleaded for your life. I've had your every comfort tended to while you were here so you wouldn't end up in the dungeons with the rats. Instead, you run away and hide behind Dev like a selfish little coward."

Her eyes burned as hotly as her cheeks. "Shut up. You have no idea what's really going on here. "

He closed the space between them and grabbed her by the shoulders. "I even thought if I treated you differently than most women, you'd…" His voice trailed off, and he shoved away in disgust.

"I'd what? Sleep with you and suddenly be converted to your cause? Sweet Lady Moon, it was all a trick. Everything. You actually made me think you cared about me." Revulsion clawed at her skin, making her feel as soiled as a two-lora whore. She reached into her hair and yanked the comb out. "Take your gifts and your lies," she said as she hurled it at him. It clattered on the floor. "I'm finished with your games."

He bent down to retrieve the comb, tracing the individual tines with his finger. "It's not a game, Arden," he replied in a husky voice.

A stray tear broke free. She swiped it off her cheek. "Yes, I know. Politics, I believe is what you called it. Go away, Kell. I don't want to even look at you right now."

"As you wish." His eyes never left the floor. "I'll go try to talk some sense into my father. I promised I'd keep you safe, and I won't let them give you to Sulaino, even if you decide to leave."

He quietly let himself out of the room, leaving her alone with the strange ache building in her chest. More tears slipped out of her eyes, and she no longer fought to contain them.

Dev ran into the room and pulled her into his arms. "Don't cry, Arden. Everything will be all right."

She buried her face into his chest and sobbed. Dev held her close and stroked her hair. After several minutes, her pain lessened enough for her to speak. "I can't believe I trusted him."

"Some lessons in life are harder to learn than others."

She wiped her nose with the back of her hand and looked up at him. "You're the only one I can trust. Please don't betray me, too."

He wiped the last tears from her cheek with his thumb, the color of his eyes reminding her of the fir trees that remained green even in the bitter cold of winter. "No, I'll never do that," he said solemnly. "You're stuck with me until one of us draws our last breath."

Hope, an emotion she'd almost forgotten, bloomed inside her once again. She tucked her head under his chin and let him hold her a bit longer. As long as she had him, she wouldn't have to face her demons alone. "Thank you, Dev."

Chapter 31

Dev waited until Arden's body stilled before he released her. He spent the last hour fighting the urge to castrate Kell. The only thing that held him back was the sobbing woman in his arms. How did she manage to stir such strong emotions in him? Anger, jealousy, fear, lust. All things he'd buried deep inside when he swore his oath to protect the Soulbearer over a century ago. And yet, she managed to resurrect them to a height he never thought possible.

"I'm sorry, Dev. I didn't mean to keep you here so long."

He knew the tone in her voice well enough now to hear the tinge of anger in it. "Don't be too harsh on yourself. Kell didn't come by his reputation by waiting for women to throw themselves at him. At least you learned his true intentions before you fell into his trap."

She nodded, staring at the floor. Her bottom lip quivered.

Damn, he didn't mean to upset her again. Awkwardness twitched in his muscles like dozens of worms. "You should get some sleep."

She nodded again. "I need to change first."

She sounded so innocent that something ached deep inside him. Shit, this couldn't be happening. Not like this, and definitely not now. He didn't need this kind of distraction. He needed to remain numb and detached if he was going to figure out a way to get them out of this mess, not wanting to rip apart anything that tried to hurt her. He backed away from her to clear his mind. "I'll step out for a moment, then."

He rubbed his eyes. The skin around them felt too tight. The long nights sleeping in the chair next to her bed were taking their toll. He glanced at her bed and longed to lie with his body curled around hers. His sleep seemed so much more peaceful when she was near him.

Damn it. Pull yourself together, man. You're beginning to sound like one of those whiny, lovesick fools the bards always sing about until you want to puke.

"Dev, could you help me for a moment?"

He jerked his head around.

She sat on the bed with her arms behind her, reaching for the knot in her laces. "I'm having trouble untying my dress, and I don't want to have to call Katie at this hour."

It took three swallows to open his throat up. Did she have any idea what she was asking him to do? To help her remove her clothes and not explore the creamy flesh that lay under them?

She's just been betrayed by Kell. I don't need to pick up where he left off by trying to get under her skirts.

He took a steely breath and kept his eyes on the knot. If he focused there, maybe he wouldn't notice the rest of her body. The smell of roses wafted from her skin. Longing threatened to seize control of him. *Steady. Keep your game face on, and don't let her know how close you are to slipping the fabric from her shoulders and tasting her skin.*

"Done," he announced and stepped back toward the portal. The sooner he got away from her, the sooner he could regain what few threads of self-control he had left.

"Thank you." Her swollen and red-rimmed eyes watched him with confusion.

The way she held the loose bodice to her chest under the light of the three moons made her look even more like some helpless waif on the street. Protective urges like he'd never felt before clawed their way to the surface. His heart began to beat faster. "I'll be back in a few minutes."

"No." The one word froze him halfway through the

portal. "You need some real rest tonight, Dev, especially if we need to make a quick escape or battle undead tomorrow. Why don't you sleep in your bed instead of the chair?"

"I need to protect you."

"But you placed wards on the windows and the doors. No one's coming in tonight unless they know how to break them."

Thank Jussip she could think more clearly than him at the moment. "You have a point."

"Please, rest, and don't worry about me. I'll be fine in the morning."

Realization jolted through his body. She was pushing him away. *Probably for the best,* he told himself as he nodded, but it didn't dull the sting of her rejection. "If you need me, I'm right on the other side."

"I know."

He entered his empty room and stared at the perfectly made-up bed. He pulled back the covers and crawled under them fully clothed and armed. The hard metal of his concealed weapons dug into his ribs, making it difficult to find a comfortable position.

***

Sulaino drummed his fingers on the message box, waiting for the glow announcing a new message. Three hours had passed since he gave his terms to Gandor. The snotty little prince seemed all too happy to give him what he wanted. Greed did odd things to men's minds. Gandor seemed so focused on claiming his father's crown that he never realized the golden-haired witch's worth.

"Shame on him for being such a fool, but lucky me." He plucked a late-season grape off a plate. The first frost of the season crystallized the sugar inside, creating a sweet syrup when he popped it into his mouth. "What do you think, Yessling?"

The former lord answered with a blank stare.

He laughed. "Oh, I forgot. You're undead now. No more talking. I think I'm coming to enjoy it."

The message box began to glow like an oil lamp. "Oh joy!"

The contents of the note met his expectations. The king refused to hand over the Soulbearer, but a mutiny was forming right under his nose because of it. He'd have her before the deadline he set.

Sulaino laid the paper aside with a grin. He could afford to be patient now. One more day, and everything would fall into place.

He stepped outside and began to cast. Thick fog rolled in from the river banks, shrouding his entire forces from the prying eyes of Heodis' forces. Tomorrow night, the people of Ranello would know the true meaning of fear.

***

Arden looked out the window, watching the fog cover the three moons. Was Sulaino leaving? The continued icy dread that filled her heart answered her question. He was still out there, waiting for her.

She'd managed to cry herself to sleep earlier and woke up alone her bed. Well, technically, not alone, Cinder's coarse fur remained within reach if she needed reassurance. She ran her fingers through it and savored the warm heat radiating from his body.

Dev's behavior tonight bothered her more than an inn full of rowdy drunkards. Whether he was angry or disgusted by her reaction to Kell's betrayal, he couldn't wait to get away from her. Of course, she didn't blame him one bit. All this time, he'd warned her to stay away from the prince, that he only meant to use her, but she'd blindly ignored him. The bitter truth was hard to swallow when she learned it.

Cinder's head popped up, and his ears perked forward. A low growl rumbled through his body.

"What is it, boy?" she whispered.

He crouched as still as a statue, staring at the portal.

She sat up and grabbed the switchblade Dev had given her. Something didn't feel right, but she couldn't place her finger on it. After slipping her feet into the suede slippers by her bed, she tiptoed closer to the portal. "Dev?"

Chaos erupted on the other side of the wall. The sounds of furniture creaking and muffled voices filtered through the portal. Cinder bolted past her, disappearing into Dev's room. A man cried out in pain.

Her heart beat faster than a hummingbird's wings. It was the only thing in her body that dared to move. Fear paralyzed the rest of it.

The struggle continued in the other room. Then Dev's voice shouted, "Trouble, run!"

The mortar holding her feet to the ground cracked. Dev was being attacked, and she was standing there like a coward instead of running in to help him. Sour disgust rose into her throat. She flicked the blade of her knife open and ran blindly into the next room.

A grunt greeted her as she buried the blade into the first body she collided with. Thank the Lady Moon it wasn't Dev. A pair of hands grabbed her from behind, but she slashed any piece of exposed flesh she could get to.

Three men struggled to restrain Dev to the bed. A pair of dull silver manacles circled his wrists with a chain between them, but that didn't stop him from punching one of his captors. "Trouble, get out of here."

"No." She punctuated the word with another stab into an attacker. Warm, sticky blood coated her hands, and the smell turned her stomach.

"Stop messing around and get the witch," Larenis commanded from the doorway. "And remember, she needs to be alive."

A crack, followed by a thud, came from the bed. Dev's limp body lay unmoving on the sheet. Her throat closed up. *No, not Dev.*

Now that they'd subdued him, they turned on her. Three of them pushed her toward the corner, cutting off her escape. The faint moonlight glittered off their weapons. The acid stench of sweat mingled with the metallic smell of blood in the small room. Their chests heaved, but they all stood still as if they waited for the signal to attack her.

Flames replaced the fear inside her, spreading through her limbs like a wildfire. They may have swords, but she had magic. She'd burn the palace to the ground if she needed to.

Another cry of pain pierced the silence. A soldier struggled to wrench free from Cinder's jaws, but the wolf held tight. Seeing his determination to keep fighting strengthened her resolve.

"Get the girl and kill the wolf," Larenis barked from a safe distance of the brawl.

Coward, her mind hissed.

One of the men lunged at her. She held her breath and twisted to avoid his hands, only to find herself face to face with another's blade. He slashed at her. A squeal escaped her lips as she jumped back.

Cinder released his victim at the sound and ran toward her.

"Look out," a voice warned just before the wolf sank his teeth into the thigh of one her attackers.

"Get it off me!" The man's sword clattered to the ground, and both hands gripped Cinder's head.

"Gladly," one of his comrades answered, plunging his blade into the wolf's chest.

Time stood still. Her vision blurred with tears. "Cinder!" her voice screamed, but it seemed to come from a distant place. Blood rushed in her ears, growing louder as her rage built inside her. Her magic begged for release. A string of curse words erupted from her mouth in sync with the bolts of blue lightning from her fingertips. The soldiers flew across the room when it hit them, leaving holes in the plaster walls from the impact before crumpling into unconscious heaps.

Arden sank to her knees. Everything around her faded from view except the bleeding wolf at her feet. *Damn stupid, loyal wolf.* Sobs choked her throat. She ran her hands through the blood-soaked fur, searching for the source of the red river flowing across his body. "I'm not going to let you die," she whispered.

Her fingers sank into the squishy flesh of the wound, and her stomach heaved. This was more serious than Ortono's wound. Cinder's chest still moved up and down but grew fainter with each breath. Time was running out. She focused on the wound and saw the layers of torn tissue in her mind. Her magic took hold of her, flowed into Cinder.

She managed to staunch the heaviest bleeding before someone grabbed her from behind. A cloth doused in something that stank like overly fermented fruit covered her mouth and nose. The interruption ripped her from the healing spell, draining her energy with it. She tried to struggle, but with each inhalation of the sickening smell, her eyes grew heavier.

"Grab the chains before she casts another spell."

I can't give up. Need to keep fighting. Won't surrender. Her thoughts became slurred, and her muscles refused to obey her mind. Blackness closed in around her as the cold metal circled her wrists.

Chapter 32

Kell poured another glass of wine and stared at the dim light that filtered through the fog. He wanted to feel giddy drunk or at least numb, but the wine didn't have its usual effect. Every time he closed his eyes, he saw the betrayal on Arden's face. It ate away at his gut like a gallon of vinegar.

"Damn it!" he shouted and hurled the glass at the wall. The crash echoed in his mind, wine-coated shards tinkling across the floor. He'd been so close to having it all come together perfectly. So damn close...

His head ached, and the pounding at the door only made it worse. "By the light of three moons, stop."

"Unlock the door then." Bynn. Of all the times to have an overly concerned friend, this wasn't one of them.

"Leave me alone."

"Not likely." A series of clicks came from the other side, and the door sprang open. "I knew learning how to pick a lock would come in handy one day."

"You're in. I'm alive. Now piss off."

"You're drunk, and you look like shit. I'd be a bad friend if I let you continue to drink alone." He sat down at the table next to him and eyed the untouched food. "Let me guess: dinner?"

"I lost my appetite."

"Listen, if this about Sulaino—"

"Sulaino can go fuck Gandor for all I care." The image of that flickered through his mind, and he snickered. His self-absorbed brother deserved it.

"Ouch!" Bynn poured a glass of water and shoved it

into his hand. "Drink this instead. You need to sober up if we're going to form a plan to deal with that mess out there."

"I don't wanna sober up. I wanna feel something other than what I'm feeling now."

"And what's that?"

He wasn't drunk enough to admit it out loud, even to his best friend. Instead, he just pulled the gold and sapphire comb out of his pocket at tossed it onto the table.

"Ah, the lady witch."

Calling her a witch rankled his insides as much as the smell of stale piss. "Stop calling her that."

"What happened between you and Arden?"

"Why the fuck do you care?"

His friend pouted. "That's a bit uncalled for."

"Well, so is you picking a lock to get in here." Every lash of his anger relieved some of the pain inside his chest. He wondered how much longer Bynn would sit there and take it.

"I'm not leaving until you're better."

He gulped the water in the glass, and his stomach lurched. "Why do you have to be such a pain in the ass sometimes?"

He shrugged. "Because you'd do the same for me. Now, tell me what she did."

"She let me down."

"Because she didn't want to risk her neck? Not too surprising."

"Then she accused me of playing games with her to recruit her to my cause." While the rest of his mind felt as foggy as the weather outside, he remembered every word of their argument with crystal clarity. "She told me she didn't want to look at me anymore."

"Can't say I blame her. You *were* using her."

Kell rubbed the greasy stubble on his cheeks. "It started out that way, Bynn, but then, things changed."

"Who'd have thought she'd be the one to snare you?"

"Yeah, who'd have thought it?" he muttered. He

reached a shaky hand across the table and refilled the water glass while Bynn went to the door to speak to one of the servants. When his friend returned, he added, "I wonder what my father's going to do with her now."

"Gandor's campaigning pretty hard to turn her over to Sulaino. He's got most of the lords on his side, too."

"Including your father?"

Bynn snorted. "He remembers when your father burned Sulaino's family. It happened in Nevarro, after all. The only thing I've heard him say about the matter is that we should've burned him with the rest of them."

"Too bad we can't go back in time and fix our mistakes." He knew the one thing he'd do—not let her get under his skin like she did. If he could manage that, then he wouldn't be wallowing in wine-induced self-pity like he was now.

"When pigs fly and Elslyn learns to smile."

A snicker worked its way past his lips.

Another knock came from outside. "That's awfully fast for breakfast," Bynn said and opened the door.

A pale-faced Ortono stood in the hallway, his shaking hand wrapped around a piece of paper. "May I have a word with you, Your Highness?"

Kell rubbed his aching brow. "What is it?"

He glanced at Bynn and gulped. The faint light of suspicion filled his eyes. "It's a private matter concerning Lady Arden, Your Highness. If it pleases you, I'd prefer to speak to you alone."

"You don't trust Lord Bynn?"

He stared at the floor. "I know he's not too fond of her, Your Highness, and I have reason to believe something bad has happened to her—"

Kell bolted from his chair so quickly, it landed with a bang that reverberated through his head. He closed his eyes and clutched the table to steady himself. "What?" he asked through clenched teeth.

"She's disappeared, Your Highness."

Those four words stole his breath away. He leaned

back to sit and would've fallen flat on his ass if Bynn hadn't shoved a chair under him in time. He sobered up quicker than he ever had in his life. "Come in here and tell me what happened."

Bynn added another chair to the table. "Have a seat."

Ortono's face went from pale to ashen, and the awkward way he shifted from foot to foot revealed his uncertainty at being treated this way by nobles. "I'm not sure if that's proper."

"Just sit," Kell ordered in a tone he used with his dogs. "This isn't a time to be overly concerned with formality."

The young soldier's eyes still flickered to Bynn. "I went to the east wing to check on her this morning and give her a small token of appreciation my wife made for saving my life, and I thought it odd there were no guards outside her room. I knocked, and the door swung open. Her bed looked like it'd been slept in, but she was gone."

Now it was Kell's turn to glare at Bynn. "Do you know anything about this?"

He raised his hands in the air, palms forward. "I swear to you on my life, Kell, I know nothing of this."

"Wait, Your Highness, there's more." Ortono's hand trembled as he gave the piece of paper to him. "I saw this on her desk. It was addressed to you."

Kell yanked the note out of his hand and ripped open the wax seal. He perused the contents and frowned. It contained just a few simple lines about how Sulaino was his problem and how she and Dev were leaving for Gravaria while they could, but it felt wrong. The writing was too crisp and the letters too well-formed to be Arden's. He'd seen her attempts at learning how to write yesterday.

"What does it say?" Bynn took the note and read it.

"It doesn't matter what it said. Arden didn't write it."

"Don't delude yourself, Kell. She ran away while she could. I don't blame her one bit."

He pounded his fist against the table so hard, both men jumped. "You're not using your head. I'm drunk, but I still remember that she's nothing more than a simple barmaid. Dev spent the last two days teaching her to read and write her own name. This doesn't look like the handwriting of someone who was just learning her letters."

"So Dev wrote it for her."

"Bynn, think. Take a good look at that note. Does the handwriting look the least bit familiar to you?"

His brows knitted together as he studied it, and then rose in sync with his gasp. "Kell, you don't think…"

"I don't think—I know. You said yourself he's campaigning to get rid of her. What better way than to make it look like she's escaped?"

"But he's your brother."

"He's an ass, and we both know it." He stood and, for the first time this morning, the room didn't sway when he did. He grabbed his sword in one hand and the soldier's tunic in the other. "Ortono, let's go investigate her room. Something's very wrong about this."

"I'm coming, too." Bynn halted when they both turned to him. "What? So maybe I was a bit suspicious of her at first, but she's shown that she's not dangerous. Besides, what kind of nobleman would I be if I didn't help find the damsel in distress?"

"Just remember, she's my damsel." Kell gritted his teeth together and followed the young soldier.

When they came to her room, it was just like Ortono had described. No guards stood in front of the doors. An unnatural silence filled the room. The sheets chilled his fingertips when he ran them over the unmade bed. Hours had passed since she'd slept there. He searched the room for more clues but found none. No signs of a struggle.

Bynn shuffled through the papers on her desk. "I can see what you mean about her learning how to write," he said, holding up a piece covered with her gawky letters.

"There's nothing here. Let's go next door."

"Dev's room?"

"Yes. Remember, where she goes, he goes, too."

The hairs on the back of Kell's neck stood on end

when Ortono turned the unlocked handle. The mess inside made his already-sensitive stomach want to heave. Blood splattered the floor and the sheets. Furniture lay in splintered pieces around the room, and a wounded wolf raised his head to growl at them. He froze inside the doorway and cursed under his breath.

"Sweet Lady Moon, what happened here?" Ortono's wide eyes mirrored his own.

"Well, you were right about one thing—something bad happened to them." Bynn ventured into the room, carefully stepping over the remnants of a broken chair and keeping a safe distance from Cinder. "Or at least to Dev."

"You'd think if they killed him, they'd leave the body behind." He followed his friend's trail into the room.

Ortono seemed to be the only one brave enough to come near Cinder. He extended a shaking hand and crouched low to the ground. The wolf regarded him with glittering golden eyes and finally leaned forward to lick his fingers. The soldier smiled, ran his hands through the matted fur. "They left us one clue."

"What's that?"

"Cinder. He never left her side, so if he's in here, that means she was, too."

Of course. How could he have forgotten how the wolf wouldn't let him kiss her last night? "Ortono, you're well on your way to a promotion."

His grin widened. "My wife would like that."

"So, we think she was here with Dev. That doesn't explain how she got out of her locked room, past two sets of guards, and into his locked room." The smug expression on Bynn's face quickly vanished as he went to lean against the wall and continued falling through it.

"But that does." Kell rushed over to the place where his friend's legs emerged from the wall. "I was wondering how Dev managed to get into her room without being caught."

Bynn jumped to his feet, brushing off his clothing like hundreds of spider webs covered it. "Damn magic!"

Kell reached forward. A cold tingle raced up his arm where it disappeared through the wall. He took two steps forward and found himself standing in Arden's room. "Very clever. It's like the wall doesn't exist."

"Kell, get the hell back in here. I don't like not being able to see you."

He walked back into Dev's room with only a slight rush of air grazing his spine to let him know he'd passed through a wall. "I'm beginning to like this."

"Only because you'd have a way to sneak into ladies' rooms undetected." Bynn's scowl almost soured the experience.

"Don't tell me you wouldn't use it if given the chance."

"Your Highness, I don't mean to interrupt, but shouldn't we be looking for Lady Arden?"

The worry in Ortono's voice jerked him back to the problem at hand. "Good point. Any ideas, gentlemen?"

"You've already pointed out our number-one suspect," Bynn said. "This reeks of Gandor."

Kell nodded. "He's the only one I can think of, too. I doubt Sulaino could have snuck his undead in here and left without turning the whole palace upside-down."

"I know Captain Larenis wasn't too fond of her, either, Your Highness." Ortono continued to stroke Cinder while he spoke.

"And Larenis has his lips firmly glued to your brother's ass in hopes he'll get a title when Gandor takes the crown."

Kell closed his eyes to gain control of his swirling thoughts. The metallic scent of dried blood filled his nostrils when he inhaled, and his stomach lurched. "Let's talk about this more in my chambers. The less ears that overhear, the better."

"What about Cinder?"

"How bad are his wounds?"

Ortono ran his hand across the wolf's chest. "Not too bad, but when I touch them, my fingers sting like my arm did when Lady Arden healed it."

"Magic?"

He shrugged. "Maybe, Your Highness."

Kell crossed the room and knelt beside them. Just as Ortono described, something felt different when his hand neared the wound, as if the air around was charged with energy. "Dev once said something about being able to heal himself. Maybe Cinder's the same way."

"Yes, Your Highness, but I feel bad leaving him behind like this. Could we ask Cero to look at him?"

He caught the wolf's gaze and held it. Neither one of them blinked for almost a minute. "Fine, but if we take care of you, Cinder, you need to drop the guard-dog act around me."

He responded by giving him a wolfish grin, complete with his tongue hanging out of the side of his mouth.

"Come on, Bynn. Let's carry him back to my chambers and put our heads together. Ortono, I want you to stick to Larenis' side like glue. Tell him I sent you to work with him today. If he so much as sneezes a hint about Arden's whereabouts, I want to know about it. Got it?"

The soldier jumped his feet and nodded.

He caught him just before he dashed out the door. "And another thing, Ortono, don't let anyone know what we suspect. Play along with their story of her running away. You'll find out more if their guard is down."

"Yes, Your Highness." He disappeared out of the room.

Bynn knelt on the other end of Cinder and lifted him with a grunt as Kell slid a sheet under the body to use as a sling. "You owe me for this. I never thought I'd be playing nanny to a wolf."

"It's no different than carrying one of our wounded men back from battle. Besides, if you play nice with him, he'll play nice with you."

"Lovely."

They wrapped Cinder up in the sheet and carried him back to the west wing. Kell's mind whirled the entire way, trying to figure out what his brother did with Arden. When he found out the truth, there'd be hell to pay.

Chapter 33

The steady drip of water echoed through the darkness. Arden opened her eyes, then immediately shut them. The lone beam of light that pierced the darkness shone right in her eyes. She smacked her fuzzy tongue against the roof of her mouth and wished for something to drink.

"Would you like ale or a nice red wine?" a deep voice asked.

"Loku! You're back."

"I never went away. I've been with you during this whole disaster. Serves you and Dev right for containing me."

"How can I hear you now when I couldn't before?"

"Check out your new jewelry. That's magic-imbued mithral you're wearing. Not only will it be all the rage next season, but it's also great at blocking any magical powers, including any old spells you've cast."

Arden looked up at the manacles around her wrists. The chain that ran between them wrapped around a hook above her. No matter how she tugged, she couldn't wrench it free. She tried to summon her fire, but nothing flared within her. Her heart pounded. *"Loku, did they destroy my magic?"*

"No, just blocked it. Sort of how you and Dev blocked me from warning you about Larenis and his goons." The bitter accusation in his voice made her cheeks burn.

"Would it help if I apologized?"

"I want more than an apology."

"I'm scared to ask what." She tugged on the chains again.

"Trouble?" a weak voice rasped a few feet away from the darkness.

"Dev? You're alive?" Tears sprung in her eyes. She searched the darkness while waiting for her vision to adjust to it.

"You didn't sound that happy when you found out I was back."

"Jealous?"

"Depends—is this the void?" Dev asked with his usual cynicism.

"Would we be chained in the void?"

"Good point." He groaned and rattled his own chains. A whispered curse followed a few seconds later. "I can't summon my magic."

"That makes two of us."

"Speak for yourself," Loku interjected.

"Can you channel your magic through me?"

A snort shook her body. *"As if I would want to help you after what you did to me."*

She stiffened. If he wouldn't help them, who would? The acidic tang of hopelessness closed her throat. She forced herself to breathe. When she exhaled, it came out as a shudder. "I'm sorry," she said to both Dev and Loku.

"Sorry for what?"

"For getting you into this mess."

"Trouble, this isn't your fault."

"Yes, it is. If I had just thought before I acted, if I had listened to you and Loku, I wouldn't have gotten all cocky and ran head-first into battle that night. Then, we wouldn't have gotten captured, and we wouldn't be rotting in this dungeon." A memory from the previous night stabbed her chest like a knife. "And Cinder would still be alive."

"Cinder? What happened to him?" His voice grew tense with worry.

"He ran in front of me and got stabbed. I tried to heal him, but there was so much blood."

"Did he catch on fire?"

"What?" When he repeated the question, she

wondered if the blow to his head addled his brain. "No."

"Then he's still alive. Or was, anyway, when you saw him last. Fire wolves burn themselves into ashes when they die. If you healed him enough to slow the bleeding, chances are, you bought him enough time to heal himself."

Some of her despair retreated. Cinder could still be alive. Thank the Lady Moon for that small blessing.

"As for me, I've already told you before that I admired your bravery. You chose to face Sulaino when the odds were stacked against you. You came out on top then, and the same could happen now."

"Are you talking about luck?"

"I think Lady Luck is smiling on you, or you wouldn't have made it this far."

She stared out into the darkness, and the smell of death and mildew filled her nose. "But what if my luck has run out?"

"Do you really think that, my little Soulbearer?"

"Well, you're still pissed off at me."

"I can be very forgiving at times if someone shows me they're truly sorry."

"I'm sorry we contained you, but you were trying to take me over without my permission. It scared me."

"Apology accepted for now, but I'll remember this incident. I may call on it in the future when I want you to do something for me."

"Then it's not really forgiveness. It's blackmail."

Her shoulders ached from keeping her arms above her head for who knows how long. At least she was sitting. Across the room, Dev stood against the wall with his hands manacled like the top of a huge Y. She couldn't see his feet. "How are you holding up?"

"I've been better."

Guilt gnawed away at her gut. "I hate to see you suffer because of me," she whispered.

"I'm your Protector. It's my duty to do all in my power to keep you safe."

"But you hardly know me. I'm just some girl who got

too close to the previous Soulbearer when he died."

His sigh echoed through the cell. She wished she could see the expression on his face. Was he angry with her? Frustrated? Biting his tongue to keep from hurting her feelings? When he finally spoke, his voice turned husky with emotion. "With the previous Soulbearers, I felt that way. I protected them because I swore an oath to, not because I wanted to. It was my punishment to bear. But with you, Arden—" His voice broke. "With you, I'd protect you even if you weren't the Soulbearer."

Her heart raced, and warmth flooded her body. Could cold and callous Dev have feelings for her? "Why?"

"Not because you're easy to live with." He sounded like his old self again, and part of her grieved for the loss of the man who spoke to her just seconds before. "You've been a constant pain in my ass since I've met you. But you're different from the others, too. Instead of using your power for yourself, you've chosen to use it to help others."

"Except when I told Kell I wouldn't help him fight Sulaino."

"Forget about that. You're only a human, and you have limitations. You weighed the risks of letting Loku gain control of you and made your decision. I can't fault you for that. You've done more for these ungrateful Ranellians than most would expect of you."

"But why do I feel like I let people down?"

"Piss on them."

She laughed in spite of herself. Just having someone to talk to made this place more bearable. She stretched her leg out, brushed his foot with her toes. The brief contact sent another warm wave of hope through her. "If I have to have someone stuck down here with me, I wouldn't pick anyone but you."

"That's not magic making you feel all warm and fuzzy."

Her cheeks burned despite the cold damp of the dungeon. *"And what is that supposed to mean?"*

"You know as well as I do that you have feelings for

Dev. Let's not have this discussion again."

"Of course I do. He's the one friend I have. He's the only person I trust."

"I mean something deeper than that. I may have been contained, but I witnessed every little exchange between you two over the past few days."

Dev didn't reply to her compliment. An uneasy silence settled over the room, making her doubt Loku's observations about Dev even more. Her mind battled her emotions and quickly buried them. They were stuck here until their jailors decided what to do with them. She tried to think of an escape plan, but her eyelids grew heavy, and she dozed.

***

The clank of keys, mingled with men's voices, woke her. The beam of sunlight that blinded her before had vanished, throwing the cell into complete darkness. A damp chill invaded the room and her aching muscles. She stretched, grazing her foot against Dev's again.

"Shh," he hissed.

"Move quickly," a voice ordered on the other side of the door. "We don't want to keep him waiting."

"Yes, Your Highness."

Arden lifted her head and peered into the abyss. Could someone have found them? Which of the princes stood outside? Were they taking her to the king? Her heart pounded. If they were still down in the dungeons, the news probably wasn't good.

The door opened, and torchlight filled the cell. Faces came into view, none of them friendly. Captain Larenis wore his usual sneer. He crossed the room, dropped his torch into the holder near her, and began to unhook her chains.

"Are you sure the manacles are on properly?" the first voice asked. The firelight illuminated his gaunt features and cast sinister shadows over the recess of his face. Gandor.

"They're on both of them, Your Highness. I have the

only key."

"Good. I don't wish to have anything go wrong tonight."

"And what are you planning, you sick son of a bitch?" Dev's words echoed off the walls and startled the eldest prince.

"That's no way to speak to royalty, elf." He backhanded Dev, drawing a grunt. "Perhaps when I'm king, I'll pay your empress a visit and teach you Gravarians proper manners."

"Good luck."

Dev's defiance inspired her. As soon as she felt some laxity in the chains, she whipped them around, catching Larenis in the face. He stumbled back with a cry and covered his cheek with his hand. "You little bitch!"

She swung again, putting all her meager weight into it. Then struck him again.

Before she could get a fourth swing in, something caught her chain and jerked her backward. She tumbled to the ground. A wave of pain ran up her back after the impact, forcing the air from her lungs.

"That's quite enough from you, witch." Gandor pressed the tip of his sword against the center of her chest. "If Sulaino didn't want you alive, I'd kill you myself."

"That makes two of us," the captain of the guard muttered as he rubbed his nose.

"Larenis, if you can't handle a simple girl who's chained and has her magic repressed, how can I expect you to lead my men?"

"Men are easier to control than this wench," he said with a jerk of the chain. He tightened his hold on it, and the prince withdrew his blade.

"I see the key. It's in the pocket just inside the Captain's overtunic on the right side."

"I'm hardly thinking about picking his pocket when I have a sword above my heart, Loku."

Dev laughed in the background. "And people wonder why I call her Trouble." Even in the dim torch light, she could see his eyes narrow. "So, you're planning on turning her over to Sulaino? And let me guess—Daddy doesn't approve?"

That comment earned him another slap to the face. At least the prince shook his hand and winced after the blow. "Next time, I'm using my sword."

Dev's tongue darted out, licking the blood that trickled from his busted lip. "What do you hope to gain by working with him?"

Gandor's icy fingers outlined her jaw, sending a shiver down her spine. "What's rightfully mine. I give over the girl. Sulaino helps me become king. Simple trade."

"But you're already heir to the throne," she replied. "Why can't you be patient and wait for you father to die naturally?"

He snorted. "We've all seen how he fawns over his bastard." When she looked at him in confusion, he raised a brow. "Surely, you knew? If my father hadn't disposed of his first wife—my mother—Kell would've been born a bastard. As it was, his mother's belly was already swollen with him when my father married her."

"He's still the third son. He'd have to kill off you and your brother before he became the heir."

"Wrong. All my father has to do is change his heir, and the throne is Kell's. I'm going to make sure that never happens."

"So this all comes down to jealousy." She narrowed her eyes and regarded the eldest prince with disgust so intense, it made her happy to have an empty stomach. "Figures. You're half the man Kell is."

He yanked her to him. The smell of stale wine flowed from his mouth when he spoke. "Is that so? Perhaps I should have a little dalliance with you, too, just to prove you wrong. Sulaino only said I need to bring you to him alive." His tongue flicked across her ear lobe, and her breath hitched. "He never said I couldn't have a bit of fun with you first."

A stream of words in a language she didn't understand

spewed from Dev, followed by a kick to Gandor's face that sent the prince sprawling. She would've fallen to the floor as well if Larenis hadn't held on to her. "You keep your hands off of her." Dev punctuated each word with another kick, bringing his knees up to his chest and catapulting them forward until his chains restrained him.

Gandor rolled away and drew his sword in one fluid movement. "You've outlived your purpose, elf."

Everything around her moved in slow motion again. A scream sat poised on her lips as the tip of the sword punctured Dev's gut. She didn't remember if she released it or not. Her heart ached as though the blade had pierced it instead of Dev. Her pulse stopped for a few seconds. An agonizing eternity passed while she watched the sword go deeper and deeper into his flesh. The smell of blood stung her nose, and tears burned her eyes. The room began to swirl into blackness. *No, please, not Dev.*

Gandor withdrew his blade with a sickening wet slurping sound, and Dev slumped forward.

Chapter 34

Kell crouched in the darkness. Bynn's heavy breaths throbbed in his ear. He jostled him.

"What?" Bynn whispered.

"I said I wanted silence, not the sound of an old man's dying wheezes."

"You know how much I hate the dark."

"Hate" would be an understatement. Kell could almost smell the ripe stench of his fear. "Pull yourself together."

"Do you have any idea what you've put me through today? First, you force me to be nice to Gandor and follow him around. Then, how long were we hanging on to that narrow ledge outside his window when he almost caught us going through his things?"

Kell rolled his eyes. "You whine more than a baby. Besides, we weren't hanging on to a ledge. We crept along it until we came to my window. And it gave us the perfect opportunity to overhear his plans."

A wave of nausea rolled through his stomach as he remembered the conversation between his brother and the captain of the guard. He wished he could blame it on his overconsumption of wine last night, but treason packed a stronger wallop than alcohol. At least they learned what they were planning on doing with Arden, even if they couldn't discover her location.

"Do you really think this is going to work? What if they have more men with them than expected?"

Annoyance prickled his skin. "Do you want to lose the element of surprise?"

Gandor had stressed the importance of secrecy. There

would only be the two conspirators and their hostage in the tunnel tonight, and Kell had Ortono and Bynn with him.

He closed his eyes and mentally mapped out the cavernous room. Four tunnels all met here under the palace. One led to the dungeons and traditionally served as a way to dispose of the bodies of those who perished there. One led up to the west wing of the palace. The other two served as escape routes in a time of siege. He didn't know which one Gandor would be coming from, but he knew which tunnel he'd take—the one leading to the outermost wall of the city. From there, he'd hand over Arden.

He tightened his jaw until his teeth ached. Part of him wished he'd told his father of Gandor's plans, but the king would've sent a score of men down into the tunnels to intercept them. His brother would catch wind of the ambush and probably abort his plan. No, the smaller group that waited with him was much better. They all knew of Gandor's plot and agreed recovering Arden was their first priority.

Voices echoed from the tunnel leading from the dungeon. Kell coiled his muscles, ready to spring as soon as they came into view. Torchlight flickered off the walls. He turned to his left. Bynn seemed to be holding his breath. To his right, Ortono slid his hand over the hilt of his sword. He braced his feet against the stone, feeling for a dry spot so he wouldn't slip. They were more than ready.

As the other group neared them, sobs mingled with the angry male voices, and his heart wrenched.

"Larenis, shut her up. We're coming to the main cavern, and I don't want anyone to hear us."

Something muffled Arden's cries, and he moved forward to rescue her. A hand grabbed him, pulled his back. In the dim shadows, Bynn shook his head. *Not yet.* Damn it, his feelings for her almost made him run head first into battle without thinking. He turned to his friend and nodded in thanks.

Fire illuminated the group when they stopped at the entrance of the cavern. Gandor stood in front with a torch in his hand. Behind him, Larenis held Arden, his hand clamped tightly over her mouth. A set of dull grey manacles with a chain stretched between them bound her wrists. She writhed against her captor.

Kell sunk deeper in the shadows, waiting until they came closer.

Gandor studied the three remaining tunnels. "This is the one that leads to the outer wall," he said as he pointed his torch toward them.

Now was as good a time as ever. Kell motioned for the other two to remain hidden and drew his sword. "Going somewhere, Gandor?"

Larenis howled in pain and shook the hand away from Arden's mouth. Two lines of teeth marks dented the flesh of his fingers.

"Kell." Fear twisted the way she said his name, but relief eased some of the tight lines of her face.

Gandor fumbled for his sword. "What are you doing here?"

"I could ask you the same thing."

As if on cue, Larenis drew a knife and pressed it against Arden's throat.

"Step aside, or she dies." Gandor's eyes glittered in the firelight.

"If I remember correctly, she's no use to Sulaino dead."

"We have you outnumbered, little brother."

"Oh, is that so?" Boots of his comrades thudded against the rock behind him, and he smiled when his brother's jaw dropped and the captain's knife wavered.

Arden took advantage of the distraction and jabbed her elbow into Larenis's ribs. A whoosh of air escaped him. She lunged forward, only to cry out in pain. A line of red appeared on her upper arm, spreading along the fabric of her tunic like spilled ink on paper.

Kell tightened his grip on his sword and hissed through his teeth. He'd have Larenis' head after everything he'd done to hurt Arden. "Let her go, and I'll plead your case to Father. Maybe he'll show you mercy, too."

"If I take her to Sulaino, I'll never have to worry about Father's mercy."

Arden frantically clawed at something, although he couldn't see what. Larenis repositioned the knife against her throat. She held her gaze with Kell's when he met it. Her lips trembled, but the determined set of her jaw told him she wasn't ready to surrender.

"Why are you doing this? Are you trying to become some kind of hero?"

"He's plotting to take the crown, Kell," she answered, despite the blade pressed against the place where her pulse throbbed. "He's trading me in exchange for the king's death."

"That's quite enough from you," Larenis growled, and a new line of red appeared on the side of her cheek.

Anger seared his veins. His baser instincts wanted to tear Gandor and Larenis into shreds and feed them to the dogs, but he had to be careful not to hurt Arden in the process. "This is your last warning, Gandor. Let her go. Don't become a pawn in Sulaino's game."

"Like you've become a pawn in your little witch's? I think not." He swung his sword at him, following it with a counter-swing of the torch.

Kell jumped to the side. Two breezes tickled his skin from where they fanned the air, first cool from the blade and then warm from the flames. He lunged toward his brother, not caring if he killed him.

Gandor caught his blade between his sword and the torch and tossed him to the side. Kell hit a wet patch and slid into the cavern wall. Stars bloomed on the fringes of his vision. The clang of metal behind let him know one of the others had stepped into his place, buying him enough time to get to his feet before attacking again.

Larenis used Arden as a shield against Ortono. "I'll have you executed for failure to obey orders," he told Ortono.

"I answer to the prince, not you." The young soldier's

eyes darted from side to side, looking for a weak point without harming her. His sword remained poised as he slowly forced his captain against the wall.

Bynn's grunt pulled Kell away from Arden and back to the other fight. His friend grimaced as he strained to keep his face from being singed by the torch. Bloodlust clouded his vision. He sprang toward his brother. Gravel crunched under his feet. Gandor turned just in time to avoid his strike. Kell swerved to the side to prevent hitting Bynn. Frustration knotted his shoulders, and he cursed his lack of sleep for slowing his reflexes.

The clank of metal and an ear-piercing scream halted them. His blood turned to ice, and he shivered when he turned in its direction. Steam rose from Larenis' face where Arden pressed her hands against it. The thick hum of magic pulsed through the cavern, seeping into his soul. The scent of burning flesh made Kell gag.

"It's time you knew the fury of a witch," Arden said in a low, cold voice. When she released him, two blackened handprints marred his cheeks. Larenis stumbled to the ground and continued to wail in agony.

Then she spun around and faced him, kicking away the chains that once bound her wrists. For a brief second, he understood why people feared witches. The green halo in her eyes flashed, and her expression hardened, making her appear like she was something other than human. She became a goddess of vengeance. An ominous feeling hung in the air around them as they all waited for her strike. White light glowed from her fingertips. "You'll pay for what you did to Dev."

A bolt of magic ripped through the room and connected with Gandor's chest. He flew across the room and hit the stone wall of the cavern with a crunch. His eyes widened, and a strangled cry escaped his lips before he slumped to the floor.

A gust of wind blew away the remnants of the magic, leaving a panting Arden in its wake. Her eyes widened when she surveyed the damage. Her hands trembled.

Blood trickled down her cheek and dripped on her shoulder, but she made no effort to staunch the bleeding. Was she even aware of what she did?

Kell took a step toward her, but she backed away. "Arden, it's all right," he said as he coaxed her toward him. "You're safe now."

Something small clattered to the floor near where she stood. A sob choked her words. She whirled around and ran into the tunnel leading back to the dungeon.

He started after her, but his feet remained planted to the ground. As much as he loathed his brother, he didn't want him dead from a witch's spell, especially when he wanted to get Arden out of Trivinus alive. "Is he breathing?"

An ashen-faced Bynn knelt next to Gandor, checking for a pulse. "Yes, but I'm sure he's got a few broken bones."

He didn't need to ask if Larenis was still alive. The incomprehensible blubbers that came from the opposite side of the cavern told him the captain of the guard still lived, although he'd probably be scarred for the rest of his life. "Ortono, Bynn, take them up to my father and explain what happened."

Bynn jumped to his feet. "If we tell him the whole truth, she'll burn."

A lump formed in his throat. Up until this moment, she'd only used her magic to help others. Now, she'd unleashed her wrath against the captain of the guard and the First Prince of Ranello. To pardon her could lead to a major upheaval in the order of things. He swallowed past the lump and pushed it down until it sank into his stomach like a brick. "They both deserved what they got."

The hardness in his voice frightened him almost as much as his intense fear for her. A dull ache formed in his chest when he realized the only way she was going to survive this was if he let her go. He had to sneak her out now before his father changed his mind and before Sulaino's undead army swarmed the city. He picked up the small key that she'd dropped. "I'm going after Arden. I'll be back in a few hours."

"A few hours?" Bynn let the unconscious Gandor flop back to the floor in an undignified heap. "What the hell are you planning now?"

The corners of his mouth twitched. "I'm going to rescue the damsel in distress." He grabbed a torch and ran down the tunnel to the dungeon.

Chapter 35

Arden tripped over a stray rock and went sprawling across the damp stone floor of the tunnel. Pebbles dug into her palms and chin, but she ignored the stinging pain that came with them. Her mind focused on one goal—to get back to Dev. Maybe if the Lady Moon smiled on her, he'd still be alive, and she'd be able to heal him.

Her lungs burned from running and the sobs that tried to force their way to the surface. She refused to cry. Tears wouldn't solve anything. Action would.

"Keeping going, my little Soulbearer. You're almost there."

She picked herself off the ground and began sprinting. Darkness obscured her path, but she felt as though something other than her eyes guided her through the twists and turns.

"Turn left and you should see the first torches at the edge of the dungeon."

She followed Loku's direction and quickened her pace when she spied the faint orange glow reflecting off the wet walls. Her heart pounded. *Please let him still be alive.*

She ran along the line of cells, peeking through the small slats until she found the right one. She tugged on the door, then shouted in frustration when she found it locked. Magic flooded her fingertips and blew the door off its hinges.

"Your magic grows more impressive with each passing second."

"Shut up, Loku." She crossed the room in a few steps and cupped Dev's cheeks in her hands. His clammy skin

sent a chill down her spine, turned her stomach into knots. "Dev?"

A faint groan answered her, and she finally let her tears fall. *Thank the goddess!* She reached up to unhook his chain and lower him to the floor, silently cursing the fact that she'd dropped the key to the manacles back in the cavern. His eyes remained closed, the sound of death rattling his breath. Sticky blood coated his tunic and gathered in a puddle at their feet. "Hang on, Dev. I'm not going to let you go this easily."

She pulled him close to her and pressed her ear against his chest, focusing on the faint thumps of his heart. Every fiber of her being pulsated with magic as she directed it toward his wounds. A strange emotion glowed within her.

She doubled her efforts to heal him. She wouldn't let him die until she drained all her magic into him. Images of the damaged organs filled her mind. A bright white light shone from the holes in them, becoming smaller and smaller as they knitted closed. It was working.

The magic began to ebb as though the well containing it had run empty, and only a trickle flowed from the cracks. *Please let this be enough.*

A pair of arms wrapped around her to answer her prayer, and the steady beat of Dev's heart vibrated through his chest. "Shh, Arden. I'm here."

Sobs wracked her body when she heard his voice, and he tightened his embrace. She hadn't lost Dev. He was alive, and she was safe in his arms once again. Giddy elation made her head swim, and laughter mixed with her weeping.

"Sweet Lady Moon," Kell gasped behind them. "Dev, are you…" His words trailed off before he finished his question.

"I'm fine now because of her." His voice sounded raw, and she dared to lift her eyes to see him. Just as she saw in her room that one morning, a myriad of emotions swirled in the dark green depths of his eyes. Awe slackened the normally sharp contours of his face. He traced the wound on her cheek. "You're hurt."

"Just a few scratches. Nothing compared to what Gandor did to you."

"I'll rip his heart out for this."

"Actually, Larenis did that to her." Kell knelt beside them and pulled one of Dev's hands off her. A click of a lock echoed through the cell. One of the manacles fell to the ground. "I'm glad I picked this up when you dropped it."

So was she. Numbness filled her fingers, making them clumsier than usual. The magic had leeched all her energy. She leaned against Dev and closed her eyes while Kell removed the chains.

"Where are they?" Dev asked.

"Bynn and Ortono are taking them upstairs to my father." A faint breath tickled the back of her neck. "Arden, are you well enough to travel?"

Travel? All she wanted to do was fall asleep right here.

"She will be," Dev answered for her. Warmth radiated from his hands and chased away some of her fatigue. The pain in her arm vanished, and she sighed. "Better?"

She nodded her head, too tired to thank him for healing her in return.

"Let's get out of here while we still have time." Kell wrapped one arm around her back and pulled her to her feet with Dev. "Sulaino said he'd attack if we didn't hand her over by midnight, and I want you as far away from here as possible before then."

His plan managed to snap her out of the sleepiness that threatened to overwhelm her. "What?"

Kell half led, half carried her out of the cell. "One of the tunnels leads to the front wall of the city, but there's another that goes under the river. If I can get you there, you should be halfway to Boznac before Sulaino realizes you're missing."

Her legs stiffened, and she jerked to a stop. Something had changed.

"He no longer wants you as his weapon, my little Soulbearer."

Her chest tightened. She hadn't expected this from him. "You're helping us escape?"

He simply nodded.

Before she could ask another question, Dev spoke. "I'll need to be better armed, then, if I want to get her safely to Boznac."

"There should be your choice of weapons in the main guard room. I'll start leading Arden down the tunnel. Meet us there when you're done."

The world seemed to be turned upside-down. Dev jogged into another room like he was in the prime of health. Never mind he'd nearly bled to death minutes before. Her own legs barely cooperated with her, and Kell was leading her to a place where she'd be free. She shook her head, trying to make sense of it all.

"You tend to do that sometimes."

"Do what?"

"Make men question themselves and change the course of their lives."

She almost laughed. Instead, she leaned closer to Kell and drew comfort from the subtle smell of bay leaf that rose with his own scent. So different than Dev, but just as familiar. Her mind mulled over everything that had happened in the last day. How could he have gone from trying to seduce her to helping her bruised and battered body out of a dungeon?

He cleared his throat. "Cinder's healing remarkably quickly. Is he magical, too?"

She halted again. "Is he well enough to come with us?" The thought of moving to a strange land without her beloved wolf almost made her want to start crying again. *Damn, I need to pull myself together and stop acting like an over-emotional child.*

"You've been through a lot. Don't be so hard on yourself." A sensation of someone hugging her filled her with warmth and comforted her.

"Not yet. I'll keep him with me until I can return him to you."

She turned and searched his face, looking for some sort of clue in his transformation. Last night, he'd acted like she betrayed him by not wanting to fight. "Why are you doing this, Kell?"

He sucked in a breath through his teeth. His face revealed his inner turmoil, tightening one minute, then going blank the next. "Arden, I—" He stopped, glanced at the floor, and licked his lips. When he looked back at her, he tried again. "That is, I—" Again, he struggled to find the right words. He pulled her into his arms and crushed his lips against hers.

His kiss wasn't like any of his previous ones. It seemed raw, gritty, demanding. When she gasped in response to it, his tongue filled her mouth, pleading with her to allow him this moment to express his feelings for her. She yielded, and the rhythm of the kiss changed. It grew more tender, almost sad, as if he hated saying goodbye to her but knew it had to be done. Each stroke of his tongue and lips spoke of his desperation and told her that his heart was breaking.

Something in his kiss frightened her more than the threat of the necromancer waiting outside the city walls for her. Kell really did care for her. Maybe even loved her. But she knew her heart belonged to someone else. Someone who would never show her this type of intense emotion. Someone who valued duty above everything else.

A moan came from the depths of his throat, and he finally withdrew. He held her face in his hands, wiped the moisture from it. "Please don't make this any harder than it already is."

"Kell, I'm sorry."

He shushed her and placed a gentle kiss on her forehead. "Right now, the only thing that matters to me is getting you out of here alive. I'll deal with Sulaino, and I promise I'll find you if I survive."

The end of his sentence pierced her already aching

heart like an arrow. *If he survives.* An image of Kell's
hazel eyes staring lifelessly up at the heavens sent a shiver
down her spine and made her skin burn where he touched
her. She wrestled free of him and turned away, unable to
bear being this close to him and keep herself together.
Confusion swirled in her chest, making it hard to breathe.
How could she care this much for him when she loved
Dev?

*"It is possible to love two men in entirely different
ways, my little Soulbearer."*

She chewed her swollen lip and tasted his kiss. Steel
formed in her veins. She knew what she needed to do. She
wasn't going to let Kell die, either. Not when she could do
something to save him.

"Arden, did I say or do something wrong?"

She looked at him, and her heart wrenched when she
saw the pain etched on his normally carefree face. She
took one of his hands in her own and caressed his cheek
with the other. He brought their hands to his chest. The
steady beat of his heart helped her find the right words.
"I'm not leaving."

His pulse quickened, and his fingers tightened around
hers. "Don't be ridiculous. It's the only way."

She shook her head, grinning. It was time to stop
playing the coward and destroy Sulaino once and for all.

*"Ah, vengeance suits you. Of course, we'll cause a
little chaos along the way, right, my dear?"*

"I can't do this without you, Loku."

The god's squeal of delight widened her smile and
renewed her energy like a good night's sleep.

Kell's fingers fell slack, but he didn't release her even
when Dev joined them. "Talk some sense into her. She's
refusing to leave now."

Dev lunged for her as if he wanted to throw her over
his shoulder, but she easily danced away from him. A
scowl twisted his mouth. "Trouble, stop playing games."

"I will once I'm done with Sulaino." She took a deep
breath and stared at both of them with her back straight

and gaze steady. "I'm going to fight, and you're either with me or against me."

For a moment, neither man said anything. A heady delight, almost like having too much ale, rolled through her.

"Trouble, don't be ridiculous."

Kell nodded. "Dev's right. There's no way you can take on that army alone."

She stubbornly lifted her chin and crossed her arms. "I won't be taking them on alone." She let her gaze rest on Dev to let him know exactly what she was planning.

His face hardened. "Don't even consider it. The consequences—"

"Are mine alone to bear. Personally, I'd rather live in an insane state of bliss knowing I did something to help others rather than have guilt slowly consume my mind."

"I have half the mind to beat some sense into you." He took another step toward her and swiped his hand, hoping to catch her arm. Instead, he only fanned the air.

"What kind of protector would you be if you did that?"

"One who kept you alive."

"Do you doubt our power?"

"That's right. Remind him I'm still a god, even if I'm trapped inside your body."

"Dev may be able to use magic, but I'm just an ordinary human."

"She's not talking about us." Dev clenched his hands into fists. "Don't do it, Trouble."

"You're not changing my mind. I told you before: I'm a Ranellian, and I won't sit back and watch my homeland overrun with undead."

"Damn it, woman, it's a suicide mission."

"Perhaps, but I'll take my chances. Besides, I'm the Soulbearer. You're my protector. Time to remember that oath you pledged."

Kell's forehead wrinkled in confusion. "Am I missing something?"

"It's none of your business, Your Highness." Dev's

face darkened, and he stared at her as if daring her to challenge him further.

"Let's just say I have an ally I can call upon when needed." She looped her arm through Kell's. "Now, if you would be so kind as to show me which tunnel leads to the city wall, I'd greatly appreciate it."

He shook his head, but his feet moved with hers. "This is insane."

Her lips curled up into a smile. "Exactly. Sulaino will never expect it. It's the only thing we have to our advantage." She paused and looked behind her. "Are you coming, Dev?"

His knuckles glowed white in the torchlight. "You're going to be the death of me, Trouble."

Her laughter sounded hollow to her ears, but she needed to bolster her courage if she was going to go through with this. "Nonsense." Once they crowded into the dark, narrow tunnel, her smile faded. *"I hope we know what we're doing, Loku."*

Something that felt like a hand pressed against the small of her back in a possessive gesture. *"Trust me. Now that I'm no longer restrained, I won't let anyone hurt us."*

Chapter 36

The smell of death overwhelmed her other senses and made her want to retch. She pinched her nose as they neared the outer wall, thinking it would block the stench, but it still filled her mouth. Even if she ignored it, she still couldn't escape the coldness that crawled along her skin and tried to smother her soul. She fought off the despair and doubts that plagued her mind and put one foot in front of the other.

"Any ideas yet, Loku?"

"A few. I need to see the layout of the land first."

"I thought you were an all seeing god."

"And you're a cheeky little barmaid."

Her giggle caused both her companions to turn and stare at her as if she was losing her mind. Kell shook his head and continued down the tunnel, but Dev lingered next to her, studying her like a scholar would a book. "Are you sure you want to do this?"

She nodded, and pushed past him.

He grabbed her arm and tugged her back. His breath tickled her ear as he said, "Is this your decision or someone else's?" His eyes flickered to Kell.

"You heard him earlier. He wanted me to leave." She shook her arm free. "This is my choice, Dev. Not his. Not Loku's. Mine."

Her words bolstered her courage for a moment, and she strode down the tunnel like she was going to a reception in her honor instead of her possible execution. A few feet later, she ended up chewing her bottom lip and playing with her pendant. *"Loku, are you sure we can do this?"*

His laughter vibrated through her body and chased the chill away. *"If you can believe Dev's story, I almost destroyed the world once. Even if Sulaino's a necromancer, a mere mortal doesn't stand a chance against me."*

"But you had your own body then."

"Yes, but if you're a willing conduit for my power, then it's almost the same thing."

"Almost?"

"Well, I didn't have tits then."

A slight breeze blew across her breasts, and her nipples hardened. She crossed her arms over them. *"You're such a pervert."*

"I don't think you mind."

The tunnel ended abruptly in a narrow alley that was barely big enough for one person to fit in. "This is it," Kell whispered.

"Is there a way for me to see what's on the other side?"

"Here." He slid a metal slat to the side, and the rotting corpse smell rushed into the small space. Even Kell looked slightly green in the torchlight. He squeezed past her to other end of the alley. "Have a look."

She stood on her toes to peer out the small opening. Dozens of red eyes illuminated the landscape. Only two of the moons shone overhead, but they gave her enough light to survey the land. *"What do you think now, Loku?"*

"I think it's time we test your elemental power with earth."

"What?"

"We need to get outside to where you can touch the ground."

"And then?"

"Then we give those living corpses a proper burial."

"What about Sulaino?"

Loku took longer than expected to answer that question. *"We may need help with him."*

She turned back to the other two. They'd retreated from the wall and sought the cleaner air back in the tunnel. "If Loku and I get rid of the army and distract Sulaino, do you think you can finish him off?"

Dev stared at Kell's sword. "Is that the same one you had the night we first met?"

He nodded. "Why?"

"Because it can pierce magical shields. Nine to one, Sulaino will have one in place, making my spells and weapons useless until he lowers it. You would have to make the first strike before I could do anything."

"So we have a plan then?"

The men exchanged glances, and each nodded.

She took a deep breath and wondered where all her spit had gone. "Good. I'll go out and do my part. When you see a chance to go after Sulaino, take it."

Dev held her shoulders and pushed her against the wall of the tunnel. "You're not going out there alone, Trouble. I won't allow it."

Her heart pounded from the intensity of his expression. It felt like he wanted to bend her to his will with only his eyes. "You have to. I don't want him to know about you and Kell until you're right on top of him. Please, it's the only way this plan will work."

A muscle rippled along his jaw before he looked away and released her. "Fine, but I'll be right behind you."

She drew another breath. This one shook her to her very core. It was time to see what she could do with the god inside her. "How do I get to the other side?"

Kell held up a large key. Rust roughed its surface, and when she took it, flakes crumbled into her hand. He covered her hand with his own. "I meant what I said about not wanting to lose you, Arden," he whispered low enough so only she heard him.

Her heart did a little flip-flop. "Stick to the plan, and we won't fail."

"You could have been an actress, my little Soulbearer. You have them convinced that you know what you're

doing, and this whole time, you're so terrified, you're about to wet yourself."

"Shut up, Loku." She entered the alley alone. After some pressure, the key fit into the lock and groaned to a click. She closed her eyes and counted to ten before pushing the hidden door in the city wall open.

"Shields up."

She followed Loku's instructions and took a step out.

The undead that milled around the wall parted and let her pass. Their expressionless, half-rotted faces bore little resemblance to what they must have looked like alive. Her heart ached for them. Where they as tortured as Dev said they were?

"Are you ready, my Soulbearer?"

"Ready as I'll ever be."

"Then let's begin." Magic gathered deep inside, pushing against the confines of her body and threatening to explode.

She gritted her teeth, tried to contain it until the right moment.

"Don't fight me. Give yourself to me, and we can defeat him."

She nodded and surrendered to the chaos god inside her. The magic pulsed stronger and stronger with each beat of her heart, coming in like waves crashing against a dam. Now was the moment. "Sulaino," she shouted into the crowd, "if you want us, come and get us."

Her voice deepened with each word until it was no longer her own. Loku now controlled her. Her vision blurred, and the last thing she remembered was slamming her palm against the ground and the rush of magic that poured from her fingertips.

***

The first roll of the land caught Kell off balance. The second one knocked him off his feet. "Sweet Lady Moon, what's she doing?"

Dev snatched him by the collar and dragged him out of the way from the showers of rock that crumbled from the walls. "Earth magic."

The next wave collapsed the tunnel behind them. The bitter taste of fear filled his mouth. His heart jumped into his throat. "Let's get out of here."

"For once, I agree with you, Your Highness." Dev shoved his shoulder against the door, opening it just wide enough for them to pass through one at a time. "After you."

He fell through the opening and landed face-first in the mud. Disgust oozed from him like the muck between his fingers. Some way to treat a prince. If they survived tonight, he needed to have a talk with the arrogant elf.

When he lifted his eyes, his jaw dropped. Arden crouched less than ten feet ahead of him. Waves of bright green magic pulsated from her hand into the ground, each one turning into a rumble of the earth that radiated out like ripples in pond. As the first waves struck the undead, they knocked them to the ground. Then the subsequent waves formed large clay hands that sucked them deep into the earth. The land outside the city instantly turned into a mass grave.

"Look out!" Dev jumped in front of him and rolled him to the side. A warm blanket of magic wrapped around him, deflecting the boulder-sized chunks of the outer wall that fell around them.

Magic crept along his skin, but it no longer unnerved him like before. "You're using one of those shield things, aren't you?"

"Yeah, but I sometimes wonder why I bother. You seem to be in a hurry to have your head cracked open."

"Remind me to thank you later." His stomach heaved as if he were on a boat in rough seas. He closed his eyes until the waves became less violent.

The earth storm waned after several agonizing minutes, and when he opened his eyes, only two figures stood in front of him: Arden and Sulaino.

"Ready?" Dev released him and reached for his sword.

The film of magic that surrounded him retreated,

exposing him once again to the icy chill that sucked all the happiness from him. He pushed himself up from the ground and noticed that the mud hardened and cracked as though it had been frozen. His fingers wrapped the hilt of his sword as he focused on the necromancer in the distance. "Ready."

"Remember, you have to strike first."

He nodded, casting a glance at Arden. She'd risen to her feet now with her arms outstretched in front of her, aiming the tendrils of green magic at Sulaino. Her grimace revealed her efforts to keep fighting, but the slump of her shoulders showed that she had almost reached her limit.

Ahead, a small mound of earth encased the necromancer's lower body. The same clay hands that effortlessly sucked the undead underground minutes before clawed at his arms and his robes. They tugged at him, but he shrugged them off. Jagged red streaks of light that shot out from his fingers pummeled an invisible wall a few feet from Arden. With each second, they pushed it further back.

Kell tightened his jaw. "Let's get him before he hurts her."

He sprang to his feet and raced toward Sulaino. Footsteps crunched against the hardened clay behind him, letting him know Dev was right on his heels. He raised his sword, ready to strike as soon as he got close enough.

The necromancer turned to him with shock clearly on his face. The red magic dimmed from his fingers, and the earthen mound climbed up his chest. A snarl curled his lips as a bolt of magic snaked across the field at him.

Another blanket of magic encircled Kell, but the blow still knocked him off his feet as if he'd been punched in the gut. The taste of blood filled his mouth.

Dev grabbed his arm and pulled him up. "Keep running. I'll protect you from him."

He looked back and saw Arden drop to her knees. His mouth went dry, and his throat constricted. The wall now only stood inches from her face. He fought the urge to turn around and protect her.

"Stop wasting time," Dev growled behind him. "If her shield breaks, she's dead."

That was all the encouragement he needed. He dug his toes into the ground and ran until his lungs felt like they were going to burst. More bolts of red magic bounced helplessly off the shield Dev cast around them as they closed the distance between them. Time to kill that bastard before he took the one thing on this earth that he cared about. He aimed the tip of his blade straight at Sulaino's heart and didn't slow down until the crunch of bone vibrated up his arm.

Arden's cry of exhaustion echoed across the plain in harmony with the necromancer's death shriek.

Kell threw the weight of his body behind his sword and continued to press through Sulaino's flesh until the bloodied tip appeared on the other side. He stared into the face of the man who caused so much terror and destruction through his kingdom. "Time for you see what waits for you in the void," he spat with one final shove of his sword.

Sulaino's mouth hung open, and his eyes bugged out. A spasm racked his body. His one hand grasped Kell's. "Fool..."

"Step back, Kell," Dev ordered. His sword sliced through the air and lopped off the necromancer's head in one clean swing.

Flames engulfed the beheaded body, forcing Kell to jump back before they ignited his clothes. The ashes disintegrated and dispersed in the wind. Now there was nothing left of the necromancer.

Relief surged through him. They'd done it. All three of them. Sulaino was nothing more than a memory.

An eerie silence hung in the air as if everyone inside the city was scared to breath. His lungs burned, and a stitch in his side reminded him of how hard he pushed himself tonight. But there was still one more thing he needed to do. He sheathed his sword and stumbled back to Arden.

She lay face-down on the ground. When he rolled her over, her pale face appeared grey in the moonlight. He gathered her into his arms. Seconds ticked by as he watched for the subtle rise and fall of her chest, fearing the worst.

"She's not dead," Dev said as he approached. The necromancer's head dangled from his hand. "I would know it if she was."

"How?"

"I'm her protector." If he knew his vague answer perturbed Kell, he didn't show it. His lean face seemed tense when he knelt next to them. "She needs to sleep for a day or two, and then we'll know more about her condition."

"What do you mean?"

"I warned you that if she channeled Loku, there could be dire consequences, and I didn't mean the collapse of the outer wall." He visibly struggled with the next sentence. "She may not be the same person when she awakens."

Kell traced the outlines of her cheekbones and jaw. She appeared to be the same as before, no different than the first night he saw her. Just a skinny girl with hair the color of sunshine. His chest tightened, and he pulled her closer until he felt her warm breath on his neck. He had to hope for the best. "She'll be fine, Dev. You'll see. She's stronger than we give her credit for."

Chapter 37

Dev stared across the sunny room at Kell. The young prince rubbed his sagging eyelids for the third time in the last five minutes, but he refused to leave Trouble's side. "Get some sleep. She's not going to wake up any time soon."

He shook his head like a stubborn child. "I want to be here when she does."

"I'll send for you the minute she stirs." It was a lie, but one he wanted the prince to believe. He didn't want Kell to witness her mental deterioration before he had a chance to evaluate her. After her display of power last night, she could've well turned into Robb. His gut clenched at the thought.

"You promise?"

The corner of his mouth twitched. "I give you my word as a knight."

Kell snorted. "We both know what kind of knight you are." He brushed a stray piece of hair off of her face. "But unless I can crawl into bed next to her…"

Dev crossed his arms. He'd allowed the prince's doting so far, but he drew the line with him sharing Trouble's bed. A twinge of guilt stabbed him when he remembered how much he enjoyed lying next to her, but he saw no reason for Kell to know about that. Instead, he glared at him until the prince retreated from her.

"Fine, I'll sleep in my own bed. But remember, you'll send for me the moment she starts to wake up."

"Of course, Your Highness."

Kell bent over and pressed his lips to Trouble's

forehead, causing something to clench in Dev's gut. He envied how freely the other man could show his affections for the girl. But he knew the reason why more than ever now. If he'd allowed his feelings for Trouble to get the better of him last night, they'd all be dead. His head, not his heart, had protected them from Sulaino's magic. He just hoped he'd made the right decision letting her fight Sulaino instead of locking her up in the dungeon.

"I'll be back in a few hours, then."

Dev nodded and waited until he was alone before he sat in his chair next to the bed. Dark smudges circled the lower half of her eyes, creating a stark contrast to her waxen complexion. If he didn't see her breathing, he would have sworn she was dead. He resisted the urge to hold her in his arms while she slept. Was it selfish of him to want to be the first person she saw when she opened her eyes?

She sighed softly and nestled deeper into the pillows. A smile played on her lips.

He tensed, preparing to send for the prince, but when made she made no movement afterward, he relaxed back in the chair. A dream. That's all it was. He wondered what it was about. Hopefully, nothing like the dream Loku sent him. He didn't know if he'd be able to resist this time.

"What do you have in store for her, Loku? You've won her over. How much further are you going to push her?"

The god didn't answer.

He pressed his knuckles into his chin. Even if she was awake, the king still declared them prisoners. After last night, no one would deny that she was a witch. The entire city watched her destroy the necromancer's army. It took a small band of men surrounding them to get them through the city streets and back to the palace. People pressed up to them, their cries of gratitude mingling with their cries of fear. He balled his fingers into a fist. Yes, the Ranellians were happy to be alive, but they didn't want to thank the witch that saved them.

Even the king shared their reaction, only he seemed more troubled. Bynn and Ortono had brought Gandor and Larenis to him before she saved the city. He'd seen their battered and burned bodies and knew the savior of the kingdom had also attacked his heir and the captain of the guard, two symbols of his authority. Heodis spent most of the night with his gaze flickering back and forth between her and Sulaino's head while he listened to the series of events. The first rosy fingers of dawn had pierced the sky before he waved them away, saying he needed to sleep before he reached a conclusion.

Dev rubbed his temples. At least Heodis wasn't making any rash decisions. He just wished time wasn't ticking against them. Thick frost covered the land and coated the windows this morning. Storm season would be coming early this year.

He mused over their situation until the sun rose higher in the sky. A beam of light crossed the window, flashed on her pendant when she rolled her head to the side. He waited for a few seconds to see if she stirred again before placing the flat gold square in his palm. She'd always kept it hidden from him, but now he had a chance to study it.

His eyes widened when he saw the Elvish writing on one side. No wonder she just dismissed it as random etchings. He peered closer at the inscription. "To Alisa, the brightest star in the sky." He flipped it over. His blood turned to ice when he saw the Milorian Rose, a symbol of one of the oldest Elvan families in Gravaria, on the back.

He released the pendant as if it burned him. The room swayed, forcing him to close his eyes. How could she be connected to the Milorians? She was just a barmaid from a remote corner of Ranello. The political ramifications alone boggled his mind.

When his eyes opened, the first thing they focused on was the scar on the top of her ear. He brushed his fingers against it, eliciting the same trembling reaction as before. He traced his own ears. The light touch sent tingles through his body that grew more intense as he neared the tips. A shudder ripped through him. He stopped, jumped to his feet, and gripped the windowsill to steady himself.

None of this makes any sense. He searched his memory for any information she'd given him about her parents or the pendant. Her father had seduced her mother while she worked in the palace nearly twenty-two years ago, the same time the last Gravarian delegation visited Trivinus. By Jussip, if her father was a member of the Milorian family…

His breath hitched. He already feared losing her to Loku. Who knew what twisted plans the Milorians would have for her once her heritage was discovered? She'd become a pawn in their games.

An image of her lashing out her frustrations at her absent father flickered in his mind, followed by her stream of heated words. She wanted nothing to do with him, whoever he was. Relief cascaded through him. He'd protect her from the Milorians.

At least that explains a few things, he thought grimly. Her power, her appearance, her grace and quick reflexes. All signs of a heritage he'd refused to acknowledge until now. When he brought her before the Empress or the Mages Conclave, would they notice? Once again, the name "Trouble" suited her all too well.

Outside, fat white flakes started to fall from the clouds above. He frowned. No ship would sail from Boznac until the spring. At least it gave him time to research the members of the last Gravarian delegation and learn the identity of her father without raising too many suspicions.

***

Arden's stomach growled loudly enough to rouse her from her dreams. How many days had it been since she'd last eaten anything? She opened her eyes and lifted her head. The familiar east wing room surrounded her, complete with Dev dozing in the chair next to her bed. Her mouth curled up into a smile, and she covered his hand with her own.

He jumped at her touch. Once he blinked the sleep

from his eyes, he leaned forward and searched her face. "How are you feeling?"

"He's trying to see if you've gone mad."

"Have I, Loku?"

"No, my dear Soulbearer. I promised you I wouldn't do that to you." He paused and added, *"But that doesn't mean we can't have a little fun with him."*

Laughter welled up inside her, threatening to explode. After everything they'd been through, could she possibly play a trick on Dev?

"Trouble, why aren't you answering me?" He tightened his grip on her hand and practically hovered over her. "What's Loku telling you?"

"Who's Loku?" she asked in a dazed voice. "And who are you, for that matter?"

A curse flew from his lips. He tried to untangle his fingers from hers, but she held on and yanked him to the bed. He froze as he rolled on top of her, pressing her deep into the soft mattress.

Dev's weight didn't feel as uncomfortable as she'd imagined it would be. Instead, it stirred something deep inside her, dredging up feelings of desire and contentment. Fire raced along the length of her skin where he touched her. She traced the sharp angle of his jaw with the tip of her finger, reveling how strange it felt with its lack of stubble, and inhaled the blend of spices and leather that made his scent unique.

"Arden, are you well?" He licked his lips, but his gaze never left hers. A hard ridge pressed into her stomach.

"Ah, see? His desire matches yours."

The hunger grew in his eyes, widening the black centers and darkening the remaining green rims into the color of cypress trees. Every muscle in his body tensed. He seemed to be waiting on her.

She needed to taste his lips, to know if they affected her the same way Kell's did. "Yes, Dev, I'm perfectly fine here with you." She lifted her face to close the gap between them.

"Damn it, Arden." He shoved her shoulders back into the mattress and flew from the bed. Agitation replaced the hunger in his face as he paced the room and ran his fingers through his hair. "What kind of joke are you trying to pull on me?"

"It wasn't a joke." She sat up and plucked the loose threads on the embroidered coverlet. "I just wanted…" What exactly did she want?

A greedy voice inside her mind answered, "*Dev naked in your bed.*"

"What did you want?" He stopped pacing and crossed his arms.

One look at him told her all she needed to know, but she still replied, "I wanted to know if there could be anything between us, if you could feel for me what I do for you."

His lips parted, and the knob in his throat bobbed up and down. Maybe she'd been wrong about him. For several long seconds, neither of them said anything. Then he spun around on his heels and stared out the window. "No," he said, his voice strained with what sounded like regret. "I'm your protector, Trouble. Nothing more, and nothing less. I'm forbidden to let anything distract me from my duty."

"But if you weren't my protector?" She held her breath while she waited for his answer. Her heart strained against her chest, thumping wildly in her ears.

He blinked several times as he looked back at her. She knew his face well enough now to tell what he was thinking. Fear, confusion, and lust all passed in waves before the smooth mask of composure settled into place. "My oath binds me for the rest of my life. Would you have me lose my honor and go back on my word?"

A heaviness descended over her and threatened to crush any joy she might have experienced with him. Tears gathered in the corners of her eyes. "No, Dev, I wouldn't ask you to do something dishonorable."

"Trouble, I—"

He reached for her, but she retreated. She didn't want his pity. She wanted something he could never give to her.

"Don't give up hope, yet, my Soulbearer."

A conversation filtered through the closed door. She heard Kell's name, followed by the deep timbre of his voice.

Another curse flew from Dev's lips. "I was supposed to send for him the moment you woke up."

"Don't worry. I'll pretend to sleep a few minutes longer and wake up." She lay with her back turned to him and pulled the covers up to her chin. Her body balled into a little cocoon, easing the ache that throbbed throughout her entire being from her bruised pride. "Please, let's forget this conversation even happened."

Heavy silence stretched between them before he answered hoarsely, "If that's what you wish."

The door creaked open, and she closed her eyes. A stray tear leaked out, and she wiped it away on the pillow before anyone could see it.

"Any change?" Kell whispered.

"She's been tossing and turning. I suspect she'll wake up soon."

Cool fingers stroked her temple and brushed her hair from her face. "And she'll be just as she was before, Dev. You'll see."

No, she wouldn't be the same person. She'd fought a necromancer and won. She no longer feared giving herself to one person. She'd opened her heart up to Dev, but he'd crushed it.

"Go get some food and some rest. I'll stay here with her for a while." The mattress sagged next to her, and a pair of arms wrapped around her. Soft velvet rubbed against her cheek. The smell of roses and bay leaf wafted up from Kell's clothes.

"Arden, are you waking up, my dear?"

My dear. The onslaught of emotions that came with those two words almost terrified her. When she looked up into Kell's face, she saw everything there that Dev had struggled to contain, and the ache in her heart intensified. Why couldn't she have fallen in love with him instead of Dev? It would have made her life much simpler.

He pressed his lips against her forehead. "How are you feeling?"

Lost, confused, uncertain. Those were just the emotions on the surface, but he didn't need to know that. "Hungry," she finally answered.

"I can only imagine. Perhaps we should send for some food?"

When Kell made no movement to release her, Dev stomped to the door with his jaw clenched tight and his mouth forming a thin line. He disappeared into the hallway to find a servant.

"At last, some time alone with you." He lowered his head, aiming for her lips this time.

"No, don't." She buried her face into his tunic and clung to him. "Please, you promised not to rush things."

Instead of becoming angry or frustrated with her like she had expected, Kell gently ran his fingers along her cheek, discovering the lingering wetness there from the one tear she allowed to betray her. He lifted her chin until she met his gaze. The sober light in his brown eyes tore at her conscience. She saw so much of herself in his hurt expression. "You're in love with him, aren't you?"

She pulled away, using her hair as a shield. "Dev is my protector," she repeated, her words sounding hollow. "Nothing more, nothing less."

"He's a fool."

"For once, I agree with the prince." A pair of invisible arms wrapped around her. *"Give Dev time to come to his senses."*

"And if he doesn't?"

"Then forget about him. You already have a man who's not afraid to love you."

She glanced up and studied Kell. What would have happened if she had met him first? Would he have captured her heart? "Kell, I'm sor—"

He cut her off by placing his finger on her lips. "Don't apologize, Arden. I knew from the beginning you cared for him. It didn't stop me from falling for you."

She took his hand in her own. "Please, Kell, what I really need right now is a friend."

"Then you shall have one." He pulled her back into his arms, his hold on her less demanding than before. "I'll give you time and space if you need it, but I'm not going to stop trying to win you over."

The door opened, revealing Dev. He stiffened as he stared at the two of them, his knuckles turning white. Then he swallowed hard, the tension easing from his body. "A dinner tray should be up shortly."

The door closed as quietly as it had opened, but Arden would have preferred him slamming the door, yelling at her, showing some display of anger. At least then, she would have known he cared for her. Instead, he appeared to have surrendered any claim he had on her.

"He's made his choice. I can't say I didn't warn him."

"What, Loku?"

"Never mind. Go back to your prince."

"Arden, when I almost lost you, well…" Kell combed her hair. "It made me realize how much you've come to mean to me in the past few weeks. And I don't mean because of your magic. Or your body. I meant you—simply you." He cupped her face in his hands. "I hope you're not in any hurry to leave me."

Thoughts of getting to Boznac and completing her training filled her mind, but when she followed his gaze out the window, she saw the thick white flakes that danced in the wind outside. "I guess I'll be spending the winter in Ranello. That is, if your father decides to pardon me."

His hazel eyes practically glowed with mischief. "Don't worry—he will. I won't stop pleading your case until he does." His lips brushed against the tip of her nose. "Besides, it gives us plenty of time to take things slowly, my dear."

Her gut knotted at those two words again. She didn't

know where things would go with Kell, but she hoped she would keep him as a friend. She listened to the calm beating of his heart and kept telling herself that things would work out in the end.

Epilogue

Dev slammed the door to his room. Loku's warning mocked him with each step. He'd held his chance for happiness in his arms, and he'd pushed her directly into Kell's.

He covered his face, sinking onto his bed. The words had hung on the tip of his tongue. He'd almost told her how much he'd come to care for her, how much he wanted to abandon his oath in favor of a lifetime with her. Now she was lying in Kell's arms, and he was left with this dull ache that threatened to drive the breath from his lungs.

In truth, he couldn't fault her. Kell had surprised even him by offering to set her free the other night. He was a good man, someone Dev could respect if he didn't know that he was a rival for Arden's affections.

And Kell could give her everything he could not.

He rubbed his chest. *When did someone who started out as a pain in my ass become a pain elsewhere?*

He drew in a cleansing breath. Things were not as dismal as they seemed. He would just make sure he stayed by Trouble's side as much as possible during the next few months. If he never allowed her to be alone with Kell, then there was still a chance he could prevent her from giving her heart to the prince. Then once they were back in Gravaria, he'd work on regaining her affections. Maybe one day, he could even be relieved of his oath.

Dev stood up, brushed the wrinkles from his tunic, and strode toward the portal to her room. He wasn't going to give her up that easily.

The Soulbearer Trilogy contines in…

A Soul For Chaos

Life is dull without a little Chaos.

Trouble is more than just a nickname for Arden
Soulbearer. It seems to follow her wherever she goes. She
mistakenly thought that by moving to Gravaria to learn
more about magic and how to control Loku, life would be
simpler.

Wrong.

Not only is her heart continually torn between the knight
sworn to protect her and the prince who woos her with a
tenacity she can't escape, but now it seems that a group of
powerful mages have banded together to rid the world of
the disembodied chaos god once and for all. Of course,
that means they have to destroy Arden in the process.

Coming December 2012

Dear Reader,

Thank you so much for reading *A Soul For Trouble*. I hope you enjoyed it. If you did, please leave a review on Amazon, Barnes and Noble, or Goodreads.

I love to hear from readers. You can find me on Facebook and Twitter, or you can email me using the contact form on my website, **www.cristamchugh.com**.

If you would like to be the first to know about new releases or be entered into exclusive contests, please sign up for my newsletter using the contact form on my website, **www.cristamchugh.com**.

--*Crista*

Author Bio:

Growing up in small town Alabama, Crista relied on story-telling as a natural way for her to pass the time and keep her two younger sisters entertained.

She currently lives in the Audi-filled suburbs of Seattle with her husband and daughter, maintaining her alter ego of mild-mannered physician by day while she continues to pursue writing on nights and weekends.

Just for laughs, here are some of the jobs she's had in the past to pay the bills: barista, bartender, sommelier, stagehand, actress, morgue attendant, and autopsy assistant.

And she's also a recovering LARPer. (She blames it on her crazy college days)

For the latest updates, deleted scenes, and answers to any burning questions you have, please check out her webpage, **www.cristamchugh.com**.

Find Crista online at:

Twitter: **http://twitter.com/crista_mchugh**

Facebook: **http://www.facebook.com/CristaMcHugh**

The Tears of Elios
by
Crista McHugh

Shape-shifters' Rule #1: Don't let the humans know you still exist.

Rule #2: If a human finds out about you, silence them.

Some rules were meant to be broken...

Ranealya ruthlessly plays by the rules and has outlived most of her race because of it. If she wants to survive, she'll have to stick to them, especially with a genocidal tyrant hell-bent on destroying all the non-humans in the realm. But everything falls apart when a human saves her life.

Gregor knows he's inviting trouble when he helps a wounded shape-shifter, but he can't pass up the opportunity to study one before they become extinct. She disturbs the quiet order of his scholarly existence, vexes him in more ways than he can count, and encourages him to break enough of the kingdom's laws so that not even being the king's cousin will save his head. The problem is, he's already lost his heart.

Excerpt follows...

CHAPTER 1

Ranealya smelled death. It called to her from the body of an old man lying in the road ahead, over-powering the stench of unwashed bodies that clung to most humans. She approached it with caution and stared into its dull blue eyes. Freshly dead. The corpse remained in pristine condition otherwise, signaling she was the first person to stumble across it.

Her stomach growled, reminding her she hadn't eaten in days, but she refused to feast on the bounty before her. Let the other beasts have him. There were far more civilized ways to scavenge.

She sniffed the air and surveyed her surroundings, making sure she was alone before she shifted. The thick fur of a wolf melted from her body as she took a familiar form, one of a middle-aged man, and dragged the corpse deeper into the woods. The icy wind prickled her bare skin, and she cursed humans once again for their lack of hair.

A search of the body's possessions revealed a change of fresh clothes in his pack, a small dagger, and enough money to buy her a hot meal and a night in an inn. *Just in time*, she thought as the first flakes of snow started falling. Winter behaved like a spoiled child in this part of the kingdom, moody and unpredictable. The only reason she stayed here was because the remote location offered protection from those who hunted her. Staying on the fringes of society had allowed her to survive this long, even though the isolation ate away at her soul as the years passed. But she could endure it. She had for centuries.

While she dressed, she tested her voice to find the

right pitch to go along with her disguise. Weeks of dormancy made it sound gravelly, but after a few sentences, her vocal cords loosened up.

Once she finished taking all she found useful from the old man, she began walking to the nearest town. A new scent caught her attention after she'd travelled about a quarter of a mile down the road, and she froze. An icy chill raced down her spine. She wasn't alone.

"Hello, traveler," a voice cried out from the trees.

She stared at the figure that appeared out of the lengthening shadows. As much as she wanted to avoid any human contact, running away would only rouse his suspicion. "Greetings."

"Headed into Poole?"

She nodded, hoping he would accept her answer and leave her alone as she continued on her way.

"Mind if I keep you company the rest of the way?"

She gritted her teeth, but shook her head. As long as she made it clear she wasn't in a talking mood, maybe he wouldn't discover what she truly was.

"It looks like there's a nasty storm brewing. Might shut down the roads for a few days." The lanky, grizzled man fell into step beside her and studied her through narrowed eyes. "You're not from Poole, are you?"

"Just passing through."

"So your appearance here has nothing to do with the reports that there may be a shape-shifter in the area?"

She fought to control her emotions, to keep her voice flat while she feigned disinterest. "Shape-shifters are just a story made up by the elves to frighten humans."

The man pulled a pipe out of his pocket and packed it with tobacco. "They ain't legends -- they're true. My grandfather participated in the Great Hunts. And there's one in this area. I've seen proof of it -- tracks that change or disappear without explanation, normal animals acting strange when it's around." He lit his pipe. "Pray you never run across one."

Ranealya's jaw tightened. This man knew a little too

much for her comfort. "How could you distinguish a shape-shifter from an ordinary person or animal?"

"Look 'em in the eye. They'll never have normal looking eyes, no matter what form they're in. Even when they pretend to be human, their eyes are still wild."

She lowered her gaze and rubbed her arms, trying to shake out the ice forming in her veins. She could still smell the burning flesh of the murdered shape-shifters. Her companion needed to be silenced before he revived the madness of the hunts from half a century ago. "You seem to know a lot about shape-shifters."

He lifted his chin. "Some people refuse to believe the legends, but they're real, I tell you. Dangerous, too. People would rather forget what they don't see."

She nodded and came closer, her hand wrapping around the hilt of the dagger she stole from the corpse. "Maybe it's better they forget."

"King Anilayus believes in them. He even sent out the Azekborn to find it. The area's been crawlin' with them lately, but I'm gonna catch it before they do. The King's even increased the bounty set during the Great Hunts. Soon, there won't be a non-human left in the realm."

Her pulse increased. Years of being a huntress had sharpened her senses. He seemed so caught up with telling her what he planned to do with the bounty that she couldn't smell any fear on him. Now was her chance to act, before he realized what she was. She slid her blade from its sheath and hid it in the folds of her cloak, ready to silence him permanently. For a second she hesitated, wondering if she could get away with scaring him into silence. Too much blood had been shed between humans and shape-shifters over the last century.

He jerked to a stop and pointed to her face. "Your eyes!"

She laughed softly as her body slid into its natural form. After all, he should see a real shape-shifter before he died. Fur rippled down her arms, and her fangs grew long enough to press into her bottom lip. She reveled in the few precious seconds she was allowed to be herself, to strike fear into a human and not worry about hiding her true nature. "You were saying?"

His eyes widened, and his Adam's apple bobbed up and down several times before he found his voice again. "I'll kill you and collect enough money to make me a rich man." He drew a hunting knife that dwarfed the small weapon in her hand.

Survival instincts took over, and the blade of her knife sliced through his vocal cords, preventing him from uttering another sound. She stepped to the side to avoid the blood spraying from the severed neck arteries. A twinge of regret passed through her chest as his body collapsed in the middle of the road. Would killing ever become easier? But now there was one less human who knew her secrets, one less human who would hunt her. Survival always came at a price.

The blood gurgled from his throat and stained the surrounding snow. She cleaned the knife on his trousers and stood. The sound of riders approaching sent a trickle of paranoia through her veins. Her heart skipped a beat from the smell of brimstone that followed. There was no mistaking scent of the King's servants. The outlines of three figures raced toward her.

Ranealya fled into the trees, sure they could hear her pounding heart. *That's just my luck*, she thought as she tore off her clothes. As much as she hated running away, attacking three Azekborn alone would be suicide. It had taken hundreds of casters to drive the drae into another realm, and those drae didn't have the demon-infused powers the Azekborn did. Her body shrank into a skinny mutt, never breaking stride as she ran.

Even the thick snow couldn't muffle the heavy gallop of hooves sounded behind her. *By the Goddess, will they ever stop chasing me?*

The sound of rushing water filled her ears. The river was close, flowing between the walls of a steep canyon it had carved out the land centuries before. She could cross it without a bridge, but they couldn't. She turned toward the sound, darting between trees in an effort to throw them off her trail.

A dark figure jumped in front of her, followed by the hiss of a blade through the air. Ranealya tumbled head first into the snow, shifting into a snow leopard as she regained her footing. If they wanted to play rough, then so be it. Her tail twitched as she crouched close to the ground.

The Azekborn lifted his sword and charged after her. Her sides heaved, but that was the only motion she allowed until he was almost on top of her. She sprung, fearing only a coward's death. The bitter, black blood of the Azekborn filled her mouth, and they tumbled to the ground together. Her jaw locked, sending her fangs deeper into his sword arm. A cry filled the air when she pulled the flesh from the bone.

She lifted her head just in time to see a crossbow bolt embed itself into her prey's chest, barely missed her cheek. She backed away, the Azekborn's arm still clutched in her teeth. She tossed the limb at the other two hunters. *Who's next?*

The standoff dragged on for several long seconds. Behind her, the rush of the river sang a song of escape, if she could only reach it. She growled and continued to back away, already beginning her next shift. Feathers replaced her fur, and her body shrank. In less than a blink of an eye, she was up in the air, flapping her wings to quickly gain altitude. The leopard's snarl morphed into the shrill call of a hawk that echoed off the canyon walls as she flew toward her freedom.

A crossbow bolt whizzed toward her from behind and buried into her wing. Her body stiffened in pain. The sharp rocks below raced toward her. With one final flap of her wings, she propelled herself forward and crashed into the trees on the other side of the river.

Her feathers melted away as she shifted back into her normal form and pulled the bolt out of her shoulder. The effort sent waves of pain throughout her body. She bit back a scream.

On the opposite side of the canyon, the two Azekborn stopped at the edge. She glared at them with satisfaction. Once again, she'd escaped them, but not completely unscathed this time.

Blood flowed from the wound in her shoulder, and the surrounding skin burned like hundreds of burning splinters had been buried into it. Hykona leaves would draw the poison out if she could find them this late in the year. Casting one more glance at her would-be hunters, she ran deeper into the snowy woods.

CHAPTER 2

An irritating trickle of moisture streaked down Gregor's back. He shook his cloak out in frustration. Somehow, he missed the sapling in front of him, and its branches showered him with their freshly accumulated snow when he'd collided with it. He brushed the flakes off his book and resumed his simultaneous reading and walking.

Ahead, a large gray dog with loose wrinkled skin bounded through the drifts, his tail wagging with excitement. To the normal ear, the dog only barked, but Gregor could hear the dog's thoughts. *"Snow! Snow! Snow!"*

Although he looked forward to his daily hike through the woods, the wind grew icy after half an hour. With a sigh, he closed his book and began to turn back to his house. He whistled for his dog to follow him, but Duke stood still in front of a small cave. "What do you see, boy?"

"Deer-not-deer," came the gruff reply.

Gregor took a few steps forward, puzzled by the dog's cryptic response. "What was that?"

Duke bounded over to him and yanked on his cloak. *"Deer-not-deer. Hurt. Come see."*

Gregor stumbled forward. His toes had gone numb, and all he wanted to do was finish his translations in front of a nice warm fire. If he could somehow prove to the King that the Clearances could be harmful to the realm, maybe he could save both lives and knowledge. He couldn't care less about a wounded deer.

What he found in the cave, however, was not what he expected. Fine fur like a doe's covered the figure from its neck to its hands and feet, but the face and body were human. And the nude body was undeniably female. His face grew warm as he covered her breasts with his cloak and kneeled closer to examine her.

For a moment, he feared she was already dead, but he felt a weak pulse at her wrist and saw the shallow rise and fall of her chest. She was only sleeping. The wound on her left shoulder had bled profusely for a while, judging by the mounds of red-tinged leaves beside her. Hykona leaves with blackened edges protruded from the opening.

Duke licked her face, and she moaned. "*Take deer-not-deer home?*"

Gregor pushed his glasses up and leaned back on his heels as he studied her. She was unlike any other creature he'd ever seen. Her face was human with smooth skin, but a pair of distinctively elvan ears protruded from her wild tangle of brown hair. He peered closer. Were those feathers in her hair? He hesitated when he saw the nails shaped like claws on otherwise normal human hands. They could be dangerous weapons if she was truly as wild as she appeared.

Duke whimpered beside her. "*Deer-not-deer hurt,*" he reminded him.

"Yes, I can see that." Gregor wished for once he couldn't hear the dog's thoughts. She needed help, but he worried about how she came by those injuries. And if what he'd read was correct, he was almost certain he'd found a shape-shifter. He'd been led to believe they'd been hunted to extinction decades ago. Would learning more about her race be worth the risk she posed? He'd almost faced the ax before for defying the king's orders, and helping her would definitely earn him a death sentence. He rubbed his hands together to warm them as he pondered his options.

"Well, I can at least heal her." He reached over the wounded shoulder. White light flowed from his palms in iridescent threads, but the wound didn't heal. He frowned.

This was unexpected. The only time he had ever seen a wound not healed by magic was when a person was already dead. He checked for her pulse again and found it still beating.

She moaned and reached for her left shoulder, eyes still closed. The gracefulness of the action mesmerized him. It surprised him that despite her wild appearance, there was something very regal about her. If he ignored the rest of her body and focused on her face, she was actually quite lovely in an odd sort of way. Her cheeks were soft and smooth, her lips full, although pale from her recent loss of blood. Thick lashes cast shadows under her eyes.

But the beauty of her face was marred when she parted her lips and revealed razor-sharp canines, destroying the warmth that had briefly flowed through his veins.

"Deer-not-deer waking up?" The dog began licking her arm.

"Let her rest." Gregor rose from his desk and tugged on the loose skin around the dog's neck, trying to pry Duke away.

She groaned and turned her head in their direction.

Gregor froze. He should have known better than to expect anything normal about her. Golden irises covered most of the visible surface of her eyes like a hawk's. When her gaze focused on him, the pupils constricted into slits, becoming more reptilian. A feral growl emanated from deep within her chest, and she curled her lips to flash her fangs.

He held her gaze as she scrambled back to the wall of the cave. She tensed, ready to pounce if approached, but her face grew more ashen with each breath. She didn't have the strength yet to put up much of a fight, and some of his fear eased.

"I'm sorry to wake you," he said, tightening his grip on the dog.

She never blinked when he spoke.

"I'm Gregor -- Gregor Meritis. I -- well, Duke here, actually -- found you here." His tongue flopped around in his mouth like he was an awkward youth asking a lady to dance for the first time. *Why should I fear her? I am a master mage, after all.* Once he tapped into his magic, his confidence returned. "I was trying to heal the wound on your shoulder."

When he reached toward it, she lashed out with her right hand, swiping her claws across his arm. Another growl rose from the back of her throat as she scrambled up the cave wall to a standing position only to collapse in a crumbled heap before she took her first step.

Duke wrestled free from Gregor and ran to her limp form. She didn't move as he nudged her with his nose.

Gregor examined his arm. The claws had drawn blood, but the wounds weren't deep. Kitten scratches. "That went well."

Duke looked up and thumped his tail on the cave floor.

"I suppose we should put her back in bed." He lifted her off the ground and arranged her gangly limbs on the bed of leaves she'd made for herself in the cave, smoothing his cloak around her shoulders. She wasn't so intimidating now. "Let's hope she's in a better mood the next time she wakes up."

Next time? He shook his head at where his thoughts were travelling. He should leave her as he found her. Everything about her screamed trouble.

But when he saw her wince in her sleep, his heart softened. She was hurt, and he knew how to help her. But first, he needed more hykona leaves. Judging by the mass of blackened leaves in her wound, she'd been hit by something tipped with poison, and he wouldn't be able to heal her completely until he removed all traces of it.

He stepped back and surveyed the cave. She'd probably appreciated a fire, some warm clothes and maybe some food, too. A mental list formed in his mind, and he repeated the items under his breath over and over again on the way back to his house so he wouldn't forget them. It wasn't a commitment. Just give her a few things until she got on her feet again. Then she'd go back into the wild.

But a small sliver of his mind hoped she stayed a bit longer.

***

Night had fallen when Ranealya opened her eyes. Dancing flames illuminated the sides of the cave walls, and the smell of roasting meat turned her stomach into a growling beast. She sat up and let the fur blanket fall to her waist. Then she tested her left shoulder, cringing when she moved it. It hurt less than before, and the image of white magic and a man's face flashed across her mind.

A log crackled in the fireplace, and she flinched. Her gaze darted around the area, looking for any signs of movement. A man sat across the fire, the same one she thought she'd dreamed up earlier. The one who called himself Gregor.

He feigned a yawn. "I guess it's time for me to go home." When her gaze never wavered, he began to squirm under scrutiny. "There's some leftover quail here, if you're hungry. I mean, I'm sure you're hungry – but if you want something to eat--" He ran his fingers through his hair. "No one knows you're here, and I'm sure you prefer to keep it that way, so don't make too much noise or attack anybody or anything like that."

His rambling amused her to no end. He was trying so hard to be brave in front of her. As if she could harm him. She couldn't shift as long as the Azekborn's poison flowed through her veins, and she was too weak to kill him. But he'd seen her in her natural state. Surely, he wasn't so dense as to not know what she was. And as such, she needed to silence him. But why did the idea of his lifeless hazel eyes staring back her cause a deep ache in her chest? He was just a human, after all.

He approached her with caution slowing his movements, carrying fresh hykona leaves, water, and a soft cloth in his hands. He knelt beside her. When he removed some of the blackened leaves stuffed in her wound, she flinched and grabbed his arm, digging her nails into his flesh.

To his credit, he didn't scream. His face tightened for a second before he drew in a deep breath and exhaled. "I need to clean the wound out," he explained in a surprisingly calm voice. "The hykona leaves are black now."

Her grip loosened, and her eyes flickered to her wound. So, he knew about healing. Perhaps he would prove useful after all. She could always delay his death long enough for him to finish healing her. A few seconds passed before she released him. Then she turned her head to the side, allowing him full access to the wound.

"So, you've finally realized I'm not trying to hurt you." He removed the remaining leaves in one saturated clump, causing her to gasp. "Sorry, I --" He sponged the edge of the wound with a damp cloth, but she tensed further, waiting for the burning to ease.

He sighed and sat back on his heels. When she peeked back at him, his mouth formed a perfect circle. What did he find so fascinating about her? Then he shook his head and wiped his hand across his face. "Do you trust me to use magic on you? I can try to take the pain away, but I may end up causing you to fall asleep."

She said nothing but loosened her grip on the fur blanket she'd been clutching the whole time.

His hand shook as he reached across her. At this angle, she could easily rip his throat out if he tried anything. Misty white light flowed from his fingers to the injured shoulder. The pain vanished, and a purr of appreciation vibrated deep in her chest. By the goddess, she hadn't felt this relaxed in years.

He withdrew his hands and reached for the cloth. This time, she allowed him to work without interruption.

"What injured you?" When she didn't answer, he continued, "Did you get into a fight?" He packed the wound with the leaves. "What kind of poison is this? Where did it come from?"

She snarled in response, and Gregor jumped back. He was asking far too many questions. The less his kind knew, the better.

"I think I may be able to heal it tomorrow, though." He stood and held out a tunic. "I ask that you please -- um -- wear this. Even though you seem more animal than human, I can still tell that you're a female, and…"

His cheeks flushed in the firelight as he struggled to find the right words without embarrassing himself further. Despite his efforts, his eyes kept returning to her body. Did he really find her fur covered breasts attractive? When was the last time he saw a naked woman? Judging by his appearance, quite a while. Stubble covered his thin cheeks, and his pale brown hair hung loose, curling around his shoulders in a somewhat tangled mess that matched his wrinkled clothes. But underneath it all, he had a handsome face, as far as humans went. And the fact he didn't find her repulsive almost made her feel sorry for what she needed to do to him eventually.

He draped the tunic over her body and shook his dog awake. "I suggest you put that on while the spell is still working so it isn't too painful. Duke and I will be back in the morning to check on you."

He paused at the entrance of the cave and muttered something under his breath. A flash of blue filled the opening, leaving behind a filmy curtain in its wake.

Ranealya's gut twisted. Just when she was beginning to think she might have found a human worth trusting, he locked her in this cave with a magical barrier. He probably wanted to keep her prisoner here until he returned with the Azekborn.

She waited until she could no longer smell him before approaching the barrier. Sparks crackled on her fingertips as she raked them across it. When it didn't waiver, she pressed her palm against it and leaned closer. The barrier was as solid as a dungeon door. She had become his prisoner.

***

Ranealya sighed and pressed her head against the damp cave wall. Dawn was approaching. She was still too weak to shift into any intimidating form, although she might be able to try something small, and there was nothing in this cave she could use as a weapon if he attacked her. Part of her knew she would have to kill him for seeing her in her natural form -- humans should never have that kind of knowledge of shape-shifters -- but she hesitated. If he knew what she was, why had he gone through all the trouble to heal her?

Complicating matters was the way he stared at her as if she was a normal woman and not a fur-covered monstrosity. Even members of her own family had turned their backs on her when they saw what she'd become, calling her the cursed one. When she remembered the intensity of Gregor's gaze, though, it almost took her breath away. No man had ever had this kind of effect on her. Why him?

Regardless of anything else, she was indebted to him for saving her life, and the idea left a bitter taste in her mouth. She may be little more than a beast, but she still remembered the code of behavior she'd followed before she'd been changed into what she is now. If his life was ever in danger, she was obligated to defend him.

She would spare him for now and see what he did. Yes, it may be breaking the rules to watch and wait but if he meant what he said about not wanting others to discover her, though, her secret might be safe with him. If he told others, his life would forfeit.

But she refused to remain his prisoner.
***

The dark clouds in the distance forecasted a possible storm within the next few hours. Gregor pulled his cloak tighter around him and trudged back to the cave with the wounded shape-shifter inside. Sleep had evaded him most of the night. Every time he closed his eyes, he saw her. The sensual curves of her body. The haunted glow of her eyes. The way she alternated between being a fierce huntress to a showing him a glimmer of trust. She still puzzled him. He wondered what she would do now that her injuries were healed. Despite her odd behavior and the risk she posed, he wanted to know more about her and hoped she would stay in the area a bit longer.

Duke continued his usual routine of digging in the drifts and running through the trees, unfazed by the cold wind or the falling snow. He paused at the barrier of the cave and wagged his tail, appearing almost as eager as Gregor was to check on the wounded shape-shifter.

He lowered the barrier and expected to find her where he left her. Instead, an empty cavern greeted him. The fire had burned down the embers, leaving an icy chill to permeate the space. The woman had vanished.

Gregor knitted his brows together and rubbed his chin. *How could this be possible? The barrier should have kept her here*. The mystery of the wounded wild woman widened threefold. Only a Master Mage could disrupt the barrier he cast last night, and even then, it would take hours to do so. She could barely stand when he left her.

Duke's barking interrupted his thoughts, followed by a flutter of wings that came close enough to Gregor's head to tousle his hair. Duke chased after whatever flew out of the cave, leaving him to stumble through the drifts after the dog. When he came to the tree Duke was barking at, he saw an owl high in the branches. The wind ruffled its snowy feathers as it watched from above, unmoved by the dog below. "It is just an owl, Duke. Leave it alone."

"No. Different owl."

Gregor took a second look at the owl. A sudden chill that was not due to the wind raced down his spine. Yes, there was something different about this owl. Something about the eyes. He focused his mental energy and asked the owl what it was doing. Its silence only added to his unease. Most animals responded to his questions. Instead, the owl flexed its talons and hissed at him.

He grabbed Duke by the loose skin on his neck and pulled the dog away. If it was his wounded shape-shifter, she was making it very clear she wanted to be left alone. "Time to go home." His voice sounded calmer than he felt.

"Leave the owl alone."

He could not escape the feeling that he was being watched the entire journey back to the house. Every time he looked over his shoulder, though, nothing was there. Unease seeped into his veins and coiled in stomach. His pace increased with the beating of his heart. He was running up the stairs to his study by the time he returned home.

***

Ranealya landed on a tree branch outside of Gregor's cottage and shook with silent laughter. And here she worried that the form of an owl wouldn't be enough to spook him. Obviously, he'd been told too many tales of the evil shape-shifters as a child.

Good. That will keep him from telling anyone about me.

Her shoulder throbbed, reminding her that her wounds hadn't completely healed. She glided down to the ground and shifted back into her normal form. The wound appeared almost closed on the outside, but it would probably take another day or two to form a pink scar across her flesh. Wounds from the Azekborn always took longer to heal than ordinary ones.

She sniffed the air for the scent of brimstone, offering a quick prayer to the goddess Elios that the Azekborn wouldn't find her until she had fully recuperated from her injuries. When she discovered no traces of them in the immediate area, she turned her attention back to the problem a few hundred feet away. Gregor Meritis knew what she was, and until she figured out what to do with him, she had no plans on leaving the area.

CPSIA information can be obtained at www.ICGtesting.com
Printed in the USA
LVOW111630170412

277996LV00001B/12/P